DARK STAR

WHITE HAVEN HUNTERS BOOK THREE

TJ GREEN

Dark Star
Mountolive Publishing

©2021 TJ Green

All rights reserved

ISBN 978-1-99-004723-7

Paperback ISBN 978-1-99-004734-3

Cover Design by Fiona Jayde Media

Editing by Missed Period Editing

This is a work of fiction. Names, characters, businesses, places, events, locales, and incidents are either the products of the author's imagination or used in a fictitious manner. Any resemblance to actual persons, living or dead, or actual events is purely coincidental.

No portion of this book may be reproduced in any form without written permission from the publisher or author, except as permitted by U.S. copyright law.

Contents

1. One	1
2. Two	9
3. Three	16
4. Four	29
5. Five	41
6. Six	48
7. Seven	58
8. Eight	71
9. Nine	82
10. Ten	92
11. Eleven	103
12. Twelve	114
13. Thirteen	128
14. Fourteen	139
15. Fifteen	148
16. Sixteen	157

17. Seventeen	169
18. Eighteen	183
19. Nineteen	195
20. Twenty	204
21. Twenty-One	214
22. Twenty-Two	226
23. Twenty-Three	239
24. Twenty-Four	251
25. Twenty-Five	262
26. Twenty-Six	271
27. Twenty-Seven	279
28. Twenty-Eight	291
Author's Note	301
About the Author	304
Other titles by TJ Green	306
	311
	312
	313
	314

ONE

SHADOW STUDIED CALDWELL FLEET, the Grand Adept of The Order of the Midnight Sun, and decided he was more pompous than JD, and that was saying something.

She leaned against the wall of the large reception room in the order's Marylebone headquarters, watching him talk to Gabe and Harlan, and wondered how much power he may have. Probably no natural magic, likely to be more of a ritual magician than anything else.

He looked to be in his early forties, slim and of average height, but fine-featured, with high cheekbones and sharp, appraising eyes. He was currently draped in his ornate ceremonial robes, no doubt to impress them with his position and influence, and his thick curly hair with a widow's peak was swept back from his face, revealing a tight expression.

"I'm sure you can understand my reticence to share too many details about this object," he said to Gabe and Harlan. "It's quite rare, and I would like to get it back as quickly as possible."

Harlan's expression was just as tight. "If you're hiring us to find this stolen object, then we really do need some details, Caldwell."

"I understand that! But of course, I expect complete confidentiality."

"And you already know that we provide that," Harlan said impatiently. "Can we get to the point, please?"

Caldwell stood abruptly and turned his back on them. He walked to the empty fireplace that dominated the room, tapping his fingers on the marble surface, while Harlan and Gabe exchanged annoyed glances.

It was close to nine o'clock on Friday evening a week before the summer solstice, and Shadow, Gabe, Niel, and Nahum had driven to London that afternoon at Harlan's urgent request, after he'd been contacted by Caldwell. Gabe hadn't been entirely sure of what they might face, so he'd opted to bring Niel and Nahum just in case. But things were tricky in White Haven right now, and Shadow was worried about her friends. However, she couldn't pass on the job either, and knew it wasn't anything that the other Nephilim couldn't handle. Niel and Nahum were outside, checking for access points and generally surveying the area and the layout, leaving the three of them to attend the meeting conducted on luxurious upholstered chairs that were arranged in a cluster in the centre of the rapidly darkening room. Their only light was from low lamps, adding a suitably gloomy atmosphere to the whole proceeding.

As one, Gabe and Harlan stood too, and Harlan said, "I think we should leave until you've had time to think about what you want. But just so you know, you will be billed for this evening, including transport. These guys have travelled a long way to see you."

Caldwell whirled around. "No, stay! Sorry. This is the first time we have had such a theft, and to be quite honest, it's a bit of a shock. This place," his arms encompassed the room and the building, "is alarmed, so I'm still trying to work out how it happened." He strode back to them, gesturing them to sit again as he also resumed his seat, and then looked up at Shadow uncertainly. "Would you like to join us?"

"No, thank you." She'd been sitting enough in the car on the way here, and had no wish to sit any more. Besides, being outside of the group allowed her to inspect the room while they talked. Aware she sounded rude, she smiled in her most charming manner and said, "Carry on, please."

Caldwell's gaze swept across her coolly and then returned to Harlan and Gabe. "The object in question is an astrolabe that was made in the thirteenth century. It is extremely beautiful, and its design makes it quite expensive, but there is another reason for its importance." He paused and cleared his throat. "Its design incorporates the latitude and longitude of Europe, and points the way to our place of origin."

"The origin of your order? Don't you know that?" Gabe asked, confused. "And why would anyone else be interested?"

Caldwell straightened his shoulders. "We do not know specifics, and therefore it's very important to us. We had humble beginnings, but we quickly grew in stature."

"Hold on a minute," Harlan said, clearly confused. "I thought your order was founded in the sixteenth century?"

"Ah, that." Caldwell gave a small shrug as if that was of no consequence. "We used another name originally, and it was changed in the 1500s for various reasons. We disassociated ourselves from the original identity as our goals changed."

Harlan narrowed his eyes at Caldwell, but Gabe pursued the original question. "But that doesn't explain why someone else would be so interested in your origins...unless it's a rival organisation seeking to annoy you. Or," he stared at Caldwell, "there's something hidden there? Something valuable."

Shadow had been listening while her gaze idled on the huge oil paintings covering the walls, detailing previous Grand Adepts all wearing ceremonial robes, occult symbols worked into the images. But she now walked around the room's perimeter to where she could see Caldwell's face.

His intense eyes stared back at Harlan and Gabe until he finally said, "It is rumoured that a great treasure can be found there."

Shadow perked up. Now that sounded more interesting.

Harlan leaned forward in his seat. "What do you mean, rumoured? You don't know?"

Caldwell licked his lips. "No. Books on the origin of our order suggest there may be treasure, but it is veiled in mystery. As is the astrolabe, which was a recent acquisition, and long searched for by us. We found it only months ago, thanks to one of our scholars. The time is approaching when we can use the astrolabe to pinpoint the place. Someone obviously knows that and seeks to get there before us. You must get it back."

"Is this a solstice thing?" Gabe asked. "Because that's only a week away."

"No, it's not, but it is a planetary thing. Sorry." He shuffled, his eyes dropping to his hands before quickly looking up again. "It's called a large planet parade, in fact, and it occurs next week—*before* the solstice. I realise this is short notice."

"What the hell is a large planetary parade?" Harlan asked, alarmed.

"It's when five planets line up in a section of the night sky. The more planets in a line, the rarer it is," Caldwell explained. "We need to read from this alignment."

Gabe stifled a curse. "What happens if we miss the deadline?"

"We lose our chance for years—and of course, whoever has it could find the place first."

"So," Harlan said, his American drawl becoming more drawn out, "you're saying this is one of those aligning-of-the-stars moments, hence the timeframe."

"Exactly."

Gabe stood and started pacing, his huge build dwarfed by the large reception room. Thick carpet muffled his footfall, and the lamps threw his shadow across the room. "You better be able to tell us something about who stole it, or we're going to run out of steam on this pretty quickly."

"I can tell you they are an accomplished thief," Caldwell said, rising to his feet too and striding across the room to the door. "I take it you're willing to help?"

Gabe looked over to Shadow, a question in his eyes, and she nodded. "Yes," he answered, "provided we have something to go on!"

"Follow me."

Caldwell led them back into the round hall that was at the centre of the eighteenth-century building, through a door at the rear, and into a long, winding passage that eventually led to stairs leading downwards. While they walked, Shadow inspected her surroundings, noting the opulence of the reception was not repeated in these back rooms. Although the mouldings were fine, the decor was far more pedestrian.

At the bottom of the stairs was a sturdy wooden door with a keypad next to it that Caldwell tapped a number on, and the noise of locks clicking preceded the door swinging inwards into a dimly lit room. Thick black carpet was underfoot, the walls were painted a matte black, and on the far side was a large safe door set into the wall.

"This is our securest room, where we keep our most prized treasures."

Harlan whistled. "Is that a walk-in safe?"

Caldwell nodded. "It is. There's just one room beyond there, and that's where the astrolabe was stolen from."

"You said the building has an alarm?" Shadow asked, already examining the safe door.

"It does. Plus, there's the keypad to this door, and that state-of-the-art safe door to which only three of us know the code—and I trust them with my life!" Caldwell folded his arms across his chest. "And yet nothing was set off! We're not even sure of the exact time the theft occurred."

"When did you last enter the safe?" Harlan asked, watching Shadow and Gabe prowl the room.

"Monday evening when the astrolabe was put back in there after our Senior Adepts meeting, and then this morning when we discovered the theft."

Shadow extended her fey magic, ignoring their conversation while she tried to detect anything unusual, and felt rather than saw Gabe move next to her.

"Feel anything?"

She ignored him for a moment, passing her hand over the safe door, and then dropped to her hands and knees to examine the carpet. He crouched next to her, and she finally looked at him and said softly, "Wild magic. Shifter magic."

"*Shifter*?" His eyes widened and he inhaled deeply, as if he would smell it, too. "I don't sense a thing."

She closed her eyes, feeling for it again. It was subtle, had almost faded completely, but she just about caught it. "Definitely. It reminds me of Hunter's magic." She sprang to her feet and turned to Caldwell. "You need to open the safe."

He broke off from his conversation with Harlan and turned to her, outraged. "I'll do no such thing! That is private."

She shrugged and made as if to walk out. "Then we can't help you."

"But you said you would!" He drew himself up to his full height and blocked her exit. "We had an agreement."

Her knife was in her hand in seconds, her blade at his throat. "Don't ever block my way."

He swallowed and moved aside, apologising swiftly. "I'm sorry. We're desperate."

Tempting though it was to slap him for his cheek, she put her knife away. "We said *if* we had something to work on. I need to see inside the safe, to see if what I sense out here will be clearer in there."

Caldwell looked at Harlan for guidance. He nodded and said, "They're good. I suggest you trust them."

Clenching his jaw, Caldwell marched across the floor, and shielding the safe, swiftly entered the code before pulling the enormous door wide. He stood back, silently watching Shadow stride past him, Gabe waiting on the threshold.

The safe itself was a long, narrow room, lined with shelves that were filled with several old books, rolled scrolls, and locked boxes. It was temperature-controlled, and therefore cool and dry. Several silver and gold goblets and candlesticks were also there, as well as some more unusual curios that Shadow barely glanced at. "Where was the astrolabe?"

"Down the far end," Caldwell instructed.

Shadow prowled deeper inside, cursing the thermostat that dispelled interesting smells and clues, but the scent of shifter was strong in there, especially on the shelf where the astrolabe had been. It was hard to say if it was a wolf-shifter, but she definitely scented the magic that indicated a being that could change form. Unfortunately, there were no other clues at all.

She strode back out again, addressing Caldwell. "Your thief was a shifter. Have you managed to annoy one lately?"

"A *what*?" he said, alarmed. He turned pale, a bead of sweat appearing on his upper lip.

"A shifter. A being that changes form." She studied his discomfort. *Maybe he'd never heard of one.* She spun, inspecting the room again, but only saw a small ventilation grill high in the wall. "I think it came into this antechamber through that and then opened the safe. I presume once it was inside it could leave by an easier route, perhaps, without setting your alarm off."

All three men were looking at her, surprised.

"What kind of shifter are we talking?" Harlan asked.

She shrugged. "I don't know, but something that can shift into more than just one form, I think. But there's nothing else here that I can detect. Gabe?"

He shook his head, too. "No. But that's something to go on. Are you sure you don't know any shifters?" he asked Caldwell. "Someone you've upset, or may know about your supposed treasure?"

"No. Our members are human. Respectable!"

"Well, that's not very nice," Shadow told him. "I know some lovely shifters." She exuded a flutter of glamour and saw Caldwell blink with confusion. "We accept the job, with a payment upfront for expenses, but we will need photos and details of the astrolabe. I'm sure it will be a pleasure working with you."

TWO

GABE EYED HIS PARTNER across the table, noting her easy, nonchalant confidence that was incredibly sexy, and she smiled back at him triumphantly, saying, "Remind me again of how lucky you are to have me."

"I'd rather I didn't." He sipped his pint, holding her gaze and refusing to back down. "You're lucky I put up with you."

Gabe, Shadow, Nahum, Harlan, and Niel were seated in a small pub a short distance from the headquarters of The Order of the Midnight Sun, talking through their options.

"Shut up, both of you," Nahum said, amused. "You've accepted the job, so I'm hoping you have more than just shifter magic to go on."

"Not yet, but we will," Shadow answered Nahum, not looking in the least bit concerned that they had so little information.

"Know any shifter thieves?" Niel asked Harlan.

He huffed. "No! I don't know any shifters at all. I know they exist, and that there's a community of them in London, but I don't know where they are." He sipped his pint and eyed them all over the rim of his glass. "I need to ask Maggie."

Gabe shook his head, recalling the conversation with Caldwell. "He doesn't want the police involved."

"I'm not involving them! But Maggie will know the community, or a few individuals at least. It's her job to know. I won't tell her anything about the theft, obviously."

"She has a nose for trouble," Shadow said uneasily. "She'll suspect something."

"She can suspect all she likes. I won't tell her a thing!" Harlan laughed. "If anything, she'll be glad to keep out of it. She's probably busy enough."

Nahum caught Gabe's eye. "Sounds like a plan. Once we know where to look, we can start asking more questions."

Gabe had a feeling this was going to get messy, but Nahum was right, and so was Harlan; they needed more to get started. "Agreed. But just because they're a shifter community, doesn't mean they harbour thieves. It could be an outsider."

"But," Niel argued, "it's likely they will have heard something." He turned to Shadow. "Did you pick up anything outside the building?"

"No. It's been too long, and there are too many other distractions. I could barely pick it up inside."

Harlan nudged his pint aside and rested his folded arms on the table. "What exactly are you 'picking up?'"

"Magical energy. I don't have a superhuman nose, so it's not scent I detect, but I can feel magic, and shifters have their own signature."

Gabe nodded, thinking of the wolf-shifter who was dating Briar, the witch in White Haven, but who lived in Cumbria with his pack. "Like Hunter, who you think has a kind of fey blood."

"Sure." She leaned back. "There are a few types of shifters in my world—birds, deer, bears and wolves, mainly, but there are others. Hunter is *not* fey—there's no doubt about that—but his ability to shift gives him a fey quality."

"Interesting," Harlan said, intrigued. "So, he's like a hybrid?"

Shadow wrinkled her nose. "No, not really. More likely that he— and his kind—are diluted. A remnant of fey-shifters that probably bred with humans forever ago and have changed over hundreds of years." Her eyes widened. "Hunter has a good nose...he would be able to scent another shifter really well!"

Gabe could see where this was going, and held up his hand. "Slow down! Let's see where we get first. We can think about Hunter if we need help."

"I take it," Harlan said, "that you guys can't pick up this 'signature?'"

Niel shook his head. "That's not what we do, I'm afraid."

Shadow winked and looked smug. "That's why they have *me*!"

Niel grabbed a crisp from the packet on the table and threw one at her. She caught it and popped it in her mouth with a crunch and a grin.

"So, tell me, Little Miss Fey," he said with a raised eyebrow, "what about shifters who take multiple forms?"

She chewed and swallowed. "There are very few who can take multiple forms. We call them chimera-shifters. It will make life harder, certainly, but if we get his—or her—magical scent, we should be able to track it. Or at least trace its movements."

"I presume," Nahum said, "that this shifter was also hired. I can't see why a shifter would be interested in the origin of The Midnight Sun. Which reminds me, tell me more about this astrolabe."

Gabe reached into his jacket pocket and extracted the bundle of folded papers that Caldwell had given them. "This is it." He selected a few and spread them on the table, and everyone leaned closer to look at the photos and schematics. "It's made of brass, but inlaid with silver and rose gold, and has tiny black pearls along the limb," he pointed to the engraved rim around the astrolabe. "The pin in the centre has a pearl set in it. It's called the Dark Star Astrolabe."

"Dark Star?" Nahum asked, leaning closer. "That's intriguing. I've read about these things. They seem complicated."

Harlan grunted. "That's because they are. Although, they are a brilliant invention. I believe they were created in the east before they became widely used across Europe in the twelfth century and onwards. They made travel easier. From what I know, these things are like the modern smart phone...they have up to a thousand uses." Everyone looked at him expectantly, and he shrugged. "Don't ask me what! My knowledge is basic, at best—although, I have bid for a few in the past." Harlan pointed at the picture closest to him. "This thing, the ornate plate with the squiggly pointers, is called a rete, and it aligns with the plate underneath, which has a fixed latitude and points to stars. It allows you to find your way by fixing on constellations. You can use it with the sun, too. And that's it! I have no idea how you use it, or how these guys could use it to find their place of origin."

Gabe stared at the page, not really seeing it, but thinking of their job ahead. "It was made specifically for the order—that seems clear. But that doesn't concern us, and we don't need to use it. We just need to find it before the end of the week."

"Because?" Niel asked, not privy to their earlier discussion.

"A rare planetary parade is occurring soon," Shadow answered, "and they need to fix on it for their directions. If they miss the opportunity, that's it for years!"

"Bloody typical," Niel groaned. "Did he say where they need to read it?"

"No," Gabe admitted, intrigued more than he cared to admit. *What was so mysterious about the origins of the order, and was there really any treasure?* "But we don't need to know." He said that more to remind himself than anyone else. He drained his pint. "So, you'll contact Maggie tomorrow, Harlan?"

"Yep, and I'll be in touch. You guys still happy to stay at Chadwick House?" He looked uncertain, which wasn't surprising. "It's all clean and aired out. I think you're the first people to stay there since Chadwick died."

Shadow finished her drink, too. "Is it still filled with his stuff?"

"Of course, but we have created a couple more bedrooms." He shrugged. "It meant rearranging some of his collections, but essentially we have honoured the conditions of his will. You'll have access to his extensive library, too. And—" he shot Shadow an accusatory glare. "*Nothing* goes missing! We know what's there."

She looked affronted, and Gabe tried not to smirk. "How dare you! I wouldn't steal from you!"

"Yeah, right," he muttered into the dregs of his pint.

Gabe stood, his chair scraping across the floor as he stretched. He'd never been to Chadwick's house before, so was suddenly anxious to see it. And the lure of a whiskey before bed sounded great. "Come on guys, let's get moving."

Harlan steeled himself to call Maggie 'ball-breaker' Milne on Saturday morning.

He'd had a fitful night's sleep worrying about shifters and where this search might lead them, and also what Mason might say. What he hadn't told Shadow and the Nephilim was that he hadn't run Caldwell's request past Mason like he would normally do. His relationship with him was tricky at present, mainly because of JD.

After the experience with JD the previous month, when he'd found out exactly how fickle and untrustworthy he was—and to be honest, downright annoying—Harlan couldn't help but question what he knew about Mason, especially as he realised how close they were. Harlan might have known Mason for years, but recently, every interaction he'd had with him had felt edgy, and Olivia had reported the same issue. If anything, Olivia had been angrier than him, demanding Mason looked after their interests, and consequently he and Olivia were prone to having secret meetings down the pub. Although, it would be fair to say that nothing untoward had happened, and life at the guild had pretty much continued as it had before. Jobs came in, he attended auctions, followed up acquisitions he could handle alone, and brought in others when needed.

This job had come when Caldwell phoned Harlan directly. It seemed that Kent Marlowe had been impressed with Gabe and Shadow, and Harlan too, after the affair with Kian. Harlan had decided that it would be too subversive not to include the guild, but he just quietly got on with it, including booking Chadwick House for the team. He knew he was risking Mason's wrath, but at the end of the day, the guild would still get paid. Now that the job was going ahead, he debated whether he should come clean to Mason, but for some reason that he couldn't pinpoint, he decided to keep it quiet. If Mason went looking through the records he'd find it, but Harlan would worry about that later.

Maggie's phone rang several times before she answered with a clipped, "Hey Harlan, I presume you have some new shit to land on my doorstep."

"Actually, no. And good morning to you, too!"

"Whatever. What do you want? I've got a fucking vampire tearing through the East End, and I need to get moving."

"I need to know where to find shifters in London."

"What the fuck for?"

Everything Maggie said suggested she took every word as a personal affront. It was exhausting. "Because I think one has committed a theft, and I need to find it."

"A theft where?"

"It's a private matter...and I thought you were busy?"

"All right," she grumbled. "Wimbledon, like the bloody Wombles."

"Wimbledon? The shifters are rich?" For some reason, Harlan had presumed they'd be short of cash.

"I don't bloody know! But it's close to the common and Richmond Park. I figure they like green spaces."

"Have you got someone we can talk to? A contact?"

She sighed, impatient to get moving, he could tell. "Maverick Hale. He's annoying but useful, and likes to keep the pack clean."

"Wolf-shifter?"

"And Alpha. He's got the usual swagger. Thinks he's a fucking rock star. I'll text you his number."

"Thanks, Maggie. I really appreciate this."

"You owe me."

She hung up on him and Harlan sighed. That actually went better than he'd thought. And he had a number. Maverick Hale. *What sort of name was that?* He wasn't lying when he said he didn't know any shifters. He knew many people who used The Orphic Guild for business, and while they were a diverse bunch, shifters hadn't been part of them...not that he knew of, anyway. Rather than second-guess himself, he called straight away, but the phone rang and rang and eventually went to voicemail. Reluctant to leave a message, he hung up and decided to try again later.

Harlan made another coffee and then decided to search the Internet for any reference to Maverick, and was pleased to find an early hit. *No wonder Maggie called him a rock star.* He owned a club in Wimbledon called Storm Moon. Harlan sniggered. *Seriously?* It was a live music venue that looked to be a mix of the dark, edgy, and up-market—a potent combination—and it was just off the High Street, not far from the Ivy Restaurant.

Harlan leaned back in his chair, sipping his drink. *A nightclub made sense.* Shifters were generally night creatures, and it would be the perfect business, and a chance for Maverick to employ some of his pack. No wonder Maverick wasn't answering his phone now. He probably kept very late hours. Harlan stared at the image of its respectable façade on the search page and decided that if he didn't answer his phone, they could visit there that night. He'd update Gabe and Shadow, and then head to the gym.

THREE

SHADOW STUDIED THE PICTURES of the astrolabe that were spread across the table, marvelling at its intricacy and beauty.

"This really is magnificent," she murmured, more to herself than anyone else.

She was sitting with the three Nephilim in the kitchen at Chadwick House after having just finished Niel's usual breakfast spread, and they were debating what to do with their day.

Nahum pulled one of the pictures towards him, looking puzzled. "It's ingenious, even if I don't have a clue how it works. But Ash would be good with this. He has an analytical mind."

Shadow nodded. "You're right."

"But," Gabe reminded them, "we don't need to know how it works. We just need to find it."

Shadow frowned at him. "But I like to know how things work."

"Not the dishwasher, you don't," Niel shot back.

"Sod off. I'm a racehorse, not a carthorse!"

Gabe laughed. "Where do you get these stupid sayings from?"

"It's not stupid," she said, her ire rising as she looked at him sitting there so infuriatingly collected and calm. "It's true. Aren't you the slightest bit curious about this?"

"Slightly," he admitted with a shrug. "But it's unnecessary. We need to focus on who the shifter is, who hired him, and where he's gone now."

"And potentially what they've stolen it for," Nahum said. "Because that could indicate where they've gone with it. I mean, if they intend to find the origin of the order and the potential treasure there, they may already have a lead."

Shadow huffed, looking at Nahum like he was an idiot. "The clue is in there!" She tapped the image. "Only to be revealed on the day of the planetary alignment. They can't know where to go yet!"

He stared at her. "I mean, that they have clearly done some research, so they must know *something*!"

Niel leaned on the table, his hand rubbing over the shaved hair on the side of his head. "This could be an inside job. If Caldwell has kept this quiet, who else would know about it? It sounds like they've been searching for it for a while, and only found it recently."

Gabe gazed into the middle distance, tapping his mug. "Maybe we should clarify that. Which leads to the next questions. Where did they find it, who found it, and who brought it here? There's a trail, and trails aren't clean. Information could have leaked at any point."

Shadow eyed Gabe, impressed at his logic. He was looking good this morning. His black t-shirt fit his sculpted muscles perfectly, the colour making his olive skin glow, and his dark eyes had taken on that intensity which, she reluctantly admitted, gave her an unwilling shiver. He turned that intense gaze on her sometimes, a smoulder of desire behind them that filled her mind with thoughts of how those hands would feel on her bare skin. She blinked away her thoughts and focussed on the job.

"We need to ask Caldwell more questions," she mused.

Niel grunted. "I'm not sure we'll get answers."

Shadow considered what Harlan had asked the night before. "Remember when Harlan was confused about the date of the order's origins, and Caldwell said they'd had another name? I wonder what that was. Why would you change your name?"

"Caldwell gave a reasonable explanation," Nahum pointed out, "but it's worth investigating." He looked around the table. "This house has a study. Maybe there's something in there. And Chadwick collected ancient stuff, right? He might have an astrolabe. I'd like to see one, properly, just to get a feel for it."

"Good suggestion," Shadow said, eager to do something. "I'll search the house."

"Why don't we all take a tour?" Gabe suggested, rising to his feet. "I didn't get to see much of the place last night, and I'd like to explore it fully."

They quickly cleared the breakfast things away and headed into the dining room, where the first thing Shadow saw was the hole her knife had made in the wall. She walked over to it, running her fingers across it, before turning to survey the room.

"It's hard to believe the last time I was in here I was being attacked by Kian."

Gabe swung around to look at her. "That was here?"

"Yep." She pointed to the sofa that was next to the fireplace, now cold and empty in the summer. "I dived behind that. We were sitting at this table when Harlan and Mason fell unconscious." She was standing next to the polished walnut table, its elegance belying the violence of that night. She pointed to the large, wooden head on the coffee table. "And that's what I threw at him, too."

Niel laughed as he walked around the room, picking things up and placing them down again in idle curiosity. "I bet he didn't expect that."

"No, I don't think he did. And then of course he scarpered down the hall, and I gave chase."

The room looked like it had that night. The furniture was antique and occasionally ostentatious, and the decor was rich and challenging to the eye, although in the bright light of day it lacked the power of the candlelit evening. It was odd being back here again, but also good.

Her place with the Nephilim seemed certain now, assured, as was her friendship with Harlan. Time had changed things for the better.

She left the room, checking on the living room briefly before entering what had been the drawing room but was now another room displaying Chadwick's occult collections. It allowed a room upstairs to become a bedroom, and The Orphic Guild had converted the attic, too.

Nahum was behind her, and he said, "This place is interesting! He's got all sorts of stuff." He peered into a glass case. "Is that a poppet?"

She went to his side, looking at the rudimentary cotton doll that had been hand-sewn with crosses for eyes. It was old, yellowed with age. "He must have a witchcraft collection. Look, old rune stones and amulets," she said, pointing out other shelves.

"Is that a withered hand?" he asked, heading to another cabinet and pointing out the shrunken yellow skin wrapped around bones. "That's disgusting." He grinned at her. "Let's hope it's not cursed. You might find it creeping across your pillow at night."

She glared at him. "Funny. *You* might find it around your throat. Oh, wait, that will probably be me!"

He lowered his voice. "Gabe better not find you creeping in my bedroom. He'd get very upset."

She looked at his cheeky expression, and despite her best intentions, felt herself flush. "I'm sure Gabe doesn't care where I go at night."

He laughed. "Pull the other one. Come on, sweet sister, this is not finding an astrolabe."

"Did I hear my name?" Gabe asked, appearing silently behind them.

"Nope. Vanity, vanity," Shadow said aloofly, and then headed to the rooms that were linked with the double doors. Hearing them behind her, she said, "This is where I was almost pinned beneath the cage, were it not for my lightning-fast reflexes."

"And this," Gabe said, casting her a withering glance as he marched across the room to a collection on a low shelf, "is an astrolabe." He picked up the ornate, bronze disc that was the size of a side-plate, and headed to the large bay window so he could see it in the light. "It's bigger than I thought. Heavy."

Niel had joined them, and he said, "I looked them up this morning. That ring on the top is to hang it so you get the most accurate reading. It's made up of several different layers, all pinned in the centre."

"Are they all this size?"

Niel shrugged. "I think they vary. They are portable, after all." He pointed at the ornate, curly bronze squiggles. "These point to stars, but it can be used in the day, too."

Shadow leaned against the window frame. "So, the Dark Star Astrolabe has a specific purpose, whereas this one can be used to find your way anywhere within a certain latitude."

"It seems so," Niel agreed. He checked his watch. "I'm heading up to the study, see what I can find up there. A couple of hours should see us through to lunch."

"Good plan," Gabe said, still carrying the astrolabe. "I'll bring this with me, see if I can work it out." He looked at Shadow. "Don't pout. Come and help."

"Dusty books? Ugh!" She gestured out the window. "It's beautiful out there! We should go out."

He stared at her with his implacable gaze. "Are you part of the team or not?"

"Spoilsport," she said, reluctantly following them up the stairs. "You owe me a pint."

Harlan finally managed to speak to Maverick Hale at about three that afternoon, and he didn't sound as he'd expected. His voice was smooth, almost a purr, whereas he'd been expecting a growl.

"Mr Hale, my name is Harlan Beckett and I've been given your name by Maggie Milne." He deliberately left out her title, but he was pretty sure Maverick would know her name.

Maverick paused before answering. "Maggie? That can only mean trouble."

"I hope not for you," Harlan said swiftly. "But I gather you're the Alpha of the local pack, and I need your advice about a shifter."

"She told you what I am?" he asked, a dangerous edge to his voice.

"I work in the occult world. Your secret is safe with me."

"It better be. One of *my* shifters?"

"We don't think so. A rare object has been stolen, and my colleague thinks a shifter is responsible, but it's not a wolf-shifter. We need a lead and thought you could help."

He laughed dryly. "We are not the only pack in London."

Harlan faltered for a moment, and then pushed on. "Obviously you're the only one Maggie trusts enough to send me to."

"Sorry; she misled you. I can't help."

"What if this brings trouble to your door?"

"We can deal with trouble. And besides, why should it? You said it's not a wolf-shifter."

Harlan was losing him; he was clearly on the verge of ending the call. "But you own a bar. Surely you have all sorts of people hanging out there. And you live in the paranormal world. One of your pack may know something."

"What is it you do, Mr Beckett?"

"I'm a collector for The Orphic Guild. Occult acquisitions. I have many contacts, and we're good at what we do."

"I've heard of you, although I have never had need of your services before. If I help you now, perhaps I'll get a better deal if I do need you in the future?"

"Of course," Harlan said eagerly. Deals were part of the game.

"Then come to the club tonight at ten. I'll leave your name at the entrance." And then he hung up, leaving Harlan murmuring his thanks into the dial tone.

Gabe was back at The Order of the Midnight Sun on his own.

He'd left the others to while away the afternoon while he questioned Caldwell. Despite the fact that Caldwell had engaged their services, he hadn't seemed that keen to speak to Gabe again, which was curious.

The front door was locked to the public, but a casually dressed man admitted him to the reception room and then left him to wait alone. Gabe could have asked his questions over the phone, but he wanted to see Caldwell's expression. He could get a better feel for his responses that way. He walked around the room while he waited, noting the large oil paintings, the heavy furniture, and the rich silks and brocades that on close inspection were worn in places, their colours faded. Maybe they were short of money and needed this treasure—if it even existed. Or maybe it wasn't a monetary treasure, but another type of treasure entirely.

His thoughts were broken when Caldwell came in, this time wearing ordinary jeans and a t-shirt—no ornate robes today. His plain attire removed some of his mystique, making him look smaller, too.

Caldwell crossed the room quickly, shaking his hand as he asked, "Have you found anything?"

Gabe shook his head. "In so few hours? No. But we have a line of inquiry." *Bloody hell*, Gabe thought, *I sound like the police.* "My team were talking this morning, and realised we had more questions."

Caldwell sat, inviting him to do the same. "Of course. What do you need to know?"

"First of all, how many people here know about the astrolabe?"

"All of our Inner Temple. That's only twenty-one people."

"And they are what you called the Senior Adepts, correct? The ones who met on Monday night?"

"Yes. They are utterly loyal, and privy to our innermost secrets." He looked affronted. "They would never betray us!"

Gabe wasn't so sure of that, but he continued, "And the three of you who hold the code combinations are part of that group?"

"Yes. Myself, the Major Adept, and the Secretary of the order. All of us have been members for decades."

"And the rest of the Inner Temple?"

"Many for years, others are more recent, but all have earned their place."

"How do they do that?"

Caldwell laughed. "That's a secret. There are tests to undergo, rituals I cannot divulge."

"Okay. How many others belong to the order?"

"I couldn't say exactly off the top of my head, but close to a hundred." Gabe must have looked shocked, because Caldwell said, "They are spread across the country. Not all live in London. We have many initiation levels, and some members who have been with us for years only progress a short way, while others can progress rapidly depending on their...abilities."

Herne's horns. It already sounded like mumbo jumbo, but Gabe kept his face carefully neutral. "And you're sure no one else would know about the astrolabe?"

"No one." He shook his head decisively, his curly hair bouncing as he did so.

"It might be that I need the names of those in the Inner Temple."

Caldwell stuttered. "Not a chance."

"Well, we'll see how we get on, won't we?" Gabe answered calmly. "Who found the astrolabe, and who was part of the search?"

"Again, it was a member of our Inner Temple—he was unaided. One of our greatest scholars and researchers who has made it virtually his life's work. He found it in France, in the south."

"And I presume he brought it here with him, in his luggage?"

"Er, no actually." Caldwell looked downright uncomfortable now, and he cleared his throat. "He feared it would be seized by customs, so arranged another method for its shipment."

Gabe's lips twitched with amusement. "He stole it, then?"

Caldwell's eyes dropped to the floor. "I didn't ask for details."

"Of course you didn't. Was it stolen from a private residence? Because potentially," he said, forestalling any lies, "they sent someone to get it back."

"The adept in question assures us he was discreet."

"Maybe he wasn't as discreet as he thought." Gabe groaned. This was getting more complicated by the minute. "And how did he ship the astrolabe?"

"He used Kernow Shipping. They are also very discreet."

Gabe froze. "Kernow Shipping, based in Cornwall?"

"You know them?"

"Sort of." At least Gabe should be able to access the records. Gabe was wearing an old, worn leather jacket, and he reached into an inner pocket for a pen and paper. "I need the dates of shipment, and ports. And also the address it was stolen from."

Caldwell jutted his chin out. "I told you, I can't get that."

Gabe settled back comfortably in his chair. "And I'm not leaving until you do."

Nahum, his two brothers, Shadow, and Harlan were in the beer garden of the Dog & Fox Pub & Hotel in Wimbledon, and had already finished a hearty pub meal. They were now sipping drinks and sharing news, while keeping a watchful eye on the comings and goings along the High Street.

It was a warm summer evening, and to Nahum it seemed as if the entirety of Wimbledon was outside. The beer garden was packed, and the street bustled with people who strolled up and down and in and out of the various bars and restaurants. There was a thrum of activity, a bustle of energy that made the place seem exciting, a very different feel to the seaside charm of White Haven. Nahum had lived in many cities in his lifetime, and he enjoyed their energy and the mix of characters that lived in them. London was no different, and he felt comfortable there.

Nahum turned his attention to the table, and particularly to Gabe and Shadow, trying to hide his amusement. They were sitting next to each other, as they often did, a studied indifference to their features that belied the chemistry between them. The air almost crackled around them sometimes—much to the amusement of himself and his brothers. They argued, fought, teased, and slid each other sly glances that they thought no one else would see. They were trying very hard not to admit it, but they were clearly attracted to each other, and he knew that only the business was keeping them apart. Neither wanted to wreck what was clearly turning into a profitable and entertaining enterprise. *Well, that and their mutual stubbornness.* He had known Gabe his entire life, and hadn't seen him like this with a woman for a very long time. *Then again, why should he wish for the entertainment to be over?* They were all running side bets on how long it would take for them to get together. Which reminded him—he should let Harlan in on the bet.

Harlan was proving to be a worthwhile ally. He had great contacts, a good work ethic, and a strong moral code, all of which meant the Nephilim respected him. And he had a great sense of humour, thank the Gods.

Harlan was looking at Gabe, incredulous about his visit to Caldwell. His mouth gaped open, his pint suspended halfway to his mouth. "Caldwell actually gave you the information? Just like that?"

"No! Stupid bastard thought I was going to go and that he could somehow talk me out of needing to know who they stole the astrolabe from." Gabe too looked incredulous. "What an idiot! What about me looks like someone could force me to leave?" Gabe threw his shoulders back and spread his hands out. "I pointed out that he had employed me, so he'd better run along and do as I asked."

Niel laughed and slapped his shoulder. "I always knew your stubbornness would be an asset."

Niel had shaved the sides of his head again, taking the long hair left into a high ponytail. His good looks were attracting his fair share of attention, especially paired with his booming laugh.

Nahum leaned his elbows on the table, wishing he'd met Caldwell. "It is odd that he would not want you to have as much information as possible. Sounds like he's in denial."

"It sounds," Shadow suggested, "that he wants to keep the image of the order as above reproach."

Gabe nodded. "I suspect that by the time this is over, he'll have trouble smoothing over the cracks. I think they're broke, too. In the cold light of day, that place isn't nearly so impressive."

"So," Harlan pressed, "who did they steal the astrolabe from?"

"A house in Nice, in the south of France. I have the address, but I haven't looked it up yet. It's owned by a Madame Raphael Charbonneau." He shrugged. "I don't know anything about her, either. But at least we have a name now."

"She may have nothing to do with the theft at all," Niel pointed out.

"True, but it's something to bear in mind." Gabe took a deep breath. "It was sent from Marseilles using Kernow Shipping, which is great for us, because it means we can get shipping details—like who booked it in."

Shadow laughed. "Like the thief, you mean?"

"Exactly," he said, meeting her eyes. "It will help us build up a picture. I've already asked Barak to look into it."

Harlan nodded enthusiastically. "Fantastic. I agree. The more we know, the better. Did you find out the order's old name?"

"No. And to be honest, it isn't my most pressing question right now." Gabe gave an easy smile. "But I will find out."

Harlan sipped his pint, nodding thoughtfully. "I take it you couldn't find their history in Chadwick's study?"

"No," Nahum answered, remembering how daunting that room was. "But we have time to look. That room is pretty chaotic."

"Yeah." Harlan looked sheepish. "It's been catalogued in a very basic fashion, but not organised. We haven't had time. Their history is something I can look into, and let you concentrate on the rest."

"Fair enough," Nahum told him. "You had success, though. Well done."

Harlan looked to the roundabout a little further down the road and nodded. "Storm Moon is down the street across from here— Church Road—in a very unassuming building. It opened at eight, and there's a band on at nine. A rock band, I think."

"I take it you've scoped it out?" Shadow asked, already looking like she wanted to jump out of her seat and leave.

"Only briefly. It looks like there's a bar on the ground floor and the club below ground. There's a big parking lot to the side, and around the back, too." He shrugged. "I didn't go in, but it looks flashy and edgy from the pictures on the net."

"I suggest," Gabe said, "that Niel and Nahum stay outside and check the exits, and we three will go in. That okay with you?"

Nahum and Niel nodded. They were used to running surveillance, although Nahum would love to look inside the club.

Gabe turned to Shadow. "Do you think you can pick up a distinct magical energy in there?"

"Maybe. It depends on how many shifters are around. I can certainly detect them now."

"You can?" Harlan asked, looking uncomfortably around him. "Are they close?"

"At the table in the corner, I think. Far enough away they shouldn't be able to listen—although they have exceptionally good hearing."

"But there's a lot of background noise," Niel said, angling his body casually so that he could look behind him. "I see them. The half a dozen in the corner."

Shadow nodded, and Nahum glanced around too, seeing four men and two women, all enjoying drinks and food. They looked harmless enough, and he said, "I'm sure they're just enjoying their Saturday night like everyone else here." He turned back to the others. "I think the club will be packed tonight. And frankly, the thief may have no connection there at all. Or they will be long gone."

"Unless they live here," Gabe suggested. "Once the goods were passed on, there's no need to run."

Niel drained his pint. "At this point, there are numerous ways this could go, and it's all pointless speculation. Let's have another drink and see what transpires later."

FOUR

STORM MOON was much bigger than Shadow anticipated. They entered the bar through sturdy wooden double doors that led into an ornate foyer where one heavily muscled bouncer, unsurprisingly a shifter, gave them a cursory glance before they headed through the next door into the ground floor bar.

Harlan, Shadow, and Gabe all paused just inside the threshold to get their bearings. The windows were blacked out, and the lighting was low. The long bar that ran across the far side of the room was topped with polished copper, and the back of the bar was mirrored and lined with rows and rows of spirits. The walls were covered with dark-patterned, opulent wallpaper, the floor space was filled with tables, and around the sides were cushioned booths upholstered in teal velvet. The light gleamed off the polished tables, many of which were already taken, and there was a cheerful, chatty atmosphere. An area in the middle of the right-side wall was free of side booths, creating a clear section that housed a door that had *Storm Moon Club* on it in gilt letters.

"Nice place." Harlan said, taking it in slowly. "Should we go down there already?" He nodded at the door.

"May as well," Gabe said, leading the way.

As they crossed the floor, Shadow felt a few curious gazes fall on them, and detected a few shifters in the room, especially behind the bar, but far more of the customers there were normal humans.

Gabe opened the door, revealing a staircase leading down to a reception area with a cloakroom combined with a ticket office. Again the decor was dark, illuminated only by low lights. A couple of staff stood behind the counter, one taking coats from two young girls, and another large bouncer guarded an ornate door. *There was clearly no expense spared here*, Shadow noted, *as even the reception areas were designed to impress.*

Harlan addressed the young woman behind the ticket counter who was casually dressed in jeans and a black t-shirt. "Maverick Hale is expecting me, and I have two colleagues with me."

Her eyes raked over them. "Let me check with Maverick." She turned her back as she picked up the phone.

The bouncer studied them too, and Shadow detected his shifter magic. She leaned against the wall, aware of where her blades were in case she needed to pull them quickly, and stared back. Gabe stood with hands thrust into his pockets, relaxed but alert. As usual, she was fully aware of his heat and physicality, and wasn't sure whether it was comforting her or distracting her.

The bouncer was tall and lean, his eyes watchful, and he carried himself with an easy grace, but he wasn't threatening. He opened the door for the two girls who had just checked their coats, greeting them warmly, and making Shadow think they were regulars as they passed through, giggling.

The call the woman made was brief, and she turned back to them with renewed curiosity. "That's fine, you can all go through, on the house. Head across the floor to the passageway and up the stairs on the right."

Harlan murmured his thanks and led the way inside.

The loud music assaulted them immediately. The club was full, a crowd of seething people standing in front of the stage on their right, situated at the rear of the building. A rock band was playing, clad in leather, jeans, and t-shirts, and the dull thud of the base guitar and drums resounded through the floor and equally through Shadow. She smiled as she looked around, the energy infectious.

Shadow hadn't been to a live music venue since she'd arrived here, and she knew she'd missed out. The room was large, and as well as the crowd in front of the stage, there were a few booths and tables by the bar at the other end of the room, but not many, and all of them were taken. Opposite, across the dance floor, was the passageway the woman had told them about. Harlan was already heading to it, but Shadow took her time to follow, taking stock of the room, and so did Gabe.

Gabe nudged her and lowered his voice to her ear. "Are there lots of shifters around?"

"A fair few, though less than normal people." She nodded to the bar. "Most of the staff are shifters, and the two bouncers."

"I expected as much," he said, and then steered her behind Harlan, who waited at the entrance to the narrow passage. At the far end of it was a door marked *Exit*.

As instructed, there was a shallow set of stairs at the rear heading up to a narrow landing and a door. Smaller rooms were on their left, filled with low seating and tables, half-full at present, and it was quieter here, allowing the customers to chat.

"Anything feel off?" Harlan asked Gabe and Shadow.

"Not to me," Gabe said, glancing around and looking relaxed, which was deceiving. He was absolutely on full alert.

"It feels fine," Shadow agreed. "Just a lot of people having a good time."

"Good. Let's hope it stays that way," Harlan said, heading to the landing.

At his knock, the door that was marked *Office* was opened by another tall shifter with blond hair and astute eyes, dressed in what seemed to be their uniform of black jeans and a t-shirt with the Storm Moon logo on the front, and he stepped back, allowing them entry. As soon as the door shut behind them, the noise vanished, leaving them in a soundproofed room overlooking the club. A desk was at the far end next to a couple of filing cabinets, and a seating area was at the other, along with a small self-serve bar in the corner. A large window, which Shadow hadn't noticed from the main room, looked out over the club. A couple of staff stood looking through it, while a man worked at the desk. All three stared at them as they entered.

The man behind the desk leaned back, his eyes wary, a smile playing across his lips as he studied all of them. "You must be Harlan Beckett and *colleagues*. I'm Maverick Hale." He stood and walked around his desk to meet them, shaking their hands with a firm grip.

"Thanks for your time, Maverick," Harlan said, introducing them.

Maverick appeared to be in his late thirties and was tall and lean with the athletic build of many shifters, and now Shadow knew what Maggie had meant when she'd sarcastically called him a rock star. He oozed self-confidence. His black t-shirt clung to his broad shoulders and powerful deltoids, and his thick, shoulder-length hair, which was a dirty-blond colour, had a slight curl to it. Shadow realised that Maverick was supremely aware of his power, but he didn't try to overwhelm them, as many Alphas might. She liked that about him. He reminded her of Gabe in that respect. It was Gabe he studied most, perhaps because of his build and height. His eyes narrowed as he greeted him, and Shadow was pretty sure he detected something different that he couldn't quite place.

Maverick gestured them to sit in the lounge area and headed to the bar. "Drinks? Whiskey, gin?" He smiled at Harlan. "Bourbon?"

"You read my mind," Harlan said, taking a seat.

"It was the accent that suggested it," he admitted, pouring his shot, and then getting a whiskey for Gabe and gin and tonic for Shadow.

Rather than sit, Shadow accepted her drink and stood at the window looking down to the club, saying, "I didn't see this window from the other side."

"You're not supposed to," Maverick told her. "It's a one-way mirror with a non-reflective surface on the other side, so it blends in with the wall in the dark. It's useful for my security team to keep an eye on things." He gestured to the two people who had returned to surveilling the club—one man, one woman—but didn't introduce them. He sat down, sipping his whiskey. "You think I can help you find a shifter?"

Harlan nodded. "A chimera-shifter who was responsible for a theft on Thursday night. We were hoping that he—or she—might have passed through here."

Maverick swirled his drink, the ice clinking against the glass. "A chimera-shifter? I presume you mean a shifter that can change into many forms?" At Harlan's nod, he continued, "That's an interesting name for them, but we call them therian-shifters. And how do you know it's a therian?"

Harlan glanced at Shadow, a questioning look in his eyes, and she said, "Because I could tell. It's one of my skills."

"Care to share?" he asked, meeting her eyes.

"Not really. But I can tell that you, your man on the door—" she gestured to the man who had let them in and now leaned against the wall watching their exchange, "and the woman are wolf-shifters, but the other man—" she pointed to the burly man who had been looking through the window but now stared at Shadow, "is human." He grinned and returned to surveilling the club, and Shadow said, "I also know most of your bar staff and bouncers are shifters, but most of your clientele is human. Although, I would need a good look around to say for sure."

"Consider me impressed," Maverick said, raising his glass in salute. "And you can tell the difference in types of shifters?"

She kept it brief. "Yes. You all have a certain *quality*."

Maverick watched her for a few more seconds, his amber eyes warm like the whiskey he swirled in his glass, and Shadow felt his magic flare. But her glamour was firmly in place and she waited until he nodded and addressed Harlan and Gabe. "You can see how busy my club is. Sometimes less than savoury characters pass through here, but in general it's a safe place for the supernatural people of this world. However, I don't keep track of everyone. We are open to all, as long as they don't cause trouble."

"But you are the only pack in the area, and shifters like to be together. It's natural you might have heard something," Harlan suggested.

"Wolf-shifters like to be together...on the whole. There are loners. Therian-shifters are very different creatures altogether. Have you ever met one?" They all shook their heads, Shadow unwilling to admit she knew them only in her own world, and he shrugged. "Trust me. Much like their ability to change form, they are slippery at best, downright troublemakers at worse. All indulge in some kind of crime, most petty, but not all. So, if I'm honest, it doesn't surprise me that your thief is a therian."

Gabe leaned forward, speaking for the first time. "Is there a community of therian-shifters around here?"

Maverick laughed. "They don't even trust each other." He dropped his smile, becoming serious. "You're going to a lot of trouble to find this guy. What did he steal?"

Now it was Harlan's turn to laugh. "I'm not telling you that, but rest assured it is expensive and precious to the people who hired us. And if I'm honest, we don't know exactly what it can do, so I think it's safer back with the people it belongs to."

Not exactly true, Shadow thought, *but close enough*. Suddenly, the thought of the astrolabe in the hands of a rogue shifter and whoever had hired him made her feel very uncomfortable.

After another moment of studied concentration, she presumed Maverick came to the same conclusion. He looked over to the woman who was as tall as Shadow, dressed in black leather from head to toe with long, tawny hair and green eyes. "Domino is my head of security, and Grey, next to her, is her second. She, more than anyone, knows of the comings and goings here, and the wider community. Tell them what you've heard, Dom."

She leaned against the glass, arms folded across her chest. "A therian-shifter called Blaze came sauntering into the bar on Wednesday night. Edric was on the door that night and questioned him before letting him in—just casually. He's been here before, and generally causes us no problems, but he has a dubious reputation, like all of his kind. He said he was down here on a job and all he wanted was a drink, so he let him in." She nodded behind them. "He sat in one of the smaller rooms for a few hours, drinking and chatting up girls. He's good looking—if you like dodgy, bad boys." Domino did not look impressed. "Anyway, one of those girls he chatted up is actually one of ours who we pay to circulate to get information." She smirked. "We like to know what trouble may land on our door, and this is one way of keeping tabs. Apparently, he was staying close by, although the job was across the river. He didn't specify what it was and she didn't push. He just said it was tricky and needed his particular expertise." Domino rolled her eyes. "He looked very pleased with himself. Bragging impresses some people."

Harlan looked excited. "Across the river sounds promising. It could be our guy. Any idea where he was staying? And why here? Wouldn't he want to be closer to the job?"

Domino shrugged. "He didn't say. But, if I remember correctly, there's bad blood between Blaze and the North London Pack. And maybe he likes to keep his distance from the job, too."

"Maggie said they weren't as amenable as you guys," Harlan admitted.

Maverick advised, "Unless you like drug dealers, lowlifes, and brawlers, it's best to avoid them."

"Are they the ones based in North Finchley?" Harlan asked.

Maverick gave a tight smile. "Yes. A good distance from here, fortunately. We don't get on."

"This guy, Blaze," Gabe said, drawing them back to the shifter in question. "From where up north?"

"Yorkshire, if I recall," Domino told him. "In his mid-thirties I'd guess, average height, slim build, longish dark hair."

"That's great, thank you," Harlan said. "Have you seen him since then? Or did your girl get an address?"

"No address, but you can talk to her if you like. She's working tonight." She looked at Maverick, who nodded, and then turned to her second. "Grey, can you fetch her?"

Grey's long stride carried him across the room, and while they waited, Maverick topped up their drinks. Shadow watched the dance floor, hearing the other three continue to chat. She filtered them out, concentrating on the scene below her.

The band had finished their set and were clearing their instruments from the stage. Another raised area opposite that she hadn't noticed when they walked in was where the DJ was set up, and from the dancing she could see below, it looked as though he had taken over from the band.

Domino was still studying the club, and Shadow said, "Do you have a band on every Saturday?"

She nodded. "And Tuesdays and Thursdays, most weeks. It's a popular venue for both established and smaller bands."

"All rock?"

"Mainly, but the DJ does 80s nights, too. That's always fun."

From the expression on her face, Shadow assumed she was not an '80s music fan. "Do you ever have disco nights?"

Domino looked sharply at her. "Don't tell me you're a fan?"

"I'm partial to Donna Summer and the Bee Gees." She shrugged. "Weird, I know, but what can I say?"

A broad smile spread across Domino's face. "Well, I'd pay to see you on the dance floor dancing to that!"

Shadow lowered her voice and moved closer. "How did you come to lead security here?"

"I earned it through hard work and a gift for diplomacy. And I fight well too, which helps."

"And do you really see only a little trouble here?"

"Really!" Domino nodded to the mass of people below. "This place is about fun and security for those in the paranormal world."

"And how come you have a human as part of your team?" Shadow asked, genuinely curious.

Domino studied her. "The worlds mix, as you well know. Grey was here one night as a patron when there was an incident. He's ex-Forces and leapt in to help, and managed to impress me and the boss. We felt it was a good idea to have humans on our staff, too. It adds perspective, and it has worked out well. What's your story?"

"Essentially, I was looking for new work, too and fell in with these guys."

Domino looked her up and down and inhaled. "There's something different about you."

Shadow smiled. "Not really." *Time to change the subject.* "Do you know Blaze?"

Her face hardened. "Only slightly. Arrogant shit, but there's no doubt he's good at what he does. He may be from up north, but he gets around a lot."

Their conversation was interrupted by the arrival of Grey and a pretty, young, dark-haired woman dressed in black—a fitted short-sleeved top, short skirt, and high-heeled ankle boots. Her arms were tattooed, and she reminded Shadow of El because of her makeup, piercings, and jewellery.

"Ah, Jet," Maverick said, gesturing to a seat. "Come and join us. Drink?"

She grinned at him as she sat, her bangles clinking together. "I better not if I want to stay sharp. Maybe in another hour."

"Trouble?"

"Just some interesting arrivals I want to chat with."

He gestured to his visitors and introduced them. "Tell them what you remember about your conversation with Blaze the other night."

She groaned and laughed. "He was at his most charming, which meant he was also at his most smug."

"You've spoken to him before?" Gabe asked.

Her eyes ran over Gabe, assessing him. "Sure, several times. I've worked here for a few years now and he's down every few months on one job or another. Sometimes he's here with other girls, but if not, we catch up."

"Sounds like you have a pretty good relationship with him. He tells you stuff."

"Depends how much alcohol he's had and how big his ego is, but generally, yes."

"Even though you work here?"

She smiled. "He might suspect it, but it doesn't bother him."

"I gather he said his job was over the river," Gabe asked. "Did he say where?"

"He said he had to acquire something from a bunch of old men with God complexes. I asked him if he was stealing from a cathedral and he laughed his head off! Said it was more old school than that." Jet huffed. "I thought he was pissed, because it made no sense to me."

Shadow took a seat. This was sounding more promising. Harlan placed his empty glass down on the table and leaned forward. "Did he say who employed him, or where he was delivering it to?"

She shook her head. "No. Even when he's had a few drinks he never says that."

Shadow had another idea. "If he's down here regularly, he'll have friends here. Is there anyone he sees in the club?"

Jet's gaze became distant for a moment, and then she focussed quickly. "Yes. There are a couple of guys I see him talking to. Neither are shifters, and I don't know how they know him, but they seem reasonably friendly."

"You don't know them?" Maverick asked her.

She shook her head. "No—just a passing 'hi' and 'bye.' But one of them is in here tonight. I saw him about an hour ago with a girl, watching the gig."

Gabe stood immediately. "Show me."

They all headed to the window and looked down on the dance floor below. It was more crowded now, and groups congregated together in front of the bar, chatting, and that's where Jet pointed after scrutinising the club.

"That's him. He's short-ish, talking to a blonde woman in jeans at the corner of the bar. Scruffy guy."

"We need to talk to him," Gabe said, watching him. "Got a name?"

Jet smirked. "Typhoo."

That stopped Gabe in his tracks. "*What*?"

"As in Typhoo Tea?" She looked at him quizzically, waiting for the penny to drop. "Tea-leaf—thief—it's his nickname."

Grey sniggered as Gabe rolled his eyes. "Are you serious?"

"Yes—it's a Cockney thing."

"Fuck's sake," Gabe muttered, as Harlan and Shadow exchanged amused glances.

"Don't cause trouble in my club," Maverick warned them, his amber eyes starting to glow.

"No trouble. We just want to talk," Gabe said, wide-eyed with innocence. Shadow almost snorted. *As if anyone would believe that.* "Any other exits I should know about, just in case he decides to run— other than the one outside your office?"

Maverick's lips pursed, but he couldn't hide his amusement. "One behind the bar—but he can't get to that. And one next to the stage door."

Harlan shook Maverick's hand. "Thanks for your help. I appreciate it."

"Good rates at The Orphic Guild then, should I need you?" Maverick asked smoothly.

"Of course."

Gabe was already striding to the door, Shadow next to him. She threw a smile over her shoulder and found everyone watching them.

"Next time."

FIVE

GABE ALREADY HAD A plan, and he addressed Shadow first. "Call my brothers. Make sure the rear exit is covered. Position yourself close by because you'll be quickest to follow him—especially if he heads to the main exit. And keep out of sight!"

"And me?" Harlan asked, rolling his shoulders.

"With me. Let's try the nice approach first. But if he runs, let him. We don't want to make a scene here." He'd found he liked Maverick and his club, and didn't want to piss him off and get himself banned. Although, from the amusement on Maverick's face, he had a feeling they would be watching from the window above, like he was here to provide entertainment. *This was no time to fuck up.*

Shadow gave him a knowing smile, and for a second he felt a stab of desire that he quickly quenched. She was at her sexiest when she hunted, but now was not the time. He saw her reach for her phone in the quiet of the corridor, and he made his way slowly to Typhoo, aware of Harlan keeping pace. He loved these moments of pursuit when everything was so unpredictable. Gabe was pretty sure he would run, but he had every faith that they would get Typhoo outside. He groaned. Even saying that stupid name in his head felt ridiculous.

Typhoo was still at the corner of the bar, talking animatedly to a short blonde woman, and Jet was right. He was scruffy. There was clearly no dress code at Storm Moon, because although many chose to dress up, Typhoo wore old jeans, trainers, and a worn Motley Crew t-shirt. *Ugh. Bad rock.* Gabe hated him already.

Gabe approached him casually, Harlan circling to his other side, and Gabe leaned in and raised his voice. It was quieter here by the bar, but the music was still too loud for comfortable conversation. "Typhoo, I need a word."

Typhoo's head jerked up, his eyes narrowing with suspicion. "Who the fuck are you?"

"I have a question about Blaze."

Typhoo stepped away from the blonde woman, who was watching with equal suspicion and dislike, and glared at Gabe, not in the slightest bit intimidated by his size. "You didn't answer my question. Who are you?"

"You don't need my name," Gabe told him, aware of the looks they were getting. "I understand you saw Blaze this week, and I just need to know where he is."

Typhoo took his time looking Gabe up and down before settling on his face again, arms crossed. "I ain't telling you nuffin'."

Gabe leaned in, nose to nose. "It sounds like you have something to hide, Typhoo. I can assure you that it's in your best interest to tell me what you know."

"Or what?"

Good question. Typhoo clearly felt very confident in the bar surrounded by a crowd, and obviously didn't expect Gabe to do anything in such a respectable place, and he was right. "You have to leave at some point, Typhoo, and me and my friends will be watching and waiting. It's much easier if you just tell me where Blaze is." He shrugged. "That's all I want."

At the mention of friends, Typhoo looked around uneasily, finally noticing Harlan. Then, unexpectedly quickly, he threw his pint at Gabe, punched Harlan, shouldered through them in the confusion, and ran. With lightning-quick reflexes Gabe ducked, though beer still landed on him, and he saw Harlan stagger from the punch, his hand on his jaw. But Gabe was triumphant. Typhoo had done exactly as he wanted. Ignoring the stares from the people immediately around them, he turned his attention to the blonde woman, but she had vanished.

No matter. They made their way through the crowd, most of them completely unaware of the altercation, and because of his height Gabe was able to see Typhoo weaving towards the rear exit by the stage. He couldn't see Shadow, but that didn't mean she wasn't there. He phoned Nahum, telling him where to watch, and then pushed through the exit door, finding that it led to a small courtyard area and a broad set of stairs heading up to the car park.

The rear stage doors also led to the courtyard, and a few band members were lurking outside it, smoking, their attention drawn to the sound of shouts from above. Gabe and Harlan raced upwards, and as they reached ground level, saw that Nahum and Niel had pinned Typhoo to the ground, and that Shadow was standing over them.

She looked at Gabe and Harlan, hands on her hips. "He's a slippery little shit."

"I can see that." Despite Niel and Nahum's strength, Typhoo was wriggling like an eel, yelling curses, and although the area was deserted except for cars and the band's van, it still felt too public. Gabe pointed to the rear of the car park where low-branched leafy trees provided some privacy. "Take him over there."

Niel and Nahum hauled him to his feet, and because he was still yelling, Niel gave him a quick punch. Typhoo's head flew back and he fell silent. They lifted him clear off the ground and carried him to the corner.

"Did you have to punch him?" Gabe remonstrated, watching Typhoo's dazed expression and blood trickling from his nose.

"He was yelling!" Niel pointed out. "Do you want the police around here?"

"Fair point," Gabe grumbled. "I guess it will soften him up."

Harlan grimaced. "I can't see him talking. He's belligerent."

Shadow already had her blades drawn. "I'm sure he will, eventually."

Harlan looked at her, alarmed. "Nothing serious, I hope."

"That depends on him."

Nahum sniffed the air and frowned at Gabe. "You smell of beer."

Gabe glanced down at his stained t-shirt, feeling the dampness on his skin. "He threw his bloody pint at me."

"Better that than a punch!" Harlan said ruefully, rubbing his chin again. "He was quick."

"Admirable, really. Not too quick for me, though," Shadow said, tongue in cheek and earning two fingers from Harlan.

Typhoo was still being held up by Niel and Nahum, but his head sagged down. Avoiding the blood, Gabe took his chin in his hand and lifted his head. "Wakey wakey, Typhoo. I have questions."

"Fuck off," he said, groggily, and Niel sniggered.

"Tell me where to find Blaze and we'll let you go," Gabe repeated. "That's all I want—an address!"

"Who the fuck are you?" Typhoo demanded, finally focussing and glaring at all of them, blood and spit running down his chin.

"Blaze has stolen something from some very powerful men, and they have hired us to get it back." Despite the flecks of blood that threatened to hit Gabe's face, he leaned closer, deciding to layer the threat. "This could get Blaze killed. He has no idea what he's messing with, and neither do the people who have hired him. If you value your friend's life, you'll help us."

"Blaze has been involved in dodgy shit his whole life. He can take care of himself."

Gabe eased back, shaking his head. "I'm not sure he can, with this."

Typhoo swallowed, his eyes nervous, but he remained silent. Gabe nodded at Nahum. "Release one arm, let him clean himself up."

Nahum let him go, and immediately Typhoo grabbed his t-shirt and used it to wipe his face, sniffing loudly.

"We're not the police and we're not the enemy," Gabe continued. "We're his guardian angels. Tell me where to find him."

Shadow was still playing with her blades, twirling them in her hands, and Typhoo watched them uncertainly. "All right. He's been stayin' at a small hotel, but he's not there now. He left yesterday, heading to the drop off point." He shuffled nervously. "He hadn't worked for these guys before, but he said they had a lot of money and he was getting paid well."

"That's good," Gabe said, nodding encouragingly. "Did he say a name, or tell you where the drop off point was?"

"Something about Black Cronos. Another bunch of posh nobs, apparently, but he'd only met one guy."

Harlan had gone very still, his face becoming pale. "Black Cronos? Are you sure?"

"Yeah! I'm not an idiot," Typhoo complained, wiping his arm across his still bloody nose. "He kept making jokes about a God of chaos and disorder."

Harlan exhaled and stepped back a pace. "Yeah, that's him. And the drop off point?"

"Oxford. That other bloody posh nobs place."

"It's a big city, Typhoo. Narrow it down."

"I didn't ask for a bleeding address, did I?" Typhoo answered belligerently. "What am I? His mother?"

Gabe studied his shifty face, convinced he knew more than he was saying. "He's your mate, and mates talk. Where is he staying?"

At his extended silence, Shadow placed her knife against his throat, the blade tickling his skin as fey glamour rolled off her. Typhoo's eyes widened and then swam as if he'd been drugged. Shadow's voice was like honey. "He's in danger, and that means that you are too, so tell me where he's staying, or I'll gut you like a pig."

Typhoo's voice when he finally answered was barely more than a squeak. "The Griffin Inn. He's used it before and he knows the owner."

"Well done," Shadow said, stepping back. "That wasn't so hard, was it?"

Gabe nodded, satisfied. "That's all we need. Let him go." Once free, Typhoo ran across the car park, disappearing into the darkness along the edge of the road as Gabe said, "He'll phone Blaze as soon as he gets a chance, so that means we need to go to Oxford tonight." He turned to find the others watching him expectantly. Well, all except for Harlan, who looked preoccupied. Gabe quickly came to a decision. "I'll go to Oxford with Shadow tonight, but you three stay here. Nahum and Niel, I want you to keep watching the order. I want to know what members are in the Inner Temple—or whatever the hell they call themselves."

Nahum frowned. "That's going to be very hard. Is it worth it?"

"Yes! Someone is leaking information out of the inner circle, and I want to know who! Even if Caldwell Fleet is in denial about it."

"But," Niel reminded him, "it could be that Madame Charbonneau found out who stole the astrolabe. She could be behind it."

"She might," Gabe acknowledged, "but I want to cover all bases. While our primary job is to find the astrolabe, the more we know, the better. I don't want to find us on the end of a double-cross. In fact, we should be careful about what we share of our investigation to Caldwell, because we don't know who he's telling."

"Good suggestion," Shadow agreed.

"Who's looking into the Madame?" Niel asked.

"Barak, which leaves Harlan free to follow up on the origins of The Midnight Sun."

"And Black Cronos?" Nahum asked.

"I'll do that, too," Harlan said, finally seeming to focus. "I know that name and I can't think of why, so leave it with me. Unless, of course, you happen to come across something."

Gabe headed towards his SUV, pulling his keys from his pocket, and the others followed. "If we find the astrolabe tonight, we'll be back in Cornwall tomorrow."

"Sure," Shadow said, snorting with laughter, "and Herne wears tinsel at Yule."

SIX

SHADOW LOOKED OUT OF the window as they drove along the main road into Oxford, the landscape silent around them. She was already excited to be visiting a new city.

It was close to two in the morning. As soon as they had dropped the others off, she and Gabe had grabbed their bags and driven straight here, the roads quiet at this hour, and they had made good time. It was rare for them to spend so many hours alone, and it had felt strange at first, both uncomfortably aware of each other. Gabe radiated strength, and she was acutely aware of every move he made. She couldn't help but notice his strong hands gripping the wheel, and she thought of the way they had felt on her skin in the bathroom in Angel's Rest, and the way his corded muscles had felt beneath her fingers. Banishing those thoughts, she had fallen into safe talk about the case, and then she had looked up Oxford, telling him that it was an old city that housed one of the oldest universities in the world—a suitable place for a meeting to pass on a mysteriously occult object.

"What do you think will be at the place where the order's origins lie?" she asked him.

"Probably a bunch of old stones and nothing else."

"You think they're chasing ghosts?"

He shook his head. "I don't know. The cynic in me says yes, but the fact that the astrolabe has now been stolen twice in recent months mean there has to be more to this. Maybe something alchemical, knowing what these guys are like."

Personally, Shadow hoped it would be old treasure or arcane weapons, because that would be more interesting than old documents and buildings, but she had to admit that Gabe's alchemical suggestion was the more likely assumption.

They passed through the leafy outskirts of the city, and Gabe asked, "How far now?"

"A bit further along yet, in the centre," she instructed, checking the directions on her phone. "Just keep going on this road. I must admit, I didn't expect we'd be leaving London so soon."

"Or me, if I'm honest, but an early lead is a bonus." Gabe glanced at her, the streetlights illuminating half of his face. "You don't think this will be over tonight though, do you?"

"No. This has the feel of something dark and twisty, and I think tonight will just add to that."

"It will be good if you can pick up Blaze's magic. We might be able to track his movements from his hotel."

"I think I'll have trouble. Besides, he might have already left," she reminded him. "He was only coming to drop off the astrolabe."

He grunted. "He seems like a party person. I reckon he'd stick around to socialise on a Saturday night."

"True," Shadow answered thoughtfully. "We always liked to celebrate a win."

"We?" he asked, shooting her a quizzical glance.

"My team back in the Otherworld. Every successful job was celebrated, as soon as we'd split the money."

"And how many were there of you?"

"Four of us. Me, Bloodmoon, who's another fey, Cheloc, a satyr, and Rowan, an Aerikeen."

"What's one of those?"

"A bird-shifter." It was odd talking about her old team; it gave her a pang of homesickness, and she hoped that they were all okay. She'd mentioned them before, but no one had asked for details then. It was almost like an unspoken pact that they didn't discuss the old days, because she really didn't ask the Nephilim too many questions about the past, either. But here, the dark, quiet confines of the car invited confidences. "He was handy for break-ins."

Gabe smirked. "Of course. And the satyr?"

"A good fighter, utterly loyal, with the best connections in the business. And he loved gambling—was good at it, too."

"And Bloodmoon?"

She smiled at the memory of him. "Charming, handsome, excellent swordsman, great horseman, and very funny."

"More than a friend?"

"No. Just a very good one. Although, he was an outrageous flirt." She stared through the windscreen, the Oxford streets suddenly replaced with memories of her team. "I wonder what they're doing now. I wonder if they miss me."

"Of course they do, Little Miss Fey," Gabe teased. "In fact, I wonder if they get anything done at all without you."

"Well, that's true," she said breezily, shooting him a grateful glance. Sometimes Gabe was unexpectedly kind. *No, she shouldn't think 'unexpected'—he was always kind.* It was an admirable quality. She focussed on the present, deciding now was not the time to ask Gabe about his wife. She wanted a whiskey in hand before broaching that topic, and needed him to be more relaxed than he was now. She brought the conversation back to Blaze and checked her phone again. "Take the next left," she instructed.

He turned onto a road leading into the city centre, where it was much livelier. Young people exited nightclubs and pubs, the sounds of laughter and shouting filling the air.

"This place is busier than I expected," she said, watching a group stumble down the street, obviously drunk.

"It's a city, and it's full of students—and students like drinking."

She checked the GPS. "Take the second right, and the hotel should be on the left."

In another couple of minutes, Gabe passed an elegant, eighteenth century building with The Griffin Inn displayed on a sign swinging above its entrance. He cruised down the street, turned, and then found a spot to park.

After studying the hotel, Gabe suggested, "We should check in here. It looks good. And I think there's a car park around the back."

Shadow nodded. "Well, most hotels have around the clock reception, so we should be okay. And it is convenient."

"Plus, it gives us a good reason to nose around."

"It looks pricey, though. I hope Harlan doesn't object."

"It's the order who are paying, and they want their astrolabe back." He gave her a lazy smile, and Shadow's stomach flipped. "Besides, we're worth it."

"I am, you mean," she said flippantly, and gave him her cheesiest grin as he started to scowl. She scooted out of the seat and grabbed her bag from the boot. "Check us in then, oh great leader."

"You always like to push it, don't you?" he grumbled, grabbing his own bag and following her.

When they entered the hotel, they found a couple of staff seated behind the counter at the rear of the lobby. While Gabe went to check them in, Shadow strolled around, noting that the interior of the building was all cream wooden panelling, polished floors, and tasteful furniture, and Shadow could already feel the power of wealth creeping up on her. It was a good feeling. She liked money. It meant you could stay in nice places and eat good food. And she liked that money meant she didn't need to worry about the tedious stuff...like bills.

What surprised her was that Blaze was staying here. His friend, Typhoo, didn't look that well-groomed, but she assumed that Blaze's acquaintances must be broad. So far, though, she could not detect any shifter magic, which was frustrating.

Gabe joined her. "Anything?"

"Not yet."

"Well, I've got us two rooms on the third floor, so let's drop our bags off and do some snooping. Of course," he said, as they entered the lift, "he might have already left, if Typhoo got hold of him."

"Maybe Typhoo hasn't got his number. I wouldn't give it out if he was just my casual friend who I bumped into in a club occasionally."

Gabe nodded. "Good point. You sure you're not too tired to search tonight?"

"Oh, no. Night hunts are the best."

Gabe gave her a slow smile as they exited the lift and walked to their rooms. Unnervingly, Gabe's room was right next to hers, and she could hear him moving around as she dumped her bag and used the bathroom. This *thing* between them hadn't abated since they'd returned from Angel's Rest, although they both ignored whatever it was. It was easier when they were at home with the others around them, but there was something about staying somewhere else that just stirred up her blood—and his, too. She could tell. He had that glint in his eye again.

She took a deep breath in and out, cursing her hormones, and then went to meet him in the corridor as arranged. "Okay, where to first?"

"Let's prowl the corridors, starting with this one."

They found nothing on their own floor, or the second, but on the first floor Shadow paused as she detected the faint swirl of shifter magic. She walked along the dimly lit corridors slowly, pausing outside each room, until she reached the end. "I think he's on this floor, but I can't tell which room. And I don't know if the magic is fresh or not, either."

"So, he's either in bed or out somewhere, and without barging into every room, there's no way to know." Gabe looked pleased anyway. "But at least we have *something*. I noticed there's a bar and restaurant at the back on the ground floor, but it's closed now, so he definitely won't be there."

"That's a shame," she said, realising she was hungry and thirsty. "I could do with a drink."

Gabe steered her towards the stairs. "Let's head out and find a bar, then. Even at this hour, I'm sure we'll find something."

Since their arrival, the centre of town had quieted again, and Shadow feared they'd be too late to find anything open until Gabe searched on his phone, finally leading them down a narrow side street to a place called Plush Oxford.

"This is the only place open now. Cocktails, beer, wine, and bar food. This work for you?"

They were standing in front of another fine, eighteenth century building where a set of steps led down to a door.

"It's set under the brick arches of the medieval city." He grinned at her. "And it's a gay bar, but it doesn't bother me. They're all-inclusive."

"As long as they have food, I don't care either," Shadow said, following him down the stairs.

Once they'd paid their way inside, they heard the loud thud of music, and Shadow found they were in a warren of corridors with rooms set on either side, as well as a large dance floor still heaving with people. They managed to find a table in the bar under the stone arches that formed the roof, and Shadow eyed the eclectic groups of people around her while Gabe brought cocktails.

"Herne's horns," she said when he returned with margaritas. "I love this place!"

"Two clubs in one night," he said, laughing. "I thought my clubbing days were behind me."

"You went clubbing in ancient Mesopotamia?"

"Not quite like this. But obviously there were late night bars, music, revelry, drinking, dancing—"

"And food?" she broke in hopefully.

"Chips are on the way—lots of them."

She chinked his glass. "Thank you. If Blaze is still in Oxford and not in bed, then there's a good chance he's here. As soon as we've eaten, I'll scout the place, and see if I can feel him."

"And we have a sketchy description of him," Gabe reminded her.

After they had eaten their food and started on the next cocktail—she'd decided they were too good for just one—she detected shifter magic. "He's here," she said softly, scanning the room as casually as she could. Not that it was really an issue. Everyone was so busy letting loose, they weren't really watching their table.

In seconds she saw him leaning across the bar as he ordered a drink, exactly as Domino had described him. He was tall and slim, his shoulder-length brown hair curling slightly on his shoulders. It was warm in the club, and he only wore a t-shirt with his jeans, revealing a Celtic-style tattoo on his forearm, but a messenger bag was slung over his shoulder, and it looked heavy.

"Far end of the bar, with a bulky bag."

"I see him," Gabe said, trying to hide his excitement. "I think he's brought it in with him."

"And he's buying two drinks, too," Shadow noted. "Is he handing it off in here? There must be better places!" she said, incredulous. She was always a fan of secluded places for dodgy exchanges herself, but there was no accounting for taste.

"Maybe he's killing time until the meet up."

"I'll follow him back to his seat," Shadow suggested, "on the pretext of heading to the ladies."

As soon as Blaze left the room, she followed him at a distance, watching him weave through the crowd before finally ducking into a dark side room, where he sat next to a young woman with long, dark hair. Unfortunately, her back was to the door and Shadow couldn't see her face, but he seemed to settle in, draping his arm around her shoulder, and she returned to Gabe.

"He's with a woman, but I don't think she's the one. They're too intimate."

"We need to watch them. We're too far away here." Gabe picked up his drink and stood, grabbing her hand. "Time to play."

"What are you doing?" she asked, glancing at his hand and then staring at him pointedly.

"We're going to find a nice seat and get cosy."

"We're going to do *what*?"

"This is no time to argue. Just remember, I'm irresistible, and you can't keep your eyes off me. Or your hands."

He looked insufferably amused with himself and she narrowed her eyes at him, his heat already radiating up her arm.

"You have got to be kidding me!"

"If you don't move right now, I'm going to kiss you."

"I'll stab you first."

He leaned in closer, his head bending and his lips closing in on hers. Barely thinking about what she was doing, she turned and dragged him with her, almost feeling his amusement. *Bastard.*

She pulled him along the corridor. The club was beginning to empty, but those who were still there were glassy-eyed and raucous, and several couples were clasped in close embraces. Feeling hot at the thought of getting close to Gabe, she pulled him into the low-lit room and onto the squashy leather sofa just inside the door. It gave them a good view of Blaze, who was busy flirting with the unknown woman.

Gabe pinned her in the corner of the sofa, his arm already across the back of the seat and curling protectively around her shoulders, pulling her to him. His eyes drifted over her lips.

"Well, this is nice."

The heat he radiated was almost overwhelming, and it took all of her willpower not to sink into his arms. Unwillingly she stared at his lips, noting how full they were, and thought how very good they'd probably taste. Keeping a smile pasted to her face, she said, "I'm glad you think this is funny, when the reality is that I'm in the middle of my very own hash-tag Me Too moment."

His smile spread as he put his lips next to her ear, his warm breath making her giddy. "Really? Because I can hear your heart pounding right now, and I don't think it's with fear."

He planted feather-light kisses along her neck as her eyes closed, her breathing becoming shallow. *Herne's horns.* That felt way better than she'd imagined, and she'd imagined it plenty.

She forced her eyes open. "You really should stop that."

"Then say it like you mean it," he murmured through his kisses that were now melting her insides. His hand slipped into her hair as he stroked the base of her neck.

"I'm trying to focus on Blaze," she hissed, watching him kiss the mystery woman across the room.

"Trying? So I'm putting you off, then? That's good to know."

The one good thing she had to admit was that no one was taking the slightest bit of notice of them—least of all, Blaze. The woman was almost straddling him now, and Shadow closed her own eyes again, swimming in the heady scent of Gabe. He smelt of a peppery spice, warm and inviting.

Focus, she chastised herself. When she next opened her eyes, the woman was pulling away from Blaze, and he looked like Shadow felt —drugged. She couldn't see his face, but he seemed to loll against the back of the sofa. *Something was wrong.* She could feel it. And now that she was closer to them, the woman felt all wrong, too.

"What's going on?" Gabe mumbled, lifting his head to look at her. His back was to Blaze, but he didn't look around. "You've become tense."

The woman eased back slowly, her hand reaching towards the messenger bag that was wedged behind Blaze. "Shit. I think she's the one. And she's done something to Blaze."

As Shadow spoke, the woman turned, giving Shadow the briefest glimpse of black eyes—flat and far from human—and as she swung around even more, Shadow grabbed Gabe's head, her hands in his thick hair, and pulled him in for a long kiss. He leaned against her, pinning her to the back of the sofa, his lips exploring her own. For a second, she almost forgot what was happening, but then she felt the woman walk past. Waiting for a beat, she then pushed Gabe away.

Blaze was insensible on the sofa. In fact, from here he looked dead. Shadow again moved Gabe off her and pulled him out of the room. "Fuck it. She's gone!"

"She can't have gone far," he said, following her down the corridor.

They spotted the woman heading through the exit and hurried after her, emerging onto the street where a few people loitered by the entrance. They hurried to the deserted entrance of the lane, the woman already ahead on the main road. Gabe began pulling his t-shirt off, and he thrust it at her, his wings expanding.

"I'll follow from above—and be careful."

Shadow glanced back anxiously at the club entrance, but they were out of view for now. "But what's the plan? Are we aiming to just take it from her—presuming the astrolabe is in the bag—or find out where she's taking it?"

"Part of me wants to know who's behind this, but that's not really our job," he said, clearly anxious to get moving. "Let's wait until she's somewhere quiet, and just take it."

She grabbed his arm. "I don't know what she is, but she's *not* human."

He nodded and then soared upwards, leaving Shadow to follow on foot.

SEVEN

HARLAN WOKE IN THE middle of the night after a poor sleep that had been disturbed by dreams of shifters and the information they had found out from Typhoo.

He lay on his back, staring up at the ceiling and thinking about what Black Cronos was. He had brooded all the way to his flat, sitting in the back of Gabe's SUV in the dark, watching the lights of London flow past like a river. Gabe and the others had asked him a few questions, but he'd batted them off, telling them he needed to think. He had heard of Black Cronos years and years ago, but the mention was more of a rumour than anything substantial, something mysterious and ephemeral. However, the name was also so unusual it had stuck with him. He wondered if Olivia knew anything, or Mason. Or even JD might, but for obvious reasons he didn't want to involve either of the latter.

Harlan's mind was too busy to go back to sleep, so he rolled out of bed and headed to the kitchen to make coffee, and then took it to his small office and library. A few months before, he had found a collection of documents and notes in the guild's library, and had been so intrigued with them that he made copies for his own reference. It was these he wanted to read now. The notes had been amassed by the collectors who had gone before him. There was intelligence on rival organisations, such as The Order of Lilith and others like it. It included members both past and present, structure, headquarters, and whatever was known about them. He was sure he'd read the name in these. They now stored the files on the computer too, but he liked to handle the old, paper ones. It was as if they stored impressions in the pages that a computer failed to impart.

After the job at Angel's Rest, Harlan had added his own notes to the file for The Order of Lilith, updating their address and the members who had died. He hadn't seen Nicoli since. After the theft of the astrolabe he'd wondered if Nicoli was behind this problem, but it hadn't seemed the right fit for him somehow, and he was glad his gut feeling had been proven right. He paused, remembering Jensen's broken body in the Chamber of Air, and the fact that Mia's body had been lost forever, and shuddered. The Temple of the Trinity had not been what he expected, and he hoped this particular investigation wasn't going to play out the same way.

He checked his watch as he settled in his chair. Gabe and Shadow would be in Oxford now, and he wondered if they were still up and whether they'd had any success. It was better that they followed their lead quickly, which meant he needed to find answers quickly, too. He opened the file, and settled in to read.

Gabe hovered high over the lane, watching the mysterious woman move swiftly through the centre of town.

The streets were empty now, but it didn't make her easier to keep track of. She was like Shadow; she blended into the darkness, and even under streetlights seemed to look insubstantial. He couldn't even see Shadow now, but he presumed she was maintaining a safe distance in her own pursuit.

Shadow said she wasn't human, so what did that make her? Another shifter, or something else? And how had she killed Blaze? One swift look was all it took to see that he was dead. Soon enough, someone would find him as the club closed, and then all Hell would break loose.

They should have stopped it. But then again, how? They couldn't make a scene in the club; that would have got them into all sorts of trouble. And why couldn't he tell there was something different about her? Probably because he was enjoying himself too much with Shadow. Even now, he could feel Shadow's soft skin. He was an utter fool.

Instead of getting lost in those thoughts, he concentrated on the scene below. The colleges of Oxford jostled around shops and lanes, their old buildings imparting a weight of ages. There were so many churches, squares, and cloistered grounds it was bewildering. The woman turned into the leafy garden of a church, and he realised this was their chance. He soared downwards, dropping on her from above, and pinned her to the ground, facedown, the bag squashed beneath them.

The woman was slender but strong, and she twisted beneath him as she tried to throw him off, but he lay across her and attempted to pull the bag out from under her. She bucked, unbalancing him, and just as he wondered where Shadow was, she arrived.

"Grab the bag," he said, still restraining the struggling woman.

But as Shadow leaned in, the woman turned and looked Gabe full in the face. He gasped, almost releasing her in shock. The woman's eyes were utterly black, and as she stared into his, he felt as if she was staring into his soul, feeling a tug deep within him.

Shocked and disorientated, he lost his grip and she wriggled free, but Shadow didn't hesitate. She punched her, and as the woman fell back, Shadow grabbed the bag, wrenching it from her grasp. She threw it over her shoulder, and pulling her two knives out, circled the woman.

The thief dropped and rolled, kicking at Shadow. She dodged her easily, and Gabe lunged at the woman. But she was like a wraith, and again she stared at him, exerting her strange power, and he felt his breath catch in his chest.

The sound of sirens broke up their fight, and police cars streamed past, their blue and red lights playing across the gravestones. All of them dropped to the ground in an effort to stay hidden, and by the time Shadow and Gabe stood again, the thief had vanished.

Shadow whirled around. "Where has she gone?"

Gabe scanned the area, but there was no sign of her. "I have no idea, and I daren't fly again. Did she hurt you?"

"No, and I still have the bag." She peered inside it and grinned. "And the astrolabe."

"Good." He retrieved his t-shirt and put it on again. "We need to get off the streets. They must have found Blaze, and strolling around at this hour won't look good."

"But the woman?"

"Let her go. We have what we came for."

Shadow looked disappointed. "So it's over already?"

He shook his head. "I don't think we should drop this just yet. I want to know more about this Dark Star, and why someone is prepared to kill for it. Don't you?"

She lifted her chin, her eyes firing with excitement. "Absolutely."

Harlan rubbed his hand across his face and muttered to himself. "Damn it!"

He was still sitting in his library, and the previous hour had flown by. He'd found the references to Black Cronos, and admittedly although they didn't tell him much, they said enough to know the group needed to worry.

The first record that mentioned Black Cronos was made in 1894 by Rosamund Fairchild, a collector for The Orphic Guild's Rome branch. She was outmanoeuvred for an artefact called the Handmaid's

Chalice, a suitably intriguing object that promised that whoever drank from it could bewitch anyone they chose. It was also intriguing that a woman was a prominent collector at that time. Harlan imagined she must have had independent wealth and enough status to allow her to travel where she chose. Maybe she was married to an enlightened man, or perhaps she was a rich widow. Whatever her background, it seemed she spoke fluent Italian and had helped set up the branch.

Rosamund had recorded the encounter in a flowing script, noting that she had been followed for weeks by a shadowy figure who she struggled to lose. She had finally found the chalice in an old palace in Florence, after searching for it for months for an unnamed client, and within days it had been stolen from a secure location and her pursuer vanished. During that time the Rome branch's director had received a note from Black Cronos, telling them to stop their search or there would be consequences. They hadn't, and other than being trailed, Rosamund had been unharmed. Harlan rolled his eyes at the suitably Machiavellian threats. Rosamund went on to say that they had never found out anything else about them.

Then during the chaos of the First World War there had been another mention of Black Cronos in London, the entry made by another collector named Peter Shelley. The guild had been threatened, again by letter, to stop searching for a collection of papers. Peter had ignored it and was then attacked one night and badly beaten, but he couldn't identify his attacker, and he never found the papers. And then the same thing happened again just before the Second World War, a threat this time to stop searching for an old diary.

Three letters, all sent to the director. That was weird. Had The Orphic Guild sufficiently threatened them to warrant such a warning? And why bother to warn at all?

Harlan flicked through the few remaining documents, pleased to see the letters themselves had been kept. Initially, he was disappointed. There were no clues as to who had written them, obviously, revealing no name other than Black Cronos, and they certainly gave no indication of where the organisation was based. *Or maybe it was an individual? Possibly even a family affair?* But then laying them out side by side, Harlan had a shock. The handwriting was identical. He blinked as he spread them out. Three letters, sent between 1894 and 1937. Not too long of a period, so potentially the same person would have been alive then and working for the organisation the entire time.

Damn it. He needed to see the original documents, and that meant going to the guild, but that would have to wait until later. He was exhausted and needed more sleep. Before retiring again, his phone rang, startling him in the silence of his flat. "Gabe. Is everything okay?"

"We have the astrolabe, but it wasn't secured without difficulties," he said, updating Harlan on their encounter. "The thief was not entirely human, but I don't know what exactly she was."

"She killed Blaze?" Harlan asked, shocked. "With a kiss?"

"Looked that way." Gabe sounded rattled, and that was unusual. "I'll explain more tomorrow. But, I wanted you to know that we have it. We'll get some sleep and return to London later today. I also want you to know that we are going to continue to look into this, even though the job is over."

"Excellent, I think we should, too." Harlan stared at the papers in front of him, deciding to wait to tell Gabe what he had found out. "I need to head to the guild later this morning. What if I catch up with you this afternoon at Chadwick House? Say, three o'clock?"

"Perfect," he said, ending the call.

Harlan couldn't believe it. *Blaze was dead.* As awful as that was, it also made things far more complicated. They had fulfilled their obligations to Caldwell, but like Gabe, Harlan wanted to know more about Black Cronos and this strange woman. If they were prepared to kill Blaze, the likelihood was they would try to get the astrolabe again. They could hand over the Dark Star and be out of it, but he had the feeling all of their lives could be at risk—including the members of the order—and that didn't sit easy on his conscience.

The one person who may know more about all of this was JD, and he was also the one person Harlan did not want to speak to. He gazed out of the window, not really seeing the faint approach of dawn as he debated what to do. He'd sleep on it, and then make a decision.

Barak stared at the computer screen, his eyes aching. This was the first time since Gabe had asked that he'd had a chance to examine the inventory, but Sundays were generally quieter at the warehouse in Harecombe, so he took advantage of it.

It was mid-morning, and he was the only Nephilim here today. He'd told his brothers to have the day off, feeling he'd get more done alone. The security team was covering the gate and perimeter, and there was only a skeleton crew in today, so he was determined to find the information he needed.

He'd filtered the shipments by port and date, and found one large shipment on the date in question, but it was composed of lots of companies, as well as individuals. He ran down the list, knowing many of the companies now and able to dismiss some easily. He was focussing more on individuals, but without a name to go on, he was looking for final addresses.

He groaned. He'd thought this would be easy, but it was turning out to be tedious and he blinked, his eyes dry. He absently sipped his coffee as he scrolled, almost spilling it in shock when he saw The Order of the Midnight Sun listed as an address. He clicked on the details of the package. All shipped goods should be itemised, and this one was no different. Several objects were listed, but not one of them was an astrolabe, and they all had proof of purchase. He frowned. *That couldn't be right.* He shook his head, amused. They must have covered their tracks, hiding it within the other items—most likely the nineteenth century statue that was listed and was of no significant value. On arrival in port, all goods had to clear customs, and most of the time it was a formality. Drugs or guns were the most commonly smuggled items, but hidden antiquities were also big business. Barak knew that Caspian ran a legitimate business, but that he also had occult customers. Not surprising, considering he was a witch. But it was unlikely Caspian or any other member of his family would know the details of particular shipments.

Barak scrolled down the page, looking to see who had sent it, and grinned in triumph. Aubrey Cavendish. *Let's hope it isn't an alias,* he mused. Just to be sure, he checked the dates on either side, and once satisfied that no other shipments had been made to the order, he checked the arrival date, finding it had arrived two days later in the large port of Falmouth. It had been collected by hand from their office, and signed for by the same person, an ornate, fanciful signature.

He leaned back in his chair, thoughtful. Cavendish was taking no chances. Normally, items like this would be posted by courier once they had arrived. He phoned Gabe, passing on the information, and frowned when Gabe updated him on their overnight activities. "It's over, then?"

"No, because this bothers me, and I can't just drop it," Gabe told him. "Will you do me another favour, please?"

"Sure."

"See if you can find out what The Order of the Midnight Sun used to be called—pre-fifteenth century—and see if you can find out anything about a Madame Raphael Charbonneau. Harlan will do some research too, but he's focussing on Black Cronos for now."

"You think this astrolabe is more significant than we've been led to believe?"

"Maybe even more than the order suspects. But at least there aren't any angels involved."

Once the call ended, Barak stared at the screen, thinking about angels and their previous assignment, The Book of Raziel. Shadow had buried it under rock and water, and he wondered if that would be enough. The old God had once been so incensed at its loss that he plucked it from the ocean, so it being buried beneath an avalanche of rock was no guarantee it wouldn't be found again. And Raziel also had an obsession with the book—enough to build an entire temple to it.

Over the last few weeks, they'd all wondered if the search for The Temple of the Seeker was really over. *Did Raziel know his book had been found and his temple destroyed? And if he didn't, why not?* He'd spent a lot of time making it, laying clues, sending innocent men insane with the burden of his demands. Surely he wasn't about to just let it go. Maybe the war between the angels had raged long after their deaths, and had long-lasting consequences. Niel's encounter with Chassan, one of the angels of air, had been alarming, too. He *knew* the Nephilim were back. *Didn't it matter? Did no one care?* It seemed they had all been watching over their shoulders, waiting for a summons or a visitation that they desperately hoped would not come, because the consequences could be disastrous.

Barak rather liked this life, although he was itching to leave the security job, as good as Caspian had been to them. He wanted to be with the others, searching for occult goods and exploring their new world. He shrugged it off, though. Gabe had given him a job to do, so he should get on with it.

He had just started a basic search for information on the order when he heard the door below bang open and then footsteps on the stairs leading to the offices. He went to the inner office window, surprised to see Estelle, and he headed to the door to speak to her.

"Hey, Estelle. What are you doing here on a Sunday?"

"Trying to find peace and quiet, and failing," she said, glaring at him.

He ignored her jibe as she walked past him to the office that was normally occupied by Dean Ellis, the warehouse manager. She looked as good and as pissed off as usual, except that she was dressed casually today. She was wearing a fitted t-shirt and yoga pants that hugged every curve, and her hair was caught up in a loose knot, revealing the dip of her shoulder and the nape of her neck, and he swallowed. *Herne's horns, she looked good.* Barak should have found her aggressive manner off-putting, but he didn't. Beneath that tough-bitch exterior, he detected vulnerability. And then as she slammed the door behind her, he winced. *Maybe he was delusional. Or maybe it was the thought of her soft skin and long hair falling over him that gave him such idiotic thoughts.*

He leaned on the door frame, contemplating his actions. Ever since the beginning of the week she'd been meaner than usual, and somehow, more brittle, too. It had coincided with Caspian's attack by spirits, and he wondered if that had shaken her, or if it was just a coincidence. Although Caspian had been recuperating with Reuben, she had spent more time here than at her main office—and Dean was complaining. Taking his life in his hands, Barak headed to the office, knocked, and opened the door.

"What's going on, Estelle?"

She was busy arranging her phone and bag and switching on the computer, and she glanced up at him, narrowing her eyes. "Nothing. Just paperwork and a couple of shipments I want to check. I won't be here next week."

"Why not?"

She leaned her elbows on the table and met his eyes. "What business is it of yours?"

"Because something is wrong. You're always a miserable cow, but this week you're even worse. What's happened?"

Her hands clenched and he felt her magic build as she spat, "I beg your pardon! Did you just call me a miserable cow?"

Barak knew he shouldn't provoke a powerful witch, but actually, he realised, that's exactly what he wanted to do. He had a reasonable working relationship with her normally, and she had a good sense of humour when she relaxed. But most of the time, she was uptight. Constrained. Sad.

"You are and you know you are, and that worries me, Estelle." He opened his arms wide, knowing, if he was honest, that it displayed his huge, muscled chest to her often-admiring eyes. "You are rich and powerful in the business world, a skilled witch, an intelligent, beautiful woman with impeccable taste, and yet you are so fucking miserable that I just don't get it!" She sat in stunned silence, looking at him as he advanced into the room. "It's pretty clear to me that you hate your life, which begs the question—why don't you change it? You could do anything!"

Estelle's mouth trembled, her face went white, and her eyes filled with tears for the briefest moment before she blinked them away. "How dare you. Get out!"

He refused to stop or break eye contact with her. "Why are you lying to yourself? What does it achieve? If I've learnt anything in my life, it's that you have to do what makes you happy, or life is long and hard. And what's the point of that?" Her folded arms trembled across her chest, and he knew his time was limited. "I wondered if you were worried about Caspian, but you hate him, too. What a dysfunctional mess your family is—and that's saying something, considering what my family dynamics were like."

Without warning, she struck him with a bolt of energy, blasting him out of the door and over the railing that edged the walkway above the warehouse. Instinctively, he flexed his wings and they shot out from his shoulders, shredding his t-shirt, and he hovered in the air, cursing himself for not preparing for this, but mostly admiring her speed and power.

Estelle was already running to the door, her hands raised, looking as if she was about to hit him again, and then she stalled as the realisation of what she'd done spread across her face. He glanced below him, relieved to see no one was there. With luck, the staff were all outside.

Barak flew back to the walkway, landed softly in front of her, and then folded his wings behind him. "Feel better now? You're lucky I'm Nephilim, or you could have killed me."

She glared at him. "You shouldn't have provoked me, then. You know what I am."

"And you should have better control over yourself. Working with you is like working with a lit stick of dynamite." Barak was suddenly furious with himself. His provocation had risked exposing both of them, and for what purpose? *To get a rise out of Estelle? He'd done that, but what the hell had that achieved?* He turned his back on her, marching into his office and grabbing a spare t-shirt from the cupboard in the corner where they kept some company stock. He pulled it on, and when he turned around, she was standing in the doorway, watching him.

"I've never seen your wings before," she said, her dark eyes openly curious.

"Just ask, in future." He glanced at the security screens showing activity around the warehouse, and saw the handful of staff clustered outside smoking or drinking coffee, and he sighed. *They'd got away with their little tiff.* He sat in front of the computer, pulling up the search screen again, and then stared at her. "You're right. I shouldn't have provoked you, but sometimes you're exasperating. And I meant it. No one should be as sad and angry as you all the time. But I won't bother you again." He looked back at the screen, ignoring Estelle, and trying to clear his head.

Nevertheless, she was still in the doorway, her expression contrite. "I'm sorry, Barak. I lashed out, stupidly. It's just the second time this week that I've been on the receiving end of verbal abuse, and I was over it. Did I hurt you?"

"Does it look like it?" he asked. "You've just ruined a perfectly good t-shirt, that's all." Then he frowned. "And it wasn't abuse. Well, it wasn't meant to be."

"I can assure you that it was the first time." Barak was itching to ask what had happened, but he wouldn't push again. She continued, "What are you doing?"

"If I told you I was doing research for Gabe rather than working, would it earn me another blast in the chest?"

"No. What kind of research?"

"He's working a case with Harlan, for The Order of the Midnight Sun, and he needs some more background on them."

She walked into the office, perching on one of the chairs. "Why have they hired you?"

"Someone stole an astrolabe from them, a very important one, apparently. It was shipped through here originally, from France." His lips twitched. "They stole it from some French woman."

Estelle laughed, finally relaxing. "Karma, then."

"Maybe. But Gabe and Shadow stole it back again last night."

"That quick? Impressive. Go on," she said, suitably intrigued. "Tell me more."

He filled her in on the background and what they'd found so far. "Do you know much about the order?"

"Nope. But," she picked up her chair and put it next to him, hustling him along, "I'll help you look."

She batted his hand off the mouse and he wrested back again, amused. "I thought you had work to do?"

"This sounds far more interesting. Or don't you want my help?" Her eyes held his with a clear challenge.

"Far be it for me to question your wishes," he said, starting the search again, and thinking what an interesting few hours this was proving to be.

Eight

SHADOW SIPPED HER COFFEE, half slumped over on a table in the hotel's dining room, watching Gabe eat a late, large breakfast.

They had made it before the breakfast buffet closed, both trying to get as much sleep as they could before they travelled back to London. Even so, she was gritty-eyed. She and Gabe had ended up sleeping in the same room, but there were no romantic entanglements, despite the fact that she remembered every second of his lips on hers. It was purely for security.

Gabe had taken first watch while she grabbed a couple of hours of sleep, and then she took the second, wary of any movement along the corridor or on the street outside. But they were undisturbed, which was a relief. They had travelled back to the hotel quickly after their encounter with the thief, cautious of being followed, but no doubt the thief was as keen to keep off the streets as they were.

Before going to bed, she and Gabe had examined the astrolabe, curious as to what had caused so much excitement. But beautiful though it was, it gave away nothing of the secrets it might reveal. Now it sat on the table between them, wrapped in a bag.

"Have you phoned Caldwell yet?" she asked Gabe.

"No," he mumbled through a mouthful of food. "I'll do it when we get to London."

"You don't want to give it back, do you?"

"No, but I will." He put his knife and fork down, his breakfast finished, and picked up his cup. "I just want a few more answers first."

"We're thieves. It's no business of ours what he does with it, or what's there. That's the first rule of business. We fulfil our contract and move on."

Gabe frowned. "But a few hours ago, you said you didn't want to drop it and were enthusiastic to know more. What's changed?"

"Sleep and the cold light of day. Don't get me wrong—I'm curious. But if we overly involve ourselves in our jobs, we'll get caught up in crap that has nothing to do with us."

His expression softened. "I know that. But this is our business to shape as we choose. I will give the astrolabe back, but I just want to do a bit more digging."

"It's like you're marshalling an army. You've got half the Nephilim on this."

"We're not quite an army. Besides, I used to be good at it."

"I'm more worried about the woman. What was she?"

Gabe rubbed his chest. "I felt her here, like those weird eyes were trying to pull my very being out. Did you?"

"I felt something, but she wasn't really staring at me like she was you. When she stood up after she killed Blaze, I glimpsed them then and they looked soulless." She shuddered. "I'm not easily spooked, but I had the feeling that if she saw me watching her last night, all would be lost." She laughed. "Sounds dramatic, right?"

"So you kissed me."

This was the first time they had spoken about that, and she held his gaze. "Yes. You started it, and it was a ruse."

"You threw yourself into it very convincingly."

"So did you, Mr I-think-I'll-smother-your-neck-with-kisses."

His slow, sexy smile spread across his face, and once again she could feel those kisses on her neck. *Maybe this is why they hadn't mentioned it in the bedroom. The hotel restaurant was safe ground.* "Do you want me to promise not to do it again?"

That was the last thing she wanted, but she said, "Yes, I think that's an excellent idea."

Gabe continued to smirk. "Sorry, I can't. Who knows when we may need it as cover?"

"True," she acknowledged, deciding to tease him. "And I may have to do the same thing with any of your brothers, too. Or even Harlan. Who knows what weird situations we might get into?"

Shadow watched his expression tighten, her own smirk hidden behind her drink. And then he smirked, too. "You're right. I may have to do the same with Olivia. It's a useful tactic."

She couldn't help but grin. "Excellent. That's that sorted. So now what?" She lowered her cup and leaned forwards. "Do you think Black Cronos could be based in Oxford? Maybe we should stick around."

"Even if they are, it will be a waste of time. We have no leads, and if that woman is still in town, I don't want to give her a chance to steal the astrolabe again." He shook his head. "No, we need to leave, and hope that the others find us a clue. Besides, Blaze's death is all over the news now. I do not wish to be questioned by the police if we've been caught on one of the club's cameras, do you?"

The thought of being questioned again filled Shadow with dread. "No. You're right. Let's get out of here, and I'll give some thought as to what kind of creature our attacker could be."

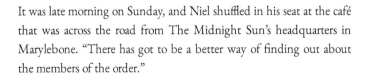

It was late morning on Sunday, and Niel shuffled in his seat at the café that was across the road from The Midnight Sun's headquarters in Marylebone. "There has got to be a better way of finding out about the members of the order."

"Like what?" Nahum asked, eyes fixed firmly on the front of the building. "We can't break in because it's alarmed."

"But what is this telling us?" Niel argued. "We can see who's going in and out, but we have no idea who they are or what their role is. It's a waste of time."

"We're getting photos," Nahum reminded him. "They could be useful."

"But we have the astrolabe!" Gabe had updated them earlier. "We'll give it back to them later, and then we can go home."

Nahum shot him a long look. "You're nuts if you think this is over already."

"But it should be. We were asked to find it, and we have. Whoever this mystery woman is doesn't concern us."

Nahum glanced around to make sure they weren't being overheard. "Blaze's death is all over the news. She was prepared to kill for that thing—and eliminated him no doubt to stop him from identifying them. They'll try again. And Gabe is onto something. We should be worried about what the astrolabe will lead to."

"I guess you're right," Niel agreed, sensing they were going to investigate the Dark Star Astrolabe regardless, and realising the reason for his ill temper. "I'm hungry."

"You're always hungry, and we're in a café!"

Niel lowered his voice, unwilling to insult the owners. "I've drank enough of their dodgy coffee, and frankly, the sandwiches just don't cut it. I want a proper lunch."

"It's not even lunchtime yet. And a sandwich *is* a proper lunch."

"It's really not." And then another thought struck him. "Didn't Caldwell tell Gabe that they had a Senior Adepts meeting on a Monday night? That's when we need to be here...if Gabe wants us to continue this stupid stake out. He may have changed his mind by the time he returns."

"He hadn't three hours ago! But that's very true, brother. And according to Caldwell, the Inner Temple are the only ones who know about the astrolabe."

"Good! That means we can come back here tomorrow evening and watch them all then. We'll get photos, and maybe Harlan can help us identify them...which leaves this afternoon completely free!"

Nahum frowned, which Niel knew he would. As Gabe's right-hand man, he hated to cut corners. "I still feel we should do something useful."

Niel cut him off before he could even start to argue. "Pub, now. Then we'll discuss options."

Half an hour later, with pints on the table and both of them halfway through a Sunday roast, Niel was feeling much more affable. "That's better," he said, poised for another bite. "This is excellent."

"Try not to inhale it," Nahum told him. "Although, I agree. This was a great idea."

Niel glanced around while he ate and felt it was only the fact that they'd arrived before the lunch rush that they'd found a table at all. They were seated in a traditional English pub that was very busy. The air resounded with chatter, and the music playing in the background meant they could talk easily without fear of being overheard. "Go on, then," he said. "What do you want to do this afternoon?"

"We're not far from The British Museum. It's a short tube ride or walk from here, and I gather they have some info in there on JD, and lots of displays of ancient civilisations. I think it's a good idea to see some of that. No one trusts JD, and I want to read and see something about him—something from his past. And," Nahum wiped his chin with his napkin, "they have a collection of astrolabes, and more importantly, statues from ancient Egypt, Mesopotamia, and Iran—Persia, to us."

Niel's curiosity flared. Since they had passed through the portal, he and his brothers had looked up the history that had passed since their time, but their research had only been online or in books. Here was a chance to see the past, up close and personal. "That's a brilliant idea. Although," he hesitated, "it could get very weird."

Nahum's blue eyes fixed on him, suddenly serious. "I know. I don't know whether to expect good memories or bad ones, but we're too close to pass up the chance."

Niel had been intending to have another pint, but now any such plans were forgotten. "I agree. Let's go."

Harlan arrived at the guild at midday, exhilarated after his bike ride through London and grateful for the fresh air, which had finally banished the fug caused by his late night. He let himself in through the back door and stood for a moment, listening.

It was quiet, the normal hum of chatter from the offices missing on the weekends, and the air devoid of the smell of coffee or food that often wafted from the staff kitchen. With luck, Mason wouldn't be here either, and certainly not Robert, the officious idiot who was Mason's secretary. Harlan walked straight upstairs, stopping by his office to grab another espresso, and then headed to the library on the second floor.

The warm scents of vanilla and old books enveloped him, and placing his coffee on a table under the window, he browsed the section that contained the originals of the papers he had looked through a few hours before, quickly extracting the letters and placing them on the table. He pulled one page out of its plastic sheet, feeling the quality of the paper, and holding it up to the light was disappointed to find no watermarks or any other interesting features. He searched the others with the same results and sighed, muttering under his breath. *What had he expected? A map?*

A thump overhead made him look up, alarmed. It came from the office and living area set aside for JD. *Had someone broken in, or was JD here?* Quickly re-shelving the papers, he exited the library and headed for the stairs. The lower floors were still silent; the only sound was the traffic, still constant in London, despite it being a weekend.

The stairs that led to JD's flat were at the end of the corridor, and much narrower than the grand sweep that led up to the first two floors. He crept up their carpeted surface, paused on the shallow landing, and listened. He could still hear shuffling and more thumps, and trying the handle, found the door was open. *Should he knock and warn the intruder? Or was it JD, and he'd give him the shock of his life if he crept in unannounced?* He'd prefer the latter.

Harlan slipped inside and found himself in a small reception room decorated with antique furniture. There were doors on each side, all partially open, and a corridor lay ahead, leading deeper into the flat. One door led to a bathroom and the other a large bedroom, but both were empty.

He edged down the corridor and realised the sounds he heard were coming from the door at the end. For a second, he thought of Gabe's warning about the mystery woman who didn't seem human, but then threw the door open regardless, leaping in and hoping to take whoever it was off-guard.

But instead of meeting an intruder, he heard a shriek and saw JD whirl around. "You idiot nincompoop! What the hell do you think you're doing?"

"Sorry, JD," Harlan said, scanning the opulently decorated room. "I heard noises up here, and thought you were an intruder."

JD was pale and had backed up to the wall behind him, a hand on his heart, his sharp features tight with anger and shock. "What are you even doing here today?"

"Research. What about you?"

A sly look crept across his face. "The same."

"Well, I apologise for interrupting you." Harlan went to leave, and then hesitated. He really needed help, and JD wasn't the enemy, as much as he'd been annoyed by his attitude in Angel's Rest. *His very dangerous attitude*, he reminded himself. *JD was not to be underestimated*. "Can you spare me some time? I have questions about one of my cases."

JD nodded, and taking a seat at a table, gestured to another chair for Harlan. "Of course."

"We were asked by The Order of the Midnight Sun to retrieve an object for them. It seems it was stolen by Black Cronos. I wondered if you'd heard of them?"

"Black Cronos?" JD's voice rose with alarm. "They're back?"

"Er, it seems so. You're familiar with them?"

"Of course I'm bloody familiar with them," JD said irritably. "They've threatened us in the past."

Harlan nodded. "I found the letters downstairs. Did you ever find out anything about them?"

"Nothing conclusive," he said blandly. "I have no idea where they are based, or who their members are, and besides, the last we heard from them was before the war. What did they steal?"

"The Dark Star Astrolabe. Apparently, it—"

But Harlan couldn't finish his answer, because JD stood so quickly that his chair crashed to the floor. "The *what*? It has been found?"

Harlan looked up at him, shocked. "You know it?"

"It points to the seat of a daring alchemical experiment that ended in disaster."

"I thought it pointed to the origins of The Order of the Midnight Sun?"

"Ha! Is that what they told you?" he marched across the room. "Dissembling fly-bitten giglets! Churlish beetle-brained gudgeons! No wonder Black Cronos stole it!"

Harlan's head was spinning. "Why would they steal it?"

"Because it's their origin, too!"

"*What*? But you just said it had nothing to do with origins! I don't understand."

JD didn't bother explaining. "Who has the astrolabe now?"

"Well, we do, actually. Gabe and Shadow retrieved it last night."

A smile spread across JD's face. "We bested Black Cronos."

"Apparently so. Their thief wasn't quite human...but then again, neither are ours."

"They must bring it here!"

"We have to return it to Caldwell."

"That simpering, half-witted fool." JD's eyes were hard. "He hasn't got the balls for this."

"Whether you think he has or not," Harlan said, knowing he was risking JD's considerable wrath, "it belongs to them."

"I don't care. I want it."

Harlan rolled his eyes. "That's tough, JD. You can't have everything!"

JD banged the table. "*I* tracked it down over two hundred years ago and then it disappeared, right under my nose. I will *not* be thwarted again!"

"Maybe you're not meant to have it," Harlan said, suddenly furious. "We have to give it back, even if they stole it," he added, suddenly wondering who it really did belong to. "Our reputation is based on delivering the goods to those who hired us. We cannot change that now, just because you want it. This is your company, your reputation, your money on the line."

"And therefore, I can risk all of that if I so choose." JD drew himself up and peered down his nose at Harlan. "And as my employee, you will do as I ask."

Shit. And this is why he shouldn't have come to JD. "What will you do with it?"

"Do exactly what they want to do. Find the Dark Star."

"What possible interest can it have for you? It's *their* place of origin!"

"Oh, no," JD said, shaking his head. "The Dark Star is a person. Or was. Bring it here now. Phone them."

"What?" Harlan's head was spinning. "What do you mean, a person? You're talking in riddles. And how do you know it's Black

Cronos's origins, too? You said you didn't know anything about them!"

JD glared at him. "Stop questioning me and do as I say."

Harlan had no idea where Shadow and Gabe were right now, but he needed time to think. "They're travelling at the moment, and won't arrive until later."

"Tonight then, up here, at seven. And don't be late."

JD turned his back on Harlan, dismissing him, and Harlan strode out of the suite of rooms, slamming the door behind him, and not caring that JD knew he was angry. *The jumped-up little shit.*

As soon as Harlan was safely in the privacy of his office, he called Olivia. "I've just had a disturbing encounter with JD."

"What's that old git done now?" Olivia's admiration of JD seemed to be over.

"He wants the latest occult object I've been charged to find. Actually, he demanded it," he added, remembering his tone. "I can't do it, Liv. It's not his, but if I don't comply I risk my job."

"Then you need to seek support from Mason. He's the director. Surely, he'll see your point. Our reputation depends on our honesty and integrity."

"I know. I told JD that, but he didn't seem to care."

Olivia muttered under her breath. "Can I ask what it is?"

"Sure," he said, filling her in on the job so far.

"You're right. JD has no say on this. You need to stand your ground, and I'll stand by you. Do you want me with you when you speak to Mason?"

Harlan leaned back in his chair and lifted his feet on to his desk. "No. I don't want to drag you into this. But thanks. I knew I shouldn't have told him, but I needed to find out about Black Cronos, and that was a bust. Shit!" He was angry with himself, knowing he should have trusted his instincts not to tell JD.

"What will you do now?" Olivia asked, her kind tone unable to calm him down.

"I'll meet Gabe as planned, and then contact Caldwell and hand it over. JD can go screw himself."

NINE

"FIND ANYTHING GOOD YET, Estelle? I feel like we've been at this for ages," Barak said grumpily.

Estelle leaned forward and tapped the computer screen. "This is interesting. It's an article on a website about old occult organisations, and it suggests that The Order of the Midnight Sun began in France."

Barak had stood to stretch his legs and make them coffee, checking the security screens as he did so. Satisfied that all was quiet, he faced her. "France? Does it give a name?"

She was still staring at the computer, absorbed in their research. "Yes, it was called Seekers of the Morning Star. *Chercheurs de l'étoile du matin*. According to this, it was comprised of a small group of men dedicated to unlocking the secrets of celestial bodies and harnessing their power for immortality and knowledge."

Barak snorted. "Nothing new there, then. Does it list any names?"

Estelle shook her head. "No. It says their members were shrouded in secrecy, with only the name itself surviving. For a while they released a few documents, alchemical of course, and there was conjecture about the membership. A landowner in Aquitaine was the most speculated about." She leaned back to look at him. "It was an area in the southwest of France, long since renamed."

"Ah, fallen empires and all that," he said, waiting for the kettle to boil.

"Something of the sort." She smiled, softening her austere features, and reminding Barak how attractive she could be when she wasn't so waspish. Oblivious to his thoughts, she turned back to the article. "Apparently, something happened and the group split."

"How do they know that?"

"Good question." She frowned and fell silent as she continued to read, and Barak made their drinks and carried them to the desk, settling in beside her.

The site she was looking at was crowded with alchemical symbols and heraldic signs and he exhaled slowly, trying not to get too excited. They had found all sorts of articles over the previous few hours, and most of them said the same thing, more or less. They talked about The Order of the Midnight Sun during the last century, and speculated on the famous figures that may have been members—a couple of prime ministers, some notorious celebrities, and members of the aristocracy. But the further these articles looked back in time, the more speculative they became.

"Do you think they tried to hide their origins?" he asked Estelle.

She absently picked up her drink. "Maybe. It's hard to know, really. History is for the winners, and the real stories or people involved are often relegated to footnotes."

"Like us?" He smiled at her.

"You're hardly a footnote. But yes," she conceded, "I know what you mean."

"We *are* a footnote," he argued, unwilling to drop it. "We're barely mentioned. We're like a fairy tale in the Bible."

"Like I said, history is for winners." She was watching him closely. "And you weren't winners, not in the end."

"No. But we were for a long time, and will be again." He nodded at the screen, happy to have Estelle scrutinise it for him as he enjoyed her closeness. "What else does that say?"

"There's brief mention of a catastrophe, and then the group split in two."

"What kind of catastrophe?"

She shrugged. "It doesn't say."

"And after the spilt?"

"It seems that some of their ex-members lay low for years, shedding their dark past and reforming under the name Seekers of Enlightenment, before finally emerging as The Order of the Midnight Sun in the sixteenth century."

"And the other half?"

"They continued on the quest they had started. A couple of names are mentioned for them too, as if they went through numerous iterations." She leaned forward to study the article again. "Hades' Path, The Dawn Star, and that's it. It suggests their organisation became ever darker, more nebulous." And then she jerked up right in shock. "It also says the Dark Star Astrolabe is attributed to them! You need to read this."

Barak leaned forward too, squinting at the screen. "'The group was believed to have lost its way in their obsession to unravel their past. There are many mysteries about them, but one in particular still has the power to draw our attention—the Dark Star Astrolabe—rumoured to have been made in the thirteenth century, but long lost to time and memory. Where is it, and what does it point to? And who will have the courage to follow its directions? Those who spoke of it do so with dread, for at its end is a monster.' What the hell..." he murmured. "A monster?"

Estelle was looking at him with an expression he had never seen on her face before. *Excitement*. "This is brilliant."

"This is insane! It's mumbo jumbo, at best."

"Why?" she asked, suddenly annoyed. "You can't possibly scoff at this."

He rubbed his face, bewildered. "No, you're right. Let's print this out and see what else we can find."

Nahum looked at the Assyrian statue of a winged lion that towered over him in the British Museum and felt a shudder of recognition. This was more than he was expecting. *So much more.*

He took a step back, feeling suddenly hot, and decided he needed to find Niel. He had left him in the Mesopotamian rooms, lost in his memories, but it was unlikely he was still there, surely.

Nahum made his way upstairs and through the galleries, feeling dizzy as the past assailed him. Many things there were from after his existence, but they were recognisable enough, their roots being found in his own time. But other things were far too close. The Assyrian lion hunts, the Canaanites, the Egyptians, the Levant, so many names... But here, fragments of their existence were right in front of him.

Almost blindly, he stumbled along, and finally found Niel in a long room staring at the Assyrian reliefs from Nineveh. He moved to his side, Niel transfixed on the images in front of him. Nahum nudged him gently. "Niel, are you all right?"

"No. I'm not." Niel turned to face him, his face pale. "This is weird."

Nahum smiled weakly. "It's unnerving, that's for sure."

"We need to bring our brothers here." Niel turned away to study the panels again, moving slowly through the room. "I'm amazed at what has survived."

"Maybe we're not out of time after all."

"Oh, we're out of time, all right. I remember commissioning things like this to be carved. The work it took, the skill, the conditions. Brother, I need a drink."

"Not yet you don't," Nahum said, steering him out of the room. "Let's look at something more modern. We came here for JD, after all."

"Right now, JD seems insignificant."

"But he's not. He's our occasional employer, and immortal, too."

Niel shook his head, his stride matching Nahum's as they headed for the galleries housing the modern displays. "These ancient remains remind me who we really are. We shouldn't be taking instructions from him! He should be grovelling at our feet."

Nahum looked at him sharply, alarmed by his tone, and grabbed his arm, pulling him to a stop. "There'll be no grovelling, Niel. We don't do that anymore."

"But you know what I mean." Niel's blue eyes stared into his own. "JD has no power over us."

"I know that, and so do our brothers. But this isn't about us exerting our authority or ancient bloodline. This is about us forging our way in the world. And potentially, JD may have just lived a bit longer than we did. And he's a lot more familiar with the past five hundred years than us!"

"So why are we focussing on the more recent past when we could be utilising what we do know?"

Nahum paused, feeling ambushed. "Because at the moment, that's where the money is. And I guess because our own time is too long ago."

"And yet..." Niel spread his arms out, almost knocking over a bystander. "It's not. It's *here*!"

"Dug out from the earth after painstaking archaeological digs. And how much has been lost? 99.9 percent of it, that's what! This is amazing, I agree, but let's be honest, Niel. Most of our history is just dust. Let's enjoy the glimpse we're getting of it and appreciate it for what it is." Nahum stared him down, knowing that Niel could be bloody-minded and belligerent sometimes, and thankful that most of the time he wasn't. "You're shocked, like I am. That's all. It's doing strange things to my head, too."

They stared at each other for another moment, and then Niel nodded. "Yeah, I'm in shock. But still..."

"Come and look at JD's stuff, and let's find some astrolabes." Nahum urged him along, desperate to move to more modern displays. He agreed that they should bring their brothers here, but what would they think? Some days being here seemed easy, when the past felt at a distance. But now, it felt like it might swallow him whole. And last month's encounter with The Book of Raziel didn't help, either.

When they finally arrived in the gallery containing JD's belongings, Nahum led them to his obsidian mirror. "It doesn't look much, does it?"

"No, but it is an old Aztec relic," Niel said, and then nodded to the wax disc next to the other objects. "And that's his Seal of God. The design given to him by Uriel, *apparently*."

"Don't you believe him?"

"Do you?" Niel asked sceptically.

"He's a wily old devil, but he did summon Chassan," Nahum reminded him.

"Like I'd forget," Niel mumbled. "At least *he* hasn't contacted me." Niel looked around the room. "Come on, let's find some astrolabes, see if someone can give us a lesson on using one, and then we can head home. I've had my fill of history for one day."

Gabe and Shadow were back in London by early afternoon, and once inside Chadwick House, Shadow headed to the kitchen to prepare a late lunch, while Gabe went to the study with the astrolabe. He'd just spoken to Barak and was disturbed by his news. He eyed the astrolabe with distaste. The object was getting more bizarre by the minute.

The rete, which depicted the celestial hemisphere, was ornate and delicate, each tip representing a star. There appeared to be a couple of plates layered in the disc, but he had no intention of dismantling it to investigate further. The centre pin that connected them all together had a large, black pearl in the centre, and its lustre shone in the sun. *Was it supposed to represent a dark star, whatever that was?* He shook his head, confused, and placed the astrolabe on the table just as Nahum and Niel arrived, both looking preoccupied.

"What's happened?" he asked them as Nahum threw himself in a chair. "You look spooked."

Niel just grunted and carried the astrolabe to the window to examine it in better light, but Nahum said, "We went to the British Museum and had an interesting encounter with our past." He updated him on what they'd seen, and for the first time in 24 hours, Gabe's thoughts left their current case.

"Really? Was it that weird?"

"Weirder, brother. But, having said that, I think you should go. We all should." He lowered his voice. "It made Niel cranky."

"I can hear you!" Niel called across the room. "And yes, I am cranky. I'm not apologising for it, either."

Nahum rolled his eyes at Gabe and he smiled. They all knew what Niel could be like. "I am intrigued," Gabe admitted, "but not right now. Why weren't you watching the order?"

"Waste of time. There was hardly anyone going in, and we decided we'd be better off going tomorrow night," Nahum said, explaining their reasoning. "But we did manage to get some basic instructions on how astrolabes work. They're complicated things, clever, very sophisticated for their time. I know we don't need to know how to use it, but—" he shrugged. "It felt like something we should do."

"Fair enough. But I'm handing that thing over later today. I'll call Caldwell as soon as I've spoken to Harlan." He checked his watch. "And that should be any minute now."

For the next short while they talked about what had happened in Oxford, until Shadow arrived in the room with sandwiches and drinks on a tray, Harlan next to her.

Harlan looked flustered, and Gabe's heart sank. "Is something wrong?"

"Just JD being his usual, belligerent self," Harlan said. He didn't sit, instead picking up the astrolabe that Niel had placed on the table again and examining it. "So, this is what's causing all our problems?"

"It is," Gabe said nodding. "It's beautiful, isn't it?"

"And a little different from the astrolabes we've been examining, including Chadwick's," Niel added. "The jewel on the disc is unusual, but from our admittedly brief instructions, it seems it would work the same way."

Harlan grunted. "As long as Caldwell is happy, I don't care. I just want it out of my hands."

"What problems are you having?" Shadow asked. She was sitting at the large table covered in paperwork with her lunch in front of her, and seemed none the worse from the late night.

For a moment, Harlan didn't answer, instead running his fingers across the engraved metalwork of the disc, seemingly lost in thought. Watching him now, it was clear to Gabe that Harlan had experienced just as disturbed a night as the rest of them. His eyes had dark shadows beneath them, stubble grazed his jaw, and his lips were tight. He seemed to be wrestling with something. Finally, he said, "JD wants me to double-cross Caldwell and deliver this to him."

Silence fell as Gabe looked at his companions' incredulous expressions, and then he laughed. "Over my dead body! I don't break deals."

Harlan grinned, finally meeting his eyes. "Neither do I, so I'm glad to hear you say that. But he did give me some interesting news."

"So has Barak," Gabe confessed, not having told his brothers Barak's information yet. "I'll start. You might want a seat."

For a few minutes they exchanged information, and by the time they'd finished, the mood had darkened.

"Can I suggest that we don't waste time, and pass this on right now?" Harlan said. "I don't want to be ambushed in this house by your mysterious attacker, or JD. Shall I call Caldwell?"

Gabe nodded. "I think we should go fully armed, too. Tell him we'll be there within the hour."

Their journey through London was relatively quick, and once again, Shadow, Harlan, and Gabe went inside the order's headquarters as Niel and Nahum waited outside, watching the building. But this time, Aubrey Cavendish was with Caldwell, the man who'd orchestrated the theft from France. He was a big, middle-aged man, soft around the edges with a paunch that indicated good living, and a very unlikely thief, Gabe decided. *Maybe he'd engaged someone else in France, or perhaps he had hidden skills.*

Caldwell grasped the astrolabe to his chest, his eyes wide. "I can't believe you found it so soon!"

"Speed was the key, and some luck," Gabe confessed. "But you need to be careful. Some powerful people want that, and I would guess they'll try again."

Aubrey prised the astrolabe from Caldwell's hands, scanning it quickly. "Is it damaged?"

"I don't think so," Shadow said, "but we did have to fight to get it."

"A fight?" Caldwell asked, alarmed. "With who?"

"Someone who was not fully human," Gabe explained, eyeing their worried expressions, but it was important they knew what they were up against. He described their encounter, noting that both Caldwell and Aubrey had gone very still, Caldwell fumbling for the chair behind him and sitting heavily.

Harlan cut in. "We believe Black Cronos is behind this. It was a name given to us by the thief's contact."

"Impossible!" Aubrey said immediately, his face flushing. "They do not exist."

"But you have heard of them?" Harlan looked amused. "Because I'll be honest, we had to do some digging to find anything on them. It seems they've been around a long time."

Aubrey and Caldwell exchanged nervous glances, and then Caldwell said, "They existed once, but a very long time ago. Your source is wrong."

"And the woman who had the ability to kill with a kiss?" Shadow asked. "If it wasn't Black Cronos, who employed her?"

"That really doesn't matter," Caldwell said, standing abruptly. "Thank you for your time and excellent service. I will arrange payment immediately, and I shall certainly use you again, should I need to."

So that was it, Gabe thought, experiencing a weird mixture of relief and disappointment. And then his phone rang. It was Nahum. "A black van has just pulled up outside, and I can see five people so far, including a woman, surrounding the building. This is not a social call. Me and Niel will try to stop them."

Gabe turned to Shadow, who was already holding her two daggers, poised for action. "Check the hallway. They've come for the astrolabe."

"*What?*" Aubrey said, already backing away as Shadow left the room. "Who?"

"Four men, one woman, and maybe more. Is there anyone else in the building?"

Caldwell shook his head. "No, it's just us."

"Good," Gabe said, immensely relieved he didn't have to worry about protecting anyone else. "Harlan, stick with these guys and leave the fighting to us."

Then a scream resonated down the hall that was abruptly cut off, and Gabe ran to the door.

TEN

SHADOW SPUN AWAY FROM the man she had just stabbed and who had fallen dead at her feet, covered in blood, just in time to dodge the attack of another man who had entered the reception hall from a doorway at the rear.

He was lean and stealthy, and like her, carried two sharp daggers. In seconds they were engaged in deadly combat. Shadow was aware of another figure approaching from the stairway, but Gabe ran to help, yelling, "Harlan, get them to the safe room!"

They fought side by side, Shadow swiftly dodging the whirling knives of her attacker. He was good. *Inhumanly good*. She felt his knife slice her arm, and she knew she'd need every ounce of her skill to defeat him.

The man's eyes were dark, and the longer they fought, the darker and more intense they became, just like the woman from the previous night. She could feel his immense concentration as he tried to back her into a corner. She dropped suddenly, rolling to the side before regaining her feet, able to slash his side with a long, deep cut before he rounded on her, a low, inhuman growl in his throat. Gabe seemed to be having a similar struggle, and she could hear his sword clashing with his opponent.

A strangled cry came from another room, and out of the corner of her eye she saw Niel stride through a doorway, whirling two swords at the same time as he aimed for their side. And then something dropped down from above, sending Niel crashing into a wall. It was chaotic, and the fight was messy. All of the furniture in the hall was upended, and the sounds of splintering wood and shattered porcelain mixed with the clash of swords and grunts of aggression.

Shadow finally managed to thrust her blade between her opponent's ribs, watching him slide to the floor, eyes wide, before the life passed out of them. She ran to Harlan's side as he hurried Caldwell and Aubrey to the door that led to the passageway and the safe room below. But they had barely walked a few feet down the hallway when the woman from the night before appeared at the top of the rear stairs, her dark eyes glowing with malevolence.

Herne's bloody horns. How many of them were there, and where the hell was Nahum?

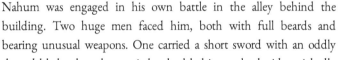

Nahum was engaged in his own battle in the alley behind the building. Two huge men faced him, both with full beards and bearing unusual weapons. One carried a short sword with an oddly shaped blade, the other carried a double-bit axe, both sides wickedly sharp, and in the dull light of the alley, Nahum could see strange engraving on the blades.

But that's all he could take note of, because the men struck quickly, clearly intending to kill him.

Nahum was suddenly glad of the sparring he did regularly with Shadow and his brothers, because he needed strength and agility now more than ever. As the axe head missed his own by mere inches, he realised he needed his wings, and damn the consequences. One man feinted to the right, trying to draw his attention, but his wings punched through his shirt, shredding it, and he used them to crush the man against the wall, throwing him with such force that the man's skull cracked and he fell, lifeless, to the ground. His remaining opponent roared with fury, his eyes bloodshot with a berserker rage, throwing himself at Nahum.

Nahum lifted effortlessly above him, grabbed the man around the neck, and hauled him off his feet. He twisted and writhed as Nahum flew higher, hoping the alley would protect him from prying eyes. His opponent flung his arm back, swiping wildly with his axe, and in an effort to dodge it, Nahum dropped him. With a strangled cry he fell to the ground, the sound cut short with a sickening crunch.

Nahum dropped to the ground, and ensuring there was no one else outside, ran through the damaged back door, across a large kitchen, and into the hallway beyond, where he saw Shadow fighting furiously with a dark-haired woman. Nahum knew who she was. Her black eyes and athleticism marked her as the woman Gabe and Shadow had fought the night before. It was unlikely she had followed them, but it was obvious that she and her companions had decided to stake out the order's headquarters.

Caldwell and Aubrey were cowering in the hall as Harlan pushed them back towards the kitchen. He eyed Nahum with relief. "I'm trying to get them to the safe room, but we're blocked." He nodded behind him. "Gabe and Niel are back that way."

Nahum didn't speak, his eyes still on Shadow and the mystery woman. Shadow ducked and rolled, striking out at the woman's legs, and Nahum took his chance. He pulled one of his throwing daggers from where it was strapped to his forearm and threw it at the woman's throat. But like she had a sixth sense, she turned, and it caught her in the shoulder. While evading Shadow, she pulled the blade free and hurled it back towards Nahum. Nahum was vaguely aware of the others dropping to the floor behind him, but the knife landed in the wall, and he grabbed it once more.

Cornered and desperate, the woman ran to another doorway, and Shadow raced after her. Nahum seized the opportunity, and hauling Harlan to his feet, asked, "Where's the safe room?"

Harlan was already leading the way. "Down here, bottom of the stairs."

Nahum checked behind them to make sure they weren't being followed, and then ran in front of Harlan, ensuring their path was safe and the room secure.

"Are you sure there's no other way in?" he asked him as he scanned the small room, noting the large safe door opposite.

"Not unless you count the air ducts."

"Good. Lock the door, and we'll come get you when it's safe."

Harlan looked as if he were about to protest, but instead just nodded.

Nahum raced back up the stairs, pausing as he considered which way to go. *Should he help Shadow, or his brothers?* Deciding that Shadow could cope admirably on her own with one opponent, and not knowing how many his brothers might be facing, he ran to the main reception hall, but both Gabe and Niel were standing over the bodies of their dead assailants, breathing heavily.

Gabe frowned. "You're covered in blood."

He glanced down, noting the blood spatter across his ripped t-shirt. "I'm surprised there's not more. So are you two. I don't think our attackers were fully human."

"Neither do I," Niel said, crouching to turn over the man at his feet. "Their eyes look odd."

"Let me guess, matte black, shark eyes?" Nahum asked.

"Something of the sort."

"Not this one," Gabe said, pointing to the man at the bottom of the stairs. "His eyes turned silvery. How many did you face, Nahum?"

"Two—brothers, by the look of them. Both huge, with matching beards. Both expert fighters."

Gabe examined the man in the corner of the room. "These were, too. Shadow killed this one. Is she okay?"

"Of course I am," she said, entering the room. Shadow looked none the worse for her encounter, although her hair had fallen loose from its knot on her head, and coils of it tumbled down her back. "Although, I lost the woman. She got out through a rear window and made it to a van on the street before I could catch up to her." She nodded to the dead men on the floor. "What are they?"

"Enhanced humans?" Gabe suggested.

"Or weird shifters?" Niel countered.

"Either way, they were strong," Shadow said. She looked at Nahum. "I take it the two huge guys out back are your work?"

"They are. Anybody else out there?"

She shook her head. "Not that I could see, but we should check the perimeter, just in case."

She had voiced Nahum's next plan, and he said, "I agree. Come with me, Shadow. Let's make sure they're all gone."

"We'll check in here," Gabe said, and he and Niel left the reception area together, leaving Nahum and Shadow to exit through the rear again.

"Did you see them arrive?" Shadow asked Nahum, as he edged down the alleyway.

"We noticed a large black van on the road, blacked out windows, very suspicious. We kept an eye on it, and noticed someone exit and head to a side window. Then the others exited and walked around the back. That's when me and Niel spilt up, and I called Gabe."

They had reached the end of the alley now, and Nahum looked around the corner and then headed to the road, checking for unusual activity. "There's nothing going on out here, and the van isn't in sight."

Shadow stood next to him, surveying the street, thoughtful. "So, we killed five, and one escaped. The woman headed to the passenger door, which means they had a driver who wasn't involved. Unfortunately, I didn't get a look at whoever it was. Did you?"

"No. I didn't have time. My priority was getting in here," Nahum said, annoyed with himself.

Shadow exhaled heavily. "We're going to have to call Maggie Milne, aren't we?"

Despite the situation, Nahum laughed at her bleak expression. "Yes, we are. But we acted in self-defence, and to protect others. Let's hope she's okay with that."

They circled around the front of the building for good measure, but the road was quiet, and the late afternoon light was dim as clouds thickened overhead. Nahum sighed, satisfied. "I think we're good for now, but we shouldn't linger. For all we know, they've gone for backup."

"They won't come near the place with police here," Shadow said. "But I agree. They'll surely try again. And Caldwell may not be so lucky next time."

--------------◄○►--------------

Harlan studied Caldwell, who sat on the floor of the safe room in obvious shock. His hand was clutching his head, pushing his hair back off his face as he stared at Harlan.

"Were all those people sent to get the astrolabe?"

"It seems so. You're lucky we were here, because you would have been dead by now. Although," he frowned as he thought through the sequence of events, "they would have known we were here. They must have wanted to kill us all. That's why they sent so many. They underestimated us."

In fact, Harlan had to admit to himself, *if he'd been without the Nephilim and Shadow, he might be dead, too.* He'd felt useless as he'd snuck past Gabe and the others. They moved so quickly they were a blur, and when he'd seen the woman waiting at the top of the stairs, his heart almost failed him. He owed them all his life.

Aubrey looked a little more composed, clutching the astrolabe as he took deep, calming breaths. "I thought the rumours that surrounded this thing were exaggerated, but maybe I'm wrong."

"*Maybe*?" Harlan snorted with scorn. "That thing must lead to something pretty special. You gonna hire an army to keep it safe? Because those people meant business."

Caldwell looked up, sharply. "You think they'll be back?"

"Of course! It's a miracle you still have it. And," he added thinking quickly, "you should tell all of your members to stay away from here for a good week, maybe longer. You don't want to risk your members being kidnapped for blackmail purposes."

"Shit." Caldwell's head dropped onto his knees. "I had no idea we would be risking so much for this thing."

"Well, I suggest you give it more thought, because clearly there's a lot at stake. Of course, if it's all too much, you could always hand it over."

"*What*?" Aubrey was apoplectic. "After all I've done to get it? I don't think so! This is ours!"

"Well, Black Cronos thinks it's theirs." Harlan looked between them both. "Who's right?"

"We are!" they said mutinously.

Harlan sat down too, leaning back against the wall, the soft carpet comfortably warm beneath him. The attack had certainly made up his mind. He was not giving the astrolabe to JD, and he was going to have to face the consequences. *Perhaps JD would be glad of it when he found out about the attack.* Harlan groaned to himself. *Who was he kidding? JD would be furious.*

When Gabe was satisfied that the building was secure, everyone gathered again in the reception room off the main hall. He'd left Nahum and Niel covering the front and rear doors, and he could hear Harlan out in the hall talking to Maggie Milne.

He felt sorry for Caldwell and Aubrey, who still looked shocked. "You need to take the astrolabe and hide it somewhere, and you should keep away from this building. They'll try again."

Caldwell rubbed his face as he paced the room. "But what are we supposed to do?"

Gabe shot Shadow an impatient look. She was leaning against the wall, watching nonchalantly, but he knew she was listening for any signs of attack. She raised an eyebrow, amused, and said, "Caldwell, you *stole* this. You must have expected repercussions."

"Not like this, I didn't." He rounded on Aubrey. "You said you were discreet!"

He looked affronted, drawing himself up to his full height. "I was! No one knew I took it."

"Wrong!" Gabe said dryly. "*Someone* knew! Either Madame Charbonneau knew and has tracked you down. Or you have a leak... which I suggested the first time."

"No one would betray us!" Caldwell insisted. "I trust the Inner Temple implicitly." He might have sounded sure, but a flicker of doubt crossed his face.

"It could be a newer member?" Gabe suggested. "Or an older member, perhaps, who feels they been passed over for something?"

Aubrey and Caldwell exchanged questioning glances, but simultaneously shook their heads.

"No," Aubrey answered. "I've known these people for many years, and they're as committed to this action as us. It has to be someone else."

"Madame Charbonneau, then?" Gabe persisted. "You were seen leaving the house, or perhaps left a clue behind."

Aubrey looked like a petulant child. "No. I planned the theft well, and knew exactly where I was going."

"If you don't mind me saying, you don't exactly look like a thief, or strike me as being nimble."

"Well, you are clearly misjudging me!" Aubrey shot back, suddenly furious.

"Enough!" Caldwell shouted. "Whatever happened, we must deal with it."

"Yes, you must," Gabe said. "But we'll be leaving as soon as we've spoken to Maggie Milne, so make sure your plan is a good one."

<hr />

Harlan's head was already pounding, and as Maggie started to shout, he felt it start to escalate.

"Five fucking dead bodies!" she yelled. "What the fuck is the matter with you guys?"

"They attacked us," Harlan pointed out, trying to stay calm. "If we, er—well, actually they—" he pointed to Gabe, Shadow, Niel, and Nahum who all stood in the reception room looking amused but trying to hide it, "hadn't killed them, *we* would be dead! And we're pretty sure they're not human."

"How do you know that? Did you *ask* them before you left their entrails all over the bloody floor?"

"It was the way they moved," Gabe said, his voice low. "They were too fast, too agile, too hard to kill."

Maggie rounded on him, looking him up and down scathingly. "Too hard to kill? What are you, a fucking assassin? Do you kill a lot?" There was a dangerous edge to her voice.

"Once, I did, but not anymore," Gabe said evenly.

Maggie's eyes slid to Shadow. "I knew I'd be meeting up with *you* again!"

"And once again, it's a true pleasure," Shadow said, her violet eyes mischievous. "Like Harlan said, we acted in self-defence!"

"Think it's a fucking game, don't you, with your smirks and cockiness? Well, it's bloody not! You have killed five people."

"Two escaped," Shadow pointed out blithely.

"That doesn't count!" she yelled. She looked at Nahum and Niel, quiet up to now, although covered in blood, and Nahum still wearing the remnants of his t-shirt. "And you two! I presume you're toeing the party line?"

"We had no choice," Nahum said calmly. "They arrived intending to kill all of us. They were heavily armed, organised, deadly, and competent, but they underestimated us. Harlan is right. We'd be dead if they weren't."

Maggie fell silent for a moment, and then turned back to Shadow. "Did you get a number plate?"

"No."

"I did," Niel said quietly. "I made sure to before I ran inside."

Maggie's attention swung back to him. "Good. You did something useful, then. Who did you say these guys worked for again?"

"Black Cronos—we think," Harlan told her. "Heard of them?"

"Nope, but you can be sure I'll be looking into them." She glared at Caldwell and Aubrey. "I'll need full statements off you two, as well, so you all need to stay put. My SOCO team is on the way, and they are very used to the paranormal, so we'll be able to find out whether they're human or not. And," she jabbed a finger at the Nephilim and Shadow, "that means you, too! I want statements, fingerprints, DNA, the works."

Maggie strode out of the room banging the door behind her, but leaving a constable in the corner of the room.

Gabe glared at Harlan. "Fingerprints? DNA?"

"Those are the rules, Gabe. Maggie will treat you better than anyone else."

Nahum nodded. "We have to expect this, Gabe. Harlan is right. It's the world we live in."

"The rules in the paranormal world are muddier than most," Harlan added. "Fortunately for us."

"I've made a decision," Caldwell said suddenly. He was sitting on the worn sofa, and had been quietly talking to Aubrey. "I would like to retain your services."

"My services?" Harlan asked. "Or Gabe's?"

"Don't you work together?" Aubrey said, confused.

Harlan saw his chance to distance himself from this, and therefore keep JD at arm's length from the astrolabe too. "Sometimes, but you can work with Gabe and Shadow's team directly. You don't need my help." He turned to look at the Nephilim and Shadow, hoping he'd said the right thing.

Gabe nodded. "Yes, you can employ us directly. But to do what?"

"Be our bodyguards. Help protect the astrolabe."

Gabe looked at his companions, who answered with nods or shrugs, and he said, "Okay. But not here. We keep you on safe ground, somewhere Black Cronos won't know. But I want full disclosure. No secrets. You must share everything you know."

Without hesitation, Caldwell said, "Deal. Where?"

"Cornwall. We leave tonight."

Eleven

HARLAN WAS NOT LOOKING forward to his conversation with JD. It didn't help that he'd had to delay it either, because of the interviews at the order's headquarters, and it was now well past eight that night.

He was relieved that Caldwell had asked Gabe for help. Without it, Harlan wasn't sure they'd have lasted until morning. He had reservations about his own safety too, but hopefully Black Cronos wouldn't know of his involvement—yet. He'd taken a long, circuitous route to the guild as a precaution, and pulling up outside, he saw the lone light on in the upper flat. With a sigh, he entered around the back, as he'd done earlier that day. He'd worked out what he was going to say on the way here, but he knew it wouldn't make any difference. JD would still be very angry.

JD was pacing in front of the unlit fireplace when Harlan entered the apartment, and he looked up eagerly, his eyes traveling across Harlan's body. "Where is it?"

"I haven't got it."

"Why not?" JD's hands were on his hips. "I've waited for hours!"

"Because we were attacked this afternoon, and only just escaped with our lives. I wasn't about to wrest the astrolabe from Caldwell at that point. It's theirs, and I wasn't about to risk my life to bring it here, either."

JD almost snarled, his hands clenched into fists. "Your life is worth *nothing* compared to that!"

Harlan looked at him, astonished. "It is to me!"

"You are employed by me, and my wishes should override everything!"

"Even my life? Are you insane?" Harlan strode across the room, wanting to shake some sense into JD, but in the end he just stood over him, satisfied at seeing him step back. "You risked everything for immortality, and still do to accumulate knowledge. How dare you think my life is yours to risk, too! I choose what risks I take. And like I said this morning, I don't back out on deals and double-cross my clients, and neither do Gabe and Shadow."

"It's a fine time to earn a conscience," JD said scathingly. "Where is it now?"

"Somewhere you won't find it. Caldwell has retained Gabe's services privately to protect them. It's out of my hands now." He stepped back, suddenly needing to put more distance between him and JD.

JD looked feral and half-mad as his eyes narrowed, a calculating look sweeping across his face. "They've gone to Cornwall, haven't they? I have their address."

"You think you can take an astrolabe from Gabe and his team? You're madder than you look." A sudden certainty struck Harlan. "You know much more about the Dark Star Astrolabe than you're letting on. What does it lead to?"

JD tutted. "Oh, no. You haven't earned the right to that knowledge. The order has no idea what they're dealing with."

Was he bluffing? Harlan wasn't sure, but he decided to brazen it out. "It's theirs! I'm pretty sure they know what it leads to, and they certainly know the risks now. And none of it has anything to do with you. I'm leaving, JD. This is over. Let it go."

Harlan turned and headed to the door, but on the threshold, JD called, "It is far from over, and if you think I'm letting it go, then you don't know me at all."

Harlan stared at him, suddenly spooked by JD's tone and the vicious look on his face, but he resolutely turned and left, not slowing until he was on his bike and well away from the guild. It was only then that he allowed himself to slow down and think about what JD had said, as the cool evening air washed over him. *You don't know me at all.*

He was right. None of them did, expect for maybe Mason, and he doubted he did, either. JD's obvious age made him seem fragile, physically incapable of acts of violence, but it didn't make him any less unpredictable or dangerous. He had five hundred years of knowledge stacked up…mystical, powerful knowledge. He had mastered immortality. And he summoned an angel at Angel's Rest when he led Gabe to believe he hadn't summoned them for years. He'd been prepared to risk Gabe's life, and had told Harlan much the same. *Your life is worth nothing.* When JD had fixed those sharp, hazel eyes on him, he felt a shudder of apprehension run through him. *What else could JD do? And had he just made an enemy of a man with dubious morals and unknown powers?*

Harlan tried to calm himself down. He was tired, and JD was angry. Everything would be fine. However, he knew a few charms and amulets that could offer protection, and he decided once he got home, he was going to ward his flat and himself. Then he'd warn Gabe, and tomorrow he would see Mason.

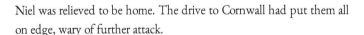

Niel was relieved to be home. The drive to Cornwall had put them all on edge, wary of further attack.

It hadn't helped that they'd needed to return to Chadwick House for their bags, as well as wait for Caldwell and Aubrey to pack and make arrangements for the headquarters, even though it was now going to be sealed for days while the paranormal division combed it for evidence.

He and Nahum were in Aubrey's car with Aubrey and Caldwell, following Gabe who travelled ahead with Shadow. When they pulled into the farmhouse's courtyard, it was after midnight and the lights were on. Their brothers were still up.

Barak flung the door open to greet them, ushering them inside quickly before locking them in. "Finally! I was getting worried."

"Just a tedious number of interviews and being fingerprinted," Niel told him as the others trudged ahead of them into the kitchen.

His eyes widened with surprise. "Really? That's shit."

"That's what happens when you kill a bunch of supernatural dudes in London."

Barak grinned. "Wow. You did have fun. I don't know if I'd say as much fun as me, but..."

Niel halted at the bottom of the stairs. "Why? What did you get up to?"

"I had the very lovely Estelle Faversham help me research our little problem." His white teeth gleamed within his wide grin. "Research has never been so good."

"You're a sneaky shit," Niel said grudgingly. "Although, Estelle wouldn't be my preferred assistant."

"Admittedly she did throw me halfway across the warehouse floor, but it was worth it."

"And?" Niel asked, wondering what else Barak had got up to with her.

"And nothing, brother. We just helped each other. I was being charming, of course."

"You obviously weren't when she threw you across the warehouse."

"I like to feel that honesty is part of my charm."

Gabe appeared at the door to the kitchen. "When you two have finished gossiping, we're having a meeting in the living room."

Niel nodded. "Be with you in five. Just moving a few things into Nahum's room—we let Barak know en route." They had agreed on the journey to bunk together, letting Caldwell and Aubrey share Niel's room until they could come up with a better solution.

"Great idea," Gabe said, looking relieved. "I was about to decide on that." He headed back into the kitchen, leaving Barak and Niel alone.

"I've already put the extra mattresses and bedding in both of your rooms," Barak said. "I presumed you didn't want to share Nahum's bed?"

"No bloody thank you," Niel said with feeling.

Barak laughed and then lowered his voice. "Any bets coming home to roost yet?"

Niel knew exactly what bets he was referring to. "Hard to say. They spent a night together in Oxford, and I'm pretty sure something happened. I'm just not sure what exactly. They are both being a little aloof."

Barak gave him a knowing grin. "Ah. We'll discuss it another time, then. Want a beer?"

"Always. Is there any food?"

"Of course—but don't rush."

Niel spent a few minutes moving his belongings into Nahum's room, eyeing the camping bed with distaste, but he'd slept on worse. The Nephilim had been lucky when they found the farmhouse to rent. It was big, with plenty of space for everyone, which meant when they needed peace and quiet and privacy, they could get it. Even so, living with his brothers could try his patience sometimes. At least Nahum was quieter than most.

As he left his room with his belongings, Nahum appeared with Caldwell and Aubrey. "This is where you'll be staying for now," Nahum explained as they looked around with relief.

"Are you two okay?" Niel asked, thinking the last few hours had taken their toll on them both. No one had really spoken in the car, and he'd presumed they'd been in shock. "That was a bad few hours in London."

Caldwell dropped his bag on the floor and sat on the bed. "To be honest, I don't think I've absorbed it all yet. And I can't get the image of the dead bodies and all the blood out of my head."

"If it's any consolation, it wasn't pleasant for us, either."

Aubrey was standing by the window, looking through the blinds at the moors beyond. He turned, his eyes bleak. Wary, even. "You were very good at it."

Nahum shuffled uncomfortably beside him. "We're warriors. It's what we did for years, but we do it less now. We don't kill for pleasure."

"No, of course not." Aubrey nodded and swallowed. "I'm not suggesting you did."

Niel tried to put himself in their shoes, and thought that actually moving in with a bunch of men you hardly knew who were very good at killing people was probably terrifying—even though they had just saved your life. "You can trust us. You're under our protection now. Take a few minutes, use the bathroom, get settled in, and then join us downstairs."

Gabe waited until everyone had settled down and had their fill of food and drink before he turned the subject to more serious matters.

His brothers had already been asking questions about what had happened in London, and although he'd given them some details, he wanted to talk to them together. Unexpectedly, they were all at home. It seemed that while he'd been away, the problem with the vengeful spirits who had attacked Caspian and the other witches had been resolved. Well, partially. Ash had told him that a couple of the Cornwall witches were involved and had disappeared. It seemed Caspian had granted them all the night off in thanks for their help with the issue, and had covered security at the warehouse with his other men.

"I think it's because we'll be called on more often in coming weeks," Ash had confessed quietly. "We could well be dragged into a witch war."

"Seriously?" Gabe asked, alarmed. "Can't the White Haven witches cope?"

Ash had shrugged. "I think they are all shocked that another witch could have been involved in the attack, and fear that this could get ugly. But yes, they can cope. I think Caspian is just being cautious."

Gabe ran his hands through his hair, wishing he'd showered, but that would have to wait. "Well, we might not be able to help, because I think this job is going to get ugly, too."

Ash was now asking their new arrivals all sorts of questions. Of all of them he was the most intellectual, and Gabe knew he'd be fascinated with the astrolabe. Zee and Eli were also watching and listening, and he presumed Barak had filled them in on his investigations already. Barak was now keeping watch outside for the arrival of any unwanted visitors, and Shadow, still streaked with blood, sat next to Ash while he chatted to Aubrey and Caldwell. Gabe was relieved to see that with some tapas and drink inside them, they were finally starting to look more relaxed.

And what the hell was he going to do about Shadow? Neither had discussed the night at the club beyond their brief chat at breakfast. The kiss. Nuzzling her neck. That had been good...too good. And he knew she felt the same, despite her protestations. But they were engaged in a wary dance, both worried about ruining a good thing. Because what they had right now *was* a good thing. He allowed himself a smile. *But it could be better.* Shadow must have felt him look at her, because she glanced up at him, a questioning look in her eye. He refused to break contact first. She gave him a slow smile before turning away again.

They all needed to sleep, but there were a couple of things he had to know first. Gabe cleared his throat and tapped his half-empty beer bottle. "We need to talk about some important things before we sleep tonight." The idle chatter stopped, and everyone looked at him. "Caldwell, you said you'd be honest about the astrolabe and your order's origins. Now is the time to share."

"Are you sure this can't wait until morning?" he asked.

"No. If by some miracle Black Cronos finds us and attacks again tonight, I at least think we should know why. I'll tell you what Barak has found out, and then you can fill in the gaps."

He summarised Barak's findings, and Caldwell grimaced. "It's mostly accurate, but sketchy. And if I'm honest, our knowledge of the order's past is, too. It seems to have been deliberately obscured." He took a deep breath. "We have heard of Black Cronos, of course. Although Aubrey is right in saying that we didn't think it existed any more. No one has heard mention of them for years, least of all us. But, yes, it could be argued they have a claim to the astrolabe, just as we do. Several hundred years ago, both of our organisations were one, and as Barak suggests, a terrible accident happened. An alchemical experiment went wrong."

"What type of experiment?" Ash asked.

"We are not entirely sure, but think it had to do with the transmutation of the soul," Aubrey explained. "There are no written details of the experiment itself, you understand, just the consequences."

Ash propped his chin on his hands, elbows on knees. "But the transmutation of the soul is one of the seven hermetic principles. It's what many alchemists strive for."

Zee snorted, looking at Ash with incredulity. "Seriously? You know about this stuff?"

"I made it my business when we became involved with JD," Ash explained. "It's been my bedtime reading."

Gabe had no idea of what Ash had been up to, and looked at him in surprise, but Aubrey appeared excited. "You understand it, then?"

Ash shrugged, understated as ever. "I understand the basic philosophy of it, that's all."

Aubrey looked slightly disappointed, but he carried on regardless. "Well, you're right, of course. It is one of the principles, but not all alchemists focus on it. It is considered the highest principle, but also the hardest to achieve. But apparently, our order found the way. Or thought we did."

Gabe stopped him. "Hold on. So you admit your order and Black Cronos at one point were one organisation. Barak's research was correct?"

"We were one until that fateful moment when everything changed," Caldwell said.

Zee butted in. "Wait! Explain this transmutation business. What does it mean?"

"Essentially," Aubrey began patiently, "it is about the soul transcending the base materialness of our body and becoming one with the universe. It is about truly understanding the mysteries of life —the assimilation of the masculine and feminine principle."

A brief silence fell as everyone struggled to understand Aubrey's explanation, and Gabe was relieved he wasn't the only one baffled by alchemy. It looked as if Zee was about to complain, but Gabe shot him a look and he clamped his mouth shut.

Instead, Shadow asked, "Is this about immortality?"

Caldwell answered emphatically, "No. It's about knowledge. About understanding how our world works."

"You're all obsessed with *knowledge*," she observed.

She made 'knowledge' sound like a dirty word, but Gabe knew what she meant. Some men went too far, but others, well...they had made the world a better place.

"So," Gabe continued, "the experiment. Someone was about to do *what*? Conjoin with the universe?"

"We believe so. To achieve the highest state of being. To find the divine within us, and without."

The divine? That didn't bode well, but he didn't voice it. "Okay. And what went wrong?"

"We don't know," Aubrey declared, shrugging.

"According to Barak, they created a monster."

Caldwell winced. "An unfortunate term."

"Isn't it just? What happened?"

"The subject—" Caldwell started.

"The *person*, you mean?" Gabe corrected, his voice hard.

"Yes, the person—well, er," he stumbled over his words, confused. "We think it was more than just their soul that was affected. We think it was their mind, too."

Niel snorted. "Like they went mad? Were possessed? What?"

"We have no idea!" Caldwell could see their sceptical faces, and he persisted. "Seriously, we don't! According to our history, the room was sealed. The experiment was never talked about again. That's what led to the division in our order. Our half vowed it would never attempt it again. The other half said that a result was within our grasp, and we had to keep trying. They went their way, and we went ours."

"So, you have no written history anywhere?" Ash asked.

"Nothing." Aubrey shook his head vigorously. *Too vigorously.*

Gabe felt like they were going around in circles, and he was too tired and too worried about the possibility of being attacked again. "So why is your order, that has so distanced itself from that murky failure at transmutation, interested in where it happened now?"

"Well, some time ago," Caldwell explained, looking ever more shifty, "our order—in particular the Inner Temple—decided that we had strayed too far from the basic principles of alchemy, and that the form had become diluted."

Aubrey nodded. "To put it bluntly, we were all show and no action. Theory, but no practical application. So, we've been trying again, focussing all our energies on this project for the last year. We want to achieve something tangible."

"You want to build on the past," Gabe said, suddenly understanding.

"Yes! We need to understand what went wrong and do it right. We know of no better way than going back to the place of that fateful experiment." Aubrey leaned forward, a fervent light in his eyes that alarmed Gabe. "There could be records there."

"But you saw the members of Black Cronos—if that's who they are," Nahum remonstrated. "They were supernaturally strong. Their eyes were *odd*. What if they progressed their own experiments, and are some sort of weird, transmuted hybrid species? They obviously want the astrolabe, too. They *made* it!"

"And we have it," Aubrey said confidently. "We need to keep ahead of them, that's all."

"That's all?" Gabe said, trying to contain his anger. "We almost died earlier!"

"But you're better than them!" Caldwell pointed out. "We can do this! We can push alchemy forward, as it hasn't been for years!"

"Hasn't been pushed by *you*," Ash pointed out. "I think there are others who have never stopped. Potentially, you have just entered a race that you are so far behind in, you can't possibly win."

"But if we don't try, we'll never know," Aubrey said, smiling softly. "I stole this because," he grabbed the astrolabe again, holding it aloft, "it will take us to our destiny."

TWELVE

HARLAN HAD SUFFERED THROUGH another poor night's sleep. He had tossed and turned, worrying about the attack and its possible repercussions, his fight with JD, and was nervous that every noise in the dark heralded someone breaking into his flat.

He was behaving like a frail idiot, and after a shower he decided to tackle Mason head-on. However, it seemed that Mason had the same idea, because when he walked through the door of the guild that morning, Smythe seemed to be hovering in the entrance hall, fussing with a huge display of flowers.

"Ah! You're here," he said in his usual insufferable superior tone and a barely-disguised look of glee on his face. "Head straight to Mason's office, please."

"Sure. I'll just take my coat off first and get a coffee," Harlan drawled nonchalantly as he headed up the stairs, refusing to look alarmed.

"But he said—"

Harlan cut him off. "I'm not at school, Robert. I'll be with him in five minutes." He smiled, a challenge in his eyes. "Let him know please, won't you?"

Robert didn't dignify that with a response. Instead, he turned and headed down the hall, his heels clicking with his disapproval. Harlan spent the next few minutes drinking his strong coffee and debating on the tone Mason was going to take, and how he would deal with it. When he thought he'd made Mason wait as long as he could, he swallowed the dregs of his coffee and marched down the hall.

"Harlan." Mason's voice was sharp as he looked up from the papers he'd been scrutinising on his huge, antique desk. The sun behind him made his hair glow in a halo of angelic light he didn't deserve. "JD tells me there was a problem yesterday." He vaguely gestured for him to sit, but Harlan remained standing.

"Yes, there was. JD seemed to think it was okay to renege on a job and double-cross our clients. That's not how we do business, Mason."

Mason blinked, the only sign of his surprise at Harlan's tone. "I agree that it put you in an awkward position, but JD does own this company."

"But he doesn't own *me*."

Mason leaned back in his chair, his eyes hard. "He employs you."

"The company employs me, and we have rules. Our reputation would be on the line. *My* reputation. I'm good at my job, Mason. Our clients trust me. Do you really want me to compromise that?"

And that was the question, Harlan mused, because Mason was both uncomfortable and furious as Harlan reminded him of something Mason had constantly used as his mantra. "The client comes first."

"I know exactly what we'd be risking, but," Mason smiled, an icy glitter in his eyes, "we are no long working for them, are we? They have employed Gabe directly now, correct?"

Fuck it. Harlan had a horrible feeling he'd made a terrible mistake in distancing himself from the job, but he brazened it out. "Correct. We don't act as bodyguards."

"Excellent, then we won't be acting against our clients, will we? JD wants you to retrieve the astrolabe. As soon as possible. He says it's in Cornwall."

Harlan laughed at the preposterous suggestion. "You want me to wrest the astrolabe from seven Nephilim and one fey? Are you insane?

And besides, we use them for jobs! They'd never work with us again —and I don't think I need to remind you of how good they are and how much we need them. They found the astrolabe within forty-eight hours. That's quite simply amazing."

Mason stared at Harlan. "That's exactly what I want you to do. And I suggest that you do it discreetly, so that we can continue to work with them in the future."

"You want me to betray our friends."

"Our contractors, not friends." A dangerous edge entered Mason's tone. "You need to consider where your loyalties lie."

Harlan folded his arms across his chest, a white-hot fury starting to build within. "And *you* need to consider where our morals lie."

"We have none, and neither do you when it suits you. Steal back the astrolabe!"

"No! The fact is, more than anything, that I am simply not skilled enough to overcome the Nephilim and Shadow and their phenomenal abilities. I won't do it! Or do you want me to die?"

"But that's the beauty of this. You won't die! They won't kill you!"

"No! Because should I actually be successful, they'll also know where to come looking for it if they suspect me. *And I will have betrayed them*!" Harlan's anger was being replaced by incredulity at the idiotic plan. "This is moronic! JD would be better off trying to come to a compromise with the order."

"But he doesn't trust them or Gabe, actually. Not after he double-crossed him with The Book of Raziel."

"Saved his life, you mean?"

Mason cleared his throat, smiling. "Well, that conversation went as I expected it to, so it's fortunate I already have a second plan in motion."

"*What*?" Harlan was struggling to keep track. He felt like he was in a hall of mirrors. "Have I just been subjected to some kind of test?"

"Yes. And I can say that you both impressed me with your logic, and disappointed me with your loyalty. You were, obviously, my first choice, but I sensed this outcome. So, I have already employed an old, valued contractor who is a very skilled thief. This thief will secure the astrolabe, and you won't be compromised." He nodded a sharp dismissal. "You can go now."

"Wait. Someone's going to steal the astrolabe? Now? *Who*?"

"I'm not that stupid, Harlan. You just go about your business. I presume you have other cases?"

"Er, yes, several," he said, recalling the stack of files on his desk he needed to follow up on.

"Good. Then you needn't worry about this any further. And of course, I thank you in advance for your discretion. You will, of course, say nothing."

Mason then studied the papers on his desk, ignoring Harlan, and just like that he was dismissed. *Just*, he thought, cursing his cockiness with Robert, *like a schoolboy from the principal's office*.

The clang of Shadow's sword against Nahum's shuddered up her arm and through her body, making her feel thrillingly alive.

Nahum was getting quicker and more deadly as they fought aggressively, kicking up dust whilst they whirled around the barn. The early morning sun sliced through the open barn doors, carrying in birdsong, and for a while, Shadow tried to forget about the astrolabe and the strange, not-quite-humans who had attacked them.

Nahum grunted as he fought, although it wasn't from being tired —he was barely breaking a sweat. It was more the effort he put into each move. Shadow, however, was silent. She had heard it made her fighting all the more unnerving, and apart from the odd thud as she landed on the ground, she didn't speak and her feet moved silently across the floor. With a dramatic whirl of his blade, Nahum sought to block her in the corner, but she swung out of the way in an unexpected turn of speed, before finally flicking his sword out of his hand and bringing her blade under his throat.

"Pretty good, Nahum. You've been practicing."

"Not enough," he grimaced. "If I'm to beat you."

She grinned. "I wasn't holding back by much. You're getting faster."

He groaned. "You were holding back?"

"Only a little. I'm fey—that makes me very fast."

"Yeah, yeah! Maybe I should use my wings next time." He grabbed his towel off the bench and wiped the dust and sweat off his face and neck.

"That's actually a good idea. It would add another dimension to our fight, and give me an extra challenge. And I'd like to see how you use your wings in combat, too."

"Please tell me I gave you a reasonable fight, though."

"You did," she reassured him, and not just to massage his vanity. She grabbed her own towel and patted her face and arms, swiping off dirt as she did so. "I'm genuinely impressed. Eli and Zee need to practice more, though. Especially now. They could be dragged into this fight."

"With Black Cronos, you mean?" Nahum sighed, placing his sword down and flexing his wrists. "Zee will, but Eli will only do the bare minimum. But you know that."

"Yes, but he can't choose who he is. I'd hate to see him injured. Will you speak to him? He won't listen to me."

"Gabe already has. But he *can* fight, you know."

"I do know. I've seen him." She'd watched him sparring with Niel a few weeks ago, and was relieved to see that despite his natural aversion to violence, he was quite skilled in combat. "But he doesn't practice as much as he should. Yesterday, we were attacked out of the blue. I feel we got lucky."

He nodded, resigned. "It's only a matter of time before they find us again."

"Perhaps we should find them first."

Nahum looked intrigued. "How?"

"Maggie. Niel gave her the van's number. She must have found out something about the owner by now." Shadow became excited at her suggestion. She'd made it idly, but now it seemed an excellent idea. She'd always rather be on the offensive. "I'll call her."

"She wanted that registration so *she* could find them, not us. She won't just give it to you."

Shadow threw her towel on the bench and started to pace. The fight had given her more energy, not less, and she needed to expend it doing something useful. "Maybe we should go back to Oxford. They must have wanted Blaze to go there for a reason."

Nahum shrugged. "And that reason could be because it's neutral ground. It's a pointless trip without a lead."

Shadow glared at him. "Why do you have to be so logical?"

"Because it saves a lot of time—and we haven't got much of it, either!"

"True. But Caldwell and Aubrey must know more than they're letting on."

"I agree." He raised his brows above his startlingly blue eyes, and Shadow thought if she hadn't already got this ridiculous thing going on with Gabe—because yes, it *was* a thing—she could easily fall for Nahum. He was calm, charming, handsome, and not half as annoying as Gabe. But she shoved that thought quickly away as he said, "Perhaps they're holding back. You know, safeguarding their privacy. They must have some idea where to go. Especially Aubrey!"

"You're right. If they know of an area we should be searching, we should make our way there quickly. Although," she paused, thoughtful, "perhaps Black Cronos has already narrowed it down, and will be there before us?"

Shadow's phone started buzzing on the bench, and she picked it up, noting it was an unknown number. "This is weird," she murmured. "Hello?"

The connection was poor, and the voice faint, but she heard Harlan say, "Shadow? Is that you?"

"Of course it's me! Where are you?"

"In a phone booth, so I'm making this quick. Mason has hired someone to steal the astrolabe. He knows you're in Cornwall. You need to either leave or prepare to defend yourself, now!"

"What do you mean, steal it?" She was staring at Nahum as she spoke, and he froze, watching her.

"Look, I'm betraying the guild by telling you this, and Mason will kill me if he finds out. I'm in Leicester Square and I'll get a burner phone soon. But just listen to me. Get out of there quickly! Gotta go."

He rang off, and Shadow pocketed her phone. "Practice is over. We need to speak to Gabe."

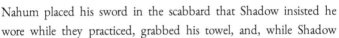

Nahum placed his sword in the scabbard that Shadow insisted he wore while they practiced, grabbed his towel, and, while Shadow headed into the main house to find Gabe, Nahum looked up to the roof of the outbuildings, pleased to see Ash sitting up there, leaning against a chimney. He flew up and sat cross-legged next to him.

Ash was leaning back against the warm stone of the chimney, relaxed but watchful. The sun had burnished his natural olive skin, giving him a golden glow. It also made his cheekbones look sharper, and highlighted his intelligent, pale brown eyes that gleamed in the light. His long hair was tied high on his head, and Nahum thought that when men talked about Greek Gods, they had probably envisaged someone who looked like Ash.

"Anyone approaching?" he asked Ash.

He shook his head. "Nothing. It's calm and quiet." He grinned. "It's a relief, after the noise of the house."

Nahum nodded and looked at the view. He had sat up here many times himself, often at night, enjoying watching the lights of houses spread across the moors, the cars travelling along the lanes, and White Haven, though most of which was hidden in the fold of the valley. Sometimes he could see the moonlight glinting off the sea, but at other times it was a swell of endless grey. In the day, however, it was easier to discern the rise and fall of the land, the gentle curves as one field rolled into another, the distant trees of Ravens' Wood, and the castle on the cliff. It was a beautiful, sunny June day and the sea sparkled, calm and flat to the distant horizon. Nahum wished he could ride Stormfall to the woods. Maybe he could later, once they had made plans.

Ash was watching him. "Are you seeking respite after your fight with Shadow?"

Nahum laughed. "A little, perhaps. She's so fast it's bewildering. She's told me to use my wings next time to add *fun* to the fight." He raised his eyebrows. "I still think I'd lose! But actually, I have news, too. We have more trouble. JD has decided he wants the astrolabe. He's sent someone to get it."

Ash muttered a curse in ancient Greek. "He has the obsessive nature of a true fanatic, which makes him a dangerous man. I've been reading about him."

"You've been reading about lots of things."

Ash shrugged. "Alchemy interests me, and I found it began a long time before JD came along—in the East. In JD's time, before his immortality, he was a very ambitious man. History suggests he could have been a professor at various universities. He made maps, you know. Cartography and mathematics were his specialties before he became obsessed with angels. He was held in high esteem by Queen Mary, and then Queen Elizabeth. I think his obsessions derailed a potentially excellent academic life. Not that I should criticise, of course. He still achieved a huge amount." Ash's gaze was distant. "You can't switch off that life. He must have continued to write and publish under other names after his 'death.'"

"Perhaps he did," Nahum agreed. "I'm sure there's a wealth of things we don't know about JD. I wonder what he wants this astrolabe for?"

"To build on the knowledge of the experiment, I'm sure, just like the others."

Ash frowned as he stared across the valley, and Nahum followed his eye line. "Have you seen something?"

"I thought I did, but it's just birds."

Nahum saw a flock of birds on the field scatter into the air, disturbed by a farmer. He sighed, wishing he could stay with Ash, but he had to find out what their plans would be. "I'll leave you to it. I suspect we'll be leaving soon."

"So be it, brother," Ash said, settling himself back against the brick once more.

Niel was preparing food in the kitchen when Shadow strode in, bristling with purpose and smeared with dust after sparring with Nahum.

In typical Shadow fashion, she was abrupt. "There's more trouble coming. Where is Gabe?"

Niel stopped chopping vegetables and looked up, alarmed. "He's in the cellar. What do you mean, more trouble?"

She ignored him, striding out of the room, and biting back his annoyance with her peremptory manner, Niel followed her downstairs.

The cellar was the place where Shadow had been held captive after they had captured her in Old Haven Church woods. Since then the iron cage had been dismantled, and the cellar was just a big, empty space used for storage. But that morning, Gabe had taken an old wooden table and chairs down there, and Aubrey and Caldwell had set up their books and research.

Shadow marched in, interrupting their conversation, and Niel leaned against the door frame, watching the animated discussion within as Shadow related Harlan's phone call.

"We should leave," Shadow argued. "What if Black Cronos tracks us here, and both parties arrive at the same time? I mean, I like our chances, but why risk it?"

"But we know this place," Gabe said. "We're on high ground, we can see people coming, and all of the Nephilim are here. Plus, the witches."

Caldwell and Aubrey looked startled and watched the exchange avidly.

"But we're sitting ducks!" Shadow protested.

Gabe rubbed his face, exasperated. "You say Harlan doesn't know who Mason has sent?"

"No. Just an old and valued contractor. It sounds like one person, but they may bring support. And we have no idea if they are human or not. And the likelihood is that Black Cronos will send a lot more people this time!"

"If they have more!" Niel argued.

Shadow shot him an impatient look. "Oh, come on. They'll have more! I suspect they have a lot of resources at their disposal, which is why they will find us here sooner rather than later." She rounded on Caldwell and Aubrey. "You two must have some idea where this astrolabe leads. That's where we should go!"

"Er," Caldwell stammered, glancing nervously at Aubrey, who looked at the floor. "Not really."

"Bullshit," she exclaimed. "Yesterday you admitted that you'd been studying this for a long time."

"And," Gabe added, "you promised us full disclosure. I promised to protect you, but if you lie, I'm out, and you're on your own."

Aubrey groaned. "Yes, okay. You have to understand that we've been very secretive about this. It's hard to share so much now."

"But someone hasn't been secretive, and that's why we're in this mess," Gabe reminded him. "However, we'll come back to your mole later. Where now?"

"We think the place of the original experiment, the place that has been sealed for centuries, is in France, in what was old Aquitaine."

"Which is where?" Niel asked, feeling excited at the prospect of leaving England.

"The southwest, bordering the Atlantic and Pyrenees, and in what now comprises the Dordogne and a few other places."

Gabe nodded, his arms folded across his chest. "The place where the order was thought to have originated."

"Yes." Aubrey pulled a map from under the papers on the table, spread it out, and pointed to an area. "Here is Bordeaux, the capital of the region, and we believe the place is close by. There are fields, woods, and a wide range of *châteaus* there, though many now are vineyards and visitor attractions."

"And Madame Charbonneau?" Gabe asked, eyes narrowing. "Where does she fit into this?"

"She lives much further south, close to Nice," Aubrey said, "and is not connected to these events."

Shadow gave a short, dry laugh. "So then why did she have the astrolabe?"

Aubrey had been hunched over the map, deep in thought, but now he straightened. "She's a rich antiquarian living on an old estate. She used to collect all sorts of things, not just occult objects. A decade or so ago she was a regular visitor to auction rooms, and has pretty much neglected her estate for her passion. Now," he shrugged, "she is old, pretty much housebound. It was sad to see how she now lives. The house is falling apart around her."

Niel felt a stir of distaste for Aubrey. His soft exterior belied the sharp brain and ruthless ambition to steal from an old woman, and he couldn't help but say, "Why didn't you just buy it from her?"

Aubrey looked at him in surprise. "We couldn't risk her not selling it to us."

"How did you track it down?" Gabe asked.

Caldwell had been thumbing through an old book while they talked, but now he gave a delighted laugh. "That was pure luck! We'd been searching for months through old catalogues of astrolabe sales going back decades, in the hope of finding ours, and stumbled upon the records for an auction in France years ago. The image was grainy, but it was enough to give us hope."

Aubrey nodded. "I did my homework, found out everything I could about her. I crossed my fingers and hoped she hadn't sold it, and then flew over to investigate. It was like the Gods willed it to be. There was hardly any security, and only a couple of staff." He shrugged. "I picked my moment and was able to hide in the house long enough to search for it. I found it in one of her rooms." Aubrey shook his head at the memory, his gaze distant. "Such a beautiful place, falling into ruin."

Shadow seemed utterly concerned about the theft and picked up the Dark Star Astrolabe that lay on the table, gleaming with intrigue under the light. "Are you sure it's the right one?"

"Yes, absolutely." Aubrey started leafing through an old leather-bound manuscript. "This diary belonged to one of our members in the eighteenth century. He'd conducted his own research, and based on papers he found, drew this image of it. Unfortunately, those original papers have long disappeared."

He showed them the drawing that had been carefully and skillfully drawn in ink, and it was clear it was the same as the one Shadow now held. Niel was confused. Something wasn't right, and clearly Gabe thought the same, because he froze.

"You two have plans you haven't told me about," Gabe accused them. "You must be planning to go to France. Why haven't you discussed this with me?"

"Er, well," Caldwell stuttered, "we thought you probably didn't need to know, and that we could just go."

"*Just go*? I bring you here—to my home—to keep you safe, and you don't think to say that you'll be going in...when, a day or two?"

Aubrey looked at him coolly. "We assumed that we were in danger here, but that once we got on a plane, we'd be safe. We have a secure place in France to go to, arrangements we made weeks ago. It's there that we shall read the astrolabe on the assigned date."

"You were going to do a midnight flit?" Gabe asked sarcastically.

"I don't know what the issue is!" Caldwell said, rising to his feet, his fine features haughty. "We thought the less we divulged, the better."

Gabe lowered his face to Caldwell's so that they were inches apart. "And in the meantime, I'm pulling *my* men from other jobs to cover you, and making plans for the next few days, and you're not even going to be here? You ungrateful shits!"

Aubrey leapt to his feet too, laying a restraining hand on Caldwell's arm. "No, not ungrateful at all! We are extremely appreciative of your protection, but equally, this is a very delicate situation. The search for something that had been lost for a long time! And of course we were going to tell you. We wouldn't just go in the middle of the night!"

Gabe rounded on him too, his fists clenched. "You don't think they would follow you there?"

"It is a secure location!" Caldwell repeated. "Only our Inner Temple know of it."

"And one of the members of which have betrayed you!"

"No!"

"You are deluded!"

Niel hadn't seen Gabe look so angry in years, but he wouldn't step in. Gabe could control his temper, and he wouldn't touch either of them, despite his menacing presence.

"Fine!" Gabe was continuing. "You get on that plane and hole up in your secret location, and you'll see just how trustworthy your Inner Temple is!"

Before anyone could say anything else, a shout disturbed them, and Niel headed to the door, yelling, "We're here! What's the matter?"

Nahum appeared at the top of the stairs, a towel around his waist and his hair still wet. "Ash has spotted a large van on the lane heading into White Haven. I think we may have company."

Thirteen

GABE STOOD ON THE roof next to Ash, following the direction of his pointed finger.

"They were on that road, heading into White Haven." Ash's golden eyes were suspicious. "It could just be a random black van, but then again…"

Gabe nodded, trying to subdue his fury from the conversation he'd just had. "Best to be prepared. Although, if it is them, surely they won't attack in broad daylight?"

"But that is both the advantage and disadvantage of being here. We're isolated."

Gabe considered their options, and the more he did, the more he realised he didn't want to run. "This is our home. If just a few of us flee, we'll leave the ones who remain behind vulnerable. I won't do it. We'll fight them off—make a stand."

Ash nodded. "I agree. Zee is still here, so we're only missing Eli and Barak."

"And we have plenty of weapons," Gabe said, thinking of the stash of swords, daggers, and axes they had, the crossbow they had recently acquired, as well as Shadow's long bow, and the couple of shotguns. He hated using guns, but had been persuaded to get them by Niel. "We could lock Aubrey and Caldwell in the cellar and keep one of us in that corridor to protect them, and then position the rest of us around the house."

"They're bound to split up. Probably approach over the fields."

Gabe nodded, taking a couple of deep breaths to calm down. He needed to put his annoyance with Aubrey and Caldwell aside, and focus.

"What's happened?" Ash asked. "You look furious."

"Bloody Aubrey and Caldwell are planning to go to France, and they didn't even bother to tell me! What is it about alchemists and their bloody secrets?"

"France?" Ash asked, confused. "Why?"

Gabe quickly summarised their conversation and saw disappointment sweep over Ash's face. "Damn it. I really wanted to be involved with this one."

"Depending on what happens tonight, we still might be. They'd be mad to continue this alone." He took another deep breath, trying to filter through his emotions. "I'm disappointed, too. I'll talk to them later."

"Would you consider me? It interests me, and I think I could be useful."

Ash looked eager, and he knew some of the other Nephilim were keen to be involved in their new line of work. Depending on what they earned on this job, maybe they should consider leaving Caspian's employment at the end of the year. That would free them up to take on new jobs, too. There was no doubt that having to cover Caspian's warehouse was starting to become a pain, but he also felt loyalty to Caspian for offering them work in the first place. The same applied to Eli, Ash, and Zee, all of whom worked for the witches, though he knew Eli would want to remain working with Briar.

Gabe nodded. "Sure, if we're still involved. I'll see if Barak wants to come, too. Niel can cover the warehouse instead. It's only fair. Although," Gabe grimaced, "I'll miss his cooking."

Ash grinned. "We'll work it out. Thanks Gabe, I'm really looking forward to this."

"Let's just hope that we can get through the next twenty-four hours, or we won't be going anywhere."

Leaving Ash on lookout, Gabe flew down to the courtyard and walked the perimeter. They had several outbuildings, the barn being the biggest. Next to it was the stable, although both horses had been put out in the fields to graze. Shadow and Nahum were the best on horseback, and Kailen and Stormfall were battle-hardened. Using them both would certainly be an advantage. There was also the building where Shadow lived, and a storage room next door. His SUV and Nahum's car were generally in the courtyard if they weren't stored in the barn, as were the bikes the other Nephilim used. A couple of his brothers could potentially hide in the buildings.

He called Eli on the way back to the house, just to make him aware of their circumstances, and Eli promised to call them if he saw anything odd in White Haven. Then he called Barak and updated him, too.

"There's a chance we might be going to France—if Caldwell comes to his senses. I'm wondering if you want to come, if we can sort everything out soon enough?"

"Are you serious?" Barak asked, sounding excited. "Did you read my mind, or something? I'd love to come. But who'll cover here? There'll be night shifts to consider."

"Leave it with me," Gabe said, sighing. "I'll see if I can work something out with Caspian."

Zee was in the kitchen when Gabe entered. He was making coffee and wiggled a mug at Gabe. "Want one?"

"Please. Make it strong."

"Where is everyone?"

"In the cellar, probably. Come on down with me while I update the group."

DARK STAR

Harlan sat opposite Olivia in a busy pub in Covent Garden, London, just a few streets away from Occult Acquisitions, the shop he needed to visit soon for one of his other cases, and hoped Olivia wouldn't think he'd gone completely mad. It was Monday at lunchtime, and he had spent the morning chasing up some other jobs, mostly for the need to do something justifiable to Mason, as his heart wasn't in it.

Olivia eyed the burner phone that sat between them on the table. "Is that really necessary?"

"Yes! For all I know, Mason can trace my calls, and I don't want them to know that I'm helping Gabe." He stared at her bewildered expression, and his heart sank. "Shit. You think I'm doing the wrong thing, don't you?"

Olivia was in her hunter attire, as Harlan liked to call it. She was wearing old jeans, boots, and a t-shirt, her leather jacket thrown across the back of her chair, and her hair was loose around her shoulders. She was, however, still wearing makeup, and managed to pull off glamorous charm, despite her clothes. She gave him a sad smile. "No, I'm sorry to say. I think you are doing exactly the right thing. I don't trust JD or Mason anymore after Angel's Rest." She pushed her white wine away, rested her elbows on the table, and dropped her face into her cupped hands. "I hate this situation, and that you've been dropped in it. But I'm not entirely sure what I can do to help."

Relief swept through Harlan. "You don't need to do a thing. I'm just glad you see my point. I thought maybe I'd lost the plot. But—" He paused, looking at her hopefully.

"Always a 'but,'" she said, resigned but still smiling. "Go on."

"I want to know who Mason has sent after the astrolabe."

She gave a short laugh. "Ha! That might be tricky, but I'll try. I can head in there soon on the pretext of grabbing some files, and if I can't manage today, I'll try tomorrow. I reckon I can worm something out of

Smythe." She smirked. "He can't help but let out how much he's privy to things."

"True, plus he likes you."

"As much as he likes anyone, which isn't much at all. I need to leave London for a few days after that."

"A case?"

Olivia nodded. "In Nottingham." She sipped her wine for a moment, and then said, "Mason didn't threaten you, did he? Or JD?"

"No, but I gotta admit, this whole thing is making me uneasy." He considered the maniacal gleam in JD's eyes, and the sneaky look in Mason's. "I don't trust them anymore. But equally, I'm good at my job, so I don't think Mason will fire me. I think I just need to lie low for a few days and let this play out."

"Okay, but if you need me, just call. I'm on your side, Harlan."

Harlan smiled and squeezed her hand. Maybe he should tell her who JD was. *It could be safer for Olivia in the long run.* If she was putting her neck on the line for him, she deserved the whole truth. "Thanks Liv. Let's get some lunch, because I have something else I need to tell you."

Barak had just finished eating his lunchtime burger when he heard Estelle's voice resonate across the warehouse and through his door. In minutes, she appeared in his doorway. She leaned against the frame nonchalantly, today dressed in a slim-fitting skirt and silk shirt. He missed her yoga leggings.

"Have you got news about the astrolabe?" she asked him.

Barak brushed the breadcrumbs from his chin and nodded. "Apparently the order was holding out on us. They have an approximate address for where they think this mysterious chamber is... somewhere in old Aquitaine, in France. They're heading there in a day or two."

"Around Bordeaux!" She sidled into the room and sat opposite him, intrigued. "So, what now?"

He grinned, unable to contain his excitement. "We might be going —if we can get flights. And if Gabe can persuade Caldwell that they still need us. He thinks they'll be out of danger once they leave the country."

"Idiots. Wait, we?" she asked, frowning.

"Yup! I'm going, too. Niel will cover here, but I think Gabe is going to try to make arrangements to cover him too, just in case he's needed." He ran his hand across the stubble of his shaved hair. "I can't wait, to be honest. I want to see more of the world—as lovely as Cornwall has been. And you, of course," he teased her.

Her eyes widened with surprise and then she suppressed a smile, a slight flush gracing her cheeks. "You're such a flirt, Barak."

"I know. But I mean it. Miss me?"

"You wish!" But she smiled as she said it, and Barak's pulse quickened.

"The only thing is, if Gabe *can* persuade them to let us accompany them, he's reluctant to use their accommodation. He's pretty sure one of their Inner Temple members has compromised them. But the possibility of securing new accommodation now is unlikely." He was aware as he was saying it that the Witches Council had just endured their own betrayal, and hoped that it had nothing to do with Estelle. He knew she hated them.

Estelle leaned forward. "You know, I might be able to help you find somewhere to stay in that area, if you're struggling."

"Really?" He leaned across the desk, catching the scent of her musky perfume. "How?"

"As you know, we have an office in Marseilles, and my Uncle Max lives close by. He has a lot of friends, rich friends, with old, rambling *maison de campagnes, châteaus,* and maybe some *gîtes*—although, they will be small."

"You really think you can get one for us?"

"There's no harm in trying, is there?" She leaned forward, too, and he felt the heat radiate from her skin, mere inches across the table from him. "But there'll be a catch."

Of course there would be. "Go on."

"I want to come, too. Caspian is back, and to be honest, I need a break from him."

"I knew something was going on between you two. What happened?"

Her eyes hardened. "I don't need to explain."

"Come on," he coaxed, his voice dropping as did his eyes to her lips. "Indulge me. I need to give Gabe a reasonable explanation as to why you want to come."

"The fact that I will find the house as a favour should be reason enough!"

"Not for Gabe."

Estelle propped her chin on her hand and looked him straight in the eye, weighing up her response. Finally, she said, "We had an argument, an unpleasant one, and he used his magic on me. I'm not sure I'll ever forgive him for that."

He raised an eyebrow. "What did you do to provoke him?"

"You think *I* provoked *him*?" Her voice rose with anger.

"Yes! I know you, and I know Caspian. He's a very reasonable man, whereas you are a firecracker. My ripped t-shirt in the bin is witness to that." He watched a range of emotions race across Estelle's face. "What did you do?"

"We argued about the White Haven witches and that stupid Witches Council, and that's all I'm prepared to say. Things got ugly."

She'd needled him about Avery. "They're his friends, Estelle. Good friends, and I like them, too. They're decent people. You should cut Caspian some slack. He could have died last week. I was there, remember? Alex saved his life."

She withdrew, easing back in her chair. "Well, he's fine now, and is back in the office tomorrow, but I need some space. And I'm due a holiday, and beautiful, sunny France will suit me perfectly. Is that enough to satisfy Gabe?"

"We'll see. Why don't you rustle up a place now and I'll let Gabe know that you're our knight in shining armour? I guess having a witch around will be handy, too. I presume you are prepared to fight with us, should it be needed? Black Cronos is a dangerous adversary."

She stood abruptly and walked to the door. "Of course I will. My anger with Caspian still burns right here." She tapped her heart. "I can't wait to let off some steam." She gave him a smile that didn't quite reach her eyes, and then gracefully exited.

For a few moments, Barak didn't move as he considered her words. As much as he wanted to, could he really trust Estelle, or was she bewitching him with her beauty and intelligence? Was he sex-starved enough to want to believe anything of her? Or, more to the point, did he really think he could melt her icy demeanour?

By the Gods, he was willing to give it a try.

He grinned and picked up his phone. *Time to tell Gabe the good news.*

Shadow couldn't believe her ears. "Resting Bitch Face has offered to help...and wants to come with us? Is this your idea of a joke?"

"No! I'm serious!" Gabe said, glancing up from the array of weapons spread across the kitchen table.

"But Caldwell doesn't want us there! Have you forgotten that?"

Gabe straightened up. "We need to persuade them to let us come."

"Why?" Shadow asked, annoyed. "The man is an idiot! They both are! Let them die. I believe it's called Darwinism."

Gabe sighed. "Shadow! That's mean."

"Don't pretend you weren't annoyed with him. You were furious!"

"Yes, I was. I hate being lied to, but I also understand that this is their big secret, and they've never dealt with anything like this before." His shoulders dropped as he appealed to her. "That's why people like them need people like us."

Shadow hated being lied to, as well. It made her feel stupid, like she'd been double-crossed. "Who cares! They had their chance. How can we trust them?"

"They're not bad people, they're just out of their depth. Besides, if we get attacked again, which I sincerely hope we don't, I think they'll be begging for our protection." He smiled, triumphant. "And that means staying in a place of our choosing."

"Hence, Resting Bitch Face to the rescue."

Gabe tried and failed to subdue a smile. "We need a place to stay, and she can help. Nahum has been looking for accommodation, just in case, and they're all booked! We're screwed without her."

"And screwed *with* her!" She groaned and threw her dagger at the wall, embedding it deep in the plaster next to the doorframe, and causing Nahum, who was entering, to flinch.

"Herne's balls, Shadow. Watch where you're throwing that!" Nahum pulled the blade out, crossed the room, and handed it back to her, saying, "I like my face just the way it is."

"I was aiming at the wall, idiot, and I don't miss." She swiped it out of his hand and slid it into the sheath strapped to her thigh, fuming. *Living with Estelle would be a nightmare.* Shadow's hands clenched just at the thought of her superior manner.

"Besides," Gabe was adding in his calmest and most annoyingly diplomatic tone, "a witch will be a useful addition to our skill set."

Shadow marched to the window and glared at the fields beyond, taking deep breaths as she willed herself to be calm. She would have to try very hard not to sink a knife into Estelle's throat, and she wasn't sure her patience would be equal to it. *Maybe she could engineer an accident...*

"Stop it right now," Gabe instructed her, causing her to whirl around to face him. He was glaring at her and tapping his head. "I can hear those little cogs squeaking around, making malevolent plans. Just don't. I rely on you. Don't let me down."

Shadow was about to argue some more, but that comment brought her up short. He'd never told her he relied on her before. She knew it, but it was something else to hear it. And that was the trouble with Gabe. He knew how to push her buttons. Every single one.

"Fine," she ground out between clenched teeth, trying not to show how pleasing his comment was. "I shall do my utmost to be polite. But if she starts something—"

"I fully expect you to rise above it. Can we move on?"

"I suppose so."

Nahum cleared his throat, causing both to turn to him. He was watching them with a broad smirk across his face. "I have news, if you're interested."

Gabe nodded. "Go right ahead."

"On the presumption that we can talk them around, I've booked flights for eight of us, at nine-thirty in the morning the day after tomorrow, taking us from Newquay Airport to London, and then Bordeaux Airport directly. Us three, Aubrey, Caldwell, and Ash, Barak, and," he grinned at Shadow, "Bitch Face."

She glowered at him. "Please don't gloat. It's unbecoming."

Nahum sniggered. "So is sulking."

Gabe ignored their bickering. "Couldn't get flights any sooner?"

"Nope. All booked. It might mean we have a tricky day or so fending off Black Cronos."

"Not if we can make a big enough impression today," Gabe said thoughtfully. "If that's even who Ash spotted."

Shadow shook her head. "It will be JD's thief we have to worry about first. Although, I'm sure a thief won't be much of a threat to us."

"Let's hope you're right," Gabe said, staring vacantly out of the window for a moment. "Would you two take the horses out and check the fields and beyond? I can't shake the feeling that someone's out there, watching us."

Desperate to get out and do something other than skulk around the house, Shadow said, "It will be my pleasure. Ready, Nahum?"

"Right with you, sister."

Fourteen

BARAK WAS STACKING THE dishwasher and doing pointless busywork after their evening meal in an effort to stop worrying. Dusk was falling, and Shadow and Nahum had been gone ten minutes, out to survey the land again. As he waited, Barak had that horrible nervous sensation, like the silence before a storm.

He had left the warehouse late that afternoon, swapping places with Niel, who had grumbled about it for a while, before insisting that it was fine. Barak knew it wasn't, and that he desperately wanted to join them. He hoped there'd be a way for that to happen.

A shout rang out across the courtyard and Barak froze, just as an arrow broke the kitchen window and embedded into the wall behind him. In seconds he'd dropped to the floor, listening for a beat, before grabbing the axe from the table.

Gabe shouted, "Barak! Are you okay?"

"I'm fine!" he shouted back, risking a peek out of the window. But although no one was in view, another arrow zinged through the window, and glass rained down upon his head. "Someone must be beyond the hedge at the back of the field!" His heart was hammering as he thought of Zee, who was now on the roof instead of Ash. "Can you see Zee?"

Gabe appeared at the doorway in a low crouch. "No. I was in the cellar. But I've secured Aubrey and Caldwell down there, and Ash is on the rear corridor."

Another crash of glass indicated they were now targeting Ash, too.

Before either of them could call out, Ash yelled, "I can see him! He's in the long grass in front of the far hedge. Shit—he's covering for about three others who are headed this way."

"Stay put," Gabe instructed Ash and beckoned for Barak to follow him.

Eli had been in the living room, but he joined them in the corridor, a sword already in his hand. "Where do you want me, Gabe?"

"We'll head to the courtyard, see if we can fan out around the house."

Barak grabbed the shotgun before racing to the front of the house that overlooked the courtyard, crouching below one of the windows. He lifted his head in time to see a bloom of debris fly up from the chimney that Zee had been next to, an arrow embedding into the brick. But there was no sign of Zee.

"Who's got the crossbow?" Niel asked.

Gabe looked grim. "Zee, but where the hell is he?"

"Sounds like he saw the shooter first, so hopefully he's on the ground," Barak reasoned. "And if there's only one of them with a bow and arrow, then we should be protected back here." He stood against the wall and peeked around the window frame, but the courtyard was deserted, and there was still no Zee. "I'm heading to the barn."

"I'll go to the right," Eli said, gripping his sword.

Gabe was on the phone to Shadow, summoning her home, as Barak pulled the door open and sprinted across the courtyard, making the barn door just as an arrow whizzed by his head and landed in the barn wall.

A second shooter.

Twilight was falling quickly now, the half-light making it harder to see, but as Barak dropped and rolled, bringing his shotgun up, he saw a figure beyond the gate, holding close to the wall. Barak was too far away to do much damage with the shotgun, but he fired regardless, and the figure vanished. Eli had made it to the empty building next to Shadow's, and he disappeared through the door safely.

But a splintering crash from behind had Barak diving to the ground, and before he could shoot, a heavy-set man was on him, a blade flashing, and he was fighting for his life.

Gabe cursed the attackers, though he was relieved to know that Shadow and Nahum were on their way back. *How had they got so close when Zee was on watch? And why the hell hadn't Shadow or Nahum seen them?*

They must have some paranormal stealth the group was unaware of. At least Zee had spotted their shooter, and had hopefully made it to safety.

With Niel in the barn and Eli in the storeroom, Gabe crept around the rear of Shadow's room. As he rounded the corner, he saw a sudden movement to his right and a strong arm snaked around his neck, choking him and trying to drag Gabe to the ground. He had a second's shock that someone had the strength to do that before he fought back, throwing his whole body backwards and cracking his attacker against the wall. The grip loosened, allowing Gabe to turn and punch. With a sickening crunch he felt his opponent's cheek break, but it didn't slow him down, and in seconds they were both rolling across the ground, trading punches.

The man was as big as Gabe, hugely muscled with the dead-eyed gaze of the men they had encountered before. He wrapped his huge hands around Gabe's neck and squeezed, but Gabe's wings unfurled, lifting them both. The man's eyes widened with surprise as his grip slackened, and Gabe pushed him against the wall, wary of flying too high. But within seconds an arrow landed in the man's chest and dropping him, Gabe spun around to see Zee at the corner of the building.

Zee just nodded, and then crept around the side of the building, his crossbow raised. Gabe headed the other way. A shout, the clash of swords, and the boom of the shotgun broke the silence, but before Gabe could respond, the black-clad woman who'd escaped from the order's headquarters emerged from the long grass of the fields and tackled him to the ground, her lips closing on his.

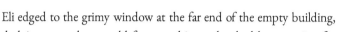

Eli edged to the grimy window at the far end of the empty building, dodging around some old farm machinery that had been rusting for years.

The shadows were dark in here, contorting into strange shapes, and he took a moment to ensure the skittering noises he could hear were just mice and nothing else. They really should get cats...he'd been telling Gabe so for months. Eli advanced slowly in a half-crouch, his sword at the ready, but also wishing he'd grabbed another weapon. He passed a large wrench on a battered work bench, and picking it up, peered through the window to the lane beyond the gate.

Like all the Nephilim, his eyesight was keen, but the grimy window both afforded him protection and obscured his view. He waited for long moments, ignoring the fighting he could hear outside, and focussed on the hedge edging the lane. Within moments he was rewarded, as another three figures sidled out of the darkness. All three were lean and stealthy, and in the dim light he could see the glint of steel in their hands, and caught a glimpse of a long bow behind the shoulders of one of them. Only one was heading towards him, and there was no way Eli could attack quietly. There was no door at this end, and the window was sealed shut. Deciding speed was his best option, he waited patiently until the man was close and then leapt through the window, glass shattering everywhere as he tackled him to the ground. With two quick slashes of his sword, the man lay dead at his feet, and he ran towards the next at the outskirts of the barn, and who was already turning to face him. But Eli's speed had given him the upper hand, and after virtually gutting his opponent, he turned to chase down the third.

Unfortunately, there were another two advancing on him, and Eli realised there were still more lurking in the shadows. Just as he was squaring up to face his opponents, he heard the whisper of an arrow in flight and he dived down, the arrow catching the top of his shoulder and spinning him around. His sword fell from his hand, but he still had the wrench...and his wings.

Eli unfurled his wings as he stood and used them like a shield, batting away a couple of arrows before his opponents were on him. He felt his blood rush as it hadn't in years, and he couldn't suppress a grin. Fighting with a wrench was inelegant, but it would have to do.

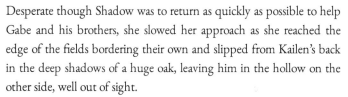

Desperate though Shadow was to return as quickly as possible to help Gabe and his brothers, she slowed her approach as she reached the edge of the fields bordering their own and slipped from Kailen's back in the deep shadows of a huge oak, leaving him in the hollow on the other side, well out of sight.

It wasn't fully dark yet, but the twilight was confusing. *Their enemies had picked a good time*, Shadow mused, *when the light was at its most deceptive*. But she couldn't work out why they hadn't seen them approach. She could only surmise that once she and Nahum left they had moved swiftly, and there was only so much ground they could both cover effectively.

Shadow scrambled up the tree to find a good viewpoint, and then melted into the dark as she attuned her senses to her surroundings. She heard the scuttle of small mammals and the swoop of the bats before they wheeled into view. The birds were settling too, the air full of their evening song.

And then she saw them—half a dozen figures, making their way swiftly through the long grass in the field where the horses grazed, and heading towards the house. By the hedge, one man was already dead; she could see the arrow in his chest and his spread-eagled pose, but another was taking pot-shots at the house to offer cover for the others. Then another figure popped up by corner of the house, dispatching a bolt that embedded deep in the shooter's chest, killing him instantly. She grinned as she realised it was one of her brothers.

The other attackers immediately dived into the grass, and Shadow realised this was the perfect spot for a sniper. She readied her bow, and moving from left to right, released her arrows in quick succession and with deadly accuracy, each earning a head shot. She waited, wondering if more would emerge. They clearly had a plan, but they had made a mistake letting her and Nahum go alive.

Shadow focussed on where she knew the lanes bordered the far end of the field, and spotted the tell-tale swish of the tall grass, indicating someone's steady progression towards the corner of the house. As good a shot though she was, the distance was too far for accuracy. She dropped to the ground, deciding to advance on foot. Tempting though it was to charge in on Kailen, in this case, stealth was her friend.

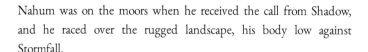

Nahum was on the moors when he received the call from Shadow, and he raced over the rugged landscape, his body low against Stormfall.

The trees were stunted from the relentless wind that blew at this elevation during the winter months, the land rising and falling and silvered with streams. He paused on a rise to study the farmhouse a short distance away, and despite the twilight, his superior eyesight meant he could see the dozen intruding figures at various points around the house, some very close and others further back, as if they were planning a wave of attacks.

He urged Stormfall forward at a trot, the thick heather masking his approach. Like Shadow, Stormfall was silent when he needed to be, and faster than any horse Nahum had ever been on. He decided to strike quickly by sweeping around the back of them, and when he was close enough, he let Stormfall race. Withdrawing his sword, Nahum charged the first man down, trampling him underfoot. He killed the next two with his sword, and then was almost unseated when a few figures rose out of the murky twilight, previously unseen. But Stormfall didn't scare easily, and Nahum wheeled him around, the horse responsive to Nahum's every need. Nahum felt the burning slice of a blade along his leg, but ignored it as he cut another figure down and then turned towards the farmhouse, deciding to charge into the courtyard.

Ash had already killed three enemies—two men and one woman—all who moved with the swift efficiency of practiced killers. Fighting in the tight confines of the rear corridor wasn't the easiest, but it hampered his opponents too, and now with all three dead at his feet as well as the shooter in the field, Ash hoped this was nearly over.

But a sound from the end of the corridor made him withdraw to the top of the cellar stairs. He risked peering around the corner, and an arrow embedded into the plaster, mere inches from his face. *Great. Now they were in the house. What the hell where his brothers doing?*

A flurry of arrows kept him pinned in position, and Ash realised he was a sitting duck. He considered retreating to the cellar with the others when crossbow bolts suddenly flew from the other direction. Ash heard a thud and then a shout.

"It's Zee! Ash? Niel? Are you there?"

"Yes, brother. I'm coming out, don't shoot!"

Zee marched towards him, his face grim. "They have sent many to attack us, all well-trained." He kept out of view of the window, but glanced towards the fields. "I think Shadow is out there. She shot the others in the field, so I'm heading upstairs to see if I can pick off some more. Are you okay here?"

Ash nodded, gesturing at the cuts on his arms and legs. "Superficial only. You carry on."

"Shout if you need me."

Ash watched Zee round the corner and settled in at the top of the stairs again. It was full dark outside now, and all the lights were off in the house. So far, there was no other movement on this side of the house, and he hoped his other brothers were coping at the front.

Zee swept the house on his way upstairs, ensuring the area remained secure.

Stepping over the dead man, he saw that the front door was partially open, another man dead on the threshold, and shattered glass lined the hall, but there were no other intruders inside. Zee raced upstairs, positioning himself at the landing window overlooking the courtyard, and witnessed mayhem below.

His brothers were fighting furiously. Eli was at the gate, Nahum was mounted on horseback, sweeping through the courtyard like the Angel of Death, Barak was just visible inside the barn doors, a shadowy blur of action, and Gabe was below him, fending off a woman. A few men had broken away from Nahum's fury and one ran at Gabe, the others heading for the open doorway. Zee raised his crossbow and began to shoot.

Gabe felt the assassin's icy lips press against his own, her hands gripping him like steel. Before she could begin to do whatever it was she had done to Blaze, he flew up and threw her off, watching her land spread-eagled below.

Her eyes blazed with fury, alleviating for a moment their blackness, and Gabe soared down, sword outstretched as she leapt to her feet, pulling a rapier out of nowhere. For the next few minutes Gabe fought furiously, the woman's lightning-quick reflexes equal to Shadow's. Her quick, darting glance behind him had him whirling around, but a flurry of bolts rained down, some finding their mark in the men behind him, the others thudding into the earth. The woman ran off, and Gabe gave chase through the fields beyond the outbuildings.

Gabe decided to risk flight, hoping the enemy shooters were dead, and soared upwards, easily keeping pace with the woman. To his left he could see a handful of figures fleeing too, all converging on a copse of trees just beyond the next field, Nahum already racing after them. He glanced back towards the woman below and blinked. She had disappeared completely. He dropped lower, searching anxiously as he skimmed over the treetops. He peered through the leafy branches, trying to see the ground below. Nothing moved and all was silent, except for the haunting screeches of a barn owl.

Glancing behind him, he saw the fighting seemed to have stopped, a slew of bodies littering their land, and for a horrible moment, he wondered where Shadow was, until he saw her racing across the far field on Kailen.

He sighed, debating if he should search for the woman on foot, but had the feeling he would not find her. *Good. Let her take back news of what they had faced*. Maybe Black Cronos would think twice about attacking again. They had lost many men today, and with luck, someone would still be alive for questioning.

Fifteen

SHADOW STUDIED THE MUSCULAR man lying on the barn floor and knew he wouldn't live much longer.

He'd been fighting with Barak, who had inflicted a deep stomach wound, and he was now bleeding out, his blood soaking into the dry, dusty ground that absorbed it like a sponge. Eli crouched next to him, pressing a bundle of cloth into his gaping wound to try to staunch the bleeding, but it wasn't from any expectation they would save him. It was only so that they could question him for longer.

Gabe crouched next to him, watching him dispassionately. "How many more are there of you?"

The man's eyes flickered as he fought to focus. "Too many. You won't win."

"The woman with the long, black hair," he said abruptly. "Who is she?"

The man gave a croaking laugh. "There are many women who fight with us."

"You know who I mean." Gabe gripped his shoulders and shook him. "Who is she?"

"The Silencer of Souls." He met Gabe's eyes. "She takes all, in the end."

"How?"

"I am a soldier. It is not for me to know."

Gabe tried a different tack. "What is so important about the Dark Star?"

"I am a soldier. It is not for me to know," he repeated.

"We have killed all of you!" Gabe said, his voice rising with incredulity. "You must know what you fight for!"

A smile played on his lips as his gaze swam. "You don't." The man had just enough about him to look at the others. His eyes were cold as they swept over Shadow who stood at his feet, Eli who was still trying to slow the bleeding, and Barak and Zee who were at the barn door, half watching the courtyard beyond. Nahum was outside, somewhere, and Ash was still guarding Caldwell and Aubrey. "You will all die in the end," he told them, and then his head lolled to the side as the life slipped from his eyes.

"Shit." Gabe rose to his feet, rubbing his face absently. "This was a bloodbath, and we still know nothing."

"Not true," Shadow said. "We know they're a much bigger group than we ever suspected, that they're organised, well-funded, and—" she stared at the man at her feet, "that they aren't quite human."

"But we suspected that anyway," Gabe said, his eyes skimming over her. "Are you injured? You're covered in blood."

She glanced down, surprised to see how much there was on her clothes. "I chased down a few stragglers at the end of the field and slit their throats. It's a very bloody way to die."

"Did you see any transport? A sign of any way at all that they approached us so quietly?"

"No, none. I suspect they made their way by foot, slowly, sheltering carefully before moving on again."

Barak grunted. "They did their homework. They knew we'd have a good view across the fields. And they are freakishly stealthy."

Gabe looked over at him, nodding. "I suspect that one of the places they sheltered was the copse of trees I just flew over. I think tomorrow we should see if they've left any clues behind."

"They won't have," Shadow said confidently. "They're too good. But," she added, noting Gabe's jaw muscles clench, "I'll look anyway."

Eli was searching the man's clothes, and then studied his face, peering into his eyes. "Look, his eyes are changing from black to brown. It's as if his humanity is returning. And his tattoos," he added, startled. "They're fading, too."

He had curious tattoos on his forearms and chest, just visible beneath his ripped t-shirt and the smeared blood. "I think they're magical," Shadow said, thinking of similar spell work she'd seen in her own world. "They imbue strength and agility in their recipient."

"But why are they fading now?" Barak asked, leaving the doorway and joining them. Like the rest of them, he was bloodied and sweaty, his clothes torn.

"Perhaps in death, the spell breaks." She shrugged. "It's just a guess."

"The Silencer of Souls has tattoos, too," Gabe mused. "What the hell kind of name is that, anyway?"

"An ominous one," Zee called over. "What are we going to do about these bodies, Gabe? We can't leave them on the fields."

"We collect them all, bring them here. And then we need to tell Newton."

"*Here*? Newton?" Shadow's hands settled on her hips. "Are you mad?"

"What in Herne's horns am I supposed to do, Shadow?" Gabe looked drained, and his dark eyes stood out against his pale face. He didn't look well at all.

"Are you injured?" she asked, changing the subject.

"No, why?"

"You look...weird."

Eli stood and stared at Gabe. "She's right. Are you sure you're not injured?"

Worry passed across Gabe's face. "I had an encounter with The Silencer of Souls. She kissed me, briefly." His hands passed over his lips. "She was like ice. But I threw her off." He shook his head as if to try and focus. "I'm fine."

"Liar!" In seconds Shadow was next to him, one hand gripping his arm, the other touching his face. "Your skin is cold. What else do you feel?"

"I guess I feel a little weak, but it will pass. I'm Nephilim. I heal quickly."

"Eli," she said, turning to him. "Is there something we can give him? A herbal drink to strengthen him? Do we need Briar?"

Eli pulled her back. "It might be some kind of poison. But yes, I can handle that."

"What if she's started to extract his soul?" she asked, alarmed, and then realising she sounded shrill, tried to calm herself down.

Gabe answered impatiently, "Maybe she did! I don't know what her weird kiss can do, but honestly, I'll be fine."

Eli propelled Gabe toward the barn door. "Let's go to the house. I have my kit there, and some goodies from Briar. And then you need to rest." He eyed the others. "I'll find Nahum. Can the rest of you start the clearing up?" But he didn't wait for an answer, and it was a mark of just how unwell Gabe was feeling that he followed Eli without question. On his way out the door, Eli shouted, "And come see me when you're done! You're *all* injured!"

There was silence for a moment as Barak, Zee, and Shadow looked at each other uneasily. Finally, Zee said, "He'll be fine. He's strong, and Eli is good. But I think it's lucky we're wearing protective gear." He indicated his black vest and thick leather gloves that all the Nephilim wore. Shadow had her own lightweight, fey-made armour on.

"But unfortunate that they were wearing it, too," Barak pointed out. He lifted the shattered breastplate that the dead man had been wearing. "This made my job so much harder."

Shadow surveyed the half a dozen men and women who lay dead around them, all similarly attired, and all with horrific, bloody injuries.

Barak's axe had done a lot of damage, and outside, in the courtyard and surrounding fields, the fallen would have similar injuries inflicted from their swords, daggers, arrows and cross-bolts. It was carnage. *Newton would be furious.*

"Let's collect the bodies and then I'll call Newton. But," she asked Zee, who still held the crossbow, "can you patrol? We shouldn't just assume they're gone."

"Sure. I'll head up to the roof again, as long as you two promise to stay together."

Barak was already dragging the fallen over to the far wall of the barn, but now he straightened, wielding his axe once more. "Agreed. Come on, sister."

Harlan stared at the ceiling, watching the play of lights from the streetlights and occasional car that passed at this late hour.

He recalled Olivia's shocked expression as she learned the truth about JD, and then her anger quickly followed. "You've known for *months* and didn't tell me? You bastard!"

"Liv, please! I was sworn to secrecy. But honestly, I wanted to tell you! And I have now," he added, pleading with her.

She'd glared at him, and then sighed. "I guess I'd have done the same in your position." She sipped her wine, her hands unsteady for a moment. "Wow. I knew JD was odd, but I didn't expect him to be—" she lowered her voice and leaned forward, "*immortal*!"

"I know. I think I've underestimated him."

Olivia picked at her food while they talked, asking, "Do you think he's as powerful as your witch friends?"

"More so in some ways, I guess. And infinitely less trustworthy."

And that's what kept bothering Harlan now, hours later at two in the morning, alone in his flat. He couldn't help but wonder, how untrustworthy was JD, and should Harlan even be here in his flat, although warded with amulets and charms? Could JD summon a demon or an avenging angel to attack him? Harlan had money. Maybe he should book into a hotel.

He still had questions, and despite Mason's instructions, he wasn't dropping this. *Who were Black Cronos, and who was the thief JD had hired?* Olivia had said she would call when she found something out, but so far he'd heard nothing. And he needed to know more about the Dark Star. He'd heard nothing at all from Gabe or Shadow, either.

Then he heard a faint, almost imperceptible noise from somewhere in his flat, and he sat bolt upright in bed. *Shit! Was someone here?* He sat quietly, trying to ignore the loud pounding of his heartbeat, and thought he detected a shuffling noise. He slid out of bed and padded silently across the room wearing only his shorts, then waited behind the door, wishing he had a weapon. *Should he try to surprise them, or scare them off by flicking on the light? If it was Black Cronos, surprise would be best.*

Crouching, he edged into the hall, where he could see his lounge and study. His breath caught in his throat as he saw someone next to the study window, rifling through his paperwork, a light playing across the desk. *Someone was in his freaking flat!*

Harlan crept forward to get a better view, and then incredulity set in as he recognised the figure. *Time for some fun.* He yelled, "Freeze or I'll shoot you! I've already called the police!"

The figure stumbled backwards. "Don't shoot! It's me, Jackson!" He turned his small flashlight on his face, showing his eyes, wide with alarm.

Harlan flicked the hall light on. "I know it's you, you thieving shit! What the fuck are you doing in my apartment?"

Jackson leaned against the desk looking sheepish. "Sorry, Harlan. I'm in a bit of bother. You haven't really phoned the police, have you?"

Harlan groaned at the typical English understatement. "Of course I haven't. I'm not telepathic. What do you mean by *bother*?"

Jackson looked as rumpled and nonchalant as ever, now that his shock had worn off. "Couldn't we chat in a more civilised manner? Over a drink, perhaps?"

"You break into my flat and expect me to be civilised?" And then seeing Jackson's chagrined expression, he groaned. "Yes, all right. I need one anyway, after that scare. You nearly gave me a heart attack."

He waved Jackson through to the lounge, pulled a t-shirt on, and then after flicking on a couple of lamps, poured them both bourbon.

Jackson prowled around with his drink, looking with curiosity at Harlan's collected objects displayed on shelves and in bookcases. "This is a nice place." He gave him an appraising glance. "You've done well for yourself."

Harlan downed his first shot, poured a second, and then sat on his sofa. "Thanks. I'm sure you have, too. We're in a lucrative business."

Jackson raised his glass in salute. "But you've done better than most."

"Well, I guess I'm good, and The Orphic Guild pays well. But rather than this bullshit chat, why don't you tell me what you broke in for? And," he added as another thought struck him, "how you got past my amulets and charms."

Jackson rolled his eyes and sat in the armchair. "Amulets and charms are not meant to stop people from breaking in, Harlan, you should know that. They're more to ward off ill intent, and you could argue they have worked. It's only me!"

"But you could have phoned!" Harlan adopted a mock English accent. "Hey Harlan, I'm in a spot of bother. Would you mind helping a chap out? I'd be awfully grateful."

Jackson looked unimpressed. "No one has spoken like that in fifty years!"

"Er, you were the one who said, 'spot of bother.'"

"I'm self-effacing, that's what us Brits do, but I said *a bit of bother*, not the rest."

Now that he had a chance to study Jackson better, he could actually see that he seemed a bit edgier than normal, despite his banter, and Harlan stopped teasing. "What were you searching for?"

Jackson sipped his drink and then said, "News flies in this world, you know that, so it shouldn't be a surprise to know that everyone has heard about the attack on The Order of the Midnight Sun."

Harlan shrugged. "Not surprising at all. There were bodies everywhere, and we had to call the police."

"But rumour has it that it's because of the Dark Star."

"Well, bully for you," he replied, keeping his face carefully schooled. "Because I'd never heard of it, so I'm amazed you have."

Jackson leaned back, rolling his glass between his hands. "I admit, I hadn't. But one of my regular clients has. We caught up for a drink yesterday, and he told me to stay clear of it. Said it's bad news."

"From what I've heard so far, I'd agree. But why did you break in?"

"It's Black Cronos I'm interested in, not Dark Star—although, I realise that right now they come as a pair." Jackson had become very serious, all trace of humour erased from his face. "I hoped to find some current information on them, without alerting you to my interest."

"They're bad news too, Jackson. From the glimpse I had of them yesterday, they aren't quite human. They're fast, deadly, and honestly, if the Nephilim hadn't been there, I would be dead right now. So would Aubrey and Caldwell. You should stay away from them."

"I can't." Jackson stood abruptly after draining his glass. "Would you mind if I topped up?"

"Go ahead."

Harlan watched Jackson pour another shot and then pace back and forth. He waited, knowing that Jackson was wrestling with something. Moments later, he seemed to come to a decision, and he sat again.

"It's ominous that they're back," Jackson told him, "because all news of them disappeared after World War II. They caused trouble searching for occult goods. Not for the Nazis, you understand, but themselves. They screwed everyone. They compromised enemy lines. I know this because my grandfather was part of a team sent to find them. He disappeared, and was never seen again."

The room seemed to shrink around them, utter blackness beyond the pool of warm, orange lamplight. Jackson's face was cast in harsh lines, and he suddenly appeared much older.

"How can you possibly know that?" Harlan asked, a sense of doom approaching. "That would have been top-secret information."

"Because I sometimes work for the government. That sort of thing runs in my family. The fact that I also work in the occult business is not chance. It's fate. And that's why I mostly work alone."

Harlan's mouth dropped open, and he had to make a conscious effort to grip his glass. "Are you a spy?"

A flicker of a smile crossed Jackson's face. "Not exactly. But the government wants all news of Black Cronos. Anything I can find, however small. The hunt is on for them—again."

"Should you even be telling me this?" Harlan's gaze flicked to the main entry as if someone was about to kick down the door.

"I can tell who I deem helpful and trustworthy enough." Jackson grinned. "And I've decided you are."

Sixteen

NAHUM TURNED OVER ANOTHER fallen enemy that he'd found halfway in the hedge, finding her throat cut. *One of Shadow's kills.* Nahum sighed as he thought of his own victims. He hadn't killed so many people in years, and he knew he'd have to kill more before this was over.

Ash must have heard him, because he called over, "Weary, brother?"

"Weary of killing. Black Cronos is like a small army."

"A well-equipped and well-trained army. It doesn't feel like a group of alchemists to me."

"No, they don't," Nahum agreed. He rolled his shoulders, feeling the deep ache in his muscles, and winced. "I think I'm covered in bruises."

"At least we're not dead."

It was the early hours of the morning, and Nahum and Ash had been working their way steadily along the farthest field from their house, while Barak and Shadow concentrated on the other direction. Eli and Gabe were in the house, trying to reassure Caldwell and Aubrey. They were, understandably, terrified. Nahum and Ash had flown back and forth in pairs, refusing to leave each other alone.

The moon was riding high now, throwing its silvery light across the fields, and the long grass around them swayed in a gentle breeze that blew in from the sea. The light also, unfortunately, highlighted the dark pools of thick, congealed blood splattered across the fallen.

"We must have faced almost two dozen, by my reckoning," Nahum said, running through the numbers. "That's a lot of people."

"And still that woman escaped." Ash chewed at his lower lip. "I'd love to know what it is she does."

"Her manner of killing, you mean? Yes, me too."

Ash made slow progress as he searched the boundary where the shadows were darkest. "I suspect their tattoos have been magically enhanced with some kind of ritual. Maybe they came out of an alchemical breakthrough?"

"Or it's just plain old magic. The witches have magically enhanced tattoos."

"How do you know that?"

"El told me a few months ago."

"But I bet theirs don't disappear after death," Ash pointed out. He grunted as he pulled another man from the hedge and slung him over his shoulder. "Surely we're nearly done now. I need a shower."

"Just that corner left," Nahum said, pointing over his shoulder. He hauled the dead woman up, wondering how she had become embroiled in Black Cronos. "Come on, let's gets rid of these two and finish up. I stink of death."

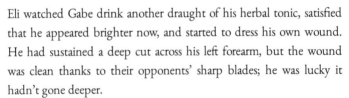

Eli watched Gabe drink another draught of his herbal tonic, satisfied that he appeared brighter now, and started to dress his own wound. He had sustained a deep cut across his left forearm, but the wound was clean thanks to their opponents' sharp blades; he was lucky it hadn't gone deeper.

Eli had set up his herbs, balms, and poultices on the long cabinet at the back of their lounge. The fire was blazing, even though the night was warm, and Aubrey and Caldwell sat before it, clenching a glass of whiskey each. They talked quietly, the astrolabe and their books on the coffee table, while Gabe stared at the flames.

Eli washed his wound with a cloth he'd dipped into a bowl of warm, herb-scented water, and once it was dressed, pulled his shirt off and cleaned his other cuts, noting the bruises blooming over his skin. He studied his face in the mirror on the wall, tentatively probing the graze across his check from where he crashed onto the ground earlier, and knew Briar would have a thousand questions for him tomorrow. As would Isabel, the woman he had been sleeping with on and off for months. *Well, one of them.* Eli refused to be tied down. It made him feel suffocated. But he was very clear on his attitude with his women. They knew he wasn't interested in being exclusive, and they either accepted it or walked away. He smiled thinking of Isabel's warm hands, and wondered if the bruises would appal her or excite her. *It was hard to know. She might enjoy ministering to his injuries.*

He pulled his t-shirt on and walked over to Gabe, crouching in front of him. His colour looked better, but he still seemed shaken, which was unusual. Gabe was generally stoic, calm, and organised, and they all took his leadership for granted. Welcomed it, even. Well, Eli did; he had no wish to order his brothers around and make the decisions. "Gabe, are you okay?"

Gabe focussed. "Yes, I just feel a little weird, that's all. I'm sure it will pass."

"You say the woman is a called 'The Silencer of Souls?'" Caldwell asked.

Startled, Gabe turned to him, as if he'd forgotten the others were there. "Yes. I still don't know what she is, but she's not fully human. She'd have easily killed you."

Caldwell looked contrite, and Eli knew what was coming. "I'm sorry we doubted you. I honestly didn't think they'd find us here, or that there would be so many."

Eli had taken them to the barn earlier to see the dead being laid out. He hadn't wanted to, but Aubrey insisted, as if he needed proof that they hadn't made the attack up—even though they'd certainly heard the fight from the cellar, and the house was a mess of shattered windows, floors covered in broken glass. They had both staggered back to the living room in shock.

Caldwell continued. "We have reconsidered our options, and agree that it would be best if you accompanied us to France."

There was no flash of victory from Gabe, just a grim nod. "Good."

Aubrey hurried on. "Not that we doubt our Senior Adepts, of course, but clearly Black Cronos have means of finding us we didn't anticipate."

"Regardless of your trust in your colleagues, in order for you to retain our services, I want a full list of every single member of your Inner Temple, and anyone else you've told."

"There really is no need," Aubrey started to say, but Gabe held his hand up.

"There is *every* need. I want every name, particularly those who know that you are here. And we will go to a new location in France. One of my choosing, that you tell no one about."

Caldwell spluttered, "But we have made plans—"

"They're changing. Those are my terms. Understood?"

They were obviously uncomfortable with Gabe's requests, but Eli knew Gabe was right, and so did they. With visible reluctance, they nodded.

"Good," Gabe said. "Write the list right now, and then we'll go through it, one by one."

The sound of an engine in the courtyard had all of them looking up, alarmed, but Eli realised it would be Newton, or Zee would surely have alerted them.

Eli stood, placing his hand on Gabe's shoulder as he made a move to stand. "You stay here, I'll go and see what's happening."

Gabe nodded his agreement, and Eli knew that he had to be feeling worse than he was admitting, or else he'd argue. Eli picked up his sword, just in case, and walked up the hall, the glass crunching under his boots. Newton's BMW was in the courtyard, and Eli suppressed a grin as he saw him already arguing with Shadow.

Newton's hands were on his hips. "Please tell me this is a joke!"

"Look at me, Newton," she protested. "I'm covered in blood, and it's some stupid hour of the night. Of course it's not a joke."

Newton looked up at Eli's approach, his eyes sweeping across his injuries. "Bloody hell. I thought you lot were invincible."

"I wish, but we do injure, as anyone does. We just heal quicker." Newton looked tired, and his hair was sticking up from where he'd run his fingers through it. "I'm sorry, Newton. I know you've had a rough week. When is Inez's funeral?"

Newton closed his eyes briefly. "Today. You better show me what's going on."

Shadow's eyes flitted beyond Eli to the door, and Eli knew who she was looking for. "Gabe is fine. Resting. Where's Nahum?"

"In the barn, which is where you need to be, Newton."

Eli followed them inside. It was better lit now, the floor swept of debris. Although, large pools of congealed blood still marred the floor, and the stench of it now, hours later, was sharp. Worse was the line of bodies laid out on the far side.

Newton gasped. "Jesus Christ! What the hell has happened here?"

Nahum and Barak were talking, but broke off as they saw Newton, and Nahum said, "We were attacked by an organisation called Black Cronos."

He quickly summarised the events of the previous few days, watching Newton examine the bodies while he listened. He shook his head occasionally as he processed the story, and when Nahum had brought him up to date, Newton straightened, already reaching for his phone. "You know I'm going to have to call my team in on this. All of these bodies have to go to the morgue and get processed properly."

"And us?" Barak asked. "This was a coordinated attack, and we were defending ourselves."

"I know, but I can't pretend this didn't happen. You'll have to make statements, but under the circumstances, that will be all. But these guys," he gestured at the dead, "worry me. Will they come back? Will White Haven be at risk?"

"They might come back for us," Nahum said, "but I don't think you need to worry about White Haven."

"I suspect that after this," Eli added, "they will rethink their strategy. They took a big hit today when they underestimated us. But," he said, trying to reassure Newton, "some of us will be leaving soon for France." He caught Nahum's questioning glance. "They've just requested our help—not surprisingly." He addressed Newton again. "If they're watching our movements, they'll know it's pointless to come here again."

Newton nodded. "They'll follow you though, and you won't be able to take your weapons with you. Have you considered that?"

This was something they had discussed at length, and now there was talk of someone driving to France and carrying all the weapons in Gabe's SUV, hidden somehow. Nahum nodded wearily. "We'll think of something."

"What does this astrolabe lead to that they want it so badly?" Newton asked.

Shadow was examining the bodies again, still clad in her armour. "We have too many theories and no real answers, unfortunately. But, knowing whether these are human or not would be good."

"Didn't you say that Maggie had taken the bodies in London?" Newton asked, frowning. "She might have results already."

"Could you find out for us?" Nahum asked. "I doubt she'll tell us, but she will surely tell you."

"Potentially we'll be working together on this," Newton said thoughtfully. "All right. Let's get started, because I want the bulk of it finished before the funeral this afternoon, and at a more reasonable hour I'll call Maggie." He rubbed his face. "Christ. I'm exhausted. This is all I need with rogue witches on the loose."

Having seen first-hand what mayhem Mariah and Zane, the two witches from the Witches Council had caused, Eli had every sympathy for Newton. "I'll still be here, with Zee and maybe Niel. We'll help if you need us."

Newton met his eyes gratefully, a faint smile on his face. "Thanks Eli, I appreciate that." He took a deep breath and punched a number into his phone. "Let's get this show on the road."

Harlan regarded Jackson, and suddenly he didn't seem the same diffident, affable occult hunter at all. There was an edge to him he'd never seen before.

"I wish I could tell you more," Harlan said after recounting their fight, "but the only other information I have on them is from years ago."

Jackson nodded. "Could I see it anyway?"

"Sure. Wait here." Harlan fetched the papers from his study, glancing nervously out of the window as he did so. He half-expected to see a figure loitering on the street, watching him like in some film *noir*, but was relieved to see that the road was deserted. Cursing himself for being jumpy, he passed the folder to Jackson and took a seat again. "I copied these records from the guild."

Jackson studied the pages for a few moments. "Old letters." He looked up. "The same handwriting, too."

"I noticed, but that might mean nothing other than they have long-serving, loyal staff."

"Could JD tell you more?"

Harlan cleared his throat. "We're not on good terms right now, but when I mentioned their name, he had definitely heard of them. He seemed surprised to learn they were back." Harlan leaned forward, sitting on the edge of his chair. "I presume you know they have the same origin as the order, but they went their separate ways."

Jackson nodded, still examining the papers. "We do. They've meddled in many things since then, and have accumulated a lot of money. But," he stared at Harlan again, "this is the first time they have been so openly aggressive in years. This is our chance to hunt them down and destroy them for good."

"*Destroy* them? That seems extreme!"

"You witnessed them the other day. You know what they're capable of. That's only a sample of their power. And it's not just in the UK. They have a presence everywhere. They may have been dormant here, but our European friends have reported their activities over the past few decades."

"What about in the U.S.?"

"They have no presence there yet, as far as we know."

"So, you have no idea where they're based?"

Jackson sipped his drink again. "None whatsoever. Any leads we think we have simply disappear into the ether." He tapped the folder. "How did you get the astrolabe back?"

"Good detective work...and some luck." He recounted their trip to Storm Moon and what they found out from Blaze's friend.

"You met Maverick Hale? He's an interesting character."

"You know him?"

Jackson wiggled his hand. "A little. I wonder if there is a Cronos presence in Oxford?" He was talking more to himself than Harlan. "I'll mention it to my contact."

"How high up is your contact?" Harlan asked.

Jackson winked. "High enough, but you won't have heard of him. Like anything paranormal, it sits under a covert operation. Hopefully though we'll learn something from the post-mortems."

Harlan blinked with surprise. "They work with Maggie and her team?"

"Hell no!" Jackson recoiled in horror. "She's not discreet enough! But the division accesses her reports and her SOCO team's findings. Most of the stuff she follows up on we have no interest in."

"We, hmm? So, you're involved with them more than you're letting on, Jackson."

"On occasions," he reiterated. He stood, shrugging on his long raincoat that he wore regardless of the weather. "Can I take these documents? I'll bring them back."

"Sure. But soon, please."

"Just give me a few hours. If you hear anything else at all, please let me know—no matter how small. And I suggest you get out of here."

Harlan stood too, walking him to the door. "I was debating that same thing. I'm jumpy as hell."

Jackson's clear eyes were troubled. "I have no doubt they would use you as leverage to get to the astrolabe, so make yourself scarce. And leave your toys behind," he added, referring to Harlan's bike and car. "They're very recognisable."

With that he slipped out, and Harlan started to pack.

Gabe was glad to see the farmhouse returned to normal by late Tuesday afternoon. He watched the last of the SOCO team drive out of the courtyard, taking all sorts of samples with them. Newton and Moore had left hours before, as had the dead once the coroner had arrived.

He had berated them for moving the bodies, but Gabe had stood his ground, arguing that they were trying to prevent panic if a passing walker found the bodies. They had all given statements, and although Gabe knew it was for the best, they all felt scrutinised and judged, and quite nervous, despite Newton's reassurance that they wouldn't be arrested. Gabe spotted Shadow emerging from her room in the outbuilding, looking refreshed after her shower, something he had yet to do.

"You should get some sleep," she suggested, walking over to join him. Her hair was still damp, looking darker than normal, and she combed it out with her fingers as she talked. "Are you feeling better?"

He nodded. "Whatever was in Eli's herbal tonic was really good, although," he rubbed his fingers across his lips. "I can still feel her touch. It's like an ice burn."

Shadow studied his face. "You'll be glad to know they look fine."

"Care to test them?"

She laughed. "Not right now, thanks."

"Later, then?"

She shot him a warning glance. "Partners don't snog!"

"Who says?"

"I do!"

"The rule you broke the other night!"

"For the cause, as you well know. And you started it." She walked into the house, swinging her hips in a way that made Gabe's loins ache, and he followed her in, deciding to change the subject while he felt he was ahead.

"Any sign of JD's thief?"

"No." She headed to the fridge and grabbed a couple of beers. "But that's not surprising after last night's debacle." She popped the caps off and handed him one. "But they might try tonight."

"They'll have to be invisible to get in. I spoke to Caspian, and he's going to manage at the warehouse without us for a few days, which means we can have a couple of lookouts tonight."

Shadow leaned against the counter. "Everyone will burn out if we're not careful."

"That's why most people are in bed right now, except for Eli. He's patrolling. Niel and Zee will be our lookouts tonight. The rest of us can sleep, and then catch the flight tomorrow."

"Niel is gutted he's not coming."

Gabe sank into a kitchen chair, his tiredness mixing with his guilt. Niel was loving their occult work, but he needed to keep the other Nephilim motivated and involved, too. "I know, but to be honest, the way we're going, he'll be joining us anyway. I guess I just want to ensure the remaining guys will be safe once we leave."

"Maybe he could follow with the weapons. *If* we can hide them well enough."

"That will be his first job when he gets up. He's going to take my SUV apart. Or," he said, voicing something he'd been mulling over, "he could fly."

Shadow looked surprised. "That's a long way!"

"It is, but we've travelled such a distance before. And it will be easy enough to do over the course of one night. He can stop and rest a couple of times, especially before he crosses the channel."

"Even carrying a big bag of weapons?"

"Yep. We'll work out some way of strapping a bag to him."

Shadow sat opposite him. "That would solve our problem. Maybe a few of you could have flown."

"I'd considered it, but there's a lot more air traffic now. And besides," he flashed her a grin, "I wanted to see what a plane was like."

She smiled at his admission, and for a moment her company was so easy and relaxed it made Gabe think that anything was possible between them. "Me too," she admitted. "Another new experience to savour in our strange, new world. Anyway, it sounds like you and Niel will be busy later, so I'll cook."

"Rabbit stew?" he teased.

"I can manage more than that!"

"I know. Thanks, Shadow. For everything. The fact you killed half a dozen of them last night really helped."

"I think you'll find it was closer to ten. I am fey." She sipped her beer, looking smug.

Gabe groaned. "Will you ever stop saying that?"

"I doubt it."

He hoped she didn't. It infuriated him and amused him equally. "You heard that Caldwell and Aubrey gave me the list of their Inner Temple last night?"

She nodded. "What are you going to do with it?"

"We went through them all, one by one, and there are a couple that strike me as suspicious. I think we should give their names to Harlan and ask him to follow them up."

"How?" She looked incredulous. "I know he has connections, but that might be a stretch, even for him."

"We haven't got time, and I think it's important. Black Cronos found us too quickly! I don't care how good their resources are."

"True. Where's the list? I'll call him."

He dug into his pocket, extracted the folded piece of paper, and handed it to her. "I've asterisked the couple I suspect. One's a newer member, and the other is the secretary —one of the members who had the codes to the lock and safe. And an eager beaver, according to Aubrey at least. One of the more fervent ones." A wave of tiredness washed over him, and he stood, leaving half his beer in the bottle. "I need to shower and sleep. So should you. You may be fey, but you're not invincible."

"I grabbed a couple of hours, post-interview." She glanced around the kitchen and grimaced at the mess. "I'll call Harlan first, and then before I cook, I'll get rid of the glass."

The mess from the shattered windows had been partially swept up by Aubrey and Caldwell who had helped with some of the clean-up, anxious to do something useful after they had taken shelter in the cellar.

Gabe checked his watch. "Shit. The glaziers are coming in the next hour or so."

"Good. I'll supervise them." She nodded at the door. "Go. By the time you wake up, the place will be almost back to normal."

"Oh, and warn Harlan that he could be in danger."

She waved him away with a flick of her hand. "Consider it done."

Seventeen

HARLAN CHECKED INTO THE Mandarin Oriental in Hyde Park, central London, a hotel that combined a satisfying mix of the old and new, equipped with restaurants, a gym, swimming pool, and bars. He had debated whether a small boutique hotel would be better, or even a basic hostel, but then decided the anonymity of a big hotel with lots of staff and security would be safer—for everyone. And besides, who was he kidding? He hated basic hotels. *They sucked.*

For added protection, he had booked in under a pseudonym, a name he had used rarely, but for which he had a credit card and passport, all completely separate from anything he used for The Orphic Guild. It was a precaution he'd taken years ago following a few hairy moments with previous hunts, and now seemed the perfect time to use it again. Today he was Bradley Harris, a suitably common name that didn't stick out.

Following a phone call on his burner phone with Shadow, where he learned the details of their horrendous night, he debated whether he should follow them to France using his current cover, but then he'd considered his conversation with Jackson Strange, and the list Shadow had entrusted to him. He decided that for now, he'd stay put. He still had his other cases that were keeping him busy, and needed to visit the office to show good faith—and hopefully see Olivia.

He examined the list he'd written down, recognising a couple of names that he suspected were high up in the order: Henri Durand and Kent Marlowe. The two names that Gabe was suspicious of were unfamiliar to him, but, he noticed with a smile, there were a couple of lesser nobility and one celebrity whose names he did recognise. *No wonder Caldwell had been reluctant to hand it over.* He considered sharing this information with Jackson, but he hadn't discussed that particular development with Gabe or Shadow yet.

He decided he'd think on it, and by the time he arrived at the guild, it was after four in the afternoon. He entered his office without anyone seeing him.

As soon as he sat down, Olivia called him, not giving him time to even greet her before she spoke. "You're here! I'm coming to see you."

In seconds she was in his office, still dressed in her fatigues, and she marched purposefully to his desk and sat down. "I stopped by your place at six this morning and you weren't there. You had me worried!"

"Six! Why were you there so early?"

"I've been worrying about everything after our conversation yesterday, and I just wanted to see that you were okay."

He smiled. "That's very sweet of you, but why didn't you call?"

She shrugged. "I don't know. I guess I was worried you were someplace where a phone might compromise you."

He rolled his eyes and walked to his espresso machine. "Drama queen. I was sleeping elsewhere, and then spent the day chasing leads on my cases."

She looked at him surprised. "Sleeping *where*? With a woman you haven't told me about? Harlan!"

"No, dummy! A hotel room, where I had the best night's sleep I've had in days. Well, the best early hours of the morning's sleep. I moved in the middle of the night and slept in."

She was on her feet and at his side instantly. "Did something happen?"

He'd decided not to tell Olivia about Jackson's visit. That would betray his trust, and possibly put Olivia in danger. The less she knew, the better. He'd decided to stick to the basic truth. "I got paranoid about Black Cronos, and," he lowered his voice and switched on his machine, the rumble helping to cover his voice, "I'm also a bit paranoid about you-know-who."

Olivia nodded and leaned against the wall. "I get that. It's a sensible move."

Harlan passed her a cup of coffee and started to prepare his own. "And I'm not going to tell you where I'm staying, either."

"Okay, well, just stay safe. These guys sound terrifying, to be honest." Olivia put her cup down and rolled up her long-sleeved cotton top, looking at him wide-eyed. She pointed to her inner forearm, close to the elbow where something was written, all the time continuing to talk. "I'm heading out in an hour, to Nottingham on that case I mentioned, so I just wanted to check in with you, really." She mouthed at him. "*JD's thief.*"

Harlan squinted at the tiny lettering as Olivia continued to chat, and although the ink was smudged, he made out the name, *Mouse*. He lifted his head abruptly, staring at her. He mouthed back, "*Are you kidding me?*"

She shook her head, and then raised her voice. "Anyway, I better get on, I have a couple of calls to make before I go." She downed her last mouthful of coffee and then walked across the room, opening the door as she called back. "You take care, Harlan, and let me know if can help with the case in the East End."

"Yeah, sure, but I'll be fine."

Olivia flashed him a beaming smile, murmured, "Afternoon, Mason. Can't stay, see you in a few days," and then she was gone, leaving Mason in her place.

Harlan sipped his drink, schooled his face into pleasant affability, and said, "Hey, Mason. Can I help you with something?"

Mason stepped inside, his sharp eyes darting everywhere. "Harlan. You've been gone a few hours. Are you okay?"

Harlan frowned, and had the horrible feeling that Mason had been following him—or was trying to. "I'm out of this office more than I'm in it, so why are you worried?"

Mason adjusted his silk tie. "Concerned about Black Cronos, of course, especially after Sunday."

"Oh." Harlan was still standing by his coffee machine, but he walked back to his chair with his drink, refusing to ask Mason if he wanted one. "No need. I've been following up leads for the Ouija board my client is after. I've narrowed it down to a couple of places."

"The East End job?"

"No, that's another one. The strange mirror with those unnerving properties, remember?" Mason had background on most of their cases, and he was aiming to bewilder him with a few of them. "Some little antique shop unearthed it, and we're researching its history. It's dark, very dark." He sipped his coffee. "I dropped in to grab another couple of files, so don't expect to see me much over the next day or so."

Mason moved idly around the room, touching Harlan's books and other objects, before asking, "No news from Gabe, then?"

"None. That's not my job anymore. Should I have heard something?" He was damned if he'd tell him about the huge attack on the farmhouse last night. Besides, Mason might already know.

"No, of course not. Glad to see you're staying out of the Dark Star business."

Harlan decided to have a little fun with him. "Your thief has retrieved it, then?"

"Not yet," Mason said, clenching his jaw. "There were some unexpected difficulties yesterday. But," he smiled icily, "it is a small delay only."

So, Mouse's attack had been thwarted by Black Cronos after all. Good. "Well, whoever it is will need some luck, but as you instructed, this is JD's business now." Harlan stood up, grabbed the large leather bag he used to carry paperwork, and started to gather some files and books together. "Is that all, Mason, because I have an evening appointment I need to keep."

"Yes, of course." Mason walked to the door. "I presume we can find you at your flat, should I need you?"

Harlan inwardly groaned at Mason's hideous subtlety and decided to mess with him a little more. "No, I've checked into a hotel until this Black Cronos business is over—personal safety, you understand."

Mason nodded, fake concern all over his face. "Of course. And where would that be?"

"I couldn't possibly tell you. It might endanger you, too. If for some reason they try to get to me through you, it means that even under torture you couldn't give me away." He shrugged. "I figure this way you could sincerely say you don't know. Obviously, let's hope it never comes to that!" Mason froze, his mouth working, but it was obvious he had no argument to that, and Harlan added, "Of course, my phone is always on if you need to talk."

"Excellent. In that case, I shall leave you to it."

In the minutes that followed Mason's exit, Harlan worked quickly, gathering anything he may need, as he had no intention of returning to his office for a while. He had no idea what might happen next, but he wanted to keep his distance from Mason and JD, and if they were trying to follow him with some hired unknown, the less he was here, the better. He had a circuitous route away from the office planned that would be even more confusing with rush hour, and the tubes would be packed. And then, once everything was safely in his hotel room, he needed to call Shadow, and then meet with Jackson.

Shadow had just told the Nephilim, Aubrey, and Caldwell who their expected thief was, and they looked at her with a mixture of incredulity and amusement. They were all in the living room after they'd eaten, and a map was spread across the coffee table, along with a pile of reference books that Caldwell and Aubrey had carried up from the cellar. Most of the Nephilim were sharpening weapons or cleaning them.

"Mouse?" Niel questioned, glancing her way as he sharpened his axe blade. "Should I be scared? That's a dumb name."

"I believe," Shadow said impatiently, "that she is so named because of her ability to get in anywhere—just like a mouse."

Ash nodded. "It's an excellent name. Mice are derided. People call them timid, but did you know that a mouse is highly adaptable to new environments, can squeeze through tiny places, is incredibly fast, can climb very high walls, and cross wires and power lines? That suggests to me," he said, reaching for another book from the table, "that Mouse will be a formidable thief."

"Well, thank you, David Attenborough," Barak groaned, "but I refuse to be intimidated by a mouse."

"Speaking of which," Niel said rising to his feet and hefting his axe, "I need to get on watch. As do you, Zee."

Zee groaned as he stood and stretched. "True. I'm sure Eli is wondering where we are."

Gabe was polishing his sword until it gleamed, but he set it aside and looked at Niel. "Are you happy with the bag arrangement?" Gabe and Niel had spent some time packing a large overnight bag with their various weapons and trialling it for flight.

"Sure," Niel nodded. "I can carry it easily, and strapped to my chest it will provide protection, too."

"All right. I'll phone you once we get to France, anyway."

"Are you sure you don't want me to go tonight? I'm happy to spend a few hours in France before you get there."

"Not on your own. And we can manage without weapons for a while. Plus, there'll be a few of us," Gabe pointed out. He walked over to examine the map and frowned. "It's a long way. Almost six hundred miles. I'm not sure you should do it in one go."

Niel paused in the doorway. "It'll be fine. I'm planning to rest on this side of the channel for a while before completing the final leg."

Gabe nodded, looking relieved. "Good."

"Well, I for one am not happy at having to travel without my daggers," Shadow protested as Niel and Zee left the room. "Planes sound stupid."

"Stupid or not, those are the rules," Nahum said, amused. "Don't you trust your bare hands?"

She looked at him disdainfully. "My hands are deadly with or without a blade, thank you. However, I feel naked without them." In fact, Shadow couldn't remember a time when she didn't carry her daggers at all times, strapped to her thighs, normally. Even when she was resting at home, like now, they were always close by. "Although, I am looking forward to trying plane travel. We have nothing like it in the Otherworld."

Nahum laughed. "Something new for all of us, except Estelle. It's a good job we have her to help us navigate the airport." He addressed Barak. "I presume she's told Caspian her plans?"

Barak nodded, although he looked worried, which was unusual for him. He was unconcerned about most things. "I have to say that I'm worried we're leaving Caspian a bit vulnerable." He reached for his beer and sipped it. "He's only just recovered from being attacked by those pirate spirits, and the two witches who were behind the whole thing have disappeared. I feel like we're running out on him when he needs us most."

"I agree," Ash said, "but the White Haven witches are closer to him now than before, so he's not alone. And they have the Witches Council behind them. He'll be fine." He leaned forward and tapped the map. "We need to focus on this."

"Very true," Caldwell said, speaking for the first time in a while. He'd been absorbed with reading a manuscript, and had been talking quietly with Aubrey. "We've studied this record before, but now that we have the astrolabe we've examined it again, and we're fairly confident that the reading we take based on the parade of planets will lead us directly to the chamber. Unfortunately, it won't be pinpoint-accurate, but it will be close."

Shadow was confused. "You had doubts?"

"Yes." Caldwell picked up the astrolabe and took out the central pin to dismantle its layers. "Traditionally, astrolabes have many plates to enable the user to choose the one suitable for the area that they are travelling in. This astrolabe only has two plates. The general European area, and France." All the Nephilim were watching now, their activities paused. "We were worried that the France plate would not be detailed enough, and we'd need another one, but now I think it will be accurate enough."

Aubrey nodded excitedly. "We just may need to do a bit of hunting at the site." He lifted one of the plates, turning it over in his hands, and the rose gold metal gleamed in the firelight. "This is an extremely detailed plate for all of France. Obviously, the places on here have slightly different names now—after all, this was made several centuries ago—but it should be easy enough to cross-match. Besides, place names or not, the directions will reveal all."

Ash frowned. "Do you think there will be other things to achieve once we're there?"

"Perhaps," Caldwell said, wiggling the manuscript. "The language on this is obscure. We can understand it, but it seems sort of like gibberish."

"Perhaps it's something Black Cronos will understand better," Nahum suggested, perplexed. "It was one of their members that designed it in the first place."

"Maybe," Ash mused, reaching forward to take the paper from Caldwell's grasp. "But maybe not. Let me study it for a while."

"Any further details about the Dark Star itself?" Gabe asked.

"None, other than vague references to the failed experiment. It's all quite ominous," Aubrey sighed. "And I must admit that after yesterday's attack, I am very worried about what we're going to find."

"It's not too late to change your mind," Gabe told him.

Aubrey shook his head. "Yes, it is. We haven't gone this far to give up now. The future of our order and all of our plans relies on this. We're not backing out."

"Neither will Black Cronos," Gabe asked softly. "So you'd better be prepared for a fight."

———◆○◆———

Harlan sipped his pint and checked his watch. Jackson Strange was late, and worry ate away at him.

He glanced around the small, crowded pub that was situated opposite the tube station in Covent Garden, full of people who'd come in for an after-work drink on Tuesday evening. He'd chosen this place deliberately. It was convenient to get to, and very popular. That meant that no one would overhear them, and it offered decent anonymity.

He glanced up as the door to the street opened, bringing in fresh evening air, and sighed with relief as Jackson entered. Harlan raised his hand, and Jackson nodded and headed to the bar, finally arriving at the table with his pint of Guinness.

"You were worrying me," Harlan admitted as Jackson sat. He looked flushed, his eyes bright, and Harlan hoped this boded good news.

Jackson took a long drink, and then brushed the foamy head from his lips. "Sorry, I got caught up in a meeting, and took a circuitous route to get here. Did you take my advice?"

Harlan nodded. "I'm staying in a large hotel."

"Good, because what I discovered today makes me very nervous."

Harlan had been about to sip his beer, but now he put it down. "Shit. What?"

"I told my superiors about Oxford, and it ties into some other knowledge they have. They've had their eye on a professor in one of the colleges for a while, but have nothing conclusive on him."

"So, what makes them suspect him?" Harlan asked, puzzled.

"His specialty is medieval alchemy for a start, and he lectures on alchemy masters—Ibn Sina, Artephius, Roger Bacon, Johann Georg Faust, John Dee, Elias Ashmole, and the Count of St Germain, amongst others." Harlan froze at the mention of JD's name, but Jackson didn't seem to notice, as he was too busy glancing at the menu. "He also comes from a rich family with all the right connections." Jackson looked up at him and smiled. "You get a nose for these sorts of things, and he hits all the markers."

"What's his name?"

"Stefan Hope-Robbins. They don't think he's the big guy, but they believe he is high up in Black Cronos. The fact that Gabe and Shadow tracked Blaze there has added weight to that."

"Wow." Harlan sipped his pint, thinking how insanely cloak-and-dagger all of this sounded. "Have they got any leads on the woman who killed Blaze?"

Jackson put the menu down, rested his elbows on the table, and knitted his fingers together. "Did you see any of that footage?"

"No. Did the club release video?"

Jackson nodded. "There was nothing inside the club, but there was some footage recorded from outside the entrance. It was blurry, all the images unreadable. But this is England, and there are cameras everywhere. They caught sight of the woman with long, black hair heading through the town, but again, anything too close became fuzzy."

"She was able to destroy the images?"

"It seems so. Or it was your friends. I know Shadow and Gabe fought her. Some wildly blurry images of that were caught, too."

Harlan felt his breath catch in his throat, and wondered if they had even considered that. "They don't have clear images of them, then?"

"No. Although," he looked amused, "it looked as if someone had landed from a height."

Harlan gripped his pint glass. "Gabe."

"Don't worry. Like I said, everything was blurry. Shadow is fey, isn't she? She should have magic that could do that, even if she used it unconsciously."

Harlan didn't answer, instead asking, "Did you tell your friends about them?"

"Sorry, but I had to. But they're not interested in them...yet. However, they think they know who the woman is."

"Ah," Harlan said, feeling guilty. "My guys know, too. Shadow told me they questioned one of the men before he died. Who do you think she is?"

Jackson took a long sip of his Guinness as if to fortify himself. "She's called The Silencer of Souls, because of the way she kills."

"Yep, that's what Shadow said. Does she kill a lot?"

Jackson regarded him steadily. "Unfortunately, yes. She has left other victims behind, but in less crowded circumstances. All they ever catch is a glimpse of her, and then she's gone. This was in Europe, you understand, not the UK."

"And she really kills them with a kiss?" Harlan asked, horrified.

"Yes, but the mechanism of it is unknown."

Harlan's mouth grew dry, and he sipped his pint again, feeling horribly out of his depth. "This is not what I expected, Jackson. Not at all. I know our job can be dangerous, but this feels next level."

"It does to me, too, if I'm honest." Jackson ran his hands through his hair, leaving it ruffled. "I also have the autopsy results back, courtesy of my *friends*, too. They are all human."

"The men who attacked us? Impossible. They were too...*different*."

Jackson shrugged, apologetic. "Maybe they were just well-trained."

Harlan considered their strange eyes. "No. I'm sure there was something inhuman about them."

"Nothing that an autopsy picked up—at least not yet. There are some tests they're waiting on. Toxicology, for example."

"By the Gods! I was hoping for good news, and instead you bring me shit."

Jackson gave a dry laugh. "You were kidding yourself. Why would I have good news? This search has been going on for decades. They can't swoop in on them in mere hours!" He glanced down at the menu. "I'm starving. Do you want anything?"

Harlan had read the menu while he waited. "Yeah, the steak. Rare, please." He put some cash on the table. "Pay with that."

"My treat," Jackson said. "I have a favour to ask."

Harlan groaned, wondering what new level of Hell his life was about to descend to while Jackson placed their order, and as soon as he sat down again, he said, "Well, don't keep me hanging."

"Your friends killed many men and women yesterday in Cornwall. It was quite the bloodbath."

"I know, Shadow told me." Harlan felt guilty he hadn't been there to help, and also relieved he was left out of it. "I'm just glad they're okay."

"They've impressed my superiors."

Jackson was looking at him calmly, but his words seemed weighted with import. "That's bad, isn't it?"

Jackson smiled ruefully. "Depends how you look at it. And it depends on the outcome of the Dark Star investigation. If Gabe, Shadow, and their team end up on top, my superiors would like an introduction. They will be the only ones who've been up close and personal to Black Cronos in years who have lived to tell the tale. They'd consider them useful allies."

"I get it. If they die, well...never mind, but if they win, they're recruited into the fight?"

"Sort of. Do you think they'd be interested?"

"They might be. Depends on the pay and conditions." Harlan thought they'd probably jump at the chance, especially Shadow, but he could be wrong. *Best to be cautious.* "They do work for us too, remember?"

"But Dark Star is a private gig, right?"

"Well, it is now."

Jackson studied him for a moment. "Why did you pull back from this one?"

"The order wanted them to be bodyguards," he answered warily. "The guild doesn't do that."

"It was nothing to do with JD, then?"

Now Harlan was really alarmed. "No! It was my decision."

"Just checking if you were under any pressure at all. You did say you were on bad terms now."

Harlan was increasingly aware he had no idea who these mysterious friends were of Jackson's, or who they really worked for. He believed Jackson to be trustworthy. Although now it seemed he was some kind of part-time spy, but what did he really know? He had no idea who he should trust, and was it really better to trust in the devil you knew? At least he had history with Mason and The Orphic Guild, and he trusted Olivia and Aiden implicitly, and Shadow and the boys. The list was in his pocket, ready to discuss with Jackson, but he decided to keep it to himself, for now.

"No," he said firmly. "No pressure at all. We're on bad terms because JD was such a shit a few weeks ago, over the trinity. I just thought it was best to continue with my other cases and let them pick up the bodyguard business. All I'm doing now is protecting myself from further attacks by Black Cronos...just in case they recognised me on Sunday."

"That's good, then," Jackson said breezily as took the letters he'd borrowed from his inner pocket and slid them across the table. "And thanks for these. There are a few things I need to do now, but nothing to involve you, you'll be pleased to know."

"I have a question," Harlan asked as he scooped the papers up and put them in his messenger bag. "If they consider Black Cronos so dangerous, and the Dark Star something to be avoided, why aren't they trying to stop them from reaching it?"

"I'm not privy to all of their decision making," Jackson pointed out. "They might be. I suspect they're tracking your friends, at least. And where they go, Black Cronos will follow. Perhaps you should warn them, just in case."

Harlan nodded his agreement, deciding he needed to call Shadow as soon as his dinner was over, but before he could comment, they were interrupted by one of the bar staff bringing them their food, and they paused until he left the table. When they spoke again, Jackson changed the subject with a grin.

"I have some gossip about Andreas Nicoli, if you're interested."

Harlan laughed, happy to have a reprieve from the mysterious intrigue, but part of him couldn't help but be disappointed Jackson didn't need him, or wonder if he knew something about JD he wasn't letting on.

Shit. His life was so complicated.

Eighteen

NIEL WAS SITTING IN the lee of the chimneys on the main farmhouse, trying not to shuffle with discomfort, and thinking longingly of his bed.

The fields around him were dark, lit only by the occasional flash of moonlight when the clouds cleared enough to let it through. *Rain was coming.* He could smell it on the air and feel the dampness intensifying. The ever-changing light made his lookout job difficult, despite his good eyesight. The hedges whispered with night creatures, the trees swayed in the strengthening sea breeze, and the scream of the foxes and screech of the barn owl blocked out more subtle sounds. *They sensed the rain, too.*

But it was beautiful, and Niel felt a calm ease over him. He glanced behind him, around the chimney, and stared at the dark roof of the outbuilding to his rear, reassured when he spotted Zee sitting motionless. Zee was facing the other direction, covering the gate and fields beyond, the crossbow resting on his lap. Niel returned to his own view, scanning the fields.

Unbidden, a memory came to him of a night like this, with scudding clouds and glancing moonlight. A night he had spent in a loggia with Lilith. A night of love and laughter. It seemed like a jewel now. Something to be polished and examined from a thousand different angles, and yet he would never see into the heart of it. He could only feel that. Ever since Harlan had mentioned her name in passing at Angel's Rest, these memories had returned more and more frequently, a bittersweet reminder of what had once been.

Lilith, and his life with her, had been complicated. Her life was far longer than her first husband's had been, and that was due to the magic of The Book of Raziel that had leaked into society. Magic she had accessed through private groups, studying in the depth of night, mastering secrets meant for the Gods alone to exact a revenge she never carried out. She was called a witch, amongst other names, for a reason. And Niel was still haunted by the memory of the angel, Chassan, his breath on his cheek, his unspoken welcome that resonated through his head. The weight of the memories felt as if it could crush him sometimes.

A tapping noise through his earpiece was a welcome break from his thoughts. *Zee had spotted something.* Niel tapped in response to acknowledge the message, and scanned his surroundings again, sweeping left to right. For a few moments he saw nothing, and then as the moon disappeared beneath the clouds again, he noticed a slow, almost imperceptible movement through the long grass bordering the hedge, moving ever close to the house.

Niel didn't move a muscle, refusing to break eye contact, and was rewarded when he made out the slim, creeping figure, arms and legs materialising out of the blackness.

Zee tapped five times in rapid succession. *He was on the move.*

Niel scanned the fields again, ensuring this wasn't part of another coordinated attack. Reassured, he then turned back to where the figure had gained ground, fully in the shadow of the house now. Niel crept forward on hands and knees just below the shallow apex, his head down until he reached the edge, sheltered by the final chimney. He spotted Zee to the left, crouching behind an old, crumbling wall. He had descended silently from the other roof. Niel was impressed; he hadn't heard a thing.

Niel focussed on Zee stalking the unknown attacker, and then he was on him or her, Zee's strong hands immobilising the figure completely. Not even a cry escaped.

Niel extended his wings and dropped behind them, folding his wings away again before moving into view. Zee had caught a woman. She was lithe and petite, dressed totally in black. She was wriggling and kicking but Zee had his arm wrapped around her, lifting her off the ground. His hand was over her mouth, and to Niel he said softly, "Let's take her to the barn."

Her eyes widened with alarm, but Niel raised his fingers to his mouth, shushing her. "We won't harm you. Calm down."

Neither he nor Zee wanted to alert the others, preferring to let them sleep, so they carried the woman to the far side of the barn, well away from the house, before speaking to her.

Zee still had a firm grip on her, and Niel quickly patted her down. She was wearing slim-fitting trousers and a top, with a balaclava on her head, revealing only almond-shaped eyes. "No weapons. Just lock picks," he told Zee. He met the woman's terrified, yet angry gaze. "Mouse, I presume?" She immediately froze. "We're going to release you now. No screaming, please." He lifted his sword for good measure. "Or you'll feel this."

Zee lowered her to the floor, and then took his hand from her mouth. As soon as she was free, she backed away, her eyes darting everywhere before finally settling on them both.

"What now?" Her voice was low but firm, with no hint of the unease she must be feeling.

"Good question," Zee said, amused. He folded his arms across his chest. "It depends on you. Are you Mouse? I suggest you be honest with us."

"How do you know the name?" she immediately countered, her chin up.

"We have good intel. Your name?" Zee insisted.

"That's one of them," she admitted, a hint of amusement in her eyes. "You're very quiet for big men. Both of you. I didn't see you or hear you."

"Good," Niel said, warming to her, even though she was trying to steal from them. "Nice to know we haven't lost our touch." He glanced at Zee. "Perhaps we should check for backup?" Zee nodded, and without another word left the barn. Niel stepped back, thinking Mouse might be more amenable with more space between them. "What do you want, Mouse?"

"You know what I want. The Dark Star Astrolabe."

"You can't have it. Tell JD his actions are dishonourable to his colleagues."

Her eyes lifted and he knew she was smiling. "Not JD."

"Mason, then. How were you going to deliver it?"

"Does it matter?"

"I guess not. Leave it be, Mouse."

"And that's it? You're letting me go?"

"Yes. If you'd threatened me with violence, I might have been provoked to do something else. But you didn't, and we don't kill mere thieves. Go, but I suggest you be careful. You're not the only one after the astrolabe."

"I know that." Her eyes darkened and her stance stiffened. "I watched them last night—for a while. I almost stumbled into the middle of it before running for my life. You killed many."

"Then you know *exactly* what we're capable of." Niel stepped back again, allowing her to access the open doorway. "Don't come back here, Mouse. We might not be so accommodating next time."

She walked past him, as quick as her name, but paused at the door to look back at him. "Last night there were more in the lane beyond here, way across the fields. I saw them as I was fleeing, but they didn't see me. A man with white-blond hair seemed to be coordinating them."

Niel crossed the barn, pausing when he was a few feet away. "How old was he?"

"Hard to say. Mid-forties perhaps? Hard-faced, fit. Furious. I suspect he will strike again."

"How many others with him?"

"Three that I saw. They were in a big, black van."

Niel wondered what had prompted her to share her news. "Thank you. I appreciate it."

"What's your name? You have mine."

He smiled. "Othniel, but everyone calls me Niel."

She nodded. "Stay safe, Niel, and perhaps we will meet again."

"Will you try again?" he asked, unwilling for her to leave so soon.

"I don't like to fail, but it depends on my instructions," she said softly. "Good luck."

She slipped out the door, and Niel realised that he had no idea of her real name, what colour her hair was, what shape her mouth was, or whether she really was as pretty as her beautiful eyes suggested. He flew back to the roof to finish his watch with many more things to ponder on.

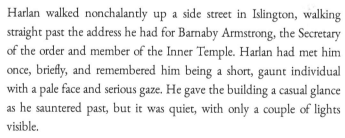

Harlan walked nonchalantly up a side street in Islington, walking straight past the address he had for Barnaby Armstrong, the Secretary of the order and member of the Inner Temple. Harlan had met him once, briefly, and remembered him being a short, gaunt individual with a pale face and serious gaze. He gave the building a casual glance as he sauntered past, but it was quiet, with only a couple of lights visible.

He'd been circling the street for the last half hour after exiting Highbury and Islington Tube Station, and nothing seemed unusual. There were no lurking black vans with darkened windows, or shady characters that looked abnormally dangerous, and he was certain he wasn't being followed. He paused in the darkest part of the road between the streetlamps, and wondered what the hell he thought he was going to find. Short of knocking on the door and marching in to ask questions, how could he know whether this man might have betrayed the order? Harlan's specialty was the paranormal and occult, not identifying dodgy people with an axe to grind.

The area was respectable, and the address in question was a narrow townhouse that Harlan suspected was split into flats. He should have a dog with him, under the pretext of taking it for a walk, or Olivia, pretending to be having a romantic late-night stroll. That was much more preferable. Or his car for a stakeout, if it wasn't so damned recognisable.

Harlan walked up the street again and then around, finally returning ten minutes later to find the street still quiet. Impatient, he checked his list. The next suspect didn't live too far from here, easily accessible by foot, so lifting his jacket collar, he hurried onwards, passing a few people leaving the pub on the corner, and mixing in with them for a short while.

But it was when these people thinned out and their chatter faded that Harlan thought he heard footsteps behind him. Footsteps that didn't veer off, quicken, or slow down, just remained steady. *Was he being paranoid, or was he being followed?* If he looked around now, he'd alert whoever it was to the fact that Harlan knew.

There was a corner ahead, and as soon as Harlan rounded it and was out of view, he sprinted and turned right onto the road he knew led to Upper Street, the main road through Islington that went back to the tube. A figure manifested on his left, dark and huge, but he kept going, his footsteps drowning out everything else as he pounded along to the main street and turned left, running straight into a group of people smoking outside a pub.

He muttered his apologies and immediately slowed to a fast trot, glancing behind him. A broad-shouldered man dressed in black emerged from the side street, staring intensely at Harlan, but there were lots of people milling around pubs, restaurants, and the KFC, offering Harlan a brief respite. A green space at the front of Union Church was dark with shadows and the rustling of summer leaves. Keeping to the other side of the road, he saw another man emerge ahead, and Harlan knew he was screwed. The man stood between him and the tube station.

And then he spotted a black cab depositing a couple of people on the sidewalk and ran, catching the door just as it was closing, and narrowly beating someone else to it. He slid inside, and as the cabbie pulled out, looked out of the window. The two figures watched him from the pavement, one of them already on the phone.

"Where to, mate?" The driver asked, his eyes on the road.

"The Mandarin Oriental." He'd half wondered if he should have the driver take him somewhere else, but there were so many black cabs around that he felt relatively safe. And besides, he wanted to be inside his hotel room, drinking a stiff bourbon without delay.

Harlan debated his options. He wasn't suited to surveillance, not with these threatening guys around. But perhaps it meant he was on the right track with Barnaby. He might not have seen anyone, but they had been there, somewhere. Either that or he'd been followed all along, and he was pretty sure that wasn't the case. Despite his reservations, he pulled his phone from his pocket, and when Jackson answered, he couldn't hide his relief.

"Thank the Gods. I need your help."

Gabe exited the airport in the bright blue of midday Bordeaux and gasped. "Herne's horns! This is *hot*!"

Estelle was next to him in a sleeveless blouse and jeans, and she threw back her head so that her hair cascaded down her back, closing her eyes as she looked towards the sun. "It's glorious, isn't it?"

Shadow rolled her eyes, and Gabe shot her a warning glance while he answered Estelle. "It is! Is it always like this?"

"Far more often than the UK!" Estelle surveyed the group as they took in their surroundings. "How did you find your first flights?"

"Like being trapped in a tin can," Nahum grumbled. "I much prefer how we do it."

Barak shrugged, his huge shoulders straining against his shirt. "It was a bit snug for my liking."

Estelle laughed, and Gabe realised he'd never seen her look so relaxed. "That's because you're all enormous—well, except for Shadow. They design seats for the average human, not giants."

"I enjoyed it," Ash said, fixing his sunglasses over his eyes. "As new experiences go, it could be worse. But I am anxious to be out of the airport."

"Me too," Aubrey said, shuffling uncomfortably with his briefcase clutched in his hand. It contained the astrolabe, and he hadn't wanted to relinquish it to anyone else, despite Gabe's protestations.

Estelle swung one set of keys that she'd collected from inside the terminal. Gabe had the other. "Let's get the hire cars and get out of here." She led the way across the car park to where the rental cars were kept beyond the visitor parking, and stopped in front of a couple of silver SUVs. "These are ours—they should do nicely. Who's going with who?"

He and Nahum had chatted about this earlier, and Gabe was keen to keep Shadow from Estelle, and Aubrey and Caldwell separated for safety reasons. "I'll take Shadow, Aubrey and Nahum, if you take Barak, Ash and Caldwell."

"Sure. You've got the address, so if you get lost, I'll see you there."

"I'm planning to follow you all the way," Gabe reassured her as they loaded their bags into the car. "How far is it?"

"About thirty or forty minutes. It's deep in the countryside, reasonably isolated, and surrounded by vineyards. It's perfect."

After one last sweep of the carpark where nothing looked untoward, Gabe slid into the driver's seat and started the engine. "You've got the address, Nahum?"

Nahum was in the passenger seat, and he lifted his phone. "Programmed in, just in case."

Aubrey was in the back, and Gabe caught his wary expression in the rear-view mirror. "Are you okay, Aubrey?"

He looked up, startled. "I'm fine. Just paranoid that we've been followed."

"I think they're regrouping," Shadow said, looking out the window with an eager curiosity. "And licking their wounds. We'll have a brief reprieve."

"And they will be planning another attack, no doubt," Nahum put in. "That's what Mouse suggested to Niel, anyway."

"Maybe. But if I were them, I'd try stealth next," she said thoughtfully.

Gabe thought about Niel and Zee's encounter with Mouse while he followed Estelle's car. "At least we don't have Mouse to worry about, although she might have been on the plane, for all we know." He glanced at Nahum. "Can we get a description from Harlan? Niel gave us nothing except 'almond-shaped eyes.'"

Shadow grunted. "Niel really should have taken her balaclava off. Idiot. And I already asked Harlan. She's petite, and that's about all I could get from him, because her appearance changes all the time. But he did say she was of Asian descent."

Gabe felt compelled to defend Niel. "They stopped her, that's the most important thing. And she shared information she didn't need to. Niel obviously made an impression." And clearly, so had she. Niel had that look on his face when he talked about her. He was intrigued, and Niel loved a mysterious woman.

Nahum nodded his agreement. "They did well to catch her. But let's not forget that according to Harlan, we might have a government organisation following us, too."

Gabe hated to feel hemmed in, and right now, he felt like he was suffocating. "It's ridiculous. I feel as if everyone is watching us!"

Nahum smiled. "It makes me feel very important. Three groups are after us, and we're one step ahead."

"I'd like half a dozen steps ahead, please!" Gabe glanced in the rear-view mirror at Aubrey, debating whether now would be a good time to tell him about Harlan's encounter with Black Cronos while investigating Barnaby Armstrong's address. *But maybe not.* Perhaps the less he knew at this stage, the better. And besides, they might learn more from Jackson later today.

Aubrey's voice was quiet but confident as he said, "If we make it to the reading, we'll be going directly to the chamber. They'll be too late."

"One more day to go," Gabe mused. "A lot could happen before then."

Shadow gave a dry laugh. "Let's hope this *château* is more castle than manor house."

Gabe nodded his agreement; otherwise, the coming days would feel like a lifetime.

They fell silent, admiring their surroundings as Gabe followed Estelle off the main roads and onto quiet lanes, meandering through villages, past fields, old stone houses, and vineyards. Gabe was aware of the subtle differences between this area and England. The design of the buildings for a start, never mind the French road signs, which didn't really register with him as he translated them automatically. It was more the feel of the place, and a change in the air itself. He was so absorbed that the time passed quickly, and it was with surprise when they turned up a long drive edged by stone walls, and finally swept into an immaculate courtyard surrounded by a variety of outbuildings with red stone roofs and slender columns. It was very different to their own courtyard at home.

The *château* itself was built of buttery yellow stone covered in ivy, a mix of square and round turrets with gothic arches and square windows, a sign of how it had been added to over the centuries, all of it charming and soothing to the eye. Lush planting edged the buildings, vibrant with summer flowers, and as Gabe exited the car, he was assaulted by their heady perfume. The whole place exuded a serene calm, but despite that, Gabe was worried.

Nahum echoed his thoughts when he said, "This place will be a nightmare to defend."

"I agree," Shadow said, walking around the car to stand next to Gabe. She surveyed the place with her hands on her hips, her eyes narrowing against the glare of sunshine. "It's beautiful, but there are so many places someone could hide!"

"Complaining already?" Estelle said, eyeing Shadow with distaste as she joined them. She had parked the other car against the far gate that looked over a tree-filled park that bordered the property.

Gabe felt a stab of worry as Shadow cast a withering glance at Estelle. "I am merely agreeing with Nahum that it will be hard to defend. But," she said, clenching her jaw, "it is a stunning place. Thank you for finding it for us, Estelle."

A shocked silence fell over the group, and Barak's lips twitched with humour. He was behind Estelle and Shadow, so neither of them could see him, and Gabe fought back his own grin, swiftly saying, "Really beautiful, Estelle. But there *are* a lot of outbuildings that could hide Mouse, should she ever find us here. And of course, there's Black Cronos."

Estelle looked slightly mollified. "Don't worry. I can set up good defensive spells for us when we get settled. Let's head inside."

For the next half an hour they explored the quirky building, assigning rooms and unpacking, and Gabe was even more disturbed. The layout was bewildering; corridors and staircases twisted back and forth on each other, as different levels revealed themselves. And everything was beautiful and expensive. He daren't think how much breakages would set them back. They needed to set up patrols immediately, no matter how good Estelle's defensive spells were.

They met up again at a long, wooden table on a sheltered terrace, climbing plants softening the stonework and scrambling through the beams overhead, jugs of lemon-scented water set out for refreshment. Aubrey and Caldwell had lost the slightly haunted look they had carried since the night of the attack, but Gabe knew this was no time to get complacent.

"We need to scout the outbuildings and the perimeter," he said to the group. "I want us to know this place intimately. Our lives may depend on it."

"I'll cover that," Barak volunteered immediately.

"I'd like to study these manuscripts some more," Ash said. "See if we can work out a few more details about the Dark Star chamber. I still feel like we'll be stumbling in blind once we uncover the location." He looked apologetically at Caldwell and Aubrey. "Sorry, guys. I know you've been working hard on this, but we still know so little!"

They shot each other uneasy glances, but nodded their consent, and Gabe hoped they weren't concealing something.

Nahum's chair scraped back as he said, "I'm with you, Barak. Shadow?"

"Coming, too," she said, rising swiftly to her feet.

"In that case," Estelle said, calmly, "I will start my spells. Is someone going to buy food?"

"I can do that," Ash volunteered, "before I hit the books."

"Then I'll search the house," Gabe said, checking his watch. "Let's meet here again in about four hours."

NINETEEN

IT WAS MID-AFTERNOON WHEN Harlan received a call from Jackson, just as he'd the left the tube station in Soho, and he sheltered in an alleyway.

"Everything okay, Jackson?" Harlan asked, as he registered Jackson's hurried tone.

"Stefan Hope-Robbins, the professor I was telling you about, has left Oxford, and is heading to France. Bordeaux, to be precise. And he was with a woman with long, black hair."

Harlan sagged against the wall. "Shit. The Silencer of Souls?"

"We think so."

"I need to tell Gabe," Harlan said, his mind racing through the possibilities. "It could be a place they'd be going to anyway. The trail seems to lead there."

"Unless the potential leak, Barnaby Armstrong, has already shared their location," Jackson suggested. "Can you check with Gabe, see if Aubrey or Caldwell had been keeping in touch with him?"

Harlan closed his eyes briefly. This is what they'd been worried about, but Caldwell was still adamant there was no mole. "Yes, of course. I'll call him now."

"I have a favour to ask you, actually," Jackson said. "I'm heading to Bordeaux too, and wondered if you'd keep an eye on the order. Update me if you hear any news? Or news from JD."

When Harlan had caught up with Jackson again the previous night, and had finally come clean about the list, he'd also thought he should share about JD wanting the astrolabe, too. It wasn't as if he'd told him anything about who JD really was, but he was starting to cling to Jackson like he was a life raft in the ocean, and reasonably full disclosure seemed important. But being asked to keep an eye on the order seemed risky. He had no wish to meet Black Cronos again. "Me? Haven't you got guys who do this?"

"It's not MI6, Harlan. It's a small division." Jackson sounded both impatient and amused.

"But they're on to me," he pointed out, feeling Jackson was playing fast and loose with his life.

Jackson fell silent for a moment, and then said, "Yes, fair enough. Just any info on JD then, and the call to Gabe."

Harlan sighed with relief. "Okay. I'll call Gabe now."

For a few moments, in the silence that followed the call, Harlan wondered if he'd gone mad, and then chided himself. He had wanted to be more involved, so here was his chance. He called Gabe quickly, taking advantage of the quiet alley, noting only a sole kitchen worker ducking out of a bar's back door to smoke a cigarette, and when Gabe picked up, he relayed Jackson's news, and asked him about the possible issue with Barnaby.

"But look, Gabe, the fact that Black Cronos members were at Barnaby's last night might just mean they are following all key players, just in case one of them can lead them to you guys. We shouldn't jump to conclusions."

Gabe swore loudly and promised to call him back, leaving Harlan loitering uncomfortably for a few minutes, but when he did return the call, he had news.

"That stupid oaf Aubrey confessed that he has been talking to bloody Barnaby Armstrong! Thank fuck I didn't tell him the address. He swears he hasn't called since we've arrived. I've taken his bloody phone anyway—and Caldwell's."

"Shit." Harlan leaned against the alley wall. "Barnaby is sounding more and more suspicious. Just out of curiosity, who's the other Senior Adept who has the codes, and why aren't I checking him out?"

"It's Henri Durand, and seeing as he's in Devon, I thought it might be tricky. However, I haven't completely ruled him out," Gabe said.

"No, best not to," Harlan mused. "But I can't see Henri being the mole." Another thought struck him. "Are you sure you can trust Aubrey and Caldwell? One of those two could be secretly working for Black Cronos."

"Don't make me even more paranoid," Gabe remonstrated.

"Are you sure they haven't spoken to anyone else in the order?"

"Aubrey swears only Barnaby, and that Barnaby would have told no one. But—"

"Yeah, yeah, he could be lying, too. I must go, Gabe, but I'll pass this on to Jackson."

Ash had situated himself at the wooden table under the vine-covered shelter with a selection of books. He had a view of the vineyards from here, and the small park with the trees to the right. He could see his brothers and Shadow in the distance, and didn't envy them being out in the full sun for so long.

Aubrey and Caldwell were at the other end of the table, looking mutinous after Gabe had thundered through there an hour ago, asking questions about Barnaby. Both of them had fiercely defended him, but now, after hushed conversations, they were looking very worried. Caldwell had raked his hands through his mane of hair and looked like a bewildered puppy that couldn't find his toy. Aubrey, however, seemed to be flushed with both annoyance and the temperature. Unlike Ash, who had spent his entire life in the heat of the Mediterranean and the Middle East, he was sure the two Englishmen weren't so used to it.

Ash sipped his water and decided to keep out of their disagreement. He returned to the text in front of him. This particular book was a couple of hundred years old, written by a member of the order who was piecing their history together. It seemed that every hundred years or so, one of them did. *An effort to reclaim and reinterpret their past glories.* It was written in ink in mostly legible writing, but portions of it were scrawled, suggesting the pressure of time, or maybe the flow of ideas. Also, sections appeared to be copied from more historic texts, and were written in old French. Neither Aubrey nor Caldwell had understood it well, and Ash had offered to try.

The truth was that once he studied it, he translated it easily, but it was less the words than the message within them that was confusing. Ash was pretty sure that the text had been copied from a much older document, written much closer to the time of the order's beginnings, when it had just split from Seekers of the Morning Star.

A name made him pause. *Mithra, the ancient God of Persia, now called Iran.* The document referred to a chamber of worship beneath a hill, sealed to contain the power within. He searched the text again, wondering if he'd got it wrong. *Or had the scribe copied the original text inaccurately? And what had this got to do with the large planetary alignment that was starting tonight, but would be at its most accurate tomorrow when Aubrey and Caldwell were planning to read the astrolabe?*

Mithra was an old and powerful God who had gone through many incarnations. He was powerful in Ash's time; his places of worship spread far and wide, especially in Persia, and he knew from his reading that he had been popular with the Romans, who called him Mithras. He was a Sun God, and was rumoured to be the inspiration for Jesus Christ. His birthday—or day of rebirth—fell on the winter solstice. From what he could remember about Mithras, he was linked with bulls. According to some histories, a bull was sacrificed to him, or Mithras killed the bull himself. But he was sure that was a later addition by the Romans. He'd also been adopted by various groups, particularly soldiers, and because of that association, he was also linked to Mars, the God of War—one of the planets in the planetary alignment.

Ash sat back in his seat, both bewildered and excited. The Romans had marched through many countries, sweeping up religions, adopting them under their fold, and spreading their own. They were generous like that, and it was sensible, because they were accepted more easily. There could be old Mithraic chambers close by, long sealed shut, their secrets shuttered. *Was it one of these that the Seekers of the Morning Star had used? Alchemical experiments that toyed with an ancient Sun God?*

"Focus," Ash muttered to himself, looking again at the French scrawl, and he settled in once more.

Shadow had volunteered to cook once they had completed their inspection of the *château*, and was pleased that Barak had offered to help.

She watched him through the open window as he set up the barbecue at the end of the terrace, not far from the long table where Ash, Aubrey, and Caldwell were still studying. He lit the briquettes with a flourish while she prepared everything in the cavernous kitchen. Ash had brought a mountain of meat from the local supermarket earlier that afternoon, plenty of salad, and fresh, crusty bread. It would have felt like a party if only the threat of attack wasn't hanging over them.

When Barak re-entered the kitchen, he frowned at Shadow. "What's with Gabe? He looks furious!"

"I believe he found out that Aubrey had been speaking to Barnaby, the Secretary. Ash told me when I took them some beers."

"Seriously? Despite our warning?"

She rolled her eyes and started to chop the salad with relish. "Yes. Although, he insists he hasn't given the address."

Barak shook his head as he reached into the fridge and pulled out half a dozen steaks and pieces of chicken. "I know it's nice to have confidence in your friends, but it does seem stupid—all things considered."

Shadow had been considering what they were going to do if—*once*, she corrected herself—they found the chamber, and she voiced her concerns now. "I get the impression that this isn't just about finding the chamber. It's also about enacting the alchemical experiments. Is that something they do when we open it? Or can they just come back and take their time after that?"

"Providing Black Cronos doesn't swoop in and seal it off, you mean?"

"Or JD? Yes, absolutely. Because," she dumped the chopped onions, tomatoes, and cucumber into a bowl, "wouldn't that mean they need their Inner Temple?"

Barak stared at her, perturbed. "That's a good point. But surely the time scale for using the astrolabe is just finding the damn place. Once they find it, they can do what they want with it. And don't forget, our flights are booked to take us back home in a few days."

Shadow nodded and turned back to her preparations. "Good. But maybe we should clarify that, because by that reasoning, they could stay here for ages, and they might want to move to the first place they reserved. They surely can't expect us to guard them for months." As she spoke, Shadow felt a rush of magic sweep up and around her, and saw Estelle walking outside, her hands raised and her lips muttering. "Did you feel that?" she asked Barak.

He nodded as he watched Estelle's progress. "I know you're not a fan, Shadow, but I think she's useful to have around."

She smiled at him, noting his admiring glance. "Sure, Barak. But she probably doesn't glare at you as much as she does me!"

He gave his familiar, booming laugh. "I wouldn't say that! You heard about how she blasted me across the warehouse the other day?"

Shadow watched his big grin, amused. She knew he liked Estelle, for some unfathomable reason. "Is this a type of mating ritual for you? A sort of trial by combat?"

Barak laughed even more and then winked at her. "Maybe, Shadow. I think I'm thawing her frosty exterior."

"Yeah, well, let's hope one of your valuable assets doesn't get frostbite!" She glanced at his groin meaningfully, pleased she could tease him. She liked the fact that he didn't dissemble, and was planning to be open about his pursuit. It would also give her some entertainment over the next few days.

He had a wicked glint in his eye as he stepped closer, lowering his voice. "So, seeing as we're sharing intimacies, I'm going to address the elephant in the room. What's happening with you and Gabe?"

"That is a ridiculous saying. And nothing is happening!"

Barak shook his head. "Don't come that with me. You two have got a thing. He watches you, you watch him. There's this—" he wiggled his hand, "*heat* between you. What happened in Oxford?"

She scowled at him, her fingers itching to fly to her knives. "*Nothing* happened!"

"Really?"

"Has he said something?"

He grinned again. "So, something *did* happen!"

"Nothing happened," she repeated, loftily. "And if you repeat such slander, you'll find my knife somewhere unpleasant."

Barak backed off, arms raised in surrender, but still looking hideously pleased with himself. "Suit yourself. But I know Gabe, and I know what I see. And for the record, I approve."

He turned around and marched to the fridge to get another beer, leaving Shadow seething.

"For the record, I don't need your approval!"

"Good for you. Beer?"

"Yes!" She snatched it from his outstretched hand, wondering how she'd let Barak get the better of her. But she couldn't stay mad at him. He was too funny. "Are we going to get on with the food before we all die of starvation?"

"Yes ma'am!" He scooped up the meat with one arm, his beer in the other hand, and led the way outside, heading to the BBQ to prod the charcoal.

Shadow followed him with a large bowl of salad and the bread, and once she'd placed everything on the table, she surveyed their surroundings. The sun was sinking into the west, but it was still hot outside, the heat lying heavy across the landscape, with no breath of wind. The cicadas were deafening, but the heat was delicious. The other Nephilim were gathering, settling into seats around the table, and Ash, Aubrey, and Caldwell put aside their books.

Gabe emerged from the house, still brooding, and he drew her away to the edge of the terrace. He looked good, his skin already darkening from the sun. His sunglasses were pushed back on his head, and he scanned the grounds before looking at her.

"You've heard about Aubrey talking to Barnaby, their bloody Secretary?"

She nodded. "He's either an idiot, or ridiculously trusting."

"Or he's been working for Black Cronos all along."

Shadow considered his words and then shook her head. "It doesn't make sense. Why would they launch a full-on attack when he already has the astrolabe? No, he's just an idiot." She turned to watch them all chatting easily around the table. "And they looked too terrified the other night."

Gabe nodded, relieved. "Good. One less thing to worry about. Any news from Harlan?"

"No, but I imagine he's following up on a lot right now. What do you think of Jackson's involvement?"

"Unexpected! It seems everyone has secrets."

Shadow's gaze fell on Estelle, who was walking through the park towards them. She must be completing her protection spells, because her arms were still raised. "I wonder if she has any. I just hope she hasn't been working against El and the others."

"Estelle may be headstrong, but I doubt she's that devious. The trouble is," Gabe said, suddenly amused, "that you two are very alike!"

For a second, Shadow couldn't get her words out. "I am *nothing* like her!"

"Occasionally superior, brimming with self-confidence, scathing of lesser mortals, impatient, wilful, and very skilled. Am I wrong?"

"I haven't got a resting bitch face!"

His eyes travelled across her face, heat building in his eyes again, and she swallowed. "True. And generally, you are very positive, unlike the very unhappy Estelle."

Mollified, she changed the subject. "Have you heard from our brothers back home?"

"It's all quiet, fortunately. Neither Zee nor Eli have seen anything unusual in White Haven, and Niel says the farmhouse is quiet." His eyes settled on the horizon. "They're coming here. They'll have their own intel."

"We'll have to keep one step ahead," Shadow reminded him. "Come on. Let's get a beer."

TWENTY

HARLAN HAD SPENT A hot and sweaty afternoon tramping around Soho and had just emerged from the shower after an evening dip in the hotel swimming pool, when his regular phone rang. He wrapped a towel around his waist, quickly drying his hands before picking it up.

He frowned when he saw the overseas number. "Hello? Harlan speaking."

A voice with a French accent but excellent English addressed him. "Harlan, thank the Gods someone has answered. It's Jean, from the Paris branch. We met a couple of years ago."

Harlan had a sudden recollection of a slender man with light brown hair. "I remember. The hexed ring case. How are you?" He tried to sound relaxed, but he was anything but. He put the phone on speaker and continued to dry off.

"I'm good, very good, but look—we've had trouble booking JD the place he wanted in Bordeaux, and we've arranged something else. The only thing is, I can't get hold of him, or Mason. Or even that Smythe man. Can you contact them?"

Shit. JD was going to France. "Maybe they're on the flight and they can't answer?"

"*Non, non.* He should have arrived hours ago. If they are heading to the wrong place, they won't get in. I've left messages, and now I'm starting to get worried."

Several options raced through Harlan's mind, none of them good. "Was Mason traveling with him?"

"I think so. He turned down any offer of help from our agents."

"Mason hasn't been on a job in years!" Harlan said, incredulous. "Are you sure?"

"I am sure of nothing, *mon ami*. But we had a group call, and Mason said he would visit the Paris office, all being well, before he flew home. Of course, his plans may have changed, *oui*?"

Harlan rubbed the towel through his hair, raking it dry. "Did he tell you what his plans were? I mean, I suspect it's some new acquisition." He was intentionally cagey. "He mentioned something to me before he left, but I've been working on another case."

"He said he was researching the origins of an old order. He didn't say what."

Harlan should have known he wouldn't give up, regardless of whether he had the astrolabe. *Had Mouse travelled there, too? And did he know where Gabe was?* "I can try his number, but I have the same one you do."

"Fantastic, thank you. And of course, if I hear from him, I will let you know."

"Do me a favour, Jean. Send me the two addresses—the old one and the new one. I may be able to track him down with the help of some friends."

"*Certainement.* I'll text them." He paused, and then added, "Was this dangerous? He didn't indicate it was."

"Possibly," Harlan said, unwilling to mention Black Cronos by name. "I'll see what I can find out. But in the meantime, don't send anyone after them, okay? Leave both houses well alone."

As soon as he ended the call, he stood motionless, wondering what to do. Perhaps Black Cronos had kidnapped them. Maybe it was some blackmail attempt—a plot to swap JD and Mason for the astrolabe?

His phone beeped with addresses. Time to phone JD. And then, perhaps, Gabe.

Having eaten his fill of barbequed meats and salad, Gabe finally started to relax. He felt more confident now that Estelle had extended a powerful wall of protection around them, and that they had checked the house and grounds thoroughly. Even if that idiot, Aubrey, had revealed the new address to Barnaby, he'd be surprised if Black Cronos could get through. Unless, of course, they had a witch of their own, or other magic in hand.

He leaned back in the comfortable wicker chair, sipping his beer, and studied the collection of individuals around the table. They all seemed relatively relaxed with each other. Although Aubrey and Caldwell were opposite each other, they chatted easily enough to Nahum and Barak who sat next to them. Estelle sat next to Nahum, in easy conversation with him and Caldwell, and Shadow was next to Barak, half-listening to his conversation with Aubrey while twirling her knife. She and Estelle were civil with each other, but neither directly engaged the other in conversation, Gabe noticed. Gabe was at the end of the table, opposite Ash.

"Have you had a productive afternoon?" Gabe asked him.

Ash pushed his plate away, nodding. "I have. I think I have an idea as to the type of chamber we're looking for, but I haven't discussed it with Aubrey or Caldwell yet." His voice was low, but they were chatting so animatedly at the other end of the table, they couldn't hear him anyway. "I think this has to do with Mithras."

Gabe leaned forward, puzzled. "That name sounds familiar."

"He was around in our time. A Persian God whose worship ended up spreading far and wide."

Gabe nodded as his memories flooded back. "I recall he was called a Sun God."

"Amongst others." Ash glanced at Aubrey and Caldwell again. "It may be that they know this. In fact, they must, considering the amount of research they've done on it, but they haven't mentioned it yet. Perhaps they think we don't need to know."

"Is it a problem?"

"Hard to say." Ash pulled a hair tie from around his wrist and bound his hair up on his head. "I have not experienced this heat in a while. It feels good."

Gabe smiled. "It does. It makes me miss home...our old home, that is. But go on. Why haven't you talked to them about it?"

"I wanted to be sure of my facts first, and having done some more reading, I'm fairly convinced this astrolabe will lead us to a Mithraic chamber."

Gabe held his hand up. "Before you go on, should we discuss this with everyone?" He nodded, and Gabe resisted the urge to ask more questions. He tapped his glass, calling everyone's attention. "Ash has some news. Things to confirm with the order, too."

"Is there a problem?" Aubrey asked straight away.

"Perhaps," Ash said cautiously. The low sunlight was slanting in now, casting long golden rays across the terrace, and it seemed to Gabe that a stir of unease rippled around them, disturbing the calm. "I've translated that French passage you were having trouble with, and well, to be honest, it sent me down a rabbit-hole, as you say. This chamber that is at the end of our search—it's Mithraic, isn't it?"

Aubrey and Caldwell exchanged a wary glance, and Aubrey said, "We think so. Nothing that is alluded to directly, except for in the passage you read. The name crops up a couple of times."

"Hold on," Shadow said, confused. "Explain Mithraic."

"Mithra, who was later known as Mithras," Ash began, "was an ancient God of Persia. In fact, he was also called Mehr in the early days. He was a Zoroastrian angelic divinity."

"Angels again," Shadow said, shooting them an uneasy look.

"He wasn't one, though," Ash assured her. "It was because he was associated with light and truth, as many angels were."

"I've heard of Zoroastrianism," Estelle said. "It's one of the world's oldest religions, isn't it?"

Ash nodded. "Based on the teachings of the prophet Zoroaster." Excitement filled his eyes as he warmed to his subject. "The religion is the forerunner of many other religious systems, including Judaism, Christianity, and Islam. It was based on good winning over evil, judgement at death, and a type of heaven and hell. It's very old. That's why some believe that Mithra was the inspiration for Jesus Christ."

Estelle rolled her eyes. "No surprise there. Christianity was cobbled together from all sorts of religions. Most of them pagan."

Nahum smiled. "You could argue that the old Gods have many different names. They reinvent themselves for new generations, for new theories and philosophies."

"But," Ash continued, "Mithraism changed over time. Its history is long and very complex. Eventually, it was adopted by the Romans. He was particularly worshipped by soldiers."

"But, by the sound of it, he was a force for good?" Shadow asked.

"Absolutely," Ash agreed. "Mithraism became a Roman mystery religion, which essentially means their rites were private, belonging only to initiates, much like—" he gestured to the end of the table, "private orders, like The Order of the Midnight Sun."

"But we are not a religious group," Caldwell pointed out testily. "We are an organisation devoted to alchemy, philosophy, astronomy, mathematics, and many other things."

"But you seek knowledge," Barak rumbled out with his deep voice. "The power to unlock the universe and the secrets to life itself. It is a type of religion, as well as science."

Caldwell's lips tightened into a thin line. "Not at all."

"Maybe not for you now," Ash conceded, "but for your predecessors, maybe? Merely small degrees of separation. I am Greek, and our most powerful mystery religions were the Eleusinian Mysteries, veiled in secrecy. And then there was Isis later on, a female deity, and another religion that rivalled Christianity." He shrugged. "There is nothing new in this world, not really."

"What's this leading to?" Shadow asked.

Ash gestured around him. "There are probably several Mithraic chambers hidden in this area. Some may be long destroyed, but others could just be sealed. I think the order's ancestors found one and used it for their experiments. All places of worship carry power to be used —if you know how."

Estelle steepled her fingers, putting them under her chin. "Interesting. You think the alchemists found a source of power to explore. Or exploit."

He nodded, a frown crossing his face. "And it went horribly wrong. Somehow." He looked sharply at Aubrey and Caldwell again. "And of course, symbolically Mithras was linked to a few things, one of them being Mars, the God of War. I thought it an interesting link to the planetary alignment tomorrow. Perhaps it's Mars that the reading is taken from."

"We thought the same thing," Aubrey said, nodding. "But we could take readings off them all, just to be sure."

Ash tapped the old book that was at the end of the table, well away from the food, and drew it closer. "Once you have taken the reading, I presume you wish to go straight there?"

"Of course!"

Gabe grunted, thinking this was bearing a horrible resemblance to the search for The Temple of the Trinity. "You assume it will be so easy! That the directions will lead us straight there. But what if it's still hidden? Or directs us to an inhabited *château*?"

"The astrolabe is the key," Aubrey said confidently. "All will be revealed."

"I was talking to Shadow earlier," Barak said, thoughtfully. "We wondered, if we do find the chamber, what then? Surely you can't be planning to do some kind of experiment straight away?"

Aubrey looked relieved to be asked something else. "No, of course not. This is all about finding the chamber. Once it's found, our Senior Adepts will join us here. We will explore it fully. We hope to find more details on the experiments performed in there. As I told you," he looked at Gabe and Shadow, "those will be the building blocks on which to base our own research."

Shadow sipped her beer and gave Gabe an amused, sidelong glance before turning back to him. "And the Dark Star? The monster within? What if he's still there? And if he's not, how do you keep it safe from Black Cronos?"

Caldwell cleared his throat. "We wish to keep it hidden. Only we will have the coordinates."

"And you'll be on the run forever from your enemies? Of course. Sounds so logical." Her voice dripped with sarcasm.

Gabe sighed. *Shadow was right. This problem would not be resolved easily.* His phone rang then and he left the table, taking his beer with him and glad to be stretching his legs. He walked over to the end of the terrace and watched the countryside disappear into a hazy purple twilight.

"Hey Harlan, how it's going?"

"Very badly. JD is in France, and he's disappeared."

Gabe listened to Harlan with increasing worry. He felt like a noose was tightening around them, and when he headed back to the table, his expression must have said volumes, because Nahum asked, "What now?"

"I have two addresses that we need to explore. JD and Mason are here in France, somewhere, but neither of them is answering their phones. And we know The Silencer of Souls is here, with some bloody professor. It doesn't sound good," he said, relating what Harlan had shared.

"JD from The Orphic Guild?" Caldwell said, shocked. "Is he here for the astrolabe, too?"

Gabe felt sorry for him. "It seems so."

"But, does that mean that Harlan..." he stuttered, his eyes wide.

"This has nothing to do with Harlan. This is all JD," Gabe assured him quickly. "Harlan is a man of his word. JD, however, wants *that*!" He nodded to the astrolabe that sat at the head of the table, its jewels winking in the candlelight that someone had recently lit.

"What professor?" Aubrey asked, seemingly unconcerned about JD.

Gabe mentally fumbled for the name. "Stefan Hope-something, from Oxford."

Aubrey jerked so violently that he knocked his wine glass over. It shattered, wine pouring over the edge and onto the ground. Everyone jumped in shock as Barak grabbed a napkin and mopped it up. Gabe however didn't budge, staring intensely at Aubrey who had gone horribly pale.

"Do you know him?" Gabe asked, fearing he already knew the answer.

"Stefan Hope-Robbins. He was a member of our order many years ago, but it ended badly. He sought...*darker* things. Was willing to risk more than we were happy to do. It brought a darkness over us. Things became ugly when we asked him to leave."

Caldwell's hand rested on the astrolabe protectively. "Please tell me he doesn't want this."

"It seems he does. He travels with The Silencer of Souls. He's with Black Cronos."

Caldwell's voice was barely audible as he addressed Aubrey. "His experiments, do you think..."

Aubrey looked horrified. "He found a way!"

The table had fallen silent, watching them both with rapt fascination.

Gabe could feel his anger building again. "Found a way to do what?"

"Harness the power of the universe to change humans into..." He stuttered over his words again. "Well, super-beings."

"*What*?" Gabe said, now furious. He glowered at Aubrey from the opposite end of the table. "And you didn't think to mention this when we were attacked by those enhanced humans the other night? *Twice*!"

"I honestly didn't put them together. I thought Stefan was a madman, and that it was a dangerous obsession that would never work. And it was years ago!"

Gabe realised he was clenching his hands and he took a deep breath. "Well, it clearly bloody has!"

Ash spoke calmly, gesturing for Gabe to sit. "This is not the time for a deep, involved discussion on how he may have achieved this, but give us the basics."

Aubrey pulled himself together. "Alchemy is about distilling the essence of things, harnessing the power of the planets and stars, and using their correspondence at the proper times. Using celestial beings to guide us, with transformation and transmutation. Stefan was particularly interested in how they could transform the soul. Make it different. He looked at all the planets and thought their power could be harnessed, particularly Mars and Mercury—the warlike and the mercurial."

Gabe heard someone utter a dry laugh, and with a shock, realised it was him. "Can you hear yourself? Mars? *Mithras*?" He stood abruptly again. "I haven't got time for this. We need to search for JD. Barak, Nahum—you're with me. Ash," he looked at him, appealing. "Try and understand this for me, please. Shadow and Estelle, you two need to stay here, make sure this place remains protected."

"*Me*?" Shadow protested. "I want to come with you!"

"I need you here, while Ash works with Aubrey and Caldwell." His face softened, knowing part of her really didn't want to be with Estelle. "And I need to know this place will be secure upon our return.

I trust you to do this. Both of you." He encompassed Estelle with that statement.

Shadow and Estelle exchanged wary glances, but nodded anyway, murmuring their assent.

Barak and Nahum were already standing, striding to the corner of the terrace. "You realise we have no weapons, yet," Barak pointed out.

Gabe stood next to him, gazing out across the now dark sky. "We'll just have to manage."

Twenty-One

HARLAN KNOCKED ON THE door to Smythe's flat for the third time and glanced uneasily at Jackson.

"He could be out. It is only nine o'clock, after all."

"But why hasn't he answered his phone all evening?"

"Maybe he's in a busy pub, or out on a date," Harlan reasoned, trying to recall what he knew about Smythe's private life. "Although, he never seemed the social kind, if I'm honest. Or maybe that was just with me." Harlan pressed his ear to the door. "I can't hear anything."

Robert Smythe lived on the third floor of an elegant Art Deco apartment building, which suited Smythe perfectly. It was in a quiet residential area, and the whole place seemed hushed. Harlan had returned to the guild to raid the office personnel files to get his address.

Jackson was already preparing his lock picks. "Come on, let's get in there before we're spotted loitering."

Harlan hoped his ominous feelings wouldn't be proven correct. If JD and Mason had been kidnapped or even killed, there was only one person who would have known all of their movements, and that was Smythe. The lock clicked, and Jackson cautiously opened the door. They slipped inside, pausing in the small, square hall. The living room was on their right, illuminated by the streetlights from the uncovered windows.

Harlan called, "Robert, it's me, Harlan."

He pushed the lounge door open wider and stepped inside, scanning the room, and with horror saw a figure lying in the centre. As his eyes adjusted to the light, Harlan hurried to his side, confirming the body was Robert Smythe.

"I'll look into the other rooms," Jackson said, "while you check him."

Harlan didn't need to examine him to see he was dead. His sightless eyes stared at the ceiling, a horrible blue-grey tinge to his skin. But what was worse were the spidery black lines that had spread across his face and down his neck. He was still wearing his suit, and Harlan could even see the lines appearing on his hands below the cuffs.

Harlan stepped back, his mouth suddenly dry. *Robert was dead. Snooty, precious Robert.* Harlan hadn't liked his snide ways, but now he felt guilty for every horrible thought he'd had about him. *And what the hell had killed him?* It had to be someone from Black Cronos. But there had been no struggle. The flat, or in here at least, looked immaculate and undisturbed.

Jackson re-entered the room, swiftly crossing to Harlan's side. "It's clear. We're alone."

"Smythe is dead. He's covered in these tiny black lines I've never seen before."

Jackson crouched and flashed his torch across his features. "Perhaps it's poison. Or something sucked the life out of him."

"Have you ever seen this before?"

Jackson stood again, his expression bleak as his eyes swept the room. "No. There's no sign of a fight, nothing untoward at all. The other rooms are the same."

"Perhaps he knew his attacker?"

"They could have overpowered him too quickly."

Harlan stepped well away from Robert's body, pulling his phone from his pocket. "I'll call Maggie...again."

Jackson shook his head. "No. Leave it to me. I'll call my contacts first."

"Why? What will they do? I do not want trouble with Maggie!"

"You won't have any, trust me."

Jackson's voice was low as he made the call, and Harlan wondered what they should do now. He needed to update Shadow, again. And he needed to break the news to the guild staff. They would be devastated, and scared. Harlan closed his eyes for a moment, wondering if Black Cronos had caught up to him, could he have died by similar means?

As Jackson ended his call, Harlan's eyes flew open. "Did you say The Silencer of Souls was with the professor earlier today?"

Jackson nodded. "Yes, why?"

"I guess I thought she might have done this, with her weird kiss. But if Smythe was at work all day, it couldn't have been her. They must have attacked as soon as he arrived home." Harlan frowned as he considered the timeline. "Jean said they had been calling all of them all afternoon."

"Perhaps he finished work early," Jackson suggested. "He might have taken leave, seeing as Mason had left."

"This is my fault."

"Of course it's not!"

"It is. They must have known who I was from Sunday's attack."

"Not necessarily. JD has clearly been making his own enquiries. And Black Cronos has threatened your organisation before. For all you know, JD has knocked heads with them in the past for this very thing."

"I guess so," Harlan said reluctantly, still unable to shed his guilt.

Jackson started to pace again, checking his watch. "My contact will be here within the hour. Until then, we wait."

"I get to meet him? Or her?"

"Her. As far as Robert's killer goes, I'm sure they have other assassins with other interesting means of killing. In fact, I know they do."

"How?"

"As I said before, Black Cronos has been around for years. All manner of curious deaths have been left in their wake. Some like this, strange black spider webs on their body. Others are just left dead through no obvious means. Some were killed violently, but we couldn't identify any obvious weapon that was used. It's like they have manufactured weapons we haven't seen yet. No knife edges or shapes to understand."

Harlan flashed back to the fight at The Midnight Sun's headquarters in Marylebone. "When I saw them fighting the Nephilim and Shadow, they had unusual silver blades, and one seemed to pull it out of thin air. I thought at first that my eyes were deceiving me—they moved so fast! But maybe you're right. They are new, unknown weapons."

Jackson looked as if he were going to respond, but instead simply said, "Let's wait for Layla."

Nahum circled next to Barak and Gabe, basking in the warm currents of air. If it wasn't for the current task, Nahum felt he could do this for hours, the pleasure of spreading his wings was so great.

But soon they would land. Below them was the country house that JD should have been heading to, but that Jean, the guild member from the Paris branch, couldn't book. It was situated at the edge of a French village, lights on in many of the houses and their gardens, their residents enjoying the balmy evening air. There were lights in the house below too, and a couple of cars on the drive.

He flew close to Gabe. "It must be a holiday rental. They might have nothing to do with JD's disappearance. And he's hardly likely to have kicked them out, no matter how odd he can be."

"Probably not, but we have to be sure."

"Let me land. You watch with Barak."

Nahum dropped to the ground, landing in a dark corner of the garden, and folded his wings away. Blade in hand, he edged across the grass to the side of the house, feeling guilty as he peeked through the windows, uncovered by blinds or curtains. Most of the rooms were lit. In the kitchen he spied an older couple clearing plates and stacking dishes, and when he edged to the side of the patio, he heard voices from a younger couple, with two children close by. He circled all the way around the house, as much as he was able, peering into bedrooms and other areas, but saw only the belongings of a family with kids.

Sighing, he took to the air again, quickly reaching his brothers. "No JD or Mason. Just a family."

Without speaking, Gabe turned and rose higher, leading them to the place JD was expected. They hovered above another big, stone-built house, but this one stood on extensive grounds, a little to the east of where the Nephilim were staying.

"It's in complete darkness," Gabe observed. "No lights, no cars."

"He's not here," Barak said. "And I checked the roads around the last place. There's no evidence of an accident. Black Cronos must have intercepted them."

"But how?" Nahum asked. "It's not like he advertised their whereabouts."

"Smythe hasn't answered his phone," Gabe reminded them. As he spoke, his phone rang, and he answered quickly. "Harlan. We've had no luck so far. I'm above the new place right now."

He fell silent, his lips tightening as he listened, and within moments had rung off. "Smythe is dead. Which means JD and Mason were picked up somewhere between the airport and here. Let's sweep the area and then head home. I have a feeling we won't find them tonight." He nodded to the landscape below them. "Black Cronos is already here, holed up somewhere. My guess is, we won't hear from them until we've used the astrolabe tomorrow night."

While they talked, hovering high above the building, Nahum had been idly surveying the grounds, and now he saw a figure close to the walls of the house. "Wait. I think there's someone down there. The east side, by the terrace."

As he pointed, another figure strolled to join the other. They flew lower to get a better look, and saw the familiar black clothing and protective vests of Black Cronos.

"Lookouts," Barak said. He looked eagerly at the others. "They suspected that someone would come looking for JD and Mason. We shouldn't disappoint them."

A spark of interest flared in Gabe's eyes. "It could be a trap. More may be waiting under the trees. And they had a bow and arrow last time."

"But if we can pick a few off, there will be less to worry about," Nahum pointed out, his blood stirring at the prospect of battle.

"All right," Gabe said reluctantly. "We go down quickly, swoop in and out, and if they are too many, we retreat. There's no point risking our lives on this. They won't underestimate us again, so this could be tricky."

Barak grinned. "But we're better than them."

"I see more now." Nahum pointed to the driveway, where his sharp eyes could see three figures clustered together. "I'll take them."

"I'll take the others," Gabe said. "Barak, hold back, and attack whoever comes running."

He nodded his agreement, and in seconds Nahum was plummeting to the ground, his wings arrowed behind him. He was on the group in seconds, and he lifted one, throwing him into a tree, used his wings to sweep another against a high stone wall, and ran at the third, tackling him to the ground in one swift movement. None of them seemed to be expecting an attack, and they were certainly not looking above them.

Nahum pressed his arm against the man's throat, pinning him to the ground, while keeping a wary eye on the other two, but both had fallen, insensible, to the ground. "Where have you taken JD?" he hissed.

The man wasn't tall, but he was lithe and strong, the corded muscles of his neck apparent as he strained under Nahum's grip. A strange, silvery light appeared in his eyes as he unexpectedly grinned. The light grew and Nahum blinked, dazzled, and then the man reared up, throwing Nahum off as if he weighed nothing. Nahum rolled, quickly regaining his feet, and cursing himself for loosening his grip. *But his eyes...*

His opponent had his fists together, and as he swept them apart, a long silver staff appeared in them. With devastating speed, he whipped across the space between them, sweeping it under Nahum's legs, and he jumped to avoid it. This man was not like the others they had met, and Nahum realised this would be a test for him. *A test he had to win.*

Barak had circled above for mere seconds when he saw half a dozen men run to help their colleagues from the edge of the grounds. Gabe was engaged in hand-to-hand combat with the men he'd swooped on, but he could not cope with more.

Angling himself low over the ground, Barak soared over their heads, picking up a man in each hand and lifting them high. They twisted furiously, one of them slashing a blade, but Barak dropped them into the trees, satisfied as they crashed through branches to the ground. He swooped in again, but this time arrows were flying around him. He turned and spun mid-air, as graceful as a bird of prey, and continued to pick the men off, the occasional arrow glancing off his wings. He felt one penetrate his shoulder, but ignored it as he flashed towards the area where the shooter was. It was a woman, and her aim was good. She followed his movements despite his speed, one arrow catching his rib cage, another embedding in his thigh before he was finally on her, and with one swift movement, he pulled the arrow from his thigh and stabbed her in the neck. The blood bubbled out as she choked and fell to the ground. He picked up the bow and quiver, aware that his thigh and shoulder were aching with a toxic heaviness.

He flew high again, scanning the area, but it was a struggle. He looked at the arrows' tips, wondering if they were poisoned, but saw nothing obvious. Below him, there was no other movement. Gabe was standing over two dead bodies, and Nahum was limping to his side. Satisfied there were no other attackers, Barak landed next to them, noting that they looked bruised and weary from their exertions.

"We need to go," Barak said abruptly. He was feeling odd. "I think I've been poisoned." Blood was pouring from his thigh wound, and his ribs burned where the arrow had grazed him. "Have I still got an arrow in my shoulder?"

Nahum searched behind his wings. "Yes. Brace yourself." With a wrenching sensation, the arrow was finally out, and Barak felt a flush of sweat race across his skin.

Gabe's hand flew out to steady him, his dark eyes serious. "We need to get you home. Can you still fly?"

He nodded. "It's not far, but perhaps you should stick close. And we should take these." Barak held out the bow and remaining arrows. "Don't touch the tips."

Gabe nodded, taking them from his hands. "Let's go."

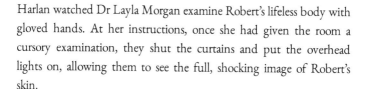

Harlan watched Dr Layla Morgan examine Robert's lifeless body with gloved hands. At her instructions, once she had given the room a cursory examination, they shut the curtains and put the overhead lights on, allowing them to see the full, shocking image of Robert's skin.

It was like something from a horror film. Robert's eyes were already covered in a filmy grey, and Layla had closed them before proceeding to examine his body. The black, spidery tracks fragmented his skin like broken pottery, and Harlan still wasn't sure whether he'd been poisoned, or if something odder had occurred.

The light also allowed him to watch Layla. Jackson had introduced them, and she had shaken his hand with a surprisingly strong grip. She was closing on sixty, Harlan estimated, a tiny birdlike woman with sharp pale blue eyes, and greying hair that still held traces of rich chestnut. She was dressed expensively, and looked as if she'd been interrupted at an evening event.

"Well," Jackson prompted her. "What's the verdict?"

"Bag." She stood and peeled her gloves off in one swift motion before dropping them into the plastic bag Jackson held out for her. It was practised, smooth, and Harlan wondered how often they had both done this. "Iron, Mars's metal of choice. I spy a pin-prick on his neck."

Harlan thought he was hearing things. "What do you mean, Mars? The God? Or the planet?"

"I have been studying Black Cronos and their death-dealing for years," she said, fixing Harlan with her piercing gaze. "They use their alchemy differently to many others. They utilise the planets and their corresponding metals as weapons. Over the years they have become more sophisticated. More deadly."

Harlan must still have looked baffled—he knew he felt it—because Jackson explained, "Alchemical correspondences. Planets, metals, astronomical timing, plants, grids, experiments...all of that." He shrugged. "Sorry. I'm no alchemist, so I can't give you details."

"I wouldn't understand this even if you did!" Harlan confessed. "How do you know about that, though?" He gestured to Robert.

Layla's lips tightened. "I know Jackson has explained our role, especially our fascination with Black Cronos. Their wartime exploits— Second World War, you understand—were horrendous, almost as bad as the Nazis. We suspect, however, it has been going on much longer. I'm referring to human experimentation, of course."

"Of course," Harlan said, nodding weakly. *What the hell had he gotten himself into?* "And now?"

"Still happening. We suspect that they recruit some voluntarily, and others...well, the vulnerable go missing every day, don't they?"

Layla was so matter of fact about it all. It was chilling. But then again, she dealt with it far more often than he did, and would have needed to find a way to deal with it.

Harlan tried to joke. "It sounds like something from a horror film. Are they making some sort of super-army?"

Layla gave him a thin smile. "Not quite. I don't think they have such lofty ambitions as to take over the world, but they are subverting and manipulating matter for their own ends."

"And you honestly have no idea where they're based?" Harlan asked, incredulous.

"No. For all the men and women that you saw at the order's headquarters and that were at your friend's farmhouse, they are actually not a big organisation. We're pretty certain of that. The man that we think is at the heart of it all moves regularly. The rest are scattered to the winds, converging when they need to. Like now."

"And the way they're converging in France," Jackson echoed.

Layla walked over to her leather bag that she'd left on a chair and pulled her phone out. "I need to call the team in."

"What about JD and Mason?" Harlan asked, hoping they hadn't already met the same fate as Robert.

"Ah, yes." Layla stared at him again. "JD. He's been interested in this for a *long* time." Her words were weighted, her gaze speculative.

Herne's horns. She knew all about him. Harlan glanced at Jackson, and saw an awareness behind his eyes too, as he added, "A *very* long time."

They were wondering if he knew. He laughed, almost maniacally. "Holy shit. You know who he really is. How long have you known?"

A broad smile spread across Layla's face, making her look suddenly younger. "A few decades."

"And you?" he asked, turning to Jackson.

"Two or three years. You?"

"A few months only. He told me himself."

Layla sat elegantly in the chair, still watching him. "Well, this makes life easier. Do you know how the secret service came to be?"

Harlan frowned. "No, why?"

"It was invented by John Dee for Queen Elizabeth I in order to help her build her empire—which, by the way, was his idea, too. He's always been bold in his thinking. He has an inquisitive, questing mind. Avaricious, almost."

"Holy shit!" Harlan repeated. "Are you telling me that he's one of you?"

Layla laughed. "No. Absolutely not. JD does not work well with others. I suppose you've noticed that?"

"Of course I have. He's infuriating!"

"But," she added, "he steps up, occasionally. Unexpectedly, too. Like now."

Harlan felt his mouth drop open. "Are you telling me that him wanting the astrolabe was for *you*?"

"Not for us. But it was to stop Black Cronos."

Harlan felt dizzy. And an idiot. "He's been liaising with you?"

"Ha! Nothing so useful. He's working on his own, but did think to inform us—ever so briefly." She rolled her eyes. "But he knows where the astrolabe could lead to. How the rumoured early experiments could enhance Black Cronos's current ones." Layla shook her head, sighing deeply. "They might even release an old monster, if the fragments of stories are true."

Harlan sat in the nearest chair, his legs growing weak. "I guess JD knows all this because of his age, right? His immersion in the occult world?"

"That and the fact he saw the results of their experiments first-hand during the Second World War. He was an ally then, for a while."

"Why the hell didn't he explain this to me?" Harlan appealed to both of them, knowing they couldn't really answer him. "I've suspected him of being a nut-job, and now it seems he's acting out of some kind of hero complex!"

Jackson shrugged. "You said it yourself. He's odd. Maybe he was trying to protect you?"

Harlan somehow doubted that, but didn't voice it. "But he's gone with Mason, of all people. He hasn't been in the field for years! He was terrible at it!" Harlan leapt to his feet, his path clear. "I have to get out there. Where the fuck are they?"

"Glad you said that," Jackson said, smiling. "I'm booked on an early flight. Want to come?"

"Yes, of course! But—" Harlan's gaze flew to Smythe. He felt responsible. "Who will deal with this, and tell the guild?"

"Leave that to me," Layla said softly as she picked up her phone.

Twenty-Two

SHADOW HAD NEVER SEEN Barak look so ill. His burnished black skin was grey, and a film of sweat covered his entire body.

Gabe had landed with him cradled in his arms after Barak had become so weak that he almost fell from the sky. He now lay unconscious on the big dining room table inside the house, his wings still folded beneath him, acting as a giant bed of feathers. The glossy, jet-black plumage shot through with blue had lost its shine, too. Shadow felt sick with worry; in fact, she was terrified they would lose him.

Gabe, Nahum, and Caldwell stood close to her, as serious as she had ever seen them, and her heart went out to his brothers. They watched Estelle and Aubrey as they tended to Barak's injuries, Ash helping them in his calm, collected way. They had already dressed his shoulder wound, cleaning out a sticky yellow substance that smelled foul. Now Estelle cleaned the graze along his ribs, while Aubrey tended the deep thigh wound. Estelle's lips moved rapidly as she worked, much as Briar's did when she used healing magic, although she had confessed it was not her best skill. Fortunately, they had travelled with a first aid kit filled with Briar's medicinal balms, as well as the herbal provisions that Eli had packed.

"This is my fault," Gabe muttered, eyes fixed on Barak.

"No, it's not. It was Barak who suggested this," Nahum said immediately, "and I backed him up."

"I sanctioned it!" Gabe rounded on Nahum. "And I asked Barak to mop up the extras."

"And he did it willingly!" Nahum shot back. "As any of us would."

Ash raised his voice, glaring at them. "Not now, and not here!"

Shadow took Gabe's arm, needing fresh air, and knowing he did, too. Besides, she should be on watch. "Come with me."

"But—"

"But nothing," she said, giving him no room to argue and propelling him out the door.

She led him to the terrace, and they leaned on the railing, looking out over the vineyards and the land around them. The cicadas had quieted, finally, and an almost full moon bathed the landscape with its silver light. But she knew Gabe wasn't really seeing it. He looked to the far horizon, but his gaze was inward.

"He's strong," she told him, more to reassure herself than him. "He'll pull through. Especially with Estelle's magic and Briar and Eli's balms."

Shadow had spent an uneasy few hours with Estelle while the three Nephilim were out. Ash had been deep in conversation with Aubrey and Caldwell, leaving her and Estelle alone. They had cleared the remnants of dinner together, awkwardly polite, before Shadow had patrolled the grounds, confident they were secure because she could feel Estelle's powerful protection spell. To Estelle's credit, she had looked as distressed as the rest of them at Barak's condition, pushing the others out of the way to help him.

"You were right," Shadow conceded. "It was worth bringing Estelle."

Gabe nodded but didn't look around. "If he dies, I will never forgive myself."

"His enhanced healing will flush the toxins out...or whatever they were."

"We're fighting something we don't even understand." He finally looked at her, his dark eyes questioning. "It's like some battle that's been raging for centuries, under the cover of darkness. Or maybe *battle* isn't the right word."

"It is, of a sort. A battle for knowledge. Advancement."

He tried to laugh. "Enhancing humans with alchemy? It sounds insane!"

"Alchemy is science, that's what I understand. And science enhances everything. They're just approaching it a different way." Shadow glanced away, the weight of his gaze feeling suddenly intimate.

Gabe gripped the railing, his arms tense as he stared over the fields again. "They pulled strange weapons on us, again. I'm trying to imagine how this will play out tomorrow, and I can't see what we should do."

"I'm sure it will become apparent once we're there."

She studied his broad shoulders and powerful arms, his sculpted chest that was visible beneath his t-shirt, and was once again aware of his heat. His thick, dark hair was swept off his face, revealing his square chin covered in dark stubble, and she wanted to comfort him, caress him, hold him. *What if she were to die tomorrow? Or Gabe?* Her heart faltered at the thought. To remain here without him was unthinkable. And they were out here, alone, serenaded with soft moonlight on a balmy night.

Without thinking it through, she slipped under his arms that gripped the rail and faced him. He looked down at her, startled, and she lifted her hands to his cheeks, pulling him to her lips with a sudden hunger. Desire raced through her, and it felt as if every nerve ending was on fire. His lips were soft but firm, exploring her mouth with deepening passion. His arms were suddenly around her, one hand in her hair, the other pulling her close, and she mirrored his actions, revelling in his heat that threatened to consume them both. He lifted her up, seating her on the wooden rail, and she wrapped her legs around his waist, pulling him closer. Time seemed suspended, everything else disappearing as Shadow realised everything felt right. When they finally eased apart, she was shocked by the longing in his eyes.

His voice was husky. "Come to my bed, now."

"But, Gabe..." Why was she hesitating? Was it because Barak was clinging to life? Or was it because their relationship would be changed forever?

"What?" he murmured, burying his face in her neck, and covering it with kisses as his hands slid down her back. She felt breathless, giddy with desire. "I know you want this as much as I do."

She tried to be rational, but Herne's horns, it was hard. "But what if it all goes wrong?"

He lifted his head to stare at her again, his face inches from her own, his passion encompassing her so completely she couldn't think straight. His voice was almost a growl. "It won't go wrong, because it's us."

And with that, she was lost. He grabbed her hand, pulling her to the stairs and up to his room.

<hr />

Ash watched Barak's motionless body, and squeezed his eyes shut. For now, they had done as much as they could do. He debated appealing to their fathers for help, and then swiftly rejected it.

"I'll watch him," Estelle said, her clipped voice firm and decisive.

Ash's eyes flew open. "You've done enough. You used a lot of magic. You probably need to sleep."

She regarded him coolly, arrogantly even. "I'm strong enough to sustain my magic."

"It wasn't an insult, Estelle. I'm trying to be considerate." He wanted to throw something at her, but instead clenched his fists. "And he's my brother."

"And he's my friend!" Her eyes were burning now, fierce with intent.

Ash noticed she wasn't touching Barak at all, but she was sitting close, her hand resting on the blanket they had thrown over him to keep him warm. They were still in the dining room, but Barak was now on a bed they had made on the floor, his head resting on a pillow, his wings still beneath him. Despite the summer night, they had the fire burning low, too. Estelle had thrown on a bundle of herbs, and their fresh healing smells alleviated the heavy atmosphere in the room.

They were also alone. Nahum and the others had headed to bed, or to the shower, in Nahum's case—he was covered in blood—and Ash had no idea where Shadow or Gabe were.

Estelle was still glaring at him, and he needed to back off. Something was going on with these two, more than he realised. "Okay. As long as you're sure."

Her shoulders dropped as she took a deep breath, releasing it slowly. "I'm sure. You should sleep, too. You've been busy all day."

Ash's mind was whirling with his earlier discussions, and now the worry about Barak. He wasn't sure he could sleep. Or if he even wanted to. "Why don't I make us some tea? Or something stronger?"

"Tea would be good, thank you."

He nodded and walked to the kitchen, the silence of the house falling around him. With only a low light on, he boiled the kettle and made a pot of tea, placing a mug, milk, and sugar on a tray. But he did not want tea. He needed something stronger. Something to take the edge off the evening. He took the tray to Estelle, saying, "I'm on the terrace if you need me."

He retraced his steps, picked up a bottle of local red wine and a couple of glasses, and took them out to the terrace where he sat at the long table looking out into the night.

It wasn't long before Nahum joined him, dressed in more casual clothes. "Good thinking," he said, helping himself to a glass. "Estelle told me you were here."

"I'm too wound up to sleep."

"Me too, but Aubrey and Caldwell have gone to bed. And," Nahum gave him a wry smile, "so have Gabe and Shadow."

Ash nodded, absently. "Good." And then he realised what Nahum meant and his eyes widened. "Hold on! Do you mean *together*?"

Nahum laughed. "Yep. That's the only thing that's made me smile all night. They don't know I saw them, though. I happened to follow them up the stairs, but frankly, they were oblivious." He took a sip of wine. "About time, too."

"The risk of imminent death always heightens one's emotions." Ash sipped too, appreciating the rich, full flavours. "Who won the bet?"

Nahum grinned. "Niel keeps tally. We'll ask him when he gets here. He should be on his way. Let's hope nothing happens to him," he added.

"He'll be fine. And so will Barak."

"Is that just wishful thinking?" All humour had left Nahum's face.

"Partly. But Barak is strong—and stubborn, just like his fallen father." Barak's father had been one of the strongest of the fallen angels, and fiercely loyal to Lucifer Morningstar who had triggered the fall. Conviction had burned in his eyes, along with a fervent loathing of the old God.

"Stubbornness is nothing though if the poison is too strong." Nahum shifted in his seat, alert with curiosity. "What did you find out from Aubrey and Caldwell?"

Ash grunted with frustration. "Alchemy has to be one of the weirdest, most complicated esoteric fields of study I've ever come across. They speak in our language, but it is almost incomprehensible!" He was frustrated just thinking about his discussion. "I've read books on it and had long conversation with two experts—two *Adepts*—but I am baffled. No wonder it takes years to be conversant with its laws and correspondences."

Nahum looked puzzled. "But I thought you were familiar with it from our old days, before the flood."

"The Emerald Tablet of Hermes Trismegistus triggered all of it, but I took little notice then. We had other things to occupy us."

"But the super-humans, what's with that?"

"Essentially, it's as Aubrey said earlier. Harnessing the power of planets, using their alignment in the sky and other astronomical correspondences and their associations with metals. Long experiments, with essences and applications."

"And they must have utilised those things to make weapons, too," Nahum said. He shook his head. "These people and their weapons make me feel old-fashioned."

Ash smiled. "There's something to be said for age and experience, though, brother."

"JD would understand it, surely," Nahum said, topping up his drink. "He's an expert."

"Perhaps that's why he wants the astrolabe. After all, he cracked immortality." Tiredness started to creep up on Ash, the quiet conversation and fine wine working its magic, but he filled up his glass again, enjoying talking to Nahum without anyone to disturb them. "Do you think we should leave a watch?"

"I'll ask Estelle," Nahum said. "But if she's still confident in her magic, perhaps we should all sleep tonight. I doubt we will get much rest tomorrow. But in the meantime," he said, smiling mischievously, "tell me what you think of Barak and Estelle."

Gabe woke up feeling the kind of languorous pleasure he hadn't experienced in years. Pale dawn light was filtering in through the partly open curtains, illuminating Shadow's alabaster skin, and Gabe couldn't stop looking at her. She was covered in nothing but a sheet, and it folded around her curves like a glove. Her right leg and arm were uncovered as she sprawled on her side, and her hair tumbled across her face. He reached for her, and then paused.

Barak.

He must have survived the night, or they would have been woken. The house was quiet, at peace. A good sign. And Barak was strong. Soon Gabe would have to get up and face the day, make decisions, but now was for pleasure. He rolled over, snaking his arm around Shadow's waist, and pulled her into him, curling around her protectively.

Last night had been more than he could have dreamed—and he'd dreamed of it plenty. Shadow complimented him in every way, and she was as fiery as he had expected. They ignited passion in each other. She stirred, and he pulled her closer, his cheek resting against her hair and then his lips nuzzled her neck. His desire was already stirring.

She wriggled in his arms, and turned to face him, her violet eyes luminous in this light, her fey otherness breathtaking. She blinked and her eyes widened, and Gabe knew she was flooded with memories of their night. For a horrible moment he thought she would pull away, her defences up, but then she smiled, pulling him closer, and her eyes said everything. She threaded her hands through his hair, lifted her leg over his hip, and kissed him, and he could think of nothing but her.

Nahum eased the door of the dining room open with his elbow, juggling two coffees, and saw Estelle stir in the half-light, her long dark hair loose as she sat upright. She had lain next to Barak all night.

"How is he?" Nahum asked softly, handing her a drink.

"Better. His breathing is easier, and his colour is good."

"Good." Nahum sat on a chair, sipping his drink and enjoying the rush of caffeine. "Did you sleep?"

"A little. I kept the fire going and repeated a few spells, and I dozed in between." She paused to sip her coffee, and stared at Nahum with a puzzled expression on her face. "Something odd happened in the night."

Nahum's thoughts immediately flew to an intruder. "Did you hear something?"

"No. With Barak. I felt him getting hot, and thought at first we were too close to the fire, but something seemed to ignite beneath his skin—like flames! He glowed. It started in his chest and then radiated out to his limbs, even through his feathers."

She pushed back her hair, and Nahum thought how much better she looked without that permanent tight-lipped frown of disapproval she always wore—her resting bitch face. He subdued a smirk, focussing instead on what she'd seen.

"It wasn't something you'd done?"

"No! I'll admit I was terrified. I thought it was a new level of the poison working. I nearly raised the whole house! But then," she looked at Barak again, confused, "I felt this ease come over him. It was like he'd burned away the poison somehow."

A sudden memory returned to Nahum, and he slumped back in his chair with surprise. "Ah. His father did that. I saw him do it once to a man injured in battle. I remember it because it was such a generous, unexpected gesture from one of the fallen. He laid his hands on him, and it was like a fire raged beneath his skin, healing every single cut." Nahum laughed with delight. "It must be inherited. He healed himself!"

"It certainly took him a while!" Estelle protested. "The poison must have overwhelmed his system really quickly." She smiled. "Our actions bought him time."

Nahum looked at his brother with new appreciation. "Maybe this event has unlocked a healing skill. These correspondences apparently link with angels. I remember JD saying so. I wonder if the poison responded to something that has to do with his angel father?"

"That's a very interesting idea, Nahum."

They were silent for a moment, considering what that meant, when Barak stirred and groaned, his eyes fluttering open. He lifted his head, trying to focus. "Where the hell am I?"

"Welcome back, brother. You certainly know how to give us all a fright."

He sat up, dwarfing Estelle next to him. "Welcome back from what?"

"Poison," Estelle explained. "Courtesy of Black Cronos, remember?"

Barak looked at her, his bed, the fire, and finally, his wings. "What in Herne's horns happened last night?"

Nahum smiled and rose to his feet, his heart light. "I'll let Estelle explain, and get started on breakfast. I'm hoping Niel is here somewhere, asleep."

"Oh, yes he is!" Estelle announced, looking apologetic. "He arrived just before dawn and found himself a room."

"Good," Nahum said, sighing with relief. He was glad to know Niel was safe, and that they now had weapons. "I was a bit worried, if I'm honest."

"He made good time—said the weather was calm and clear."

"Good, I'll leave him to sleep."

Barak had been listening, and he still looked confused. "Is Gabe okay? My memories aren't all there yet."

"Don't you worry about Gabe. He's *just fine*!" Nahum said enigmatically, and left them to catch up.

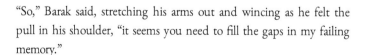

"So," Barak said, stretching his arms out and wincing as he felt the pull in his shoulder, "it seems you need to fill the gaps in my failing memory."

Estelle had edged away from him to give him room, but not too far, and she sipped her coffee, watching him over the rim. "You really can't remember?"

"No. I mean, I remember we went to look for JD's place, but after that…"

"You had a fight with some Black Cronos members and got shot with poisoned arrows. Does that jog your memory?"

His head felt woolly and confused as he struggled to remember the events, and then it struck him. *The woman with the bow and her impressive accuracy.* "Yes. I was hit while I was flying. Nahum spotted them lurking around the place JD should have been."

"It was a trap, and you ploughed right into it."

He rolled his eyes. "You are always so combative! Of course it was a trap, we knew that, but also saw it as a chance to take a few of them out. And we certainly did," he said smugly.

"So nice to know I spent my whole night looking after you, and you don't seem to care that you nearly died."

"I do care! I didn't want to die! I didn't want to be injured, either. Hold on," he said, as her words filtered through his foggy brain. He took in her lack of makeup, t-shirt and yoga pants, and her mass of tumbling hair that he wanted to run his hands through. "Are you saying you slept with me?" He patted the blanket next to him, still feeling its warmth. "Right here."

"Guilty," she teased, batting her eyelashes. "Does that make you feel a little vulnerable? I promise I did not take advantage of you."

Her eyes swept across his bare chest and down his body, and he realised he'd been cut out of his jeans, and that all he was wearing were his boxer shorts under the blanket. "I would be more than happy for you to take advantage of me, but I must insist I be awake to fully appreciate it. Deal?"

He couldn't contain his grin as she stared him right in the eye and said, "If you have to play by the rules, then I suppose so."

"Oh, Estelle," he said as a rush of early morning desire told him everything seemed to be working properly, and also made him grateful for the blanket. "You are a very naughty girl."

"Naughty *woman*, actually. Now, if you can possibly get your mind out of the gutter," she said, sipping her coffee demurely, "do you think you can explain why you seemed to internally combust last night?"

He did not appreciate the change in subject. "I did *what*?"

"You seemed to have this rush of fire just under your skin, about two to three hours ago. It started in your chest and spread everywhere. Nahum said your father did similar things. Has that happened before?"

"I don't think so!" He placed his hand on his chest as if he would feel different. "Where, here?"

"Yep. It sort of blossomed outwards." She explained their thoughts on the poison and alchemy.

All sorts of memories flooded back to Barak. His father was huge, a giant amongst the angels, and a fierce warrior. He didn't show compassion often, but Nahum was right, every now and again he healed using his hands, a flash of fire that flared from his fingers. "I've never knowingly used it, but maybe it's been latent in me all along." He stared at his hands, willing them to produce fire, but nothing happened. "I can't do it now."

Estelle studied him, puzzled. "Maybe it only happens when your body is in stress, or perhaps you just need to practice. But I'm a fire witch, so maybe I can help you."

"Well, that sounds like fun."

"Oh, does it?" she laughed, rising to her feet. "I'm a hard task master."

"I'm fine with that. Where are you going?" he protested, enjoying their quiet intimacy.

"I need a shower, and so do you."

"Is that an invite?"

"You're incorrigible," she said as she walked to the door. "No. But I'll see you later, over breakfast."

She smiled as she left him, and Barak realised he felt better than he had in years. He was pretty sure it was Estelle's doing too, rather than his father's power. It was certainly time for a shower...a cold one.

Twenty-Three

NIEL HAD ONLY TAKEN a cursory look around the *château* when he arrived. He hadn't flown so far in a long time, and he was more tired than he expected, so for a few hours he'd slept well. Now he followed the sound of voices to the long, covered terrace at the back of the house, and discovered a few people gathered around the table. Covered dishes and jugs of coffee had been placed down the centre, and the remnants of breakfast on used plates indicated he was the last to arrive.

"This is where you all are! Morning all! Wow. What a place!" For a moment he simply took in the view of the vineyards, appreciating the warmth that promised a hot day, as the others greeted him. He sat next to Nahum and poured himself coffee, glad that it was still warm.

"I thought I'd let you sleep," Nahum told him, "but everything should still be hot."

"I could eat it cold, I'm so hungry," Niel confessed, already filling his plate. He looked up at Barak, who was still not his normal self. "I'm glad to see you looking better. You were out cold when I arrived!"

Barak gave him a wry smile. "You've heard I had a run in with a strange poison, I take it?"

Niel nodded to Estelle, who sat next to Barak. She looked tired, but there was something different about her that Niel couldn't place.

"Estelle gave me a brief rundown."

"Yeah, my body did an odd thing I need to think about," he said, distractedly topping up his coffee.

"But everyone else is okay?" he said, glancing around the table.

"We're fine," Gabe and Shadow said together, almost too quickly.

Niel frowned, thinking they both looked furtive—flushed, even—but despite that, Gabe radiated a calm Niel hadn't seen in months. Shadow, however, could barely meet his eyes.

Oh. He paused, his fork partway to his mouth, and then catching Shadow's scowl, he shovelled food in quickly and turned away. Nahum and Ash were both looking at him with barely concealed smirks that told him to shut up and move on. *So, it had finally happened. About time, too.*

Struggling to hide his own amusement, he spoke quickly. "Great! So, what's the plan today?"

"Harlan will be arriving in a few hours," Nahum said. "He's bringing Jackson, and he sounded excited."

"Jackson?" Niel grunted. "Why him? Not that I mind, obviously."

"More weird connections, I gather."

Ash sighed. "Let's hope they provide a way through this mess. JD has gone missing, along with Mason."

Niel paused. "Really? How—and why?"

"He's not answering his phone," Nahum explained. "Although, he could be sneaking around and lying low."

Aubrey and Caldwell hadn't spoken yet. As usual, they were sitting close together, looking furtive and worried, but then Caldwell said, "Everything is gathering. I can feel it. The planets are aligning, and so are the players."

Aubrey nodded. "It's like a portent. When we take the reading tonight, we need to be ready to act quickly."

"You can't read it in the day?" Niel asked.

"No. After further discussion, and some thorough reasoning with Ash, we will take the reading from Mars. Once we have our new destination, we have to head to the place itself."

"And Black Cronos?" Niel studied the faces around the table. "They're here, obviously. Surely they can't follow us?"

Nahum grimaced. "Unfortunately, we're worried that they have JD and will use him for leverage."

"But we don't know that yet," Gabe remonstrated. "When Harlan arrives, we can pool our knowledge. Until then, we should use the day to rest, plan for all eventualities, and check our weapons. If we fail tonight, Black Cronos wins, and who knows what that could mean."

When Harlan arrived at the *château* in the late morning with Jackson, he felt alert, excited, and more alive than he had in days. He felt, in fact, like a spy—especially when he left his very expensive hotel and was picked up a by a sleek black Audi to be taken to the airport.

As he and Jackson passed through the gates of the property in their rental car, a wave of power passed over them, and Jackson, who was driving, grunted. "Now *that's* a protection spell."

"You don't have to keep insulting my charms and amulets," Harlan told him.

"I'm just saying it was good!"

"If they're protection spells, how come we're getting in?"

"Something to do with us not having malevolent intent, or something of the sort, I guess."

Harlan had barely time to think about that when they swept into a grand courtyard overshadowed by magnificent architecture, and Nahum stepped out from under a shaded loggia, his scabbard and sword strapped around his waist, the hilt glinting in the light.

"Good to see you," he greeted them, as Harlan exited the car.

"You too, I think," Harlan said, shaking his hand. "I'm glad to see this place seems secure. I wasn't sure what we'd find."

"Oh, we're settled and safe here, for now." Nahum turned to Jackson. "Good to see you, too. I'm looking forward to hearing your news."

"The calm before the storm," Jackson said wryly.

Nahum gave a hollow laugh. "Caldwell said something similar this morning. Something about everything aligning." Nahum led them inside the house, asking, "Any news from JD?"

Harlan's anxiety that he'd finally contained flared again. "No, even though Jackson's contacts have been trying to trace his phone. He's a wily old fox. Part of me is hoping he's gone underground and turned it off. It might still be likely, if it weren't for Smythe."

"Yeah, sorry to hear about that," Nahum said, his bright blue eyes flashing with sorrow. "Look, I'll take you to your rooms upstairs where you can freshen up, and then come and join us on the terrace. We've been virtually living out there. We're going through strategies for tonight, and it would be good to get your opinion. And of course, share your news."

Nahum led them through the warren of rooms and staircases, finally depositing them in ornately decorated bedrooms on the same hall. Harlan headed straight to the shower, sluicing off the grime from the journey, and then joined the others outside.

It was a hive of activity. A telescope had been set up at the end of the terrace, and Aubrey, Caldwell, and Ash were clustered around it. Books were sprawled across the long wooden table, and a laptop was at the far end. Barak, Gabe, Shadow, Niel, Nahum, and a woman he'd never met with long, dark hair were all sparring in a patch of shade in a grassy area below the terrace. All the Nephilim wore cotton pants only, their bare chests covered in sweat. Shadow wore jeans and a t-shirt, looking nimble and lithe next to the well-muscled Nephilim, and the other woman looked like she was dressed in yoga gear. She must be Caspian's sister, Estelle. He'd heard a little about her. She had no weapons, just her forbidding magic that she was using to fight with. Flashes of fire and bolts of energy flew from her hands, making everyone work hard to duck them or counter them.

He leaned on the railing watching them all for a moment, unnoticed. Shadow was battling Nahum and Gabe, while Niel and Barak fought Estelle, but it seemed to Harlan that Barak wasn't fighting with quite as much vigour as the others, and they seemed to be treating him gently.

"They like their practice," Jackson observed, leaning on the rail next to him. "I think it's too bloody hot!"

Jackson had finally taken off his long coat, and just wore his jeans, t-shirt, and scuffed sneakers.

"I really don't think they care. Look at them! They make me feel inadequate."

Jackson grinned. "They make me feel safe." He gestured to his regular-sized biceps. "I'm not really the workout kind. I have to rely on my wits."

"I think we'll need wits, luck, strength, and anything else we can use tonight."

He heard a shout of greeting, and saw Gabe waving. In minutes, all of them were trooping back to the terrace, using towels to wipe the sweat off themselves.

"I gather you two have some things to share," Gabe said, slinging the towel around his shoulders.

Harlan cast a sideways glance at Jackson. "Yeah, *someone's* got some interesting connections."

Jackson shrugged nonchalantly. "It's just one of those things." His gaze slid over the table, to the kitchen. "Shall I get drinks?"

Niel waved him off. "Sit, please. I'll get everything."

Despite their half-dressed, sweaty state, the Nephilim and the two women sat around the table, looking at Harlan and Jackson with interest.

"Have you met Estelle?" Nahum asked. He quickly made the introductions, and Estelle nodded briefly, her cool gaze sweeping over them.

Niel returned, handing out beers and placing down jugs of water, and as Shadow opened a bottle, she asked, "What's with JD?"

Harlan grimaced. "We have a horrible feeling that he's been kidnapped, him and Mason. He landed in Bordeaux, we know that for sure, but he's since gone missing."

"And still no response?"

"Nothing. Half of me wants to think he's keeping his head down somewhere, but I believe that's wishful thinking."

Ash, Caldwell, and Aubrey joined the group, and Caldwell said, "We have all the cards right now. We have the astrolabe and will read it tonight, from here. Unless they've found out somehow where we are, they can't follow us." He looked triumphant. "They've lost. Tonight, we'll go into the chamber."

Ash shot an impatient look at Caldwell. "But if they have JD and his life is threatened, we'll be forced to compromise. They'll kill them if we don't, and I will not have that on my conscience."

Aubrey and Caldwell looked as if they might protest, but Jackson stepped in. "Actually, we want them there, so them having a bargaining chip works in our favour."

A chorus of *whats*, *hows*, and *whys* rung out around the table, and Jackson raised his hand.

"Hear me out. I work for a division of the government on occasions —the Paranormal Interests Division—and ever since World War II they have been looking for Black Cronos, which we believe to be a small but well-funded group, dangerous, and often without scruples. You've seen that for yourself. This is our chance to catch the ringleader and hopefully stop them for good."

"*If* he—or she—is there," Gabe said.

"We think they will be. The Dark Star chamber is a big deal. It contains secrets hidden for centuries. He'll be there."

Aubrey looked pale. "Please don't tell me it's Stefan Hope-Robbins."

Jackson shook his head. "No. We think it's a man called Toto Dax. He comes from a long line of alchemists and occult dealers, but has a small group of alchemy experts as part of his group—Hope-Robbins being one of them."

"Toto Dax!" Niel exclaimed. "Is that for real?"

Jackson laughed. "Maybe not. We suspect he has several names."

Niel's arms were crossed over his broad chest. "Is he a guy with white-blond hair?"

Jackson looked at him wide-eyed. "Yes, why?"

"Mouse saw him on our back lanes on the night we were attacked at home, supervising the few survivors."

"He was in Cornwall? Wow!" Jackson ran his hands through his tangled hair, a gleam of excitement in his eyes. "For him to be so close shows how much this means to him. He's hardly ever spotted. He must be here now, too."

Nahum looked puzzled. "If you want to catch him, does this mean you have backup?"

"Of a sort." Jackson looked shifty. "The PID doesn't have any military support, not since the war. They are primarily an intelligence-gathering organisation. There's a witch who has done work for them in the past, me of course, and they've used The Orphic Guild before too, JD included. They also access police paranormal divisions, so we're more like the link for a few things."

Harlan listened, noting the word 'we' was used a lot, and a few things Jackson had already told him dropped into place. They were the link to the paranormal SOCO team and their results, Maggie's findings, Newton's, and probably other police divisions he'd never heard of. Harlan knew the occult world ran far and wide, but he'd still never really considered a government agency existed, which was stupid.

Jackson was continuing, "We only get really involved if we determine there's a big risk—and this is one. We'd like to utilise your skills, and want you to catch him for us."

Gabe gave a dry laugh. "Will you pay us?"

"Of course. I have a small unit on standby that can transport him, or anyone else you capture, out of the country. But, as I say, we're not military and don't want to involve them, either." He sighed. "They have a tendency to take over things."

"But we get to keep access to the chamber?" Aubrey asked, frowning.

Jackson's gaze swung to him. "It depends on what you want to do with it. I'm hoping you're not planning on making your own super-humans or monsters?"

Caldwell spluttered. "No! This is about transmutation of the soul for a higher purpose!"

"Potentially yes, then. You get to keep access."

Harlan watched Jackson's coolly measured response, but knew from the conversations he'd had that it wouldn't be that easy. Jackson had already told him that if the place looked too dangerous, they were going to destroy it. Or seize it for PID. Right now, Harlan wasn't sure which way it was going to go.

Caldwell was now bristling with annoyance. "This is not on! This is *our* origin. Our find! Aubrey did all the hard work in locating the astrolabe, and I don't see why someone should be swooping in and taking it from us! Our order has plans."

"I appreciate that," Jackson said smoothly, "but don't forget that a monster is rumoured to be lurking in this chamber. Safety is paramount."

Harlan realised Jackson had all the smooth, calm, competent assuredness of a man used to getting his own way. He had a quiet strength about him, Harlan had always known that, but now cast in this new light of working with the government, Harlan decided that he was probably far more involved than he was letting on. He hadn't elaborated on his grandfather's disappearance, but had intimated it was a family business. *In which case, where did his parents fit into this?*

Harlan sipped his beer, watching the interactions between everyone sitting around the table, and thought that the next twenty-four were going to prove very interesting indeed.

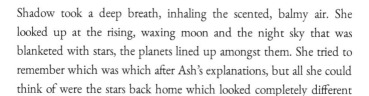

Shadow took a deep breath, inhaling the scented, balmy air. She looked up at the rising, waxing moon and the night sky that was blanketed with stars, the planets lined up amongst them. She tried to remember which was which after Ash's explanations, but all she could think of were the stars back home which looked completely different to here.

She turned to watch Aubrey and Caldwell's preparations. The time was approaching, and Aubrey was currently looking through the telescope and then at the astrolabe that Caldwell was shining a torch onto.

The Nephilim were in the house, finalising weapons and discussing tactics with Harlan and Jackson, but Shadow had left them to it. She would fight the same way she always had, and if they managed to capture Toto or Hope-Robbins that was fine, but she wouldn't worry about killing them, either.

Shadow also wanted to keep her distance from Gabe. She found that she wanted to keep touching him; he was like a magnet. All day he had been glancing at her, touching her arm and the small of her back, and her body had yearned for him. His touch had branded her skin, and now, closing her eyes, she remembered every moment of their night together, like some glorious, drug-addled dream. And this afternoon, of course, when they had managed to sneak off to shower and find some time alone.

She knew her brothers had found out. They all looked at them both in that knowing way. None of them had commented yet, but that was just a matter of time. And that was okay. She had nothing to be ashamed of. As Gabe had whispered last night—it was inevitable.

An excited burst of chatter made her look back at Caldwell and Aubrey. They were lining up the astrolabe, referring to their notes as they did so. Aubrey made a few final adjustments as Caldwell gesticulated. They seemed to be bickering. Shadow could not understand what they were doing, but after several minutes, Aubrey emitted a small whoop and high-fived Caldwell.

"You've done it?" she asked, strolling to their side.

Aubrey was beaming. "Yes. For good measure we read from all the planets, but this Mithras link makes Mars seem the perfect match." He tapped the astrolabe. "We have the coordinates."

He bustled over to the table where the detailed map of the area was secured with candles, and Caldwell shone the torch on it while Aubrey measured. He jammed his finger on the spot. "Here, next to the sea."

Shadow squinted at the map. "And we are where?"

Caldwell pointed, "Here. So about half an hour's drive." He too was frowning at the map. "It's on the grounds of an old estate, *Château de Porge*."

He pulled out his phone and tapped it while Shadow studied the map. The building was situated on a rise in an area of green, but it was impossible to see how big it was.

"As I thought," Caldwell said. "It's a ruin, a shell of a building with extensive grounds." He was already heading indoors, saying, "I'll tell the others."

"We'll need to search," Aubrey said. "The chamber could be anywhere."

Shadow huffed. "Another bloody search for an underground room. *Great*."

He looked at her, confused. "Another?"

"Just our last two jobs, but I guess that's the nature of this business, isn't it?" She straightened up. "We need to leave. Is there anything else you must take?"

"We have our bags prepared." Aubrey swallowed, looking nervous. "We have our ritual equipment, as well as torches, our reference books, and we'll take the astrolabe, of course."

She watched him dispassionately. He was an odd man, full of bluster, large, pompous, undeniably intelligent, and willing to risk everything for the Dark Star, including stealing for it. And his near miss with death—twice—hadn't fazed him, either. *Very curious.*

Everyone followed Caldwell outside, and while most clustered around the map, Ash headed to the telescope with Caldwell to look at the planets.

"Are you sure of the coordinates?" Harlan asked, a frown creasing his brow.

"Very sure. It's not some random place on the map—it's an old *château*. It could well have been owned by one of the members back then!" He looked uncertain. "I can of course check the other coordinates...we read from all the planets, but they'll be close."

Jackson nodded, his shaggy hair falling around his eyes. "Do it anyway."

Gabe glanced at her, but before he could speak his phone rang, and everyone froze. He answered it quickly. "Gabe here."

He grimaced and mouthed, *Black Cronos*. "What do you want?"

Shadow could hear a tinny voice but not what was said, especially when Gabe paced, his shoulders hunching. They had already discussed their options, so what Gabe said wasn't a surprise.

"I need to speak to him and Mason first... JD, keep a cool head, we'll meet soon—Mason, I'm afraid it's true." Gabe's lips tightened, and Shadow heard the tinny voice again. "We will meet you there, and go in together... Okay, then kill them and you will find nothing." Gabe's voice was hard, unyielding, and there was a pause as the person he spoke to considered his words. Shadow wouldn't doubt him. Gabe sounded as mean as a warrior sylph, and they would cut your throat just as soon as look at you. He continued, "I've met him a few times, and he was prepared to let me die last time. I'm returning the favour...

It's called compromise, and I guess a question of faith—in your men and mine... *No*. I'll text it when I know we're close... Because I don't trust you."

He ended the call, his lips twisting in a crooked smile. "Mason and JD are alive, and both are furious—especially Mason when he heard that Robert was dead."

"You spoke to Toto?" Jackson asked.

"That's who he said he was. Smooth and oily." Gabe checked his watch and then the map. "We can be out of here in five minutes. We'll fly, obviously, and I'll take Shadow. Flight should take us ten minutes or so. I want to do some homework and check the site before we call them. The rest will follow in the car. Agreed?" He looked at Estelle, who seemed as if she might complain, and Shadow couldn't help but feel pleased she wouldn't fly with them. "I want someone with strong magic to protect the humans. Okay?"

Estelle had changed out of her yoga clothes and was now dressed in jeans and dark outerwear like everyone else. She lifted her chin. "Okay."

"I still don't like it!" Aubrey said, and it was clear he thought victory was about to be snatched from him.

"Nobody likes it," Harlan drawled, obviously impatient. "But we play with the cards we're dealt. Let's get out of here."

Twenty-Four

GABE CIRCLED OVER THE *Château de Porge* ruins, Shadow in his arms, dropping lower and lower. Gabe's brothers were close, checking out the lanes below the ridge and the sprawl of lightly wooded grounds.

"See anyone?" he asked her.

She squirmed in his arms. "No one. It's isolated, isn't it?"

"Good. It needs to be, considering what may happen here later."

From the air they could see broken towers that were set into the steep ground that fell away to the sea, the fallen stones silvered in the moonlight. A rudimentary path ran up from the road below, and the remnants of other buildings were visible, long lines of stone crossing back and forth over the flat part of the grounds. He landed on the highest point, next to the remains of an old wall, the arched window framing the starlight. Before releasing Shadow he kissed her, pressing her back against the stone wall before letting her go reluctantly. She looked amused but pleased, and within seconds she'd drawn both her swords, and he followed suit. Her long bow was across her back too, which had made her more difficult to carry, but he didn't care. She'd faced him this time, wrapping her legs around his waist, her cheek pressed to his chest. It was gloriously distracting, but now he banished those thoughts from his mind and focussed on the task at hand.

Gabe stared over the low wall, noting the steep sides of the grassy hill that became more acute as it reached the cliff edge. Below, the surf roared against the rocks. A fall here would kill a mortal, and it was unlikely anyone could sneak up that way. He wondered how close Black Cronos was. They could take up to an hour to get there, but he doubted they'd be so lucky.

Within minutes his brothers landed next to him, all similarly dressed in military-style combat clothing, including protective vests strapped around their chests. None of them liked wearing them, but Black Cronos was too formidable not to take every precaution around. Barak had seemed none the worse for his injuries as the day progressed, and had looked annoyed at the suggestion of being left behind. They couldn't afford to anyway; he needed them all.

Barak was already surveilling the grounds. "It's impressive...and big. Did Caldwell and Aubrey narrow down the area here?"

"Of course they bloody didn't," Niel grumbled, swinging his axe to limber up. "But if it's a chamber, then it should be beneath a tower, surely?"

"Not necessarily," Ash said. "Mithraic chambers were often in the countryside, in natural caves or old tombs."

"Are there any clues at all?" Niel asked.

Ash smirked. "I have been researching *châteaus* in this area with Aubrey and Caldwell, as I'm sure Black Cronos has, too. A *château*, ruined or not, was always the most likely location when you considered the members of the group. They were rich landowners, for the most part. Unfortunately, this area has lots of crumbling *châteaus*, but this one caught our eye because of its great age and the grounds. It is one of only a few that are this old. I have an idea where to look."

"Lead the way, then," Nahum said, sweeping his arm out.

"I suppose I should call Toto," Gabe grumbled, pulling his phone free as he followed Ash. "I don't want him to get too upset and trigger-happy."

"Did JD and Mason sound okay?" Shadow asked, eyes narrowing.

"Mad as hell. I think JD's ego is bruised, but Mason," Gabe recalled the shake in his voice. "He was very upset about Smythe. And upset means unpredictable, which I don't like."

"It's Mason," she said scathingly as she fell into step beside him. "He's hardly a gun-toting, axe-wielding murderer."

"Nothing wrong with axe-wielding," Niel said, swinging his own through the air with a whoosh once more.

Gabe fell back a pace while he dialled, and Toto answered quickly. He didn't even let Gabe speak. "The address?"

"*Château de Porge*. It's on the coast."

"I know exactly where it is. Do not go into the chamber without us," he said, ringing off abruptly.

"Arrogant prick! We haven't even found it yet," Gabe muttered as he caught up to the others who were now some distance away from the main buildings, standing in the remnants of a stone tower.

"I think it's either beneath us, or in one of the other stone towers," Ash was explaining. "Or over there." He pointed to a stand of trees. "There is a stone circle in the centre. I checked when I flew over. It's almost completely overgrown now, but a stone circle suggests a place of worship."

Nahum nodded, clearly excited. "Beneath there would have held significance. Let's split up. I'll take a spade to the circle."

They had brought digging tools with them, and the car that the others were traveling in had a pick and other tools, too.

"I'm with you," Barak said. "Anyone else?"

"I'll come," Shadow volunteered. "I like your odds."

She winked at Gabe and set off with the others, leaving Gabe to start digging with Ash and Niel.

They both looked at him, amused. "Don't worry, brother," Ash said, patting his shoulder. "She only has eyes for you."

Gabe stared at them. He'd been expecting this all day. "Don't start!"

"Start what?"

"You know what! Don't think I haven't caught your smirks!"

"We're pleased for you, Gabe!" Niel said, already stomping over the heavy-set, cracked stone slabs and listening for any difference in noise. "Quite honestly, I'm glad it's finally happened. Your testosterone was close to exploding."

"Shut up!" Gabe said, wanting to throttle both of them. "It is out of bounds!"

Nahum threw back his head, laughing loudly, and an owl hooted close by. "It is *so* not out of bounds! Now, come and help us, and stop looking so bloody enraged."

Shadow studied the stone circle that was overgrown with weeds and dappled with moonlight. It was chilly beneath the trees and she shivered, sensing something evil lurking in the air.

"I think you're right, Nahum. This is the place."

He whipped around. "What makes you say that?"

"I can feel something dark here. Something unnatural."

She crouched and placed her hands on the earth, expanding her fey senses. She already picked up more wild earth energies than the others, except perhaps Briar, the earth witch, but if she became quiet and focussed, letting her senses open wide, she could pick up so much more. *Yes, she felt a displacement of energy here, and it was old.*

Taking a deep breath and holding that sensation within her, she stood again and walked across the centre of the circle. The stones were tall, misshapen, and crooked, and although the trees closed in around them, the circle itself was undisturbed, except for long grass. To the east the stones looked slightly different, and she realised they made an entrance, two of them slightly taller than the others. At their feet was a long piece of stone that she presumed had fallen from the roughly squared-off tops.

"Look," she said, striding over. "This would have been the ceremonial entrance."

Barak stood next to her. "I feel it, too. It's like the air is weighted."

Shadow turned abruptly, walking out of the circle and into the trees, expanding her awareness beneath her feet. The earth felt less dense, and she sensed air beneath her. When she looked up, Nahum and Barak were watching her.

"Well?" Nahum asked.

"I think there's a passage directly below us."

Barak's voice rose in excitement. "Where's the entrance?"

Shadow didn't answer, pacing deeper into the woods where she lost the feeling for a moment. She changed direction, retraced her steps, and tried again, keeping her alignment with the eastern gate. And then she felt the stirring of something far below her.

Nahum and Barak had followed her, watching her silently, and she lifted her head, triumphant.

"Here."

Harlan had to inch the car up the rough, overgrown lane that led to the *château*, and he had barely progressed when he saw lights behind him in the distance.

"Damn it. I think Black Cronos is here already."

"Nothing we can do about that," Jackson said. "Keep going."

"I could blast a fire ball or two at them," Estelle suggested.

Harlan caught her eye in the rear-view mirror. "Save it until we have JD and Mason safely with us."

Harlan now knew why Shadow couldn't stand Estelle. She was a prickly individual, her face prone to setting in stern, uncompromising lines, and although Shadow was wilful, there was a lightness to her that Estelle didn't have.

She continued to speak, her voice clipped. "They will try to kill us, you know that, once we are inside. They will want this for themselves."

"We know," Jackson answered, refusing to be riled. "But we remain on alert at all times." He twisted in his seat to look at her. "At some point we'll all be fighting for our lives, but until then, we wait."

"And your extraction team?" Caldwell asked, his voice tight with tension.

"They're close. Don't worry about that."

Harlan concentrated on the final part of the drive, his mind whirring over the term 'extraction team.' It sounded ridiculous.

An area of rough grass was at the top of the rutted lane, and Harlan pulled well to the side. As soon as they parked, Harlan and Jackson armed themselves with shotguns, while Aubrey and Caldwell gathered their bags. Estelle needed nothing, and sparks of magic were already firing in her hands.

Harlan was relieved to see Gabe and Ash approaching, fully armed, and said, "I saw lights behind us—Black Cronos is close. Have you found anything?"

"Shadow thinks she has discovered the entrance. They're digging now." Gabe gestured behind him. "In the stand of trees over there. I've decided that when we enter, I'm leaving Shadow, Niel, and Nahum outside, on watch."

"I think that's wise," Jackson said, loading his shotgun and pocketing some extra shells. "I presume we're sticking to the plan and waiting for them to act?"

Gabe nodded. "I think they'll wait until we're all inside the chamber. He'll want to know we're in the right place before they jump us."

"We should pre-empt them!" Estelle said scathingly. "All this playing at being gentlemen is ridiculous. We all know how it will end." She returned to her earlier argument. "As soon as JD and Mason are safe, we kill them instead. Well," she shrugged, "maybe not *kill*. Incapacitate, certainly."

"I'm glad you said that," Jackson said sharply. "If we kill them while defending ourselves, that's one thing, but we are *not* killing them in cold blood. That's not what we do—nor are we sanctioned to do! I'm not 007, and the paranormal division does not condone that type of behaviour. And," he added forcefully, "we want Toto alive! This—" he waved the shotgun around, "is a last resort."

"I hate to say this," Harlan said, "but I'll think you'll be using that whether you want to or not."

The rumble of engines disturbed their conversation as two large black vans pulled up beside them, and Harlan realised that for all their planning, Black Cronos could exit right now and kill them all, agreement or not, and he took some deep breaths to steady himself. He glanced nervously at the ruins around them, hoping there were no other members of Black Cronos creeping up the hillside.

The passenger door to the first black van opened, and a man with carefully combed, white-blond hair exited the car. For a moment, he didn't speak as his deep-set eyes swept over them, the look of the obsessive about him. And then he smiled, a shark's smirk that didn't reach his eyes, and that if anything made him look even more deadly.

"So, here we all are at last." His voice was smooth, and he frowned as he took in Gabe and Ash. Instead, he addressed Caldwell. "I see you have brought your formidable bodyguards with you."

Caldwell stepped forward, a challenge in his eyes. "Of course. We have as much claim to this as you."

"I suppose you think that, but our forefathers made the astrolabe after your half abandoned the enterprise."

"But we were there at the time of the great experiment. There is no reason we cannot work together."

Another man exited from the driver's side, and Caldwell took a sharp intake of breath. "Stefan. I wondered if you'd come."

"As I wondered if you would." Stefan was of average height and build with unruly brown hair, round glasses perched on his nose. He wore corduroy trousers and a tweed jacket, the very epitome of a professor, and Harlan found it hard to believe he was involved in such an enterprise. But he looked at them coldly, his expression aloof. "You rejected my ideas once."

"We have different ideas as to how this knowledge should be used," Caldwell said, squaring his shoulders.

Harlan was impressed. He didn't think Caldwell had it in him.

Caldwell studied the man with the pale hair. "I presume you are Toto Dax?"

"The very same."

"You seem to be leading this."

"Perhaps." He gave another cold smile. "Have you found the chamber?"

"First things first," Gabe said, interrupting them. "Where are JD and Mason?"

Dax gestured brusquely to Hope-Robbins, and he slid the side door of the van open, revealing JD and Mason inside, their mouths gagged and their hands and feet tied. Two men sat on either side of them, and with a flutter of fear, Harlan saw The Silencer of Souls, too.

"Let them go," Gabe said, "and then I'll lead the way."

Toto gave a dry laugh. "We really don't need you to lead the way. We could kill you all right now. I have brought my own team."

His words triggered approximately a dozen men and women to exit from the second van, and The Silencer of Souls joined them.

"You've tried that before," Gabe pointed out, unperturbed. "It won't go any better for you now."

Toto's lips twitched with amusement. "Mason will remain here, with his guards. Should I not return safely, we will kill him. JD, however—" he looked at him with interest, "may have something to contribute, so he can come, as long as he behaves."

The men cut the ties binding JD, and with a worried glance at Mason, he stumbled out of the van, grasping to loosen his gag as Harlan stepped forward to help him keep his balance. Both were usually dapper, especially Mason. He took pride in his well-made suits. Now he looked grubby and unkempt, but he met Harlan's eyes with a steely determination before the door slid shut, hiding him from view once more.

JD virtually shook Harlan off as he rounded on Toto. "You are an animal! You do not deserve to find the Dark Star chamber."

Toto leaned in close, his voice a low snarl. "Oh, yes I do, and when we find what's in there, you'll *all* regret coming along."

Nahum looked at the ornately carved stone slab that was set into the earth, wondering what they would find beneath it. It had taken some digging, but eventually they found the entrance about half a metre below the surface. Once they had brushed the soil away, they could see it was etched with strange symbols, and they had left it closed for the alchemists to see.

Both groups clustered around it, and he eyed Black Cronos warily. *So many guards didn't bode well.* The Silencer of Souls looked as sleek and deadly as a black panther. She was self-contained, looking at no one except Toto and Gabe, whom she regarded with a slow smile. If she affected Gabe in any way after their last encounter, he didn't show it, and Gabe met her stare with a wry smile of his own. Only Niel and Shadow were missing from the crowd. They had withdrawn into the trees, circling the perimeter, and watching from a distance.

All the alchemists dropped to their knees to examine the symbols, a fervent light behind their eyes, and for a few moments at least, it seemed that their animosity had been forgotten.

"Fascinating," JD muttered. "The entrance faces east as is befitting for a Sun God. See the ancient signs for Mithras etched in the surface?"

"And symbols of the stars and the planets," Aubrey said, nodding along enthusiastically.

Toto smiled like a shark again. "And the symbol for a journey."

Nahum took the opportunity to speak quietly to Gabe. "Where's Mason?"

"In one of the vans by the *château* ruins. As soon as you have the chance, free him."

He nodded, and Gabe turned his attention to the alchemists. "Are there symbols that warn of what we may face? Clues to a path?"

JD stood and brushed earth from his trousers. "No. This is an ornate entrance only."

"But it does carry a warning," Caldwell said, rising too, and looking unconcerned at his announcement. "It says only those who seek the truth shall be victorious." He straightened his shoulders. "And seeing as I do, I do not fear that statement."

Toto regarded him through slitted lids. "We shall see, won't we?" His subtle undertones conveyed that he knew much more than anyone else did, unless he was just very good at trying to undermine them. He gave a mock bow to Caldwell. "Perhaps you should lead the way."

Caldwell looked at him suspiciously, perhaps wondering as Nahum was, if they were sacrificial lambs, but he merely nodded and shouldered his bag, and then addressed Gabe and Nahum. "Let's remove the slab, then. It can tell us nothing more."

The slab was one huge square of stone, easily two metres across, and Nahum picked up the crowbar they had brought with them— they had come prepared for anything—and angled it beneath the slab. Gabe positioned himself, ready to lift the raised edge, as did two brawny members of Black Cronos.

It took a few moments to position the crowbar correctly; the stone was thick, and Nahum needed to slide the bar down the side until he felt it catch underneath. Then he levered it up, allowing Gabe and the other two men to flip it over, where it crashed to the ground with a judder. Stale air erupted out around them.

Gabe shouldered past Caldwell, saying, "Let us go first. It's what you're paying us for." Caldwell looked as if he might protest, but then stepped back as Gabe added, "Nahum, make sure this entrance remains open."

Nahum nodded, and Toto grimaced before speaking to one of his own men. "You stay with him."

Nahum eyed the man who positioned himself on the other side of the entrance. He was easily as tall as Nahum, his dark hair shaved close to his scalp, and he planted his feet firmly, crossing his arms over his chest as he stared back.

This could prove interesting.

TWENTY-FIVE

THE STEPS BELOW GABE'S feet were littered with soil and small stones that crunched as he went, the only sound breaking the silence. His torch flashed across the stone walls and he inhaled deeply, and then promptly wished he hadn't. The air smelled foul, was tainted somehow by something cloying beyond the scents of earth and cold stone.

The steps were wide enough that Ash could walk next to him, and Gabe murmured, "What in Herne's balls is that smell?"

"Smells like death. Not quite the shining glory of the Temple of the Trinity, is it?"

"Not really, but I prefer this one, despite the smell, if I'm honest." Gabe was more than happy to have no angel involvement here, fallen or otherwise.

They proceeded slowly, making sure the steps were firm and there were no hidden traps. He'd experienced those before—stairs falling away into a pit of spikes, or into deep holes with water far below. But everything felt stable, as it should, really, if it was a regular place of... what? Worship? Or just experiments with time, matter, and whatever else alchemists did.

He glanced behind him and saw that Caldwell and Toto were merely steps behind them, the others following in a procession—a weird, unholy alliance. *For now.*

The steps travelled deep into the earth, and they finally came to a halt on a stone landing with two enormous wooden doors in front of them. Again, symbols were carved into them—signs for air, water, fire, earth, sigils of protection, the large image of a bull, a stylised sun, and several strange patterns that he couldn't quite recognise—but more ominous were the thick iron bars that crossed the wood, and the heavy beam that slotted into brackets, sealing the door shut. However, he stepped aside, allowing Caldwell and Toto to approach it together.

"The Bull of Mithras. It is the Mithraic Temple!" Caldwell said, almost breathless. He glanced at Ash. "We were right."

"And the constellation of Lyra—the lyre of Orpheus," Toto said, his hands running across the patterns that Gabe hadn't recognised. He nodded, as if he expected as much. "To reference a journey to the Underworld, perhaps. And that one," he pointed to another cluster of carvings, "Virgo. Linked to Persephone."

Gabe could have kicked himself. Star constellations, of course, and they both referenced the Underworld.

JD hustled next to them. "References to Mithras and Orpheus? Odd."

"Not really," Toto said dismissively. "Many organisations combined different beliefs. Our order sought knowledge. Were willing to travel where others would not. I think it's time we enter."

Gabe hefted the thick beam out of the brackets and placed it to the side, and then he and Ash pulled the great doors open, allowing another wave of stale air to billow around them. A short passageway was visible ahead, the walls lined with old-fashioned torches wedged into brackets. They progressed down it quickly, and the torches flared to life as someone lit them. They arrived at another set of double doors at the end, again sealed with a thick beam.

Gabe stared at the alchemists' eager faces. "Are you sure you want to go in? These are very big doors, and must be sealed for a reason."

"Of course we're sure," Toto said impatiently. "You hardly think I'm going to change my mind now?"

It was the response he'd expected, and to be honest, despite the dangers, he was curious to see what lay beyond. He laid the beam to one side again and opened the doors to reveal a large chamber before them. Stone benches ran along either side, and in the centre was a statue of a man slaying a bull.

"The Mithraic chamber," Caldwell said, pushing past Gabe in his haste to get inside. There were more torches in here, and they flared to life as Estelle threw balls of fire at them, filling the chamber with a rich, golden glow.

But Gabe was looking beyond the statue to the wall at the end. "This can't just be it."

Ash shuffled through the gathering of men to Gabe's side, ignoring the excited chatter of the alchemists. "I agree. The Order of the Morning Star must have used this as their entrance."

Gabe and Ash clambered onto the stone benches to squeeze past the others, and Estelle joined them, her gaze sweeping along the end wall constructed of hefty blocks of stone. She pointed to an area on the right. "That section isn't as well finished. Look at the crumbling mortar."

"It's a later addition, put up hurriedly, I suspect," Ash said, running his fingers along it.

They started tapping, and found it had a hollow sound to it. By now, the chamber had quieted again, and Caldwell and Toto were right behind them.

"Break it down," Toto said, his eyes gleaming.

"Allow me," Estelle said, raising her hands and releasing a blast of power at the wall.

A rumble resounded around the chamber as a section of rocks flew backwards. A wave of dust rose into the air, and instinctively they all stepped back, shielding their faces. But when the dust settled, it was clear there was a large space beyond.

The Silencer of Souls grabbed a torch from the wall and thrust it at Toto, her gaze raking over Gabe as she did so, and for a moment, he could feel her cold lips on his again; he vowed if he had the chance later, he would kill her. Toto, however, took no notice of the look that passed between them, almost absently taking the torch as he stepped over the debris, and interestingly, Caldwell let him go first.

Shadow heard the blast and felt a rumble beneath her. Alarmed, she jumped down from the tree branch where she'd been surveying the almost pitch-black land beyond the edge of the grove, tangled with shrub and brambles. She readied her bow, wondering what the noise meant.

Niel materialized out of the shadows. "It's too soon," he reassured her. "They'll have barely got in."

"That's what worries me. What if the entrance is booby trapped?"

"I guess it's a possibility."

She glared at him. "You're supposed to be reassuring me!"

He grinned. "Oops. Worried about lover boy?"

"What did you say?" she asked, aiming an arrow at Niel's chest in a split second.

Niel stepped back, hands raised. "Just teasing. You can take a joke, right?"

"And just what is so funny about me and Gabe?" *Bollocks. She'd vowed not to rise to their taunts or confess anything, and what had she just done?* She lowered her bow with a sigh. "Don't you dare start."

"I'm just glad you two have finally...well, whatever. All that sexual tension was starting to affect me."

"Really? I'm so sorry," she said, her voice dripping with sarcasm. "It wasn't exactly easy for me!"

"But you could have acted sooner."

She floundered for words. "Well, I was worried about the business—and stuff."

"It's fine. It gave us time to place some bets," he said, grinning broadly.

She raised her bow again before he could blink. "You did *what*?"

"It was just some fun. You should be pleased I'm telling you! Now you know."

"I should shoot your balls!"

"Will it make you feel better if I tell you we've got bets on Barak and Estelle now?"

She lowered her bow and mimed gagging. "You have? Does that mean it might actually happen?"

"That's what the bet is about. Care to wager a yes or no or a tentative date?"

Suddenly, Shadow felt much better. "Okay. What are the odds?"

Before he could answer, Shadow saw the trees rustle behind him, and something flew out of the darkness.

"Get down!" she hissed at him as she simultaneously dived out of the way, rolled, and then fired a few arrows from her prone position, satisfied to hear a thump as their attacker fell out of bushes and to the ground, dead.

Shadow remained in a crouch, looking around warily as Niel crouched too, both utterly silent. Another rustle of branches sounded behind them, and a flurry of arrows embedded in the trunk of the tree only feet away. She immediately turned and shot half a dozen arrows back in quick succession.

"That's *your* fault," she hissed at him. "You distracted me!"

"I did not!" he hissed back. "You distracted me. You and your bloody sex life!"

"Shut up!"

An arrow hit a different trunk, this time from a different direction, and silently Shadow indicated she was going to go around. She cast her fey magic outward, feeling the trees' presence become stronger as she did so, responding to her earthy magic. Immediately her senses magnified, and she felt half a dozen men moving through the trees, converging on them. Once more, she cursed her stupidity for arguing with Niel about her sex life, shouldered her bow, and set about rectifying it, coming up on the closest man like a ghost and stabbing him through the throat before he even knew she was there.

She heard a strangled cry from the other direction, and knew Niel had found another. In a running crouch, she zigzagged through the undergrowth, picking off one, then another, until she found herself facing the remains of a stone wall and heard voices beyond it. She eased herself along it, finally able to see into the ruins of a room where a couple of Black Cronos members were talking, one man and one woman. She stepped out, shooting the man facing her first, but the woman was already diving to the ground as she threw a weird weapon at Shadow.

It was silver, shimmering in the light like it was molten metal, and it caught her bow, shattering it into tiny pieces. Shadow barely had time to register her shock that something had destroyed her fey-made weapon before the woman was on her, knife in hand. Shadow smacked her arm away and kicked her in the stomach, causing her to stumble backwards, and withdrawing both swords, whirled them around as she advanced.

Her opponent was slim and athletic, and her eyes had taken on a silvery sheen. She clenched her fist and seemed to draw a blade out of the air as she moved swiftly to block Shadow, and Shadow realised this would be no easy fight.

For a few moments after the rumble of the blast, Nahum and the other man guarding the entrance waited, both keeping an eye on the stairs and each other. And then out of the corner of his eye, Nahum saw a flutter of movement.

Rather than dive for cover, he launched himself at the man opposite him, slamming up against a wall of muscle. But he wasn't aiming to knock him down; he was going to use him as a shield. He dodged around him, grabbing him around the throat and pulling him backwards.

He fought back hard, but it was already too late. Nahum felt him go limp as whatever had been thrown at him hit his opponent instead. Nahum dropped him and, accessing his throwing daggers, threw them at the woman who was sprinting towards him. His daggers were on target, but something odd was happening to the woman's skin. It shimmered, and suddenly it seemed as if her skin had become a shield. His daggers virtually bounced off her.

She was within feet of him when she launched herself, hitting him like a bullet, and with a shock, Nahum realised her arms felt like metal, and her face had a metallic sheen to it. Her hands fixed around Nahum's throat and closed tightly as she leaned into him, her breath hot on his face. He clamped his hands over hers to prise her off, but she was incredibly strong.

Screw this.

Nahum's wings unfurled and he lifted them off the ground, the woman's feet flailing and her grip loosening for a second until she wrapped her legs around his waist and tightened her grip once more. *That had never happened before.* He spun around, fighting to see as his vision blackened, and flew at one of the ruined towers. He slammed her back into a stone wall, powering through it, and then into the next. An explosion of rubble ballooned around them, and in free-fall now they plunged over the cliff and spun towards the surf that crashed into the rocks below.

Niel was knocked off his feet by a blow between his shoulder blades, and he sprawled on his stomach as someone landed on his back, clasped his hair, and pulled back his head. In his peripheral vision, he saw the flash of a blade.

What the actual fuck...

Niel reared up and rolled over, pinning whoever it was beneath his considerable weight. An obviously male hand flopped on to the ground, clenching a nasty looking blade. He reached over, grabbed the thick wrist, and twisted hard before being thrown off.

The next several seconds were a blur of hard earth, muscle, blade, and the snarling face of some feral Black Cronos member who stank of dog. And then without warning, the man collapsed on Niel's chest, and blood gurgled from his mouth and onto Niel's face. Scrabbling to get clear of him, Niel threw him off and saw Shadow staring down at him.

"You okay?" she asked, holding her hand out.

"No!" he said, grasping it and hauling himself to his feet. "I am covered in this stinking cur's blood!" He wiped his face, smearing it everywhere.

"You look even worse now," she said, leading him to the entrance of the chamber. "Like some deranged zombie we like killing in those video games."

"You don't look much better yourself," he noted, seeing a slight limp to her walk and blood-soaked clothing. "Are you injured?"

"No. It's all from the woman I finally killed."

Then Niel realised her bow was missing, only her quiver of arrows strung across her back remained in place. "Where's your bow?"

"That bloody woman destroyed it!"

"Your *fey* bow?" He knew how strong her weapons were. She never let them forget it.

She grimaced. "Yes! I don't like these people or the way they fight. They pull weapons from nowhere, and grow weird armour." She paused as she saw the body on the floor. "Where's Nahum?"

Niel peered down the stairs. "Well, he's not down there." He scanned the trees again, wary of further attack, and asked, "How many did you kill?"

"Half a dozen. You?"

He looked at her resentfully. "Three."

She preened. "Never mind. I'm sure there's more. Do you think we should head to the chamber?"

"Let's wait, and if Nahum doesn't appear, maybe we'll go looking for him." He searched the sky. The moon was lower now, their surroundings darker, and he hoped he wouldn't end up stumbling across his brother's body. "Did you notice Mason wasn't with them?"

Shadow frowned. "No, I was too far back, watching the other direction. Do you think he's here somewhere?"

Niel didn't answer, instead staring through the grove towards the ruins. "They'll have driven here and have probably parked at the top of that lane we flew over. I bet Mason is insurance. I wonder if Nahum has gone looking for him." He lifted his axe, running his finger along the sharp blade. "You stay here, make sure no one else goes in, and I'll go check."

TWENTY-SIX

HARLAN WAS IN THE middle of the group that stepped over the rubble of fallen stones and ventured into the next chamber. For a second, he stood just inside, letting his eyes adjust to the light, and heard murmurs as torches flashed around the space.

It was a large cavern that was a mix of natural cave and man-made structures. His flashlight illuminated crumbling columns rising into the air, and in the middle was a dark block of something.

Estelle conjured her witch lights, throwing them high above the group, obviously not as worried about revealing her true nature to strangers as the White Haven witches were. Her lights revealed more old-fashioned torches in brackets on the columns, and again she illuminated them with a quick burst of fire, and the cavern flared into life.

Harlan's first impression was that there had been a fight in here, or some sort of earthquake. Long stone tables were placed around the chamber, the surfaces crowded with bottles and jars, braziers, and other old-fashioned scientific equipment. But some of them had been smashed, tables split into pieces, surrounded by broken glass, or upturned. His blood ran cold as he saw metal gates set into the right-hand wall of the chamber at regular intervals, dark rooms beyond. They looked like either cells or storage rooms. He hoped for the latter. Overhead, what looked to be long strings of *something* were suspended over the entire place in a spider web design. He stumbled backwards as the resemblance struck him.

"Holy crap," he murmured to Jackson, who was next to him. "This is like that room in *Frankenstein*! The laboratory where he made the monster! But it looks like there's been a struggle here...a big one."

Jackson nodded absently as his gaze travelled the room. "I agree." He squinted up at the overhead lines that fed to a structure on the far side. "They're odd, considering the age of this place. I think they're for conducting energy." He focussed on Toto, who was directing his men to search the cave. His team fanned out, some heading to the tables, others searching around the far reaches. Toto then strode to the centre of the chamber, the other alchemists racing after him.

Harlan squinted at the blocky structure that squatted in the middle. "Is that a tomb?"

"Please don't say that."

Harlan glanced nervously around, noting that two Black Cronos guards were positioned on either side of the entrance, but with relief saw that Barak was close by. He caught his eye, and Barak nodded reassuringly. Ash was with the main group, but Gabe was conducting his own search of the room, while Estelle stood slightly apart from all of them, her sharp eyes appraising everything.

Jackson hurried to join the alchemists, but Harlan decided to see what was beyond the metal gates. He took his time, studying the columns as he went. Like most other things here, they were covered in painted symbols. Some of them were geometric in design; he'd seen similar ones before in books on alchemy.

He wandered amongst the stone tables, noting the dusty, grimy bottles that were lined up in rows, remnants of dried materials visible in some. At the side of one table, where it butted up against the wall, he saw wires travelling from a huge pottery jar on the floor up to the roof. The top was plugged with a cork, and Harlan caught the faint waft of something sharp. *Vinegar*. Examining the wires closer, he saw they were attached with clips to a rod that was sticking out of the pot, and it looked to be iron. A memory flooded back of an article he'd read on ancient batteries. It was believed that ancient civilisations had found a way to generate power, a type of crude electricity. *Was that what this was? A power source?*

He scanned the room, seeing the same huge pottery jars lined up at regular intervals all around the cavern and at the base of some of the columns, and looking up, he realised the columns weren't just for show—they supported the wires. *But what did they do?* It didn't seem as if they provided light; there were no rudimentary bulbs, for a start, and the torches already supplied that. And then as his eyes followed the web of wires, he realised not only did they lead to the structure at the far side, they all led to the alleged tomb in the centre.

Harlan's mouth suddenly went very dry. This was starting to seem more and more like some mad scientist's laboratory. Barak must have been watching his progress, because in seconds he was at his side, the big man looming over him.

"Are you all right?" he asked, his voice a rich rumble.

"No! Look at these wires overhead, and the pottery jars—and where they go. Right to the middle! I think the jars are a power source...ancient batteries!"

Barak was silent for a moment as he took it all in. "We had no such thing in my time. Explain how they work."

"I have the most basic knowledge only," Harlan said trying to retrieve what he'd read. "But eighty or so years ago, some guy discovered these pottery jars outside Baghdad—"

"Persia?" Barak asked, frowning.

"Well, Iran now, but yes. Anyway, they had copper and iron tubes in them, and they looked like a smaller version of this! They dated them to be over two thousand years old, and they discovered that they had been filled with vinegar or wine, which would start a reaction. Electricity! These are just much bigger versions...and there are lots of them."

"Interesting. Ash would know more, I'd put a bet on it. Have the others noticed yet?"

"I think they're too absorbed by the tomb—if that's what it is."

"It looks to be, but it's sealed for now, and there's a pretty big argument brewing down there as to how to open it." Barak glanced behind Harlan. "Have you looked beyond those grills yet? Because there are more wires leading through them."

"Are there?" Harlan whirled around and hurried towards them, Barak next to him. He peered into the first one and played his flashlight around the space.

"There's a bench along the far wall covered in rags, and," Barak paused, his eyes narrowing. "Bones. I can see them protruding through the rotted cloth. They're prison cells."

"Damn it. I'd hoped they were storage rooms." Harlan recalled Jackson telling him about human experimentation in the Second World War, and then he glanced at the members of Black Cronos placed strategically around the chamber, The Silencer of Souls next to Toto. "That's what these guys are, Barak. They're the results of experiments, but they clearly got stuff right."

Barak was already hurrying on to the next cell, and in each one they saw evidence of human habitation, with a hard bench along the back wall. "I wonder what they poisoned me with?" he murmured. "It triggered something in my blood."

A shout from the far side of the chamber caught their attention and they spun around, Barak already drawing his sword, Harlan cocking his gun. It was Stefan Hope-Robbins, and he was next to the structure the wires fed into. He called, "I've found a switch to the batteries. It may open the tomb."

Barak lowered his mouth to Harlan's ear. "I'm going to make sure our exit is clear. Stay sharp, Harlan."

Harlan nodded and hurried to the group. He found Ash at the back watching everyone, particularly The Silencer of Souls, who studied Gabe's actions with unnerving patience. For a moment Harlan just waited with him and watched the tomb. It was a step pyramid of four levels, surprisingly large up close, and seemed to be carved from a single block of white stone. Although Harlan thought it was unlikely to be made from one piece, he could make out no seams between blocks. Ornate symbols were carved onto the surface, and they seemed to crawl and writhe in the flickering firelight.

Estelle had positioned herself on the far side, alone, her face implacable as she watched the guards. Caldwell was arguing with Aubrey, Toto was arguing with JD, and Gabe had clambered onto the tomb and was examining the topmost level.

JD was gesticulating at an ornate symbol on the lowest tier. "I'm telling you," he said, shouting and red-faced, "that the jewel in the astrolabe must sit in the middle. It's part of the trigger, and must have been incorporated into the astrolabe's design."

"I admit that that has a certain logic, but it will destroy the astrolabe," Toto said, surprising Harlan that he should want to keep it intact.

"So? We're here now! We don't need the astrolabe any longer."

"Easy for you to say," Toto shot back. "It's not a part of *your* heritage!"

"You curdle-faced milksop!" JD spat. "Like a babbling clapper-claw! It is a wonder you have got as far as you have with your alchemical enhancements!"

Oh no. When JD started spouting Shakespearean insults, Harlan knew things were getting ugly. What was really worrying was why JD was helping at all. *Jackson had suggested JD was trying to stop this, but was he really?*

Toto's eyes hardened at JD's insult. "My team are the most enhanced humans you could ever wish to find."

"And yet Gabe and his team have decimated them!" JD yelled.

"Enough!" Stefan roared, and everyone fell silent and turned to him. At their reaction, Harlan started to wonder just who was in charge of Black Cronos. "Put the jewel in position now."

"Wait!" Jackson shouted, holding his hand up in a stop sign and leaping in front of the symbol on the tomb. "Is this really wise? We have no idea of what's in there, but we've all heard the rumours of a monster." He studied the alchemists' faces. "This looks like a tomb, and we all know it! All you need is the research. You don't actually have to open this." He appealed to each of them. "You're risking everyone's lives for this."

Toto sneered. "There is no research in here. My team has searched everywhere." His arm swept up to encompass the room. "It is a damp, cold cave. The tomb must preserve their research, too."

"But what if it's not here? Perhaps they stored the research elsewhere. These symbols might be some sort of code," Jackson pointed out. "Don't you think you should study them carefully first?"

He shot a desperate look at Harlan, and he felt compelled to support him. "I agree," Harlan said, moving to Jackson's side. "Potentially, you'll lose the chance if you open the tomb."

"I'm not an idiot," JD said scathingly. "I have already made a cursory examination of these symbols while you were skulking about, and they contain no hidden messages. Neither are they particularly magical. They are standard alchemical symbols—that's all."

Harlan gritted his teeth. "JD, I wasn't skulking about. I was investigating what was behind those metal grills. They are cage doors! Dead men are locked inside them! And in case you haven't noticed, some of this equipment has been destroyed—possibly in a fight. Please," he appealed, "can we think rationally about this?"

The alchemists, despite their differences, now shuffled together as if presenting a united front, and Caldwell stepped forward, throwing his shoulders back. "You must trust us on this. The symbols tell us nothing about the research, but that symbol there—" he thrust Jackson aside, "is the symbol for a new awakening, and it's clear the jewel must sit there. There's even a seam running around it! JD is right. It's a trigger, one we must activate." He turned to Gabe. "Thank you for your protection over the last few days, but we're here now. Your job is done."

Gabe gave a dry laugh. "I'm pretty sure it's not. What if the monster is in there?"

"It's a tomb. Therefore, whatever is in there, is dead."

"I'm glad you're so confident. Okay, go ahead. We'll pull back while you do your thing." He glanced at Harlan, Jackson, and finally Estelle, who was still poised for action on the far side of the tomb. "Let's give them some space."

Jackson looked as if he might protest once more, but in the end followed Harlan and Estelle to where Gabe and Ash had retreated to a safe distance.

"Right," Stefan said impatiently. "Can we get on with it?"

Aubrey had clearly decided to follow JD's earlier suggestion, as he had been fiddling with the astrolabe for several minutes. Now he finally prised the jewel out with a small blade and positioned it carefully in the centre of the ornate design. It clicked into place, and a whirring noise sounded deep within the tomb. Simultaneously, Stefan struggled to lift a long wooden lever next to him. It seemed stiff from lack of use, but he persisted stubbornly, finally flipping it up, and immediately there was another thump and thunk, and a strange fizzing noise filled the chamber.

Gabe drew everyone back even further. "This is going to be interesting. We need to be ready to go, to possibly fight our way out." He looked bleakly at the tomb. "I think there's a lot more in there than research papers. And potentially, whatever they find, Toto will want only for himself."

Estelle shook her head in disbelief, magic still balling in her hands. "I agree. And Caldwell is a fool if he thinks he's just going to walk out of here." She studied their surroundings. "If it looks as if they are going to kill us, or trap us, I'll tackle the guards next to Stefan."

"I'll take The Silencer of Souls and the guards on the other side of the tomb," Gabe said.

"Barak is planning to keep our exit clear and deal with the guards there," Harlan told them.

"Good. Then I'll take the remainder," Ash said. He leaned closer to Harlan and Jackson. "You two may need to stop Toto and Stefan if they try to prevent our escape. I don't think we need worry about the others—except maybe to rescue them."

"And what if something comes out of that tomb?" Harlan asked.

Gabe grimaced. "We can't let it escape, and that may take a team effort."

A flash of white light above them ended their conversation as electricity started to arc from what Harlan could only presume was some kind of ancient junction box, and then a white spark danced along the web of wires as the batteries fired up. Harlan wasn't entirely sure how it was working, but there was no doubt that it was. And something else was happening to the tomb. It radiated a pale light, weak at first, but as the wires continued to charge and electricity arced across their heads it grew brighter, until with a jarring, scraping noise, the top tier of the tomb split in half and slid open.

Harlan stepped back gripping his shotgun, as did the alchemists, and a breathless silence fell as everyone watched, transfixed. And then a roar sounded from within the tomb, something so primal and wounded that Harlan broke out in a sweat as he cocked his gun.

TWENTY-SEVEN

NIEL EXITED THE GROVE and looked across the ruins to the vehicles parked in the distance. The grounds of the *château* were deserted and ominously silent, and there was no sign of Nahum, but he could see a couple of guards next to the vans.

Niel crossed the ruins cautiously, wondering how best to deal with the issue of Mason, and decided an upfront approach would be best. As he left the shadows, however, he sniffed dust and rubble, and frowned at the closest tower. *Was it his imagination, or was there more damage now than had been earlier?* He paused and listened, but heard nothing except the crash of surf below, so he set off again. With his axe secured to his belt, he held his hands up as he approached the van.

"Toto has sent me to check on Mason." He grinned. "An act of faith between us all."

Both guards looked at him suspiciously. They were tall; one heavily muscled, the other lean and mean-looking. Both had dead eyes.

The leaner one spoke. "I doubt that. Turn around and walk away. We only take orders from Toto directly."

"Oh, come on," Niel argued, half-joking. "They're all busy in the tomb. He hasn't got time to babysit you guys. Let me check on Mason."

The other man was staring beyond Niel, eyes narrowed. "Why are you alone?"

Niel shrugged. "Why wouldn't I be?"

"Our men are back there. They should have seen you approach." He rubbed his palms together and out of nowhere produced a long, slim blade like a rapier and pointed it at Niel. "Where are they?"

Niel ignored the question, instead saying, "That's a neat trick. How do you do that?"

He sneered. "We do it because we're superior to you in every way." He stared at Niel's face and chest and snarled. "Is that blood?"

Crap. He'd already forgotten about that and decided to ignore it. He feigned innocence, his arms outstretched. "I haven't seen anyone! I've just left my colleagues guarding the entrance with yours."

The man clearly didn't believe him, and he didn't waste words, because in a split second he lunged at him and Niel counterattacked, swinging his axe up to block him again and again as the man proved more agile than he looked. For the next few minutes, Niel was totally absorbed in fighting the guard. The other one just watched, his weapon at the ready, and Niel knew if he survived this, he'd be fighting him next.

Then something caught all their attention as a scream pierced the air, followed by a roar that sounded like Nahum. Niel saw a whirl of wings and feathers soaring above the cliff before it crashed through the closest tower, sending rubble flying as it headed towards them. Niel and his opponent dived to the ground, and as Niel cautiously lifted his head, he saw the other guard lying unconscious, blood pouring from his head, a huge stone block next to him.

Niel had barely time to see Nahum struggling with a woman who seemed stuck to him like a limpet, when he had to evade the jab of the rapier, and he leapt to his feet, swinging his axe with lightning-fast flexes. A blur of wings swept past him as Nahum plummeted to the ground, squashing the shrieking woman under him. He drove her onto the outstretched rapier of her fellow assassin, crushing him at the same time.

Niel jumped out of the way, and stood with his axe poised as Nahum extricated himself from the woman's grip, cursing as he did so.

"Herne's hairy bloody bollocks!" he exclaimed angrily. "She was stuck to me like bloody super glue. Legs like pincers around my hips, and her fingers were instruments of bloody torture." He gesticulated angrily at his neck and the ugly red marks circling it. "Look at it. It's a miracle I can even speak!"

"And yet you can, brother!" Niel said, amused. "The important question is, are your balls okay?"

Nahum looked down at his groin. "I bloody hope so. This may not have been my most sexually active few months, but it won't last forever."

Niel sniggered, and then quickly sobered as he looked at the dead woman, the rapier piercing her side. "You nearly impaled yourself."

"It would have been worth it to get rid of her. Have I killed the guy under her, too?"

Niel crouched and checked. "Yep. Smashed his head off a rock beneath him. That one though," he murmured, standing and pointing to the other man who had fallen first, "is still alive—just barely."

A rapping noise came from inside the van and a curt voice called, "Hello? Let me out!"

Niel pulled the door open, spotting a crumpled figure sitting inside, still partially bound, although someone had removed his gag. "You must be Mason."

The slim, grey-haired man looked up at him, alarm flashing across his face. "Yes, I am. You're not one of them."

"Nope. I'm one of the good guys," Niel said, quickly loosening the man's bonds. "Othniel at your service. And this," he gestured to Nahum, who stood next to him, "is Nahum, one of my brothers."

"Gabe's men?"

"The very same."

Mason nodded and staggered out, rubbing his limbs. "Are they dead?"

"Two are, but this one isn't," Niel said, nudging the fallen man with his foot. "He was hit by a rock."

"Well, he bloody should be," Mason said viciously, taking Niel aback. He wasn't a big man, but he exuded a lot of energy. *A man used to getting his way*, Niel realised, as he said, "Give me a knife."

"What?" Nahum asked, confused.

"A knife. I'll bloody well finish him off myself!"

Niel could barely believe his ears, and from the expression on Nahum's face, neither could he. "Are you kidding?"

"No! Knife, now!"

Nahum pulled one of his daggers free and handed it over, hilt first. Mason marched over to the man and with one swift movement, stabbed him in the throat. Arterial spray splattered out, covering Mason, but he didn't care. He wiped the blade on the guard's clothes, stood with a huge sigh, and turned to them with a grim smile.

"That's better. May I borrow this until we're out of here?"

"Sure," Nahum said, almost stuttering over the word. "Did he do something to upset you?"

"Animals. Abhorrent aberrations of nature." He shuddered. "The less that survive this, the better. Where is everyone?"

"The chamber," Niel told him. "But you should wait here. I'm going to check on them now."

"Not a chance. I'm coming, too. Lead the way!"

Niel had half a mind to tell him to stuff his attitude, but instead he rolled his eyes, glanced at Nahum with an exasperated expression, and walked away. They were only halfway across the ruins when a roar shook the ground, and they ran to the entrance.

Shadow was waiting impatiently at the top of the steps. She was pretty sure there were no other Black Cronos members loitering in the bushes, and wondered how much longer she should wait for Niel and Nahum.

Suddenly, an epic, guttural roar rolled up the stairs, and without waiting to wonder what it could be, she raced down, swords drawn. She barely took in the huge carved doors and long chamber with the statue in the centre, focussing only on the shouts and another roar coming from beyond the broken wall at the end.

She vaulted over the stones and paused inside the threshold to let her eyes adjust to the flickering firelight and the onslaught of stimuli. A loud buzzing noise filled the chamber, echoing off the stone walls, and flashes of arcing white light fizzed at points across the roof, illuminating like a horror show the scenes underneath.

A massive, monstrous figure strode around the far side of the chamber, bellowing so loudly it made her wince. For a moment, she couldn't quite make out what it was. All she knew was that people were running everywhere. Some seemed to be attacking the figure, while others were running away—or being flung away like dolls. Shotgun blasts resounded, one after another, and some men seemed to be scrabbling around a tomb in the centre. A ball of fire soared through the air, smacking the hulking figure in the chest, but it didn't seem to impede it at all. Instead, it roared again and turned to charge. And that's when Shadow made out its features.

It was an enormous giant of a man with the legs and head of a bull. It reminded her of the satyrs from her world, except they were good-natured, cheerful creatures; this beast was enraged. And it was attacking everyone.

Shadow ran in to join her team who were spread in a loose circle around the rampaging creature, all of them darting to attack it, trying to distract it in one direction while striking from the other. But it wasn't working. Despite its huge size, it was agile, and insanely strong.

A few Black Cronos soldiers were already dead, but The Silencer of Souls was still alive, sticking close to a man with white-blond hair in the centre. Next to him were JD and Caldwell, all of them scrambling into and around the tomb, Aubrey's head just visible before he ducked into it again. And then Shadow realised something else. The surviving members of Black Cronos weren't engaging the creature—they were hanging back, watching her own team risk life and limb.

She ran to Harlan, who was closest and reloading his shotgun. "What's happening?" she asked, dragging him away.

"These stupid idiots released this thing from the tomb," he said, his eyes wild. "And now we have to stop it from getting out, all while trying not to die!"

"But we're the only ones fighting it, and so far, it's winning!"

A crunching noise made them both look up in alarm, and they saw Ash hit the cave wall, before slumping to the floor. He shook himself down and stood once more, this time his wings shooting out as he soared over the creature.

"Come and help us, then," Harlan said, about to run back to the others.

"Wait!" she grabbed his arm. "What woke him?"

Harlan frowned at her. "What do you mean? We opened the tomb!"

"The wires—the white lights! What are they?"

"Rudimentary electricity. Stefan released the tomb mechanism, potentially sparking the Minotaur to life, too—it's like bloody Frankenstein's monster!"

"Who's the blond man in the middle?"

"Toto, and the other guy next to him is Stefan Hope-Robbins. Both are sneaky shits—do not trust them!"

He shook her off and ran, but Shadow looked at the mass of interconnected wires running to the large box with levers and dials at the end, and then back at the figures in the centre.

There was a victorious shout from Aubrey as he emerged from the top of the tomb, shaking a fist full of papers. "I've found them!"

Toto pushed JD out of the way, scrambled up next to him and tried to grab them, setting off a huge scuffle in which Aubrey punched Toto, sending him sprawling off the tomb. The Silencer of Souls bounded up the tomb and threw herself on Aubrey, and both of them disappeared inside, papers scattering everywhere, and the remaining alchemists ran to collect them.

Nahum arrived at her side then. Mason was hanging back, wide-eyed with shock. "Shadow, we need to get out of here!"

"Not until we stop that thing—and Black Cronos!" She looked at the wires again. "I need Estelle. I have an idea. Where's Niel?"

"Fighting Black Cronos and trying to keep our exit clear. As soon as we arrived, they attacked. They've clearly decided it's time to eliminate us." Nahum's expression darkened. "Shit. The guards are moving in on JD and Caldwell, too. Okay, I'll get the alchemists out, you help stop that thing."

Shadow ran, zigzagging through the chaos to Estelle's side, narrowly avoiding being hit by a fireball. "Estelle, can you target the wires in some way? If electricity animated that thing, can we fry it using the same method?"

Estelle barely glanced at her, focussing only on the monster. "I can't move objects, Shadow! That's not my skill!"

"But could you channel the power somehow?" She pointed at the flashes of light. "I don't know much about electricity or how this is set up, but it seems that there's a lot of energy up there, just waiting to be used!"

Estelle paused, her eyes travelling from the large contraption against the wall to the wires that snaked overhead, and while she considered her options, Shadow watched Gabe and Barak engage the creature. Barak attacked with breathtaking speed as he barrelled in, his sword flashing, and Gabe went after the creature's blindside, managing to stab it several times. But nothing slowed it down.

The creature was covered in a multitude of deep cuts and stab wounds across its body and limbs. It bled profusely, and yet it wasn't tiring. She winced as it picked Barak up like he was a doll and hurled him away. Above them was solid rock, and even if Estelle could blast some of it free, they risked being buried alive in the collapsing cavern.

"They combined it with the power of Mithras, didn't they?" Shadow said, more to herself than Estelle. "That's why it has the head and limbs of a bull, but it was so much more than they expected."

Estelle launched another flurry of magic as it turned their way, and she looked exasperated. "Which explains why none of the spells I've used will work! They've somehow harnessed the power of the God! I've tried all sort of spells on it—to immobilise it, freeze it, burn it, clot its blood...many horribly destructive things I wouldn't ever dream of using on anyone else—and none of them work!" Shadow was shocked to hear that Estelle had morals, but Estelle was already speaking again, her eye on the wires. "It's possible to use that power, but I'd need to ground myself." She stared at the floor. "We're standing on earth and rock, but I risk electrocution."

That's all Shadow needed to hear. "Well, I'll leave you to work it out and go help my brothers." And then she ran to join the fight.

Nahum waded in to break up the fighting alchemists before the soldiers did, pulling Caldwell away from Stefan, and JD from Toto. All of them were bloodied and bruising, with scraps of paper crumpled in their hands and shoved inside their clothing.

"You're all insane!" Nahum yelled. "Get out now, before we're all killed!" He pointed at the rampaging monster. "Are you all blind? Is that what you want?"

"Their research was flawed!" Toto said, his eyes icy. "I can build on it!"

Nahum hadn't got time for this. "You've made your own monsters —get out now!"

Toto faced him down. "There are more papers here. And I will get them before I leave!" He shook Nahum's hand off and clambered up the steps to the tomb, just as The Silencer of Souls emerged from the inner compartment. "Just in time, my dear. Help the guards finish these gentlemen off for me. They are not to leave this place," he said, ducking inside the tomb.

"Run, now!" Nahum shouted, pushing Caldwell and JD aside and punching Stefan out cold. *The less people who could interfere, the better.* "And drag him with you!"

He whipped around, flinging a dagger at an oncoming guard, and plunging his sword into the next.

Caldwell hadn't moved, despite the increasing threat. "But Aubrey —he was in the tomb!"

"Then he's already dead," Nahum told him. "*Go!*"

Nahum fought off another guard with deadly accuracy, and then faced the advancing woman. She was taking her time walking down the tomb, as if savouring her chance to kill him.

Suddenly, an enormous crackle of energy erupted overhead, and Nahum instinctively ducked as what appeared to be lightning flashed across the roof of the chamber, illuminating everything in a stark white light. It happened again and again, magnifying in its intensity as a huge electrical storm built up overhead. Forks of lightning flashed to the ground, narrowly missing him, but it caught The Silencer of Souls and threw her across the room, where she landed on all fours like a cat, her clothing smoking.

But she wasn't looking at Nahum anymore. She was staring at Estelle.

Estelle was standing apart from the others, and was surrounded by a nimbus of power like a gigantic Tesla ball, her bare feet dug into the earth as she radiated energy, pulling it from the wires that snaked around the cavern. Her arms were spread wide and she swept them at the monster, a massive bolt of lightning striking it in the chest and sending it flying into the cave wall. She followed it up with another and then another, pinning the creature in place with the onslaught until its body started to smoulder, and it bellowed with pain and fury.

Their team was already running for the exit—all except for Barak, who loitered by the tomb, watching Estelle. Nahum ran to his side.

"Barak, we have to leave!"

"Not without Estelle."

"But she's got this!"

"And she just might collapse because of the massive amount of power she's wielding." Barak regarded him steadily. "It's okay, Nahum. Just keep the entrance clear, and I'll see you outside." Nahum hesitated, clearly torn, and Barak's large hand clamped on his shoulder. "She didn't leave me, and I'm not leaving her. Go."

Gabe arrived at the chamber's entrance after making sure everyone was ahead of him, and he paused on the threshold, keeping a wary eye on Barak and Estelle.

The chamber had turned into a death trap. The air smouldered, and the scraps of paper and the clothing of the fallen soldiers were already smoking, some bursting into flames. The whole place was ready to go up like a powder keg.

Jackson went to push past Gabe. "Gabe, I have to get back inside. Toto is still in there—in the tomb."

"You're as mad as they are," Gabe said, incredulous. "Look at this place!"

"Which is why I'm prepared to go. We need his knowledge about Black Cronos."

"You've got Stefan!"

"But I want Toto, too!"

Gabe stared at Jackson's stubborn expression. His lips were set in a tight line, his eyes narrowed. Then he glanced at Harlan at his shoulder, looking similarly determined. "*No*. You go and meet your extraction team. Ensure *everyone* is out of here. I'll get him."

"Gabe," Harlan grabbed his arm. "She's still in there—The Silencer of Souls. I saw her on the left. Be careful!"

Great jolts of lightning were sizzling through the air, and keeping his head low, Gabe sprinted across the chamber. It was hot now, and the air was so charged he could feel his hair lifting off his head like he'd stuck his hand in an electrical socket. He ignored it and the chaos beyond as he leapt on the tomb and looked inside.

It was a huge structure, with steps leading to the room at the bottom, and it seemed to Gabe that it was the place of the original experiments, as there was a wealth of objects down there. He presumed they had built the tomb around the monster. But there was no Toto here; only Aubrey's lifeless body was inside. *Shit*.

He looked around, studying the cavern from his elevated position, but he couldn't see him or the woman anywhere. All he could see were dead soldiers and smouldering fires. He'd already explored the cave earlier. There were no hidden doorways, no exits...unless they'd found something he hadn't.

Estelle was barely visible in the maelstrom of electrical energy she'd unleashed around her, but he could see the monster clearly. It was on the floor in flames, and if it weren't already dead, it would be soon. As much as he didn't want Toto or the woman to get away, this was no time to linger. He jumped down into the tomb, picked up Aubrey and threw him over his shoulder, and then headed to the ground level and Barak's side.

"Barak! How do we stop Estelle? It's time to go!"

Barak looked at him, panic-stricken. "I don't know. It's like she's locked inside that thing! I can't get close!"

Gabe looked at the contraption of wires and levers and the batteries running through the cavern and had an idea. "We need to destroy the panel," he said, yelling to be heard over the noise, and depositing Aubrey on the floor.

He grabbed a large stone from a broken column and hurled it at the rudimentary control panel. Barak followed suit, both throwing stone after stone until it shattered, sparked, and went dead, releasing Estelle from the maelstrom of energy that surrounded her. She collapsed on the ground, and Barak raced to her side, feeling her pulse, while Gabe picked up Aubrey again.

"She's alive," he said, scooping her up. "Let's get out of here, Gabe."

They were almost at the entrance when a secondary reaction started. A large humming, fizzing noise rose around them, and Gabe paused and looked back on the alchemists' chamber of horrors. One by one the rudimentary batteries exploded, flames climbing high and starting another wave of electric pulses, but Gabe didn't care. *With luck, the entire place would ignite.* He turned his back and raced outside.

Twenty-Eight

THEY ALL LOOKED TERRIBLE, Harlan thought, as he surveyed his bedraggled team.

They were next to their car and the two vans belonging to Black Cronos. JD was sitting beside Mason, sipping bottled water and talking quietly. Neither had said much to Harlan, and he wasn't sure what that meant, but right now he was too tired to care. Barak was sitting with Estelle, who was now conscious but looked utterly drained. Nahum and Niel had just returned from patrolling the grounds, their stances still wary. Ash was talking to Caldwell, his hand on his shoulder, looking earnest but gentle. Gabe and Shadow were leaning against one of the vans, studying another larger white van parked a short distance away, this one belonging to Jackson's extraction team.

Harlan turned to watch, too. He hadn't really believed they would turn up. In the madness and chaos of this whole evening, he'd expected Jackson to be teasing him, like it was some great British wind-up on the sole American.

But he hadn't been lying. They were a unit of half a dozen men and women, with one wearing a bureaucratic suit. The others were dressed in military-style clothing, and they kept their distance from the rest of them—Jackson made sure of it. Stefan Hope-Robbins was groggy but conscious, and he had been cuffed and shoved, cursing and swearing, into the back of the van, his voice vanishing as the door banged shut on him.

Jackson returned to their group and resumed his interrogation of Gabe. "He must have been in there!"

"I'm telling you, he wasn't!" Gabe looked as annoyed as Jackson was. "I have no idea how Toto got out or where he went. I can only presume that woman helped him escape. And believe me, I am not happy she made it out, either."

"Damn it!" Jackson exclaimed, "Have we—"

"Yes," Niel interrupted. "We have searched the woods around the circle, and the ruins. They're gone. Whoever is left is dead, and you've got the bodies."

Aubrey's body and the dead Black Cronos members who had been killed in the ruins had been placed in body bags and loaded into the van, along with any equipment they could find.

Jackson sighed, and then brightened as he pulled himself together. "Sorry. You're right, we have. And we'll take their vehicles, too. With luck we'll find some more information in them. Toto would have been the prize, though. I think he's the real brains behind the enhanced humans."

Gabe grunted. "You should be able to get back in the chamber once the fires are out. I've checked the entrance. It's accessible."

Jackson grinned. "I know. We have a second team en route. This is actually better than we expected, in many ways."

"*What*?" Caldwell said, abruptly ending his conversation with Ash. He was smeared in dirt, his hair was a mess, and his clothing was torn, but his eyes blazed. "That is *our* chamber!"

Jackson folded his arms and regarded him steadily. "Your friend Aubrey is dead, and the whole place is a disaster zone. Are you really telling me that you want your Inner Temple to come here now?"

"Yes! If not to use it, at least to see it!" He looked down at the ground, shuffling his feet, and when he looked up again, his eyes were bright with unshed tears. "Aubrey was a brave soul, dedicated to learning our craft. We should honour him here. No one did more than he to find this place. You will treat his body well, won't you?"

"Of course," Jackson said gently. "We will get him home quickly and safely, and release him to you as soon as we can. And if you're sure you really want to, we'll ensure this place is safe before you return. Just be aware that we could be here for some weeks."

Caldwell patted his jacket that was looking very bulky. "And I will keep the papers I've found."

"Yes. But I want copies!"

"This is private!"

"This is the government you're dealing with now. Be grateful we're letting you keep anything."

Caldwell's lips tightened and he drew a deep breath in, but then he deflated like a popped balloon. "All right." He looked up at Gabe and Shadow. "Thanks for your help. We really couldn't have done this without you."

Gabe grunted. "One of you is dead. I don't really consider that a success."

"But we have some of the research at least, and we found the place," Caldwell insisted. "If only Aubrey and I had been here alone, that thing would have got out."

"You know," Gabe said thoughtfully, "we still haven't found your mole."

"There is no mole!" Caldwell said, annoyed.

Gabe refused to back down. "You're wrong, and now you're being wilfully blind. Someone—possibly Barnaby Armstrong—leaked that you had the astrolabe. *They* are responsible for Aubrey's death, because if Black Cronos didn't know about it, we wouldn't have been chased across England and France, and The Silencer of Souls wouldn't have sucked the life out of him."

Harlan almost felt sorry for Caldwell. He was desperate to defend his Senior Adepts, but there was no denying that Gabe was right. "I know you don't want to admit it, Caldwell, but there's no other explanation. When you get home, you need to be very careful who you trust."

"All right," he shouted. "Just leave it, please, for now. This is too much, on top of everything else."

"To be honest," Jackson said quietly, almost apologetically, "it will be something we look into. We will explore all potential connections to Black Cronos. But perhaps we should talk about that later," he added, as Caldwell glared at him.

An awkward silence fell for a second until Shadow said to Harlan, "You called it a Minotaur. What is that?"

He laughed. "It's a mythical bull-headed man trapped in a labyrinth. It's a murky tale, as all the Greek legends are. King Minos was sent a white bull to sacrifice to Poseidon, but it was so beautiful, he couldn't do it. To exact his revenge, Poseidon made the king's wife fall in love with it, and well...she had sex with it and gave birth to a bull-headed man."

Shadow looked horrified. "She did *what*?"

Gabe looked pale. "That's disgusting."

"It's a legend, of course!" Harlan said, trying to reassure them. "Not real. It's about the power of the ancient Greek Gods and the hazards of not paying them proper respect. King Minos put the Minotaur in the middle of a complicated maze, and then men were sacrificed to it."

"Is it a legend?" Ash asked, amused. "Because after what we've seen today, how can you doubt it? As you know, I am Greek, and have seen many strange things in my time. And we all know how vengeful Gods are."

Harlan did a quick calculation in his head. "The Minoan civilisation was during the Bronze age, right? Were you guys around then? Did you know him?"

"Maybe I'll keep that story for another time," Ash said, smiling. Harlan had a sudden vision of Ash in Bronze-age clothes, and thought he would suit that time very well.

Shadow, however, had heard enough. "Are we done here? I'm knackered and I stink, and after a shower, I want a drink on that stunning terrace."

"Agreed," Gabe said, stepping away and expanding his wings with a flourish. "Are you coming back, Jackson?"

"I think I will. I'll get the team to drop me off, but it won't be for a while yet." He turned to Harlan. "Can you drive everyone else?"

"Sounds good to me. Bourbon has never sounded better."

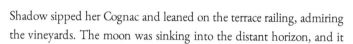

Shadow sipped her Cognac and leaned on the terrace railing, admiring the vineyards. The moon was sinking into the distant horizon, and it would be dawn soon.

She pulled a lightweight blanket around her shoulders to keep off the chill that had fallen in the early hours. It had been a long, crazy night, and she was glad that Gabe and her brothers had made it out of there alive. *Especially Gabe.* Even when he wasn't with her, he filled her thoughts. She would return to his bed later and sleep there... eventually. And she didn't care who knew it, either. When she imagined this turn of events, she thought she might feel prickly about it. Defensive, even. But actually, she didn't feel any of those things. In fact, she felt incredibly and unexpectedly comfortable about the whole thing.

She heard the Nephilim inside the house and smelled food. Despite the hour, Niel had decided to cook, proclaiming he was starving and that he would never sleep until he filled his stomach. At which point everyone else had requested food too, so now he was in there cooking bacon, eggs, and waffles with Harlan's help, who had also found bottles of whiskey and bourbon for the table.

Everyone was too wired after their exertions to even think about sleeping now. Caldwell had already settled at the end of the table with his newly found papers, half-destroyed and decaying, not surprisingly.

JD and Mason joined him, and she was glad they were here. They knew him well, better than they did, and could comfort him as he mourned the loss of Aubrey. And of course, help him study his new acquisitions.

The back door swung open, and a slight figure slipped out wearing a long, elegant cardigan, and Shadow watched warily as Estelle joined her, cradling her own glass of whiskey. She leaned on the railing too, silent for a moment. They weren't friends, and she doubted they ever would be, but there was also no doubting she was a good witch.

Shadow forced herself to speak and be civil, wondering why on Earth Estelle had come to stand next to her. "That was some impressive magic you pulled off in there. Are you okay?"

"Of course," she said brusquely, immediately annoying Shadow. "It was hard, but I was equal to it."

"So, you pass out after every time you use magic?" Shadow couldn't resist saying.

"No!" Estelle glared at her. "That was a particularly big spell!"

"Herne's balls, Estelle! Calm down! Why are you so damn prickly? I'm not doubting you. I was impressed!"

Estelle's face froze, and she turned away abruptly. "I'm tired." There was a moment's silence, and then she grudgingly said, "You're a very good fighter. Shockingly fast."

Shadow couldn't help herself as she said, "I know. I'm fey." She stared at the vineyards again, feeling Estelle's animosity rolling off her in waves; she wished she'd just sod off and leave her in peace. "That bloody monster was virtually unstoppable. I've got bruises in places I didn't know I could. I think my hair is singed, too. How do you think *they* stopped it? The original alchemists, I mean. They sealed it in a tomb, neatly packaged and tucked away!"

"Good question," Estelle said, curiosity replacing her anger. "They obviously had a fight with it at some point. When we first arrived, we found broken tables and destroyed columns. They must have employed a fail-safe that we knew nothing about. Something alchemical. Perhaps with the aid of the research, Caldwell will find out."

"Perhaps. And," Shadow added, still brooding, "my beautiful bow was destroyed."

"But you can get another one, I'm sure."

"Not like that one," she said sadly, wondering where in fact she could get one made. Something she could talk to El about, perhaps.

They fell into an awkward silence, and Shadow wondered what Estelle wanted. She would never normally seek her out for conversation. And then it struck her. *Barak.* They all knew Barak liked Estelle—hence the bet. He'd often joked about how he liked her feisty nature, but he always made light of it. Frankly, Shadow was appalled. *But maybe there was something more there—for Estelle, too. Or was it just about the White Haven witches and her brother?*

Sick of standing in silence and refusing to move—she liked leaning against the railing and listening to the murmured conversations around her, and the clatter of the others inside—she said, "Caspian must not have been that pleased at you coming here so soon after he was attacked."

Estelle looked startled at that. "Caspian? I don't think he cares one way or the other. A break will do us both good. I'll probably stay on a few days, actually. You could all stay." She offered it casually, almost tentatively.

"Could we?" Shadow thought through the possibility. They had no new jobs to rush off to, and the witches were okay, although they may need their help soon with the missing witches who had betrayed them. "I guess we could, for a few days. I must admit I like this heat, and the *château.* It's very beautiful. I guess it depends if Caspian can manage without Barak and Niel for a few days longer. They do work for you."

"They work for Caspian, not me, and I know he's arranged cover for a few days. I'm sure he can cope," she said, a hard edge to her voice.

"Well, that's good to know," Shadow answered uneasily. "I'd have thought you'd be glad to see the back of us. Why don't we ask when the others come out?"

"Yes, let's." Estelle shuffled and stared into her glass. *Here it comes.* "Is it my imagination, or do you and Gabe have a *thing*?"

"Oh, yes. We have a thing. A big thing." She smiled. "I tried to pretend it didn't exist or would be bad for business, but what's the point in that? You only live once. And it was inevitable, despite the fact that he's a big, winged idiot," she said affectionately, not thinking he was an idiot at all. "And my brothers can only tease us so many times before they get bored and move on to something new. Although, I gather there was a bet that I'm not very happy about."

Estelle still wasn't looking at her. "They do tease, don't they? All of them. It's hard to know when they're serious."

"They do, but they're good men. Honest. Despite their wings they are essentially human, which means they come with all the crap that goes with that." She shrugged, mischievous. "Not fey, obviously, which is a flaw."

Estelle rolled her eyes. "Really?"

Shadow just laughed. "And they have nice muscles, too."

The door swung open again behind them, and Gabe's arms slid around Shadow's waist as he kissed her neck. "Ladies." He nodded to Estelle, and said to Shadow, "You smell good."

"That's because I've washed the smell of roasting monster off me."

He laughed, sending a shiver up her spine. "Food's ready. You both coming?"

"Yep." Shadow wiggled out of Gabe's embrace and looked at Estelle, who hadn't moved. "Come on, Estelle. If you don't get to the table quickly, it will all be gone. They eat like horses."

She trailed after them, and while Niel, Harlan, Nahum, and Barak delivered dishes to the table, everyone else settled into seats.

Shadow decided to broach the subject first as soon as everyone sat down—well, everyone except Jackson, who still must be at the chamber. "Estelle says we can all stay here for a few more days. What do you think?"

"I think it sounds fantastic!" Niel said enthusiastically. "Fine food, French wine, the heat! Yes, please."

"This heat reminds me of Greece, so that's a yes for me," Ash said, smiling.

"Fine with me," Gabe said easily, reaching for a dish of bacon and topping his plate up. He glanced at Nahum. "What do you think?"

"I think our brothers at home will be glad of the peace."

"I'd love to stay," Harlan said, looking at JD and Mason. "But it depends on what my bosses say!"

Mason looked as if he'd aged ten years. He'd lost his confident demeanour; obviously Robert's death had hit him hard, but he nodded. "I think you should, Harlan. I, however, will head back later today. I need to sort things out regarding Robert...talk to his family, address the staff. Take a few days, but make sure you're back for the funeral."

"Of course, I will be there. And then we'll talk." He stared at Mason for a long moment, and he just nodded.

What did that mean? Shadow wondered. *It sounded ominous.* "What about you, JD?" she asked.

He too looked haunted, but he still had that stubbornness around the eyes she'd come to recognise. "I'll stay a day—if Caldwell is happy that I help him with his new research—and then I'll head to the Paris branch."

Caldwell nodded. "Of course, JD. A day or so to gather my thoughts would be good. And despite what Jackson said, I would like to revisit the chamber before I go. Then I too must deal with Aubrey's death, and the implications for the order."

Barak smiled at Estelle and raised his glass. "That sounds like a plan, then. To the next few days."

Estelle returned his smile, and Shadow inwardly groaned as she raised her glass with the others. *What in Herne's horns had she just collaborated in?*

As if Gabe had read her thoughts, he nudged her and winked. "See? She's not so bad after all."

Thanks for reading *Dark Star*. Please make an author happy and leave a review here. Book 4 will be out in May 2022. This series is a spin-off of my White Haven Witches series. The first book is called *Buried Magic,* and you can get it here for free.

If you enjoyed this book and would like to read more of my stories, please subscribe to my newsletter at tjgreen.nz. You will get two free short stories, *Excalibur Rises* and *Jack's Encounter,* and will also receive free character sheets of all the main White Haven witches.

By staying on my mailing list you'll receive free excerpts of my new books, as well as short stories, news of giveaways, and a chance to join my launch team. I'll also be sharing information about other books in this genre you might enjoy.

Read on for a list of my other books.

Author's Note

Thanks for reading *Dark Star*, the third book in the White Haven Hunters series. I really wanted to explore some of the wonderful world of alchemy in this story, and Jackson and Estelle wrote themselves in.

Estelle is such a fabulously complex woman, I wanted to see how she and Barak interacted. I also thought Jackson had more to share, and can quite honestly say I never saw his involvement with a government organisation happening until I was in the scene. I love it when that happens!

I also thought it was time for some very dangerous bad guys, and hence Black Cronos appeared. I'm sure they'll be back, especially The Silencer of Souls. The *Chateau du Porge* is a real place, but I fabricated everything about it! It was in the right place for my story, so I decided to use it.

JD continues to mystify and confuse Harlan. John Dee was a fascinating man, and is credited with developing England's spy network, but I'll share more about that on my website https:/tjgreen.nz

Shadow and Gabe had to end up together. I'm sure their continuing relationship will be eventful. I also loved writing about the other Nephilim, and their characters will continue to grow and evolve, as will Harlan's.

Book 4, as yet un-titled, will be out in May 2022.

I am still planning on writing a few short story prequels—for Shadow certainly, and hopefully Harlan and Gabe, too.

If you enjoy audiobooks, *Spirit of the Fallen*, White Haven Hunters #1, and *Shadow's Edge*, White Haven Hunter's #2, are both audiobooks, and this book will follow soon. Links are on my website – https://tjgreen.nz/

If you'd like a chance to get involved in my books and join my fabulous Facebook group, just answer the question and I'll let you in - https://www.facebook.com/groups/696140834516292

Thanks to my fabulous cover designer, Fiona Jayde Media, and to Missed Period Editing.

I owe a big thanks to Jason, my partner, who has been incredibly supportive throughout my career, and is a beta reader. Thanks also to Terri and my mother, my other two beta readers. You're all awesome.

Finally, thank you to my launch team, who give valuable feedback on typos and are happy to review on release. It's lovely to hear from them—you know who you are! You're amazing! I also love hearing from all of my readers, so I welcome you to get in touch.

If you'd like to read a bit more background on my stories, please head to my website—www.tjgreen.nz—where I blog about the research I've done, among other things. I have another series set in Cornwall about witches, called White Haven Witches, so if you enjoy myths and magic, you'll love that, too. It's an adult series, not YA.

If you'd like to read more of my writing, please join my mailing list. You can get a free short story called Jack's Encounter, describing how Jack met Fahey—a longer version of the prologue in the Call of the King, my YA Arthurian series—by subscribing to my newsletter. You'll also get a FREE copy of Excalibur Rises, a short story prequel to Rise of the King.

Additionally, you will receive free character sheets on all of my main characters in White Haven Witches—exclusive to my email list!

By staying on my mailing list, you'll receive free excerpts of my new books, as well as short stories and news of giveaways. I'll also be sharing information about other books in this genre you might enjoy. Finally, I welcome you to join my readers' group for even more great content, called TJ's Inner Circle, on Facebook. Please answer the questions to join! https://business.facebook.com/groups/69614083451629

Give me my FREE short stories!

About the Author

I write books about magic, mystery, myths, and legends, and they're action-packed!

My primary series is adult urban fantasy, called White Haven Witches. There's lots of magic, action, and a little bit of romance.

My YA series, Rise of the King, is about a teen named Tom and his discovery that he is a descendant of King Arthur. It's a fun-filled, clean read with a new twist on the Arthurian tales.

I've got loads of ideas for future books in all of my series, including spin-offs, novellas, and short stories, so if you'd like to be kept up to date, subscribe to my newsletter. You'll get free short stories, character sheets, and other fun stuff. Interested? Subscribe here.

I was born in England, in the Black Country, but moved to New Zealand 14 years ago. England is great, but I'm over the traffic! I now live near Wellington with my partner, Jase, and my cats, Sacha and Leia. When I'm not busy writing I read lots, indulge in gardening and shopping, and I love yoga.

Confession time! I'm a Star Trek geek—old and new—and love urban fantasy and detective shows. My secret passion is Columbo! My favourite Star Trek film is The Wrath of Khan, the original! Other top films for me are Predator, the original, and Aliens.

In a previous life, I was a singer in a band, and used to do some acting with a theatre company. On occasion, a few friends and I like to make short films, which begs the question, where are the book trailers? I'm thinking on it...

For more on me, check out a couple of my blog posts. I'm an old grunge queen, so you can read about my love of that here. For more random news, read this.

Why magic and mystery?

I've always loved the weird, the wonderful, and the inexplicable. My favourite stories are those of magic and mystery, set on the edges of the known, particularly tales of folklore, faerie, and legend—all the narratives that try to explain our reality.

The King Arthur stories are fascinating because they sit between reality and myth. They encompass real life concerns, but also cross boundaries with the world of faerie—or the Otherworld, as I call it. There are green knights, witches, wizards, and dragons, and that's what I find particularly fascinating. They are stories that have intrigued people for generations, and like many others, I'm adding my own interpretation.

I also love witches and magic, hence my additional series set in beautiful Cornwall. There are witches, missing grimoires, supernatural threats, and ghosts, and as the series progresses, even weirder stuff happens.

Have a poke around in my blog posts, and you'll find all sorts of articles about my series and my characters, and quite a few book reviews.

If you'd like to follow me on social media, you'll find me here:

Facebook, Twitter, Instagram, TikTok, BookBub.

OTHER TITLES BY TJ GREEN

<u>Rise of the King Series</u>

A Young Adult series about a teen called Tom who's summoned to wake King Arthur. It's a fun adventure about King Arthur in the Otherworld!

<u>*Call of the King #1*</u>

King Arthur is destined to return, and Tom is destined to wake him.

When sixteen-year old Tom's grandfather mysteriously disappears, Tom stops at nothing to find him, even when that means crossing to a mysterious and unknown world.

When he gets there, Tom discovers that everything he thought he knew about himself and his life was wrong. Vivian, the Lady of the Lake, has been watching over him and manipulating his life since his birth. And now she needs his help.

<u>*The Silver Tower #2*</u>

Merlin disappeared over a thousand years ago. Now they will risk everything to find him. Vivian needs King Arthur's help. Nimue, a powerful witch and priestess who lives on Avalon, has disappeared.

King Arthur, Tom, and his friends set off across the Otherworld to find her, following Nimue's trail. Nimue seems to have a quest of her own, one she's deliberately hiding. Arthur is convinced it's about Merlin, and he's determined to find him. *The Cursed Sword #3*

An ancient sword. A dark secret. A new enemy.

Tom loves his new life in the Otherworld. He lives with Arthur in New Camelot, and Arthur is hosting a tournament. Eager to test his sword-fighting skills, Tom is competing.

But while the games are being played, his friends are attacked and everything he loves is threatened. Tom has to find the intruder before anyone else gets hurt.

Tom's sword seems to be the focus of these attacks. Their investigations uncover its dark history, and a terrible betrayal that a family has kept secret for generations.

<u>White Haven Witches Series</u>

Witches, secrets, myth, and folklore, set on the Cornish coast!

Buried Magic #1

Love witchy fiction? Welcome to White Haven—where secrets are deadly.

Avery, a witch who lives on the Cornish coast, finds that her past holds more secrets than she ever imagined in this spellbinding mystery.

For years witches have lived in quirky White Haven, all with an age-old connection to the town's magical roots, but Avery has been reluctant to join a coven, preferring to work alone.

However, when she inherits a rune-covered box and an intriguing letter, Avery learns that their history is darker than she realised. And when the handsome Alex Bonneville tells her he's been having ominous premonitions, they know that trouble is coming.

Magic Unbound #2

Avery and the other witches are now being hunted, and they know someone is betraying them.

The question is, who?

One thing is certain.

They have to find their missing grimoires before their attackers do, and they have to strike back.

If you love urban fantasy, filled with magic and a twist of romance, you'll love *Magic Unbound.*

Magic Unleashed #3

Old magic, new enemies. The danger never stops in White Haven.

Avery and the White Haven witches have finally found their grimoires and defeated the Favershams, but their troubles are only just beginning.

Something escaped from the spirit world when they battled beneath All Souls Church, and now it wants to stay, unleashing violence across Cornwall.

On top of that, the power they released when they reclaimed their magic is attracting powerful creatures from the deep, creatures that need men to survive.

All Hallows' Magic #4

When Samhain arrives, worlds collide.

A Shifter family arrives in White Haven, one of them close to death. Avery offers them sanctuary, only to find their pursuers are close behind, intent on retribution. In an effort to help them, Avery and Alex are dragged into a fight they didn't want but must see through.

As if that weren't enough trouble, strange signs begin to appear at Old Haven Church. Avery realises that an unknown witch has wicked plans for Samhain, and is determined to breach the veils between worlds.

Avery and her friends scramble to discover who the mysterious newcomer is, all while being attacked one by one.

Undying Magic #5

Winter grips White Haven, bringing death in its wake.

It's close to the winter solstice when Newton reports that dead bodies have been found, drained of their blood.

Then people start disappearing, and Genevieve calls a coven meeting. What they hear is chilling.

This has happened before, and it's going to get worse. The witches have to face their toughest challenge yet—*vampires*.

Crossroads Magic #6

When Myths become real, danger stalks White Haven.

The Crossroads Circus has a reputation for bringing myths to life, but it also seems that where the circus goes, death follows. When the circus sets up on the castle grounds, Newton asks Avery and the witches to investigate.

This proves trickier than they imagined when an unexpected encounter finds Avery bound to a power she can't control.

Strange magic is making the myths a little too real.

Crown of Magic #7

Passions run deep at Beltane—too deep.

With the Beltane Festival approaching, the preparations in White Haven are in full swing, but when emotions soar out of control, the witches suspect more than just high spirits.

As part of the celebrations, a local theatre group is rehearsing *Tristan and Isolde*, but it seems Beltane magic is affecting the cast, and all sorts of old myths are brought to the surface.

The May Queen brings desire, fertility, and the promise of renewal, but love can also be dark and dangerous.

313

314

Printed in Great Britain
by Amazon